SO STEADY

SILVER DAUGHTERS INK, BOOK #2

EVE DANGERFIELD

∽

First published by Eve Dangerfield Books in 2019
Copyright © 2019 by Eve Dangerfield
All rights reserved. No part of this publication may be reproduced, stored or transmitted in any form or by any means, electronic, mechanical, photocopying, recording, scanning, or otherwise without written permission from the publisher. It is illegal to copy this book, post it to a website, or distribute it by any other means without permission.
This novel is entirely a work of fiction. The names, characters and incidents portrayed in it are the work of the author's imagination. Any resemblance to actual persons, living or dead, events or localities is entirely coincidental.

DEDICATION

For the food pokers. Especially Peasy.

1

"We are well advised to keep on nodding terms with the people we used to be, whether we find them attractive company or not. Otherwise they turn up unannounced."
Joan Dideon, *Slouching Towards Bethlehem*

"You do not have to be good.
You do not have to walk on your knees
For a hundred miles through the desert, repenting.
You only have to let the soft animal of your body
love what it loves."
Mary Oliver, *Wild Geese*

Nicole DaSilva sat on the couch and folded herself like lady origami—right knee over left, fingers woven in her lap. She scanned the Airbnb for loose papers and stray glasses, but every corner of the apartment was spotless. That should have been reassuring, but uncertainty quivered in her belly.

"Breathe," she told herself. "Just breathe."

But each inhalation only made her chest tighter. Impatient, Nicole stood and walked to the bathroom mirror. She scanned herself for pimples, grey hairs, chips in her manicure. There was nothing. Short of surgery, the woman before her couldn't be improved. She'd spent the day getting The Full Beauty. A cut, colour, blowout, manicure, pedicure, eyebrow threading, and tinting, lash extensions, and a thorough wax of her underarms, legs, and labia. Her makeup had been professionally done, and she'd chosen her outfit a week ago: a Country Road shirt, peach silk shorts, and Dior sandals. Pretty but not *too* feminine, the pastels contrasting her black hair and blue eyes.

She lingered at the mirror, cataloguing the things she couldn't change—her widow's peak, her slightly larger left eye, the thinness of her top lip. She'd always been hyper-aware of her flaws. When people told her she was beautiful, she wanted to demand, "What about the widow's peak? The mismatched eyes? Have you taken them into consideration, or do you think they're *quirky* or something?"

The woman in the mirror looked so unhappy, Nicole was embarrassed.

"Smile," she demanded. "You're pretty and well-off, and you have a good job. You're going to see your fiancé for the first time in three weeks. You're lucky, so *be happy*."

She drew her cheeks back, but her smile was joyless. She let her face fall back into gloom.

Aaron hadn't wanted to come to Melbourne. He considered the city enemy territory. DaSilva Country. He'd wanted her to spend the weekend at their house in Adelaide and it had taken a lot of arguments to get him to agree to fly to Melbourne.

"We're not fucking staying at your house," he'd said. "Your sisters hate me. They'll put a frog in my bag or call the cops on me at the airport or something."

Nicole wished she could have told him he was paranoid, but he was right; Sam and Tabby did hate him, and they weren't known for their subtlety. As heavily tattooed extroverts, they were known for the opposite of that. In the end, she'd booked an Airbnb as far from

Brunswick as possible and hoped her sisters were too busy for long-distance sabotage.

Nicole studied her reflection, pushing her lackluster top lip out.

I could always get some filler put in. Aaron said that girl at work has it and it looks sexy...

She imagined how her sisters would respond if she showed up to Silver Daughters with lip injections.

"Oi, someone call the council! There's a wild duck on the loose and she looks huuuuungry," Tabby would say while taking as many photos as possible.

Sam might laugh or she might be insulted. They were identical twins, after all, and her getting fillers was akin to saying Sam's top lip was too thin.

"Our mouth's not good enough for you now?" Sam might say, though she was the one who'd covered herself in tattoos and separated them into distinct individuals—the sexy artist and her boring double. As the only non-tattooist in her family, Nicole was used to being treated as the vanilla sheep, but it still grated sometimes. Although if she had lip injections...

She rolled her eyes at herself. "You'd be a boring accountant with lip injections."

It was irritating to still be wading in her teenage insecurities. She was twenty-eight and engaged, too old to resent her lack of edginess. Too old to worry about what her sisters thought of her fiancé.

We don't want to think anything about him, Sam announced. *But he's such a dickhead, he makes it impossible.*

Yeah, you can do better, Tabby chipped in. *For example, Ivan Milat is still alive.*

Nicole prodded her top lip. "Shut up. Aaron and I are getting married. We have a house together."

Tabby laughed. *Because we all know real estate is the erotic backbone of all relationships. He's so boring, Nix. His face is a Caucasian blur. Even lip injections wouldn't jazz him up.*

Nicole snorted and was instantly ashamed. When she'd moved to Adelaide, she'd broken her habit of talking to her sisters in her head, but since her return to Melbourne, Sam and Tabby had taken up their chairs in her mind and resumed commenting on everything she did with intrusive jocularity.

She'd told herself it would stop when she returned to South Australia, but she no longer knew when that would be. She'd returned home two months ago to help Sam with the family business which had edged close to bankruptcy after their dad left on a spontaneous hiatus. She'd expected to stay a couple of weeks, but Silver Daughters financial troubles were so extensive, she'd filed a remote working request so she could stay until they were solved. Her sisters were thrilled, Aaron was not.

"Your dad left the studio to Samantha and she can't manage it," he snarled down the phone. "She needs to grow up and sell it to someone who can, not keep it on life support with the help of her more successful sister."

"Please don't be mad at me," she'd pleaded. "Silver Daughters is our home. Sam and Tabby learned to tattoo here! I ran the accounts when I was fourteen! I have more happy memories here than anywhere else!"

Without warning, Aaron had hung up on her. Later he texted to say if she loved the studio so much, she could stay there forever.

They weren't doing so good, relationship-wise. The problem was, she couldn't bring herself to tell him what he wanted to hear—that Adelaide was her home and he was more important than her sisters. She knew that *should* be true, but her heart still belonged to Brunswick, to the graffiti murals and pretentious cafes and weirdos in Salvation Army jumpers. And though her sisters drove her bonkers, her heart belonged to them, too. To their blue eyes and bad language. To their easy, unpretentious love.

She wanted to miss Aaron, but every day in Melbourne was like a holiday from reality. Everything except...

She tried to keep the thoughts from rushing in, but it was too late. *He* arrived in vivid detail—big and mean, wearing black jeans and carrying a fat fantasy novel. It was Noah Newcomb as she'd first seen him, the day she'd returned to Melbourne.

"He's great," Sam said as she drove her and Tabby from the airport. "Quiet but great."

"Great at tattooing, or great in general?"

"Both. Tabby, stop kicking my seat, you dickhead."

Nicole had assumed Noah Newcomb was like her dad—a long-haired hippie, spaced out, but essentially harmless.

She'd never been so wrong in her life.

A hulking beast stood reading a novel at reception, big as a house with blackwork tattoos drilled into every inch of his skin. As she looked at him, a cold snake uncoiled in her belly. She'd grown up above the studio; she wasn't intimidated by ink, but she knew this man wasn't some tatt-happy hipster. He had tattoos for the same reason redback spiders were splashed with scarlet—a visual warning. He had a thug's face—broad brow, heavy jaw, a nose that had obviously been broken. That, too, felt like a warning.

She'd turned to Sam, half-convinced the guy had broken in, but her twin smiled, and Tabby launched herself at the guy.

"Who is that?" she'd whispered as Tabby and the stranger hugged.

"Uh, Noah Newcomb? Tattoo artist? The big guy Dad loves?"

Nicole felt winded. She took a step back, intending to go outside, when he looked at her. His eyes were green. Not muddy hazel or dull moss, but *green* like emeralds or spring grass and fringed with the longest black lashes she'd ever seen. Noah's gaze sparked with crackling intelligence.

Oh gosh, she thought. *No. No. No.*

But it was too late, excitement burst inside her like an atom bomb, making her skin prickle and her heart pound. He was so big, so beautifully scary and new.

And while mania hijacked her brain, Noah Newcomb just stood there, cool as anything, cataloguing every inch of her body. She saw him clock her engagement ring and frown slightly, but his gaze still lifted to reexamine her breasts. She'd scowled, trying to shame him, but Noah's upper lip had curled. His smile said, *Tell me you don't like it.*

And she'd tried, but her mouth was too dry. All she could think about was Noah's body on top of hers, knees shoving her thighs wide. *"Tell me you don't like it."*

Heat zigzagged down her chest and into her underwear, and as she stared into Noah Newcomb's eyes, she knew he was a problem. But that was okay. All her life she'd solved problems. She *would* stamp out her inconvenient attraction and salt the earth where it had grown. And she'd succeeded admirably... if you ignored that little slip in the hallway. And it was easy to ignore that little slip in the hallway.

Nicole's pelvic floor contracted, and she groaned aloud at her silliness. She'd done such a good job of not thinking about *him* since this afternoon. It was so disappointing that she'd caved to these stupid fantasies.

She exhaled and checked her watch. Ten minutes until Aaron was due to arrive. She returned to the lounge and rearranged herself on the white leather couch. If Aaron knew how she felt about Noah, he would... she had no idea. Though 'lose his mind' was probably the most accurate prediction. He talked about women he found attractive, had acted on that attraction more than once, but she hadn't dared to say Noah's name to him, afraid he'd hear something in her voice. If he knew about her little slip....

Her face burned hot at the memory. She'd been standing in the hallway at Sam's Ink the Night party, staring at the brooch her dad had sent in the mail, and he'd come up behind her, asking if she was okay... They were both drunk, or she was, anyway, and it had only lasted a second.

It didn't feel real enough to count as a kiss, let alone cheating, for god's sake.

Hey, why not bring up the issue with Aaron? Imaginary Tabby asked. *He'll have great insights into what is and isn't cheating, being that he's a big cheating twat-basket. Actual cheating, not just mouth-touching in a hallway.*

"That was different. Aaron was under a lot of pressure at work, and I've wholeheartedly forgiven him for the affair—"

Affairsssss, Sam said. *Plural.*

Yes, plural. But they didn't matter, at least not compared to her and Aaron's commitments, their years of being together. It was the same thing with Noah and the frankly disturbing things she imagined him doing to her body. They were daydreams. The relationship equivalent of fairy floss. Yes, they were distracting, but she could push through them. Mind over matter. Or was it matter over mind?

It doesn't matter, Sam chortled.

Yeah, never mind.

"Shut up, both of you."

Nicole straightened her top so it lay flat against her skin. She and Aaron were engaged, they were having a big wedding at Ascot Manor, then settling down to start a family. That was why the full beauty and expensive Airbnb. She would look and act so perfect that Aaron would understand she needed to stay and help her sisters fix Silver Daughters' finances. She couldn't be happy unless her family was happy, but once they were happy, she could redirect her energy into making *him* happy and their wonderful married life could begin.

There was a hard rap on the door.

Nicole stood, trying to arrange her face into a beatific 'I love you' smile. She walked to the entrance and turned the door handle. "Hey, fiancé."

Aaron's hair was tousled, his face tight. "Hi."

Her optimism about this visit crisped like saplings in the sun. "How... how are you?"

Aaron jiggled the handle of his suitcase. "Fine. Can I come in?"

Wordlessly she moved out of the way. He rolled his silver Fabbrica Pelletterie luggage into the living room. "Nice place," he said without looking. "Any chance of a drink?"

"Of course."

She nervously poured Aaron a Chardonnay as he stripped off his jacket. He worked out almost every afternoon and the muscles of his back and biceps were visible through his shirt. She watched him, willing herself to tingle, to *want* to want to touch him.

She thought of Noah's hands, thick-knuckled and scarred, covered in ugly, gothic tattoos. Her navel pulled tight, and she was furious with herself. She straightened her shoulders and handed Aaron the wine. "Good flight?"

"Good enough." He drained the glass in seconds.

"Wow. Do you want more or—"

"Do you love me more than you love them?"

Nicole stared at him, baffled. 'Him' was one thing, who the hell was 'them?' "Pardon?"

"Don't fuck around. *Them*. Your sisters and your dad." Like her, Aaron had a thin mouth, and right now, it was a furious line. "Do you love me more than you love them?"

Nicole swallowed. "I... what kind of question is that?"

"The only one that matters. It's been months since you left home."

"Barely two," Nicole corrected and instantly regretted it. There was never any sense arguing semantics in romantic relationships. Fights were about how the other person *felt,* not pinning down the facts. You never found any vindication in being right.

Predictably, Aaron's eyes bulged. "Are you fucking serious? That's the line you want to take?"

"I'm sorry, but they're my family, I need to—"

"Of course, you need to. You always *need to*. Meanwhile, I'm coming home to an empty house after work, listening to you tell me you miss me like I'm some leftover kid in a divorce. You owe me more than this, Nicole."

Tears pricked in the backs of her eyes. If he missed her, why couldn't he say that? Why did he have to make it sound like he'd hired her to do a job she was slacking off on? "I'm sorry. You know I love you."

Aaron shoved his hand through his gold-brown hair. "That's not good enough. I'm tired of living alone because my fiancée's ditched me for her sisters and a shitty tattoo studio."

"It's not shitty! It's the family business and—"

"I don't give a fuck! You made a commitment to me. It's time you came home."

Her heart was banging against her ribs, she was pretty sure she knew what was coming. "Or...?"

Aaron's nostrils flared. "Or we're done. Over."

A tear slid down her face and she was ashamed of her first thought—*I hope I don't ruin my extensions.* God, she was vain. She was vain and spoiled and selfish. She hadn't tried hard enough.

"What'll it be?" Aaron snarled.

She wiped away a tear. "Why does it have to be a choice?"

"Because I said so." Aaron grabbed the handle of his suitcase and panic shot through her. She ran to the door, blocking his path. "I love them, Aaron. They're my *family*."

"And what about our family? What about our kids?"

Having never given birth, Nicole assumed he meant 'future kids.' The ones whose names she dreamed about at night. "What about them?"

"I don't want them near your sisters or your dad. They're irresponsible druggies."

"They're not dru—"

"Your sister nearly got caught flying with pills and Samantha was arrested with a joint and your dad petitioned for the legalization of all banned substances. He was on the news, remember?"

God, that was the thing about Aaron. Any venting on her behalf was stockpiled and kept as weapons in future arguments. He never held onto the good things—that Tabby was insanely funny and smart. That Sam could tattoo like ink ran in her veins, and her loyalty was bone-deep. That her dad was gentle and kind, and he'd raised them alone without asking for anything in return.

"You don't get it! They're a part of me."

"Oh, I *get it* alright." Aaron's eyes were dark with fury. "Still got your tattoo, I see."

She clutched her left wrist. "So?"

"So, you told me it was coming off. That you didn't want to be a female with tattoos anymore."

The moment was deathly serious, but she couldn't help it, she imagined Sam's expression if she heard him talking about 'females with tattoos.' The smile that wouldn't come in the mirror slid onto her face like an enemy submarine. She clapped her hand to her mouth, but Aaron had already seen it. A muscle twanged in his jaw. "Oh, it's all a big joke, is it?"

"No, I prom—"

Aaron's wine glass shattered on the floorboards. "Is this funny? Are you laughing now?"

She gave a panicky, birdlike screech. "What are you *doing*?"

"Making myself clear." Aaron's icy gaze drilled into hers. "Me, or them, Nicole. Choose right now."

2

"**M**r Newcomb, this is Gia from the Collingwood Medical Centre calling to confirm your appointment on the thirteenth. Please ring us back as soon as you can. Bye!"

Noah deleted the voicemail. It was too early to return the call right now. He'd have to take a walk on his lunch break. Normally, he'd call at nine, but he didn't need anyone at Silver Daughters finding out about his vasectomy. He shoved his phone into his pocket and tugged out his cigarettes. He lit up, exhaling into the cool morning air. He liked Brunswick before sunrise, subdued and a little bleak. He liked smoking on the way to work, thinking about the day ahead. Though lately, all he thought about was Nicole DaSilva. The black gloss of her hair, the way her brow furrowed as she read, how she coughed whenever he got in from smoking in the courtyard. Or she had until Sam told her to shut the hell up.

"It's dangerous," Nicole told her twin, loud enough for him to hear. "Secondhand smoke and even thirdhand smoke *kills*."

She said it so prissily, as though maybe none of them had caught the word on cigarettes being bad for you. It made him want to laugh. Actually, it made him want to smoke while Nicole sucked him off, one hand tight in her hair to keep her in place.

And she'd love it. That's exactly what she wants, for me to fuck her like an animal and give her permission to like it.

Sometimes that pissed him off. He walked around daydreaming about Nicole DaSilva's hair and eyes and laugh, and the only sign she thought of him was the odd glance that said she was curious about getting drilled by the big scary man.

Sometimes that pissed him off. This morning it made his cock throb. He could just picture her bent over his tattooing chair, naked except for sky-high heels. *Please, Noah, I'm so horny I can't think anymore. Please fuck me like a dirty, dirty, girl, then send me back to my spreadsheets?*

Yeah, Nicole DaSilva was the kind of woman who distracted herself from her body with work. Ignoring her needs until she could barely cross her legs under her desk. Got all cranky with her coworkers instead of giving herself what she wanted. How many times had he wanted to go into her office on a Wednesday afternoon, spread her out on her desk and...

Christ, it was too early to get all cranked up about fucking someone else's fiancée. Noah pulled his brain back into neutral, trying to take in the sights and smells as he made his way to the studio. He was tired, but that was his fault. Kelly had texted him at ten and, wanting a distraction from endless thoughts of Nicole, he'd invited her over. When they were done, he'd walked her to the door and Paula had come into the hall in her Minnie Mouse pyjamas, primed for trouble. "Ooh, new girlfriend?"

"Get back to bed," he'd told her, but Kelly had already flashed Paula a hopeful smile. "Not yet."

He'd almost groaned. He'd been screwing Sam's tattoo model for a while, and he was sure there was nothing to it but sex, but he hadn't actually asked, and now he'd have to end things.

As he crossed at the lights outside Brunswick Bakehouse, he trialed methods of letting Kelly down easy. A call was probably over the top, but a text was pretty cold. Meeting up with her just to tell her he was into someone else seemed like a dick move. He lit another smoke and remembered something his old man used to say. "You want to get rid of a girl, just vanish, mate. Stop calling; stop going anywhere she might find you. That's the way to do it."

As he strode past a pop-up sneaker store, he reflected his dad had invented ghosting years before it entered the cultural lexicon. If his old man wasn't in Bali avoiding charges—and a massive cunt—he'd call to congratulate him. Although, Harold Newcomb hadn't invented anything. The art of wandering off to let chicks do the dirty work of dumping themselves probably went back to caveman times. His old man had just perfected it. Off the top of his head, Noah could remember three times stacked blondes had showed up at his house looking for his dad.

"I haven't seen the prick," his mum told them. "Who knew bikies were such arseholes, hey?"

Ghosting was a weak move, he decided, ashing into a street bin. He'd call Kelly tonight and tell her they weren't going anywhere. He'd leave out the obvious question—why the fuck did she want them to go anywhere? The sex was fine, but it wasn't earth-shattering. But maybe he was putting his feelings onto her. Maybe she'd been fully present when they fucked, while his mind turned like a compass needle back to Nicole DaSilva.

He'd never been so obsessed with someone and unfortunately for Nicole, that was her. Until his idiot brain finally absorbed the fact she was engaged to some dickhead from Adelaide, he had to roll with the punches. Nothing else to do. She wasn't interested. If she had been, she wouldn't have run when they kissed in the hallway at Sam's party. Not that it'd been a real kiss. More of a drunk peck.

Noah reached the scarlet façade of Silver Daughters, taking a second to admire the polished windows and the clean sidewalk. Nicole had done that herself, sweeping and polishing in her tight skirt and red-bottomed heels.

"We want to be perceived as a professional high-quality business," she said at their last breakfast meeting. "That impression starts at the door."

"Doesn't it start when the client thinks about coming to see us?"

Tabby asked. "Or does it start at the point of their conception? Come on, everyone; let's debate the nature of existence!"

Noah didn't have any brothers or sisters. Sometimes that felt like a good thing. He shouldered his way inside the studio and found Gil leaning against the reception desk, a lilac Supreme cap low on his forehead. "Hey."

Gil looked up. "Morning, big guy. Warm out there?"

"Not yet."

"Hope it doesn't get too hot today, I've got a PT session after work. Tris, back and thighs."

"Mmm." Noah had heard enough about Gil's gains, meal prep, and lifting schedule to last a lifetime. His fortieth was coming up and becoming a walking copy of *Men's Health* was how he was choosing to deal with it. That and buying a shiny black Fat Boy like the one Arnie rode in Terminator 2.

He shrugged off his jacket and hung it on the stand. "You ride in today?"

"Nah, it's too hard to carry my gym shit." Gil flashed him a grin. "Why, do you want a go? We can chuck on some training wheels if you like."

Noah ignored him. As far as the staff at Silver Daughters knew, he couldn't ride and that was just how he liked it. "Where are the girls? Aren't we having a staff meeting?"

"Yeah, not sure that's happening."

"Why?"

Gil pointed at the ceiling, where the DaSilva family apartment lay. Noah listened, hearing nothing but the birds and traffic outside. "What?"

"I heard a load of crying and banging not too long ago. There must be drama happening."

Noah stared at Gil, trying to work out if he was being funny. The DaSilva sisters were all big personalities, but they'd never canceled one of Nicole's meetings, not even the week the place had almost been burned down. "You gone up there to check on them?"

"Nah, that's not my business. No meeting means no pancake

carbs, *and* I don't have to listen to Nicole talk about the bottom line or whatever the fuck so..." Gil tugged at the brim of his cap. "I'm gonna get a keto coffee. Wanna come?"

Noah glanced back at the ceiling. He didn't want to stick his oar in, but he owed it to Edgar to check the girls were okay. "I'm gonna see what's happening. Lock up if you leave."

Gil gave him a mock salute. "Good luck. Don't let 'em talk to you about their feelings."

Pretty hypocritical for a guy who could wax poetic about whey protein for hours on end, but male tattoo artists tended to be showy, shit-talking assholes. At least they did in the commercial industry. The guys who'd taught him to ink were a whole other kettle of fish.

He headed around back to the residential entrance. He'd walked the cracked concrete path a million times when Edgar still lived here. They'd had dinner a few nights a week before Nicole or Tabby showed up. Back when Sam was single and always off with her latest fling. He and Ed would sit in the backyard drinking beers and talking about art and music. He was the only man he'd ever been able to relax around. Now he was gone, his daughters filling his absence.

Sam became his boss; Tabby took the spare artist slot and Nicole flew in from Adelaide to fix the finances and fuck his head into a new dimension. He hoped he wasn't going to run into her upstairs. Lately, she'd been leaving the room as soon as he walked into it. Smart chicks not wanting a bar of him was nothing new, but Nicole was under his skin so deep, it stung.

The minute he saw her he'd known he was fucked, not because she was taken or miles out of his league, but because she was rose gold. Whenever he looked at her, he saw the peach blush of sunset. You couldn't replicate that colour with ink or paint or even tech. There was too much light in it. It glowed.

There was too much light in Nicole DaSilva, too. Too much goodness trying to get out. She hovered around Silver Daughters, polishing over problems. Her sisters called her a control freak, but he didn't buy that. He had a feeling making other people happy was the only thing that gave her peace. And Sam and Tabby never gave her any credit. Not only was Silver Daughters doing ten times better thanks to Nicole, *they* were doing ten times better. Two months ago, both sisters looked like underfed vampires. Now they jogged and ate kale salmon salad and the shadows under their eyes were gone. They went on about how much energy they had but never thanked their sister for cooking their meals and dragging their asses to the park. And unlike a control freak, Nicole didn't want any credit. She seemed happy being rose gold, transmuting everything into a prettier version of itself.

Noah knocked on the DaSilva's front door. He could hear stomping and shouting but couldn't make out what was going on. He hammered the door. "Hello? Sam?"

There was no response, but his phone vibrated. Bemused, he pulled it out and saw the DaSilva landline number. He swiped to answer. "Hello."

"Morning, assclown."

It was Tabby, irreverent and peppy as ever. He frowned. "How'd you get my number?"

"Secret government database. Why are you standing outside the door?"

"Can you let me in?"

"I asked my thing first."

Noah waited, but Tabby just hummed the Star Wars theme. He resisted a few seconds then couldn't hack it anymore. "I want to know why the meeting isn't on. What's happening?"

"Oh, the usual stuff. Rich get richer. Poor get poorer. Climate change. The ever-repeating cycle of birth and rebirth—"

"I meant 'what's happening inside your house?'"

She sighed. "It's a long and complicated story, but essentially, we will not be having a meeting. In fact, I'm pretty sure Sam and Nicole won't be coming downstairs today."

"What's happened? Is Scott's old man back?"

A month ago, the DaSilvas' old neighbour had tried to burn their house down in revenge for not selling the place to him. Greg

Sanderson was supposed to be in a mental health facility in Queensland, but if he'd snuck out or something...

"Nah, it's not Scott's crackpot dad, it's about... well I shouldn't say..."

Noah gripped his phone. "Talk."

"I don't know, it's a pretty big deal..."

"How big?"

"Absolutely amazing. Basically breathtaking. Completely confounding. Deeply dramatic—"

"Tabby, I swear to god."

"—Epically enormous. Frankly formidable. Guaranteed game-changer. *Hectically* huge..."

"Tabby!" Sam shouted. "The fuck are you going on about?"

"Nothing!" Tabby yelled. "Just focus on keeping her away from the cleaning products. I'm scared she's going to do my room."

Noah frowned. Keeping *her* away? That sounded like... "Is Nicole all right?"

"Nah, but hang on. I'm moving to a more covert location." There was some shifting around, then Tabby cleared her throat. "Nix got dumped."

The sentence took a moment to seep into Noah's brain. "Nicole?"

"Got dumped, yeah. Well, not *dumped*. Aaron, the big dickcheese, shoved some cunt ultimatum about going back to Adelaide in her face then fucked off, even though she paid for the Airbnb they were staying in..."

Noah stopped listening. A thousand victory flags were unfolding in his mind, waving scarlet, sap yellow, and kingfisher blue. Nicole DaSilva, single. Ringless. Free to... what exactly? Where was he going with this bullshit?

"... then Nix came home all puffy and told me and Sam to hide her phone and credit cards. That was ten hours ago. We've hit peak chaos now."

"What does that mean?"

"Nix is freaking out," Tabby said cheerfully. "If she gets access to money or a phone, she'll call Aaron and ask for her ring back. So, she's under house arrest and we must stay here and make sure she doesn't make the worst decision in the world just because she's already hired wedding caterers."

Noah stared at the DaSilva's front door. He could hear more shouting now, was it Nicole calling out in grief, or Sam trying to contain her? Was she okay? Was anyone comforting her?

"Noah, mate, you there?"

He swallowed. "I thought the girl kept the ring?"

"Usually, but Aaron's such a tight arse pie-fucker he asked for it back. Hey, are you free next Saturday?"

"Why?"

"I'm planning a party. Well, more of a big drunken soirée. It's to help Nix get over her failed engagement."

That sounded like a fucking terrible idea, but what did he know? His longest relationship had lasted six months. "Sure. Well, I'm gonna go open the studio."

"No, wait!" He heard several loud footsteps and then the front door flew open to reveal the youngest DaSilva in a red silk dress and yellow gumboots, her blue hair tied into a knot. "Let's get a coffee!" Tabby said.

"Uh…"

She tutted. "Come on, man, I need to get out of the house."

"What about Nicole?"

"She's fine! Sam's just put her in the bath with a glass of straight gin!"

Noah tried not to think about Nicole in the bath, drunk and needing consolation. He tried not to think about anything at all. His head felt like it had just been stuffed with fifty hard drives' worth of information. He needed time to sort this all out. "I should go back to the studio."

"Later." Tabby grabbed his arm and steered him toward the sidewalk. Noah decided to let her, it was easier that way. They walked toward Sydney Road.

"So," Tabby said. "What's new, Nobo? You still slamming Kelly?"

Noah liked Tabby, but sometimes he wished she'd never showed up to help Sam with the studio. She didn't give him sleepless nights like Nicole, but she also didn't bring the slightest bit of structure, levelheadedness, or homemade cookies to Silver Daughters. Instead, she brought a thirst for drama, shitty nicknames, and unhelpful observations.

"Don't look so shocked," Tabby said. "I saw the two of you leave together at Scott's housewarming. Sam knows although she's all *'respect his privacy, blah, blah, blah.'* Nice work, man, Kelly's helly-hot. I would say 'hella,' but it rhymes better this way."

Noah didn't say anything, and they walked to Hammers in silence. When they arrived, Tabby strode up to the counter. "Latte for the big guy, almond milk frappe for me, please."

The barista grinned, clearly under the impression they were a couple. Fat fucking chance. Tabby was attractive but with her blue hair and colourful tats, she reminded him of a Pokémon. She was the furthest thing from his type. He fucked women who had piercings and liked it rough in bed and told stories about this ex-boyfriend selling gear for the Banditos or that cousin doing time for armed robbery. The kind of women who looked at him and saw something familiar.

Although, Nicole wasn't like that, and it didn't seem to matter to his cock. He wanted her like she was the last woman on earth.

And now she's single...

He nudged Tabby out of the way and paid for their coffee. Would he get a chance to make good on all those heated little looks Nicole shot him? Should he order her a latte, take it back and—

What? Ask if she wanted a rebound fuck? In the wake of her engagement collapsing? Christ, if she didn't skin him, Sammy would.

Get real, he told himself, as he and Tabby moved aside to wait for their order. He and Nicole had chemistry, but she was rigid in a way her sisters weren't. Conservative. He bet she'd never had sex outside a relationship, and even if she did, it wouldn't be with him. Probably consider it a reduction of her overall marriage value. He liked fantasy novels, but he wasn't dumb enough to confuse them with the real world, or the shitty past he'd climbed out of.

His pocket buzzed, but he ignored his phone. He had a feeling it'd be Imogen or Jessica. He'd been fucking around lately, wanting a distraction that never fucking came.

Tabby turned to him, her fingers steepled in a way that reminded him of TV therapists. "You must be wondering why I asked you to have coffee with me?"

He stayed quiet.

"How long could you stay quiet if you wanted to?"

Forever.

He raised his eyebrows at Tabby, who sighed. "I asked for one reason and one reason only. I need you to come to Nix's party. Like, I really need that."

"You need some stuff moved?"

"No, I mean, I *could* use a hand giving people a ride to the bar, but I also need you to have sex with Nicole."

Noah stared, convinced he'd heard wrong.

"I've got it all figured out." Tabby unlocked her phone and showed him a list. "Around midnight, Nix will be medium-tipsy, and Sam will be moderately-drunk. The DJ will play *Toxic*, which is Sam's sex jam—don't ask me how I know that—and she and Scott will leave, thus removing a big obstacle between you and Nix. At this point, if I've played my cards correctly, Nix will approach *you,* at which point—"

Noah held up a hand. "This is not happening."

"But it should! This is exactly what Nix needs."

"How do you know?"

Tabby rolled her eyes. "I'm not going to dignify that with an answer. Anyway, don't act like you don't want to be all up in Nix. We all *know* you want to be all up in Nix. Just do it. I'll buy you a box of doughnuts."

This. This was why you didn't make friends. Why you didn't get attached to places. These complications, the little things people knew about you built up so that one day they all got used against you. Noah hadn't had time to process the Nicole situation, but one thing was clear—if Nicole didn't get back with her ex, she was going to stay at

Silver Daughters Ink, making his dick hard and his life miserable. It was in his best interest that she got back with her ex, and if that couldn't happen, he needed to stay the fuck away.

"I'm not coming," he told Tabby. "Prior commitment."

"So, you won't make Nicole happy by giving it to her hardcore and keeping her from her nutcase ex?"

"You've got some fuckin' balls calling *him* a nutcase."

Tabby didn't smile. "You'll regret it if you don't come to the party. Mark my words."

Their order was called. Noah had never been so happy to be getting a latte. "We're going now."

"Fine, but don't tell anyone about my indecent proposal."

"You couldn't pay me to."

"Not even for a million dollars?"

"No."

"Not even if it would save the lives of every cancer patient on planet Earth?"

Noah closed his eyes. He liked Tabby, but talking to her made him want a vasectomy ten thousand times more.

3

Nicole tugged at the hem of her sparkly red dress. She hadn't brought clubbing clothes with her to Melbourne, and Sam's taste was more adventurous than hers. The material required her to go commando, and she was already paranoid about flashing someone.

"I can't come out tonight," she told her twin.

Sam handed her a glass filled to the brim with sparkling wine. "You can. You will. You must. You have no alternative."

"Isn't this all a bit fascist? You and Tabby forcing me to have a party I don't want?"

"Not when we're doing it out of love. Drink."

Nicole sipped obediently. For the past week, she'd been doing whatever her sisters told her: eating when they put meals in front of her, falling asleep when they turned out the lights. Either she was obeying commands, or she was in their dad's office, pushing away thoughts of Aaron with work. She'd been sure that her manic breakup energy would reveal the reason Silver Daughters almost went bankrupt, but she'd found nothing.

"Did you or Dad make any big payments in the last twelve months?" she asked Sam for what felt like the millionth time. "Anything you withdrew out of the SDI accounts and forgot to put on the books?"

Sam glared at her over her wine glass. "No work talk."

"But—"

"I mean it, tonight is about drinking, dancing and screaming the word 'woo.' That's it."

"Fine, but we're talking about this tomorrow."

"Whatever. How are you feeling?" Sam squinted at her, clearly scanning for signs that she was going to cry or keel over. Nicole would be offended, but she'd done both multiple times this week. It was embarrassing how weak she was. She was single, not experiencing a terminal illness. She forced herself to smile at her twin. "I'm fine. Where's Tabby?"

"Right here, milady!"

Tabby burst into the room, shaking her arms so violently her boobs were bouncing out of her mini-dress. Nicole felt a pang of envy. Aaron always wanted her breasts to be bigger. He once suggested she ask her friend Jackie for the name of her surgeon. For a second, she wondered if they would still be together if she'd gotten fake boobs, and she realised she was being ridiculous. She might as well be cupping her cheeks and sighing *'Aaron used to love big cans...'* She snorted at her own joke.

"What?" Sam asked eagerly. "What's funny?"

"I'm just thinking about Aaron being a jerk."

Sam and Tabby looked at each other, clearly delighted.

Nicole rolled her eyes. "Stop being so encouraged by the smallest —oof!"

But both her sisters had thrown their arms around her, hugging her with all their might.

"You're going to be okay," Sam said, sounding insanely close to tears. "You're going to be fine."

"I know!"

Tabby put the Polaroid on her bedside table. "We need more champagne. Proper champagne."

"We have sparkling, we don't need champagne!"

But she had already dashed back out of the room.

"Oh well, better make room." Sam drained her glass in one. Nicole hesitated, then followed suit. The bubbles burned in her nose and she suppressed a burp. "Tonight isn't going to be too big of a thing, is it?"

"Nah, only the people who came over when I won Fadeout Festival."

Nicole gaped at her sister. "Almost two hundred people came over when you won Fadeout Festival!"

"Oh… yeah. They did, didn't they?"

"Sam! I don't want heaps of people knowing I got dumped! I haven't told my boss or any of my Adelaide friends…"

"So, think of this as a trial run for telling everyone else. Training wheels. Besides, these guys aren't arseholes. They won't drown you in fake sympathy wanting to know all the gory details and secretly wondering if they could bag Aaron."

"My Adelaide friends aren't like that!"

Sam turned away, examining her eyelashes in the mirror.

"They're not!"

Tabby re-entered the room carrying a bottle of Moët & Chandon. "Who's not?"

"My Adelaide friends aren't arseholes."

"Ah." Tabby raised the bottle. "Champagne?"

Nicole glared at her. "No. First, you both have to admit that my Adelaide friends aren't arseholes."

"Isn't it unkind to force people to say things that aren't true?"

Nicole stamped her foot, the way she used to when she was little, and Sam pretended she'd gone invisible. "It is true! Remember, you met Jackie and Taylor and Jennica and Chloe when we did that girls' trip to the Barossa Valley for my birthday! We drank wine and talked about TV? We had fun! They were nice!"

Sam picked at her eyelashes in the mirror, pointedly ignoring her.

Tabby winced. "Ah… Jennica did give me fifty bucks for a line. That was pretty nice. Although, maybe she just doesn't know how much drugs cost?"

Nicole scowled at her. "My friends are *nice*."

Tabby tilted her head to the side. "So why haven't you told them you've chucked Aaron?"

"Because it's not the right time! But they *do* like me, and they *are* nice!"

Her sisters were many things, but they weren't unkind. They didn't let the awkward silence fester. Instead, Sam plucked the Moët bottle out of Tabby's hand. "Let's get this thing open."

"I wanted to open it!"

Tabby and Sam tussled over the bottle until Tabby succeeded in ripping it away from Sam. She sprinted around the room, unwrapping the foil, as Sam chased her.

"You're shaking it up!" Nicole said, trying not to giggle.

Tabby dropped the foil and yanked off the little wire cage. "Who cares! You just escaped the shittiest relationship ever! I should pour it over your head like it's the Formula One!"

Nicole put her hands on her hair. "Don't do that."

"Fine." Tabby popped the cork into the ceiling and as the wine rose in a glut of foam, she drank straight from the neck.

"To our sister, Nixalopolous!" she shouted, holding it up for Sam. "She's back, and may she always stay back!"

Sam drank, and though she kept smiling, Nicole felt her happiness dim. She was grateful for all her sisters had done for her this week but she didn't want to 'stay back.' She wanted to improve. Now she'd had her week of mourning, it was time to put her nose to the grindstone and make new plans. She wanted her perfect life, and she wasn't going to find it in her childhood bedroom or getting drunk with her sisters.

She touched her watch, thinking about the laser appointment she'd made for next week.

"Nix!" Tabby rushed over holding up the bottle and she tilted her head back obediently but she kept her hand on her watch. For years she'd used her silver Cartier timepiece to cover her tattoo, but if she went through with her appointments, she'd need to cover her bare skin. If Sam and Tabby knew what she was planning, they'd shave her in her sleep.

Sam wiped her mouth with her tattooed forearm. "We need music. Everyone cool with Alison Wonderland?"

"Fuck no, we need my revenge playlist," Tabby said.

"Revenge playlist?"

Tabby sprinted out of the room, returning with her portable speakers, Rhianna's *Needed Me* blaring. "I found every single song about dumping trash and put it on the Silver Daughters Spotify. The playlist is called 'Dumping Trash.' It's already got fifty-three listens!"

Nicole frowned. "Dumping Trash?"

"Silver Daughters Spotify?" Sam raised a palm to the ceiling. "When the fuck did that happen?"

Tabby ignored both of them as she put the speakers on the dresser and pulled her phone from between her tits. "Right, photo time. Everyone say, 'Aaron's a fuckwit, and I hope he falls into an abandoned mine shaft and dies.'"

"Tabby!" Nicole protested as her little sister pulled her into her side.

Sam wrapped her arm around her other shoulder. "Aaron's a fuckwit, and I hope he falls into an abandoned mine shaft and dies."

The camera flashed. The resulting image showed her scowling at the camera, stuck between her two radiant, heavily tattooed sisters. So, just normal life.

There was a loud knock at the door, and Tabby let out a scream. "That'll be Toby and Scott! Hurry up, pound back the bubbles so we don't have to share."

"Maybe we *should* share," Nicole suggested, but Tabby had already taken a long swallow and handed the bottle to Sam. "Hurry up, Tobes is huge. He could finish this whole thing himself."

Sam cast her a suspicious look. "You're not doing him, are you?"

"No! We're just hanging out. I'm showing him how to walk on the wild side."

Sam's face creased with suspicion and Tabby laughed. "Not like that. We're mates."

"You better just be mates," Sam said, swigging champagne. "He's Scott's PA. If you wreck his head, you'll have me to answer to."

"Should Scott be going to parties with his PA?" Nicole asked Sam. "I know he and Toby get along, but isn't it unprofessional?"

Sam shrugged. "It doesn't matter as long as *someone* doesn't dick him around under the guise of being his mate."

"I'm not going to dick anyone," Tabby protested. "I'm taking a break from sex. Trying to get my chakras in line. Come on, Nix, have a big drink, and then we'll take some pre-party snaps."

Nicole made a face. "We don't need snaps."

"We absolutely do. Your eyelashes still look lit despite the buckets of tears you've cried this week. I have no idea how that happened, but it needs to be documented for the ages."

IT WAS MIDNIGHT, and Nicole was dancing with Tabby. She didn't know the song or who'd bought the peach cocktail in her hand, but she was having fun. The whole night had been fun. They'd gone for chicken and margaritas at Bellville, then to a drag show in Collingwood where a queen named Bitchney Sneers had pulled Nicole onto the glittering stage. She'd serenaded her with *I Will Survive* and Nicole had almost cried with laughter and amazement.

"That was so sick," Tabby had said afterwards. "This vid is going straight to the 'gram. I'll tag you!"

"No!" she'd said, but she was secretly thrilled when Tabby did it anyway. Her engagement shot up ten-fold whenever her Instagram famous little sister tagged her in anything.

At 10pm the five of them had headed to Emerald Bar for her 'official' party. Tabby steered her right past the bouncers and into the VIP section where two dozen vaguely familiar people were waiting. They cheered when they saw her, like she was a visiting celebrity.

"Did you tell them I got dumped?" Nicole hissed but Tabby had already ducked away to the bar.

"How can she afford all this?" Sam yelled over the music. "She better not be selling gak."

"She's not," Toby shouted. "She offered the owners free tattoos. And a couple of the bartenders at Bellville. And the drag queen, I think."

Sam pressed a hand to her eyes. "Why do I ever ask? Someone get me a drink."

Scott smoothed a hand over her shoulder. "I'm on it, darling. Nicole, would you like a drink?"

Not as much as she wanted everyone to stop deferring to her, but she knew they were only being nice. "A vodka soda, please."

"You got it."

That drink had been hours ago and though people kept handing her fresh ones, Nicole didn't feel drunk. Maybe because she was dancing. Time had always felt slippery when she was dancing. She loved it. When she was younger, she'd fantasied about doing burlesque like Sam, or maybe even being a stripper, moving so well that men fell over themselves to book her for private dances. Maybe even men like—

Don't.

If there was one thing she'd gotten good at since Aaron left, it was ignoring thoughts of Noah. She had a life to rebuild and he had no role to play in her shiny new future. Her focus was firmly on removing her tattoo, getting an even better job in Melbourne, and finding the father of her children.

Only, now she'd been drinking, thoughts of his shoulders and big tattooed hands kept coming unbidden. She felt a heat washing through her body as she danced and realised, with some surprise, she wanted to be touched. It had been so long since—

"Want another drink?" Tabby shouted as Ocean Park Standoff bled into a trance-y cover of Pumped Up Kicks. "I'm pretty sure Anthony'll get you one."

Nicole laughed. Anthony was one of Tabby's friends. He was indie boy cute and had flirted with her in a way that made her feel charming rather than pressured. "He's too young for me. I've got next."

"Cheers. Rum and ginger, please."

Nicole finished the last of her peach drink and headed for the bar, weaving around young, never-been-engaged people. Where was Aaron tonight? Trying to chat up every girl in the world, probably. A few weeks of debauchery, then he'd buckle down and find her replacement.

She paused, letting other people jostle past her. Who *would* Aaron's next fiancée be? He was the only man she'd met whose standards were even higher than hers. Once upon a time, he'd called her 'the closest thing to perfect' but she'd failed, hadn't she? And she was vain enough to care.

"Excuse me," a girl said. "Can I get past?"

"Oh sorry." Nicole stepped aside. She wasn't going to the bar; she'd find Tabby and tell her she was tired and—

She felt him a split second before she saw him. An electrical fizz down her back made her shift, squinting through the crowd until she spotted him sitting beside the bar, beer in hand.

Her first thought was that Noah Newcomb was so not handsome. His bent nose and forehead were exaggerated by the strobe lights and he looked so menacing, she'd have picked him for a bouncer. But her second thought was that she was glad he'd come. More than glad. *Relieved*. Her insides warmed like she'd been drinking Christmas brandy and all she wanted was for him to look up. To see her.

As though he could hear her thoughts, Noah turned. Their eyes met, green into blue, and the heat in her middle became something akin to burning. She waved, because she didn't know what else to do. "Hi!" she mouthed. "Thanks for coming!"

Idiotic. So, so dorky.

Noah didn't deign to reply. Instead he smirked, that familiar, *'you want it, don't you?'* leer. He studied Sam's dress with lazy approval, his gaze lingering on her hemline.

She wanted to be disgusted, but sparks skittered across her skin. She stood in the spotlight of his attention, her body tingling as though his hands were on her, stroking gently. She couldn't remember a man ever looking at her like that. Like she was Marilyn Monroe, swirling her white skirt; the epitome of feminine attractiveness. The crowd surged around her, but she didn't pay them any mind. She needed to stay here, keep him watching her—

An elbow clipped her side.

"Oof!" Nicole turned to see a man in a pinstripe shirt grinning. "Sorry. Shit place to stand though."

Nicole rubbed where his elbow had caught her ribs. "Jerk."

Out of the corner of her eye, she saw Noah rise to his feet, his expression murderous. He looked like a stone giant brought to life by an evil wizard.

She waved both hands at him. "No! Please don't come over."

Noah glared after pinstripe guy and she could see the anger thrumming inside him. Panic shot through her, its taste metallic on her tongue. He looked so—she hated herself for thinking it—mean. It was the easiest thing in the world to imagine Noah taking the pinstripe man outside and cracking him open like an egg. And not because of her, though that would be the excuse, but because he could. Because it would be easy.

For the millionth time, she wondered who Noah Newcomb was. Sam and Tabby knew so little about him. *She* knew so little about him. All around him men moved aside, tucked their girlfriends under their arms. How would it feel to have that power? To be so intimidating? Did it make you mean just on principle?

Noah's nostrils flared and he sat down. Relief swamped her and, not wanting another excuse for him to get up, she turned and headed for the bar. He watched her leave. She could feel it. Her ass tingled like eyesight had a touch.

"How'd you go?" Tabby shouted when she returned to the dance floor with their drinks.

"Fine," she lied. "Noah's here. Did you invite him?"

"Yeah, but I didn't think he'd show." Tabby took a long sip of ginger rum. "Did you know he's fucking Kelly?"

Time did a little stop-reverse. "What?"

"Noah's drilling Kelly. You know, Sam's model."

Oh, she knew Kelly. Five-eleven, blonde, pretty tattoos all over her tanned skin. She'd been on the cover of *FHM* and had twenty thousand Instagram followers. Sexy, sensual, sexpot Kelly. And she was having sex with Noah. Her gut twisted like a fish on a hook. She had no right to be upset, none whatsoever, but why had he made her feel…? How could she have ever thought…?

Tabby pounded her back. "Nix, brah. You cool?"

"How could he do that?"

Tabby raised a brow. "Eh?"

She swallowed, trying not to imagine Noah and Kelly in bed together, tall and tattooed and groaning in unison. "How could Noah do that to Sam? Kelly's her favourite tattoo model. What if it ends badly and Sam can't use her anymore?"

"Sam'll live. And it won't end badly. The dark horse knows what he's doing."

"Excuse me?" She could hear herself becoming prim. She always did that when she was upset.

Tabby drank more ginger rum, oblivious to her panic. "Uh, pretty much what I said. Noah gets laid like it's his job."

Nicole gaped at her sister. "But why? He's so quiet and he's covered in blackwork and he always looks angry and he's just so not the kind of guy anyone fantasises about!"

She blurted it out like a confession, as though she wanted Tabby to solve the crime of her infatuation. But she just shrugged. "He's big, man. He's big and he's mean and he looks like he could tear a boar apart with his bare hands."

"So?"

Tabby rolled her eyes. "Christ, you're naïve. Hey, I think that's Murphy. Murph! Murph! Over here!"

Tabby darted away like a silverfish, leaving Nicole to her confusion. Noah and Kelly. Kelly and Noah. Her jealousy was so sharp she could have cut someone with it. Kelly. She could have cut Kelly with it. God, she needed help processing this. She looked around for Sam, but she and Scott were dancing to a Britney song in a way that said they were leaving as soon as it ended. She lined up for the bathroom and peed. When she got out of the stall, she splashed cold water on her wrists while she studied herself in the mirror. She looked fine. Good, even. But she didn't look sexy. She'd always struggled with sexy. It wasn't about looks—Sam was her genetic double and she was sexy. It was her *personality* that was wrong. She couldn't show she was turned on in a non-embarrassing way. The sluttiest lingerie looked girly on her and she made dumb faces during sex. Aaron said she looked like was sitting on a pincushion. She'd cried and he'd apologised, but only because he'd hurt her feelings, not because it wasn't true.

She looked at the bare finger where the ring used to be. If there was a time to give being sexy another try, the week she got dumped was a good bet. And if Noah really was a dark horse and definitely wasn't 'father of her children' material, was there any harm in exploring… that… with him?

She looked into her own eyes, silently asking if Noah Newcomb made her feel sexy.

I don't know, came the answer. He makes me feel exposed. Is that the same?

She didn't think so, but maybe it was the start of sexy; that flaying, nowhere-to-hide sensation. Maybe if she followed it, sexy would pursue.

A girl gang burst into the bathroom, chatting and laughing. Nicole left the bathroom, not thinking, just moving. She found Noah in the same place, drinking a different beer and interacting with no one. She slipped into the seat beside him.

"Hello. You're sleeping with Kelly."

Noah squinted, as though unsure she was there. "You drunk?"

"No!"

A raised brow.

"Yes! But that's not the point," she said, louder than she intended. God, of all the times for the alcohol to kick in… she focused hard on Noah's face, determined to keep her train of thought on track. "Do you want to know something?"

"Am I gonna hear it regardless?"

"Probably!" She leaned closer and his scent hit her in a rush of warm cedar. Was that cologne beneath the laundry detergent and fresh tobacco? Noah didn't seem like the kind of guy who wore Giorgio Armani but then why did he smell so delicious? Was it his sweat? Some kind of pheromone? She leaned closer, trying to subtly inhale and almost toppled off her stool.

Noah gripped her arm, holding her in place. "Do you want me to get Sam?"

"Please, no. If they know I'm drunk, she and Tabby will start mothering me intensely."

"And that's your job, isn't it?"

If she hadn't seen his mouth move, she wouldn't have believed he'd talked. Noah Newcomb saying something personal—and mildly bitchy—about her behaviour?

"I have to mother them," she said with all the dignity her drunk tongue could muster. "Our mother left, you know, when Sam and I were eight and Tabby was four."

His face softened. "I know. Sorry, Nikki."

Her heart pulsed so hard it was like her weight was shifting. She looked at him, and the pure, unadulterated beauty of his irises made her say it. "Noah, do you know I've only slept with three guys?"

The corners of his mouth twitched. "Three more than me."

"You know what I mean. That's not enough. The first two were when I was in *high school*. That's not normal."

God he was so close, so close and his eyes were the colour of a football field, so green and lovely and his lips were nice too, fuller than she'd realised. She remembered that night in the hallway, when they'd almost, kind of kissed, and a zap wove itself down her stomach and between her legs.

"Nicole." Noah's face wavered in front of her like Christmas lights. "You want some water?"

She shook her head, wanting to say it so bad, it was almost scary. She bit her cheeks and the pain incited action. "I want you... us... to... you know. Tonight."

Noah face grew stony. He looked as angry as he had when pinstripe shirt elbowed her. "Not gonna happen."

It was lucky she'd taken so many blows to her emotional system this week. The rejection hurt, but it was a dull ache, not a sting. Not anything that would make her cry. She'd go home and examine her bruises tomorrow. She stood, feeling delicate but steady. "Okay, bye."

She turned and walked away and it would have been fine, only her heel caught on a slippery thing—lime wedge?—and then she was on the floor, her knees, chin, and palms throbbing with the impact of her fall. There was a collective gasp over the music and fifty hands seemed to pull her to her feet.

"Are you okay?" a redhead asked.

"I'm fine." She brushed her hands down Sam's dress, hoping Noah hadn't seen her. That he'd had a heart attack. That she'd been imagining him this whole time and he didn't really exist. Without looking back at him, she headed for the exit, pretending she couldn't feel her throbbing skin.

A warm hand closed around her shoulder. "You okay?"

Nicole felt her eyes prickle. "Don't. Please, just don't."

Noah didn't let go. He turned her to face him, gentle but unrelenting. Nicole kept her gaze on his shoes. If he was laughing, even slightly amused, she'd die from embarrassment.

"Nikki..." He slid a finger under her chin, tilting her face up.

He wasn't smiling. His expression was as sternly neutral as it always was and that was a comfort, as real and warm as his hands.

"I'll take you back to yours," he said. "Come on."

He slid an arm around her and her whole body tingled with beautiful electricity.

4

The street outside was packed and throbbing with the music from the bar. Nicole looked around for a taxi, but Noah took her arm. "I'm parked in the side street."

"You drove?"

"Yup, only had two beers."

Her mortification doubled. He'd remember in HD sobriety the way she'd propositioned him and chin-stacked and all the other humiliating crap she'd done tonight. She shook her arm, trying to break his grasp. "I have to go back. I left my bag inside."

Noah didn't budge. "You didn't bring a bag. Come on, Nikki. When you hit the deck, the night's over. That's the rules."

She'd have told him to shove his rules, but a crowd of lads walked past, hollering and whooping to line up at the door. With Noah at her side, they acted like she was invisible, but if she had to queue to get back in, she doubted they'd be polite. And her knees and chin and palms *were* still stinging. "Fine. Let's go."

He led her to his van, walking slowly so she could match his stride. "Is your head okay?"

"I landed on my chin," she said, trying to sound like it didn't matter. As though none of this mattered. Noah's half smile said she wasn't pulling it off.

Noah's van sat white and dusty on the side-street. He opened the passenger side door for her. "You okay?"

"*Yes.*" She practically leapt inside trying to prove it. It made her wounded knees ache. She'd ridden in Noah's van before and the smell was familiar—cigarettes, dust and a cinnamon sweetness she couldn't place. It was nice. In fact, everything about being out of the noise and heat of the bar was nice.

Noah climbed into the driver seat, pulling his seat belt across his chest. The sight made her giggle. The sight and all the gin.

He frowned. "What?"

"You're too scary-looking to put safety first."

Noah didn't smile, but the lines beside his mouth got a little deeper. "You want food or something before I take you home?"

"Can't we go back to your place?" she asked, emboldened by his almost-grin.

Noah's jaw worked like he was chewing gum. "I said I was taking you to yours."

"And coming inside...?"

"No."

This time the rejection stung. She must be sobering up. "Why not? You're always looking at me like you want to see me naked. Or are you making fun of me?"

Noah leaned over, grabbing her seat belt buckle. She flinched. "What are you doing?"

He smiled then, a cold flash of teeth, and he drew the seat belt across her chest, snapping it into place.

"Oh, um, thanks."

He gave her a look she couldn't parse.

"What?"

He didn't answer, just pulled out his keys and started the engine. They set off down Greville Street and Nicole let her head loll to the side. She felt like someone had scraped a knife over her drunkenness and was determinately chipping away to the hurt waiting for her in sobriety. No sisters or work or even casual sex for distraction. It was back to reality now.

A week ago, I was engaged, she thought. *Now I'm single with two skinned knees. How did this happen?*

She heard a strange sound and turned to see Noah snapping a lighter in front of the cigarette in his teeth. She watched the end become an electric cherry.

"You shouldn't smoke in here," she said.

"It's my van."

She'd give him that one. She returned her gaze to the street. Three girls in mini-dresses were having a fight, pointing their fingers and flicking their hair. She was extra glad to be on her way home. "Thanks for the ride."

Noah rolled down the window. He looked angry for some reason she couldn't help but feel responsible for. She considered asking him what was wrong, but history dictated this would go unanswered. She tried for small talk. "Why do you have a van?"

"Because I do."

Her temper flared like the end of his cigarette. "Is it that hard to say 'I like the colour' or 'I won it in a bet?' Do you really have to be grumpy *all the time*?"

Noah looked over at her, his eyes lovely in the yellowish glow of the streetlamps. "You want to talk meaningless shit so you don't have to think?"

"I wanted to sleep with you, but that's not an option, apparently."

The corners of his mouth quirked.

"Are you laughing at me? Because if you are, I will jump out of this car."

"It's a van."

"Yeah, it is! A creepy van. Isn't it enough that you're huge and covered in tattoos? Do you really need to drive a van?"

They stopped at a red light. Noah dragged on his cigarette. The end burned like the light holding them in place. Stupidly, she realised they were alone for the first time since they'd kissed in the dark. She folded her arms over her chest, wishing she was already in bed. The silence stretching between them was excruciating. At least it was for her. Maybe Noah didn't give a damn. The light turned green and they drove on.

"How long have you smoked?" she asked because she *needed* to break the tension.

"A while."

In someone else, that might have meant a few years, but Nicole bet Noah was one of those ratty pre-teens who hung out on street corners, blowing smoke at strangers. Burlesquing as the adults they wanted to be. Silence swooped over them and she twisted her fingers in her lap. They weren't even close to Brunswick. This was *torture*.

"Okay."

Her mouth went dry. "Okay to what?" *Okay to sex?*

"We'll talk if that's what you want."

"It is."

But Noah didn't respond, just kept smoking and staring ahead. She clicked her tongue. "When you said, 'we'll talk,' did you mean 'sit here in silence, making me doubt every decision I've ever made?'"

His mouth quirked. "You're trying to be cute."

"Is that a crime?"

Noah ground his cigarette butt into a tray on the dash. "Why do you want me to fuck you?"

Nicole blinked, half-sure she'd misheard him. "Um, why not?"

"Not good enough."

She sat up a little straighter. "Do people need a reason to do sex?"

"No."

"But I do?"

Noah didn't say anything. He looked angry again. She chewed her tongue. She could call him out, but why? Her life was sad enough without trying to debate Noah Newcomb into bed. If he didn't want to sleep with her, that was his decision.

Noah opened his mouth, then closed it again.

"Ooh, what?"

He shook his head, clearly irritated with himself. Nicole turned toward him, oddly excited. "Come on, you can tell me!"

Noah grimaced. "You're scared of me."

"No, I'm not."

"You freaked out when I put your seat belt on. And you told me to stay away when that asshole shoved you at the bar."

Was this what he was mad about? Why he didn't want to sleep with her? Nicole laughed, she was so relieved. "That seat belt thing was involuntary, and that pinstripe guy wasn't worth starting a fight over. I hurt myself more when I fell over."

Noah didn't seem to think this was a good explanation. He glared out into the traffic, looking angrier than ever.

"Now you know I'm not scared of you, can we hook up?" she asked, figuring it was worth another shot. "It's okay if you're not attracted to me, but now seems like the right time. You know, since we're alone and single and we have nothing better to do."

Noah's jaw jutted. "You think I'll jam my dick into anything that breathes, don't you?"

"Isn't that... your deal?"

Bad idea. Noah's lip curled and in the shadowy light, he looked so genuinely frightening, Nicole recoiled.

"Sorry, but I thought you slept around."

"Who told you that?"

"Tabby. She says you're a dark horse."

Noah slumped back into his seat. "I haven't... that's a new development."

"Why?"

He didn't answer. Silence swelled between them again. Nicole twisted her fingers together, linking the bones as tightly as she could. "You know, if you don't think of me like that, you can just say so. I know I'm not sexy and Kelly is. And all the other girls you're with probably are, too."

This was followed by another silence, this one tight as tooth floss.

"What?"

Nicole blanched. "I... what do you mean?"

"Who the fuck told you you're not sexy?"

"Um, Aaron, kind of, but I've never been sexy. Not like Sam or

Tabby. But it's not a comparison thing, I'm just weird when it comes to sex. I pretend I'm somewhere else and I can't relax. It just doesn't work."

Noah flicked open his cigarette packet and placed a fresh one between his teeth, his movements rough and jerky.

"Are you angry because I don't think I'm sexy?"

He nodded.

Nicole's head throbbed. From the alcohol or disappointment, she wasn't sure. "Why?"

He shook his head, snapping his lighter to create another red cherry. The sudden light combined with the curl of his lips made him look rakish. Nicole pictured Noah's big mean tattoos peeking around the corners of a tailored suit. Her insides squeezed tight. They were almost at her place. She was never going to know why he wouldn't sleep with her, and tomorrow she'd be sober enough to regret everything. She twisted her hands together and gasped as a bone in her index finger popped.

"Stop." Noah's voice was hard. "Stop hurting yourself."

She untwisted her fingers. "Nervous habit."

He muttered something, exhaling a silvery stream of smoke.

"What was that?"

"Probably something your ex gave you," he said through his teeth. "Along with the dumb cunt idea you're not sexy."

"Oh." Her lips spread in an unbidden smile. "Does that mean you think I am?"

"Nicole, I swear to Christ…"

"What?"

Noah inhaled, turning an inch of cigarette to ash. "You better not be serious."

It was silly to be flattered by a non-compliment, but Nicole couldn't stop smiling. She rubbed her upper arms, trying to smooth the goosebumps.

Then a horrible idea occurred to her. "Are you in love with Kelly? Are you taken?"

Noah scowled. "Fuck, no."

Lightness, with an unpleasant aftertaste. "So why can't we... you know?"

He let out a little groan. "Nikki..."

She knew she was whining like a brat who wanted a pony, but it felt like she was edging toward an honest answer and she didn't have anything to lose. "If you think I'm sexy and we're both single?"

"Dumping your ex doesn't mean you should come looking for a fuck from me."

He did want to go home with her, Nicole realised. She could hear it in his voice, but she could also hear his resolve. She might get a reason but she wouldn't be touched, so why bother?

She rubbed her shoulders, trying to relax. You'd think the big guy with the dirty tattoos who stared point-blank at her tits was a safe bet, but you never knew, did you? She moved her hands lower; her nipples were swollen, aching from rubbing against Sam's dress. Maybe she'd take a bath when she got home and—

"Nicole."

"What?" She frowned, then realised her hands were inside her dress, massaging her breasts.

"Sorry," she said, pulling her hands away. "I'm... you know. But that's not your problem, as you made clear. And I respect."

Noah slowly ground his second cigarette into the ashtray. Something about it made her mouth dry. She turned to look out the window and realised they were on her street. Noah pulled up outside the studio and turned off the engine. She could hear crickets and cicadas, nature penetrating even the inner suburbs. Her fingers shook as she unclipped her seatbelt. "Okay, thanks for the lift—"

"Give me your hand."

His voice was low. Hard. Before she processed what he'd asked, she'd extended her palm. Noah took it, his fingers rough and warm. Then he positioned her hand on his thigh. Only it wasn't his thigh, she was touching his...

Nicole whimpered. "That's..."

"Yeah."

Heat spread through her belly like lava, but she couldn't move, couldn't do anything except clasp her hand to Noah's erection. She was breathing hard and fast like an accordion. "What are you...?"

Noah leaned across the inner console, bringing the burr of cigarette smoke with him. She didn't want to find it attractive but the edge of it, the ugliness, was making her heart pound.

"You still want me to fuck you?"

She nodded dumbly.

"No, you don't." He moved closer. So close, stubble scratched her cheek. "I'll give you nightmares."

"You *won't*." She still sounded bratty, but she couldn't help it. Her nipples were throbbing and her—god it was so hard to call it any of the words—*ached*. She had never wanted a man so badly. Why couldn't Noah just take her? Not make her touch his penis and discuss her feelings, but take control of this situation?

Noah's hand covered hers, guiding her palm along his erection. She felt him swell beneath the denim and the situation was so bright, so real. She tried to jerk her palm away but Noah's hand tightened, keeping her where she was. "You are scared of me, aren't you?"

"A little bit."

"What if I said I like that?"

Nicole closed her eyes, too turned on and overwhelmed to make sense of the question. He was so big. So big and so hard... "I don't know."

He made a chainsaw noise in the back of his throat. "You like it, too, don't you? The thought of me forcing myself on you? Making you take it?"

Yes. She felt the answer as much as she thought it. She licked her lips, her skin ten times more sensitive than it should have been. "Can we do that?"

His face was in shadow, but she could see him shake his head.

A stab of misery. "Because you don't want me?"

A snarl and her head jerked back, pain bursting at the back of her skull. Noah's fist was tight in her hair. She jerked her head forward, but he held her fast. "Because I'll hurt you, Nicole. I've wanted you for too long, too fucking bad to hold back. You let me into that little pussy, I'll fuck you until it hurts. I want it too much not to."

Her stomach tightened, she felt like she was falling, spinning through space with no fear of hitting the ground. "Noah, please?"

He gave a hard laugh. "You think you'll like it, but you don't have a fucking clue. It'll be hours, Nikki. I'll fuck you in every hole you have. You'll be so desperate you'll do whatever I want, beg for shit you've never even heard of."

She was shaking, sure if he wasn't holding her, she'd slide to the van floor. "I want that."

"Do you?"

She nodded, the movement sending pain shooting through her scalp, but it was nothing compared to the liquid heat between her thighs. "I know I do."

He bent forward. She thought he was going to kiss her, but his teeth closed on her lower lip and pain whistled through her. She gasped.

"You don't know shit. You've only fucked three guys and I bet you wanted to marry all of them. You won't want to marry me, Nikki. You won't want to *look* at me once I'm done with you."

He released her hair and she slumped back into her seat, scalp tingling. Noah eased her palm away from his cock. "You okay?"

The question confused her. Was she okay? Was anything okay? It all felt up for debate. "Kinda?"

He nodded. "Want me to walk you up?"

She looked over at him and as with their hallway kiss, she wondered if the hair-pulling and lip-biting had been a hallucination. "Will you come inside?"

But she knew the answer was no even before he shook his head. "Go to bed."

She could have stayed but in truth, she was so rattled, it was a relief to leave his strange van and the strange thing between them. To get back to the familiar un-sexiness of the real world and away from the undeniably sexy, but incredibly confusing unknown that was Noah Newcomb.

5

Nicole slept badly. She woke multiple times, her pillow crammed between her legs, the memory of Noah pulling her hair back so vivid, it might still have been happening. When she got up to pee she was still lopsided with alcohol and a guilty conscience. For once, she successfully fought the urge to be productive and got back into bed, determined to sleep her bad mood away. It didn't work. She stayed entirely conscious, replaying her ride with Noah; the tobacco and cinnamon smell of his van, the feel of his cock through his jeans, the sting of his teeth closing on her lip.

As the sun rose and her mind stayed on Noah, Nicole found her hand had idled into her underwear. She was so wet, it was obscene. Gross, but she couldn't stop. She stroked herself and was soon so swollen, her panties felt like a chastity belt. But no matter how turned on she got, she couldn't embellish her memories into a satisfying fantasy. Every time she tried, she saw Noah ordering her to bed like a strict parent and winced into her pillows. Eventually, she gave up, lying back and hating her needy body. She was a grown woman masturbating over a man who didn't even want to sleep with her. Pathetic. She got up and took a shower, scrubbing away the slipperiness between her legs. She brushed her teeth and completed her

Korean skincare regimen, an anti-pollution oil cleanse, a green tea water-based cleanse, a lemon exfoliating scrub. She applied a thin layer of AHA toner followed by floral essence. Next came Vitamin C serum and a coat of collagen moisturiser. By the time Nicole dabbed tinted SPF 50+ CC cream under her eyes, she felt renewed. The problem was, now she was out of bed, she had nothing to do. The studio was closed, Sam was still with Scott, and Tabby wasn't home. She supposed she could call Aaron about canceling the wedding, but that ranked slightly above 'cleaning the toilet' as a fun way to spend a Sunday afternoon.

She wandered to the kitchen, wondering if she should make keto muffins when her gaze fell on Tabby's iPad. There was something she could do... not the smartest idea, but compelling enough to push apart her clouds of Sundayitis.

She turned on the tablet and opened the Silver Daughters email account. After looking around fervently, she pulled up Noah's last paycheck invoice then copied his tax file number into her work accountancy program. His details came up at once. *Noah Harold Newcomb.*

Harold? Her inner Tabby cackled. *Fuckin' woof!*

It was a fairly bad middle name. She didn't know if anyone had ever looked less like a 'Harold.' Her fingers hovered over the touch-screen—to click or not to click? What she was doing wasn't *illegal*, but it didn't feel moral.

If you want to know about Noah's past, why don't you ask him? her inner Sam suggested.

Because he wouldn't tell me anything.

What do you think you'll find?

Something.

She knew there was something to find, knew it down to her bones. Noah's refusal to talk about his past was more than stoicism, she was sure of it. Then there were some of his tattoos—a spider web on his left elbow, a clock with no hands hidden inside his right sleeve, the bushranger Ned Kelly's last words *'such is life'* scrawled along the back of his neck. Noah wasn't the kind of guy who jazzed up his middle-class background with criminal tattoos, so why did he have them? She'd always been suspicious but now he'd bitten her lip and told her his fantasies would give her nightmares, she'd be an idiot not to dig. She had a moral imperative to dig!

And you're single enough to dig? Sam asked.

"Shh."

Nicole took a deep breath and clicked his name. The first thing she saw was his birthday—November 15, 1985. He was thirty-four. That wasn't a huge surprise, but it felt good to know. The man who'd held her palm to his cock had a birthday, just like everyone else.

The rest of the results weren't nearly so straightforward. Noah had only consistently filed taxes for the past five years—when he'd started working at Silver Daughters. Had he been earning so little before that he didn't meet the minimum threshold? It didn't seem likely and he didn't seem the type to have been studying or living overseas or any of the obvious explanations. Disappointed, Nicole exited the accounting website and googled 'Noah Newcomb.' The top results were the Silver Daughters website and Instagram. The rest of the Noah's were randoms.

Nicole's gnawed her lower lip. Not being able to stalk someone in this day and age was infuriating. Her research options were dwindling. As his boss, Sam could apply for a national police check on Noah, but she wasn't going to do that. As Sam's genetic double, she could pretend to be her twin and ask for the police check, but if Sam found out, she'd slap her into the next decade.

She drummed her fingers on the kitchen table, trying to think of things to Google. She added Noah's middle name to the keywords and tapped search. A wall of flaming skulls filled the screen.

An old tattoo design of Noah's? They didn't look like his style, though they were weirdly familiar... Nicole squinted and realised they weren't skulls, they were helmets. Square helmets with a slit for eyes, the same kind Ned Kelly and his bushrangers wore. Was Noah related to Ned Kelly and trying to keep it a secret? That would be kind of cute...

She scrolled to the text results and saw news articles accompanied by more flaming helmets.

Further arrests in Rangers Motorcycle gang operation.
Bikie Boss jumps bail for Bali.
Two in court on drug charges following Rangers gang raids.

A golf ball lodged itself in her chest, forcing her ribs out and away. She *did* know that flaming helmet, but not because of Ned Kelly or a tattoo she'd seen growing up. She knew it from the news.

With shaking fingers, she clicked the link that said *Bikie Boss jumps bail and heads for Bali.*

"Oh my gosh!"

The man in the image wasn't Noah, but the resemblance was uncanny. He had the same wide forehead and hollow eye sockets, though his irises were brown, not green. Nicole stared at the flabby, unshaven face and her heart gave a hot squeeze. She felt like Bluebeard's wife, standing at the door of her husband's forbidden room, key in hand. There was still time to turn away, though she knew she wouldn't.

In for a penny, Sam whispered.

"In for a pound."

She inhaled and scrolled down.

Notorious one-percent bikie boss, Harold Newcomb, is believed to be hiding in Bali's Kuta Beach. Newcomb is avoiding prosecution for manslaughter, blackmail, possessing a prohibited weapon, drug trafficking, and assault. All crimes he conducted during his reign as chapter president of The Rangers Motorcycle Gang.

Spit filled Nicole's mouth. She kept scrolling through the details of Harold Newcomb's crimes, speculation he was being hidden by fellow bikies, reminders that he was incredibly dangerous and, right down the bottom, a quote from his ex-wife, Natalie Newcomb.

I haven't heard from Harry for years and neither has my boy. P**s off the lot of you.

She stood and paced the kitchen, the tablet loose in her hands. She knew Noah was hiding something, but she'd thought it was tattooing without a license or selling weed or punching someone in a bar fight. Not a dad who was the head of an infamous bikie gang. Despite how people like Aaron regarded tattoo studios, she had never met a bikie. Her dad's policy had always been to respectfully turn away men who wanted him to do club tats. He was a hippie who took a dim view of organized crime. Yet, he'd hired the son of one of the most notorious bikers in Australia. Had he known? He couldn't have or he'd have told her or Sam. And where was Noah in all this bikie business? His mum clearly wasn't a fan of Harold. Had he grown up estranged from his dad? Outside the criminal lifestyle?

"In for a penny, in for a pound," she muttered and Googled 'Harold Newcomb,' 'Rangers,' 'Family', typing quickly, as though the words might burn her.

The first result was a website called onepercentbikers.com.au. She scrolled past the details of Harold's childhood and how he formed The Rangers in the eighties. The writing was amateurish and peppered with grammatical errors. There was no reference to Noah anywhere. She scrolled to the section labeled 'personal life.'

From 1985 to 1995 Harold Newcomb was married to Natalie Dreyer. They had a son in 1985. He's believed to have been patched into The Rangers in 2003.

Nicole's heart was pulsing, pounding. It didn't prove anything; anyone could set up a website and write any old garbage... except Noah looked like Harold and Harold was undeniably a biker and he had a son born the same year as Noah and Noah was big and scary and had big scary tattoos and...

"Oh my *god*." Nicole pressed the tablet to her forehead. "Oh my god, I tried to sleep with a biker!"

What would Sam say when this got out? She hated bullies, and bikies were just bullies covered in the skins of dead cows. And Tabby... Tabby was going to freak out. They'd be lucky if she didn't live stream herself confronting Noah and post it to every social media platform on earth.

Nicole paced back to her bedroom and locked the door. Then she curled back under the covers, shoes and all, comforted by the soft weight and the fact she was alone. That the secret was still hers. She couldn't tell her sisters what she'd discovered. They'd accuse her of snooping on and suspecting the worst of someone they liked. She needed proof.

She unlocked the tablet and searched for articles about Noah. There was nothing. She expanded her search to The Rangers, but most of the news copy were lists of crimes with few names and details added. She needed *context*. To understand how dangerous bikers could be—how dangerous Noah might be. There was that TV show, *Sons of Anarchy*, but after scanning a few plot summaries, she doubted watching it would be helpful. She doubted Noah's mother had ever murdered one of his girlfriends. She'd found an eBook, *Blood in the Gears,* that had been written anonymously by a Rangers ex-member in 2006. She bought it and downloaded the copy onto the iPad.

After a pit stop, she returned to her bed with a cup of peppermint tea and began to read. The first few chapters tracked the biker tradition from America to Australia in the 1900s. She skimmed the flabby exposition and wondered where Noah was. Home? In bed with Kelly? Riding a motorbike across the countryside because he was a criminal?

The memoir picked up slightly in chapter three. The author described how meth production and distribution boomed in the early nineties, flushing money into the gang. Everyone got new motorbikes and a three-storey clubhouse was paid for in cash. The Big Boss—Nicole assumed this was Harold Newcomb, though he was never addressed by name—threw a party with unlimited alcohol, cocaine and thirty 'prozzers.' Nicole thought of Noah's bulky, greying father and poked her tongue out. Whatever they'd paid the sex workers, it hadn't been enough. The role of women within the gang was limited and demeaning. They were either wives, granted thin status as a biker's property, or 'sluts' who hung out at the clubhouse.

"They're just holes," the author wrote. "They hang around because of the money or the drugs, or to piss off their parents. Some just want a good fuck. Most holes get what they came for."

Nicole made a face. That was the grossest thing she'd ever read, and she'd finished *American Psycho*. She remembered Noah, his fist in her hair, his mouth inches from hers. *"I'll fuck you in every hole you have."*

It wasn't the same. He hadn't been calling *her* a hole, he'd just been referring to the parts of her that *were*—

"Urgh!" She wasn't sure what was more embarrassing, her rationalisations or the fact she wanted to rationalise Noah calling parts of her body... that. Did he see her the way the author saw the women who hung around the club?

The thought should have been repulsive; but all she could think about was how Noah watched her across the bar, hungrily, disrespectfully. She closed her eyes and was back in his van, her lips stinging from his bite.

You let me into that little pussy, I'll fuck you until it hurts.

Nicole actually shivered. Her shoulders shook and goosebumps raced along her arms. Was this her fault for rejecting sex and danger? Was she now doomed to crave sex with bikers and the biker adjacent? She didn't know. What she did know was that she needed to orgasm or risk insanity, but she *couldn't*. Not now she knew Noah's secret...

Her lower body throbbed, and she brushed a hand over her sex. Just that slight touch sent another ripple of energy along her skin, making her whimper. She looked around the room but none of her silent possessions offered any assistance.

Resistance is futile, Tabby said. *Get down to business.*

Sam laughed. *The business of giving yourself the business.*

Nicole screwed up her nose. She did not need her sisters anywhere near her sexuality.

As though to assist her, their voices dissolved, and a fantasy began to play. She was standing outside The Rangers clubhouse, in jean shorts and her cowboy boots—they didn't pinch her toes like they usually did, and her makeup was natural-perfect. Her hair looked great, too, thick and lightly curled.

Nicole settled back with a smile. This was a fantasy she could get behind. Now, why was she going anywhere near a biker gang? Maybe she wanted drugs? No, that was spooky. Maybe she needed money? Yes, maybe her dad had cancer and couldn't pay for chemotherapy, so she'd hired herself out as a—

Tabby's laughter resounded in her head. *'This isn't America, toolbox. We have universal healthcare. No one needs to suck biker dick for cancer.'*

"Shut up," Nicole told her. "This is my fantasy."

Deciding to forgo the reason, she closed her eyes and imagined herself walking inside the clubhouse. It would be dark and crowded, full of faceless men. The music was loud, and she wandered the rooms, feeling uncomfortable. Red-faced men like Noah's father and Chopper Reed were looking at her, closing in around her, their mouths slack with hunger, and it made her want to put on more clothes. She was just about to leave when a door opened and Noah strode in. His face was set and he was head and shoulders bigger than anyone else. His gaze fell on her and she lit up inside, the way she had last night.

"Get away from her," he told the other men. He strode up to her, grasping her arm. "Why'd you come here?"

No, that would lead to the same 'sucking penis for cancer' problem as before. Besides, Noah wouldn't ask. He never asked anything. He'd look at her with his electric green eyes then steer her into a room with nothing but a lamp and a mattress inside. "Lie down with your legs wide."

She'd twist her hands together, wanting him, but not wanting to show it. *I've never done this.*

Fantasy Noah wove his fist through her hair, the way he had in the van, and forced her onto the mattress. *You'll get used to it.*

He knelt over her, licking a hot line down her neck. *Pull your shorts down. Show me your pussy.*

She unbuckled her jean shorts and they melted away, no awkward shuffling required, then she spread her legs, feeling her cunt separate beneath her cotton panties. She was soaking, aching. Her face was pressed into the scratchy mattress, but she didn't care, she needed him inside her. *Please? Can we...?*

Shut your fucking mouth. Noah pressed his knees between her legs, spreading them wide. Then he gripped her panties and—

A door slammed open. "Nix! We're home!"

Nicole sat up so quickly, Tabby's iPad went flying. "Hiiiiii!"

"Are you okay?" Sam called. "You sound weird."

"I'm fine!" She pulled her hand from her underwear. "How's... how's it going?"

"Good! Scott's here!"

"Hello, Nicole," Scott said in his clipped British accent. "We got Chinese takeaway if you'd like some?"

Nicole tugged at her sundress, trying to cover everything up. Her nipples were still rock hard, and her heart was racing. God, what even was her life?

"Nix?"

"That's great," she shrieked. "I love Chinese takeaway! I'll be out in a second!"

"Um, okay," Sam said. "Can you hurry up? We've got the puppies, we could use some spare hands!"

"I could use some spare hands," she muttered. But that wasn't true. She needed *fewer* hands, that way she couldn't keep touching herself. Yes, she needed fewer hands and more information about Noah. Or failing that, a time machine back to last year, when her life made sense. She got up to wash her hands and help her sister.

6

The next day Nicole was sitting at her dad's desk when something hit her in the back of her head. She turned to see Tabby leaning against the door frame, arms folded. "About time! I've been calling your name for ages."

Nicole rubbed the back of her head. "You don't have to throw things at me."

"That was a highlighter I took out of your pencil cup thing, and you didn't even notice! Do you have Mondayitis?"

"Maybe," she lied. Mondayitis wasn't her problem. Noah Newcomb was her problem. She doubted two waking minutes had passed without her thinking about Noah, The Rangers or sex. She wasn't sure which topic was the most distressing. When she was reading *Blood in the Gears,* it was the knowledge she'd lived her whole life without considering the subgroups of men cooking meth, breaking legs, and shooting each other. When she was in bed, it was the rough, filthy sex she hadn't had. Now she was at work, it was Noah acting like he hadn't made her feel his cock through his jeans.

She'd made sure she was standing at reception this morning, talking to Gil. Her lipstick was fresh, her hair blow-dried, and she'd worn a new pencil dress so tight it required skipping breakfast. A fat lot of good it did her. When Noah showed up, he barely looked at her, just grunted hello and headed down the hall.

"How was your weekend?" Gil called after him. "Do anything fun?"

Noah didn't even turn around. "Nope."

Then he vanished into tattoo room two and shouty rock music started playing four seconds later.

Nicole wasn't sure what she'd expected, but it wasn't to be brushed aside like an irritating cat. Especially since at the sight of him, her heart started banging against her rib cage. He was so *big*. Somehow that always surprised her, as though the Noah in her head was just a cardboard cutout of the man himself. When he walked past her, smelling of soap and cigarettes, she'd had to bite the insides of her cheeks to keep from calling out and demanding to know... what?

If his father was really the boss of The Rangers? If he was dangerous? If he'd spent the last twenty-four hours thinking about her, too?

"Nix! What the fuck, man?"

Nicole refocused on her sister. "Sorry, I... what were you saying?"

Tabby opened her mouth and Nicole knew what was coming. "Don't tell me to take a break! I'm too busy."

"But you're super stressed! Why don't you take a half-day?"

"Because I've got a tonne of work to do!"

"Like what?"

Like trying to work out if Noah's a bikie, she thought. *And whether he's gotten better-looking overnight or I'm losing my actual mind.*

"Nicole?" Tabby cupped her hands around her mouth. "Earth to Nicole, come in, Nicole. Nicole, can you read me?"

"Yes," she snapped. "I can't take a freaking break. There's a delivery coming and we're getting our pay system upgraded this afternoon, then I have a Skype call with Francine—"

"Your Adelaide boss?"

"Yes. I need to explain why I'm still in Melbourne instead of at my desk in head office. Then I need to continue to try and figure out why this business almost collapsed three months ago."

Tabby rolled her eyes. "God, who cares? We're fine now."

"That's not the point! If we don't know why Silver Daughters almost went under, then it might happen again!"

"Fine, but just lay off the green teas, okay?"

Nicole looked at her mug where a Jasmine teabag was idling. "What's wrong with green tea?"

"I read somewhere it's like nature's heroin."

"Wouldn't *heroin* be nature's heroin?"

Tabby shrugged. "Maybe there's more than one kind of heroin. Wow, that's deep. I should tattoo it on someone. Anyway, I'll leave you to Type A behavior. Give me a heads up when the ink gets here. I need to restock."

"There's nothing wrong with Type A behaviour," Nicole shouted at her sister's retreating back. "You should try it sometime!"

Tabby gave her the finger.

Nicole glared after her sister, then her thoughts boomeranged back to Noah. She knew she should talk to him about the biker thing. The question was could she even say 'biker' to him after spending last night screwing herself to the thought of him being one?

She hadn't wanted to do it. She'd tried thinking about grandma DaSilva, about Aaron cheating. She'd even wheeled out that awful trip to the doctors when she was nineteen. It hadn't worked. She'd let fantasy biker Noah say and do disgusting things to her. Then she'd let him do them to her *in front of the other bikers*. By 4am she was so miserable and horny and confused, she cried in her bed like a baby. How was she supposed to talk to Noah without any of that mess coming out?

She stood up, mug in hand. She was getting another green tea, and screw what Tabby said. She pushed open the door and saw Noah coming out of tattoo room two, cigarettes in hand. They froze as if being a man and a woman in a hallway was against the law. "Hey," she said, trying to sound normal. "Having a break?"

"Yeah."

She tried and failed to block the fantasy of him spreading her legs in front of the other bikers and going down on her. Not because he wanted her to feel good, but because he knew coming in front of all those men would humiliate her. He'd wanted to humiliate her. To fuck her into a thousand remorseful orgasms.

"Nikki?"

Nicole raised a hand to her cheek. "Sorry, I didn't catch that."

"Tired?" Noah's eyes glinted like two chips of jade. He looked like he knew what she was thinking, though he couldn't possibly know what she was thinking. That was not a skill he possessed.

"A little." She raised her mug to distract him from her face. "Cup of tea?"

"No thanks." His gaze fell to her lower-than-professional neckline. "New dress?"

Warmth fluttered in her chest. "Newish. I haven't worn it here before."

"I like it."

"Really?"

A glance at her tightly belted midsection. "I like you in it."

He might as well have said 'I'd like you out of it.' They both knew that's what he meant. Nicole inhaled and her breath felt like it was coming in through a straw. "Thanks."

"Anytime." Noah leaned in, eyes gleaming. "What are you doing for lunch?"

Okay, she needed to breathe. Dizziness was making her think Noah was about to ask her out, which he wasn't because dating wasn't his thing. Letting her touch his dick in his van and being weird about it afterward was his thing.

"Nikki?" A line had appeared between Noah's eyes. She wanted to touch it. She swallowed, trying to focus. "Um, I'm not doing anything for lunch. I mean, I'm thinking of skipping it. Doing some intermittent fasting. It's good for your metabolism."

Noah rubbed the back of his neck, exposing a bicep tattoo of a tree. The trunk was shaped like a naked woman. Was it stupid to be jealous of a tree woman tattoo? It *felt* stupid, but she was doing it. Did that make her stupid?

"Let's go to Greens," he said.

"Excuse me?"

"Let's go to Greens and get a burger. Fuck this fasting thing."

Nicole's heart pulsed into her mouth. He *was* asking her on a date. Or something like a date. At the very least, he was asking her something. "I..."

The door to tattoo room four banged open.

"Hey, did I hear something about Greens?" Gil called. "I'm fucking starving."

The intimacy between her and Noah burst like a bubble. Nicole shrank back into her dad's office. "I think I'll just stay here for lunch."

Noah took a step away from her, his face impassive. "Okay."

"Let's go to Greens, big guy," Gil said. "I'm almost done with Kurtis. Wait fifteen?"

"Nah," Noah said, his gaze locked on hers. "Got stuff to do."

"Fuck ya, then." Gil's door slammed shut.

Nicole compressed the mug between her fingers. "He shouldn't leave his client alone in the chair to ask about burgers."

Noah shrugged. "Happens."

And just like she was a square. A buzzkill. She was *always* a buzzkill here. In Adelaide, her colleagues followed her on Instagram and asked her advice on tricky consultancy projects. Here, everyone thought she was an anal-retentive weirdo for updating the waiting room magazines and investigating missing money.

Because why be professional when you could just swear and lose thousands of dollars and be covered in tattoos and—

"Nikki?" Noah's forehead creased. "You okay?"

Nicole gripped her mug tighter. "You know what? No. I work two jobs and I just got dumped and I can't find out where eighty thousand dollars went, and my dad has been missing ages and no one cares what I do, even though they always ask for my help and I'm so *tired*."

Noah looked up at the ceiling, clearly at a loss for what to say.

"Exactly!" she snapped. "You don't really want to know, so please stop asking. I've got work to do."

She closed her dad's office door, relieved to put something solid between her and Noah.

Two hours later, her stomach hurt with hunger, but it was good. It felt like focus. Her Skype call with Francine had gone okay. Her boss wanted her back in Adelaide, but she was happy with the work she was sending in remotely.

"This is good preparation for when you go on maternity leave," Francine teased.

Nicole smiled, though her words felt like a punch in the uterus. How was she supposed to tell her boss that her sparkly future had been canceled? How was she supposed to tell anyone? This wasn't supposed to be her life.

But getting depressed about being single and living in her childhood bedroom wouldn't help. She needed to focus on fixing her problems—starting with the suspected bikie tattooing in the room across from hers. She needed to confront him about The Rangers. She checked the staff e-roster and saw his break was over and he was tattooing a twenty-two-year-old, Daniella Bright.

She hated the burst of jealousy that went through her when she read that name. Tattooing required seeing and touching a lot of skin. Her sisters worked hard to be taken seriously despite that and she owed Noah the same respect. Only... she couldn't stop her insides from twisting up like eels. Daniella Bright was a pretty girl name and when she opened the door, she heard happy, girlish laughter coming from Noah's room.

What do you want? she asked herself, but no answers came, just nausea. Her phone rang and, eager for distraction, she picked up without looking at the name.

"When are you going to wake the fuck up and come home?"

Aaron's voice was so loud, so unexpectedly mean, she almost dropped her phone. "I... what?"

"I just got an email from Francine telling me you're doing such a great job in Melbourne and she's so excited for the wedding. You haven't told her you fucked up our engagement; you haven't told *anyone*."

"I don't know what to say!"

"Bullshit!" Aaron's voice was so loud, it was like he was on speakerphone. "You don't want to work at your dad's shitbox studio. You don't want to live with your batshit sisters. So again, wake the fuck up and come home."

Maybe it was the stress, maybe it was an excess of green tea antioxidants, but she burst into tears. Big gulping toddler sobs. She cried and Aaron shouted, neither of them listening to each other until Sam burst through the door, her tattooing gloves still on, and snatched her phone.

"Fuck off, you useless cuntlord," she snarled into it, before hanging up. "Jesus, Nix..."

She wiped her tears away from her cheeks. "Sorry."

"Don't be sorry." Sam pointed at the ceiling. "Upstairs."

"But—"

"No buts. I'm keeping your phone and Tabby's changing the Wi-Fi password. You're done working for today, so go relax or I'll fucking kill you."

Nicole knew better than to protest. She gathered up her things and headed for the door. As she passed Noah's room, she heard him say something in his rumbly baritone and Daniella Bright giggled. A stick of jealousy speared her right through the middle and she hurried out of the studio feeling like a failure.

Alone in the apartment, she considered and discarded taking a bath. Instead, she collected the rubber gloves from under the sink and started pulling the Tupperware and expired jars of mustard out of the fridge. Once it was scrubbed clean and reorganized, she moved onto the cupboards, then the laundry. She wiped and stacked and rearranged. Then she started on dinner. Tabby came upstairs just as she was browning chicken for a stir fry. "I thought you were supposed to be relaxing."

"Cooking is relaxing. Do you and Sam want rice or noodles?"

"Neither. Sam's gone over to Scott's and I'm gonna go see Radiant Spunk play the Evelyn."

Nicole felt a pang of disappointment. "Did Sam leave my phone?"

"Nope. She says you need a solid twelve-hour screen fast."

"That's not fair, she doesn't have a phone! She doesn't know how much I need one!"

"Preaching to the choir, my dude." Tabby jumped up and sat on the kitchen counter. "Hey, you know what you are?"

"What?"

"A food poker."

Nicole frowned, wooden spoon in hand. "I'm cooking!"

"You're poking. The chicken's fine, but you just keep poking it. Poke, poke, poke."

Nicole withdrew the spoon from the wok and instantly itched to return it. What if the chicken burned? What if it stuck to the metal? What if—

"Why don't you stop poking food and come out with me?" Tabby demanded. "It's only five thirty, come experience 'Radiant Spunk.'"

"I'm fine here. And 'Radiant Spunk' is a hideous band name."

"They were almost 'Intergalactic Jizz.'" Tabby hopped off the counter. "If you're not keen for the spunk, I'll head out now."

Nicole frowned. "Please don't sleep with any of the guys from 'Radiant Spunk?'"

"Cannae promise that, lass."

"I thought you were taking a break from sex? Realigning your chakras?"

"Fuck my chakras, they're too needy." Tabby's expression grew serious. "Nix, are you sure—"

"If you ask me if I'm okay again, I will give you a backhander."

Tabby raised her palms. "Fair enough. Check you later, food poker."

Nicole waited until the moment she was gone and plunged the spoon back into the chicken. Food poker. How dare she? At least she cooked actual food. The last thing Tabby made was hard candy and she was pretty sure she'd put THC in it.

She set the meat on a paper-towel-lined plate and stir-fried kale, carrot, and baby corn into the wok. She was adding ginger marinade when the landline rang. Frowning, she headed for the hall. She'd half-forgotten they had a landline, let alone that people might call it. Yet there it was, on the little table, still covered in Tabby's Barbie stickers. She'd get some eucalyptus oil and clean them off later. She picked up the receiver. "Hello, DaSilva residence?"

Nothing. Nicole could hear music playing in the background.

"Hello?"

"Yeah, uh, it's Noah."

Nicole had the bizarre urge to giggle. "Is something wrong?"

"No. Yeah. I'm still downstairs."

"Okay...?"

"I need help with the new system. I can't get my client's card to swipe."

A girl laughed in the background. The sound like nails down Nicole's internal chalkboard. Daniella Bright, no doubt. She had a brief, insane urge to hang up then took a deep breath. "You need to open up the PayWave program—"

"I've tried all that," Noah interrupted. "Look, I'm confused as fuck. Can you come give me a hand? Please?"

She looked at her pink t-shirt and cotton shorts. "I'm not dressed properly."

"Please?"

"Um, sure. I'll be there in a sec."

She turned off the burner and headed for the door, pulling her hair out of her sloppy ponytail. This was a good test of her mettle. Even without makeup and clothes, she could still be professional in front of Noah. She *would* be professional in front of him.

She found him behind the counter fiddling with the card machine, and next to him was a girl with shiny ash-brown hair and amazing eyebrows.

"Oh, hiiii!" she said. "Thanks so much for helping us!"

If Nicole had a wish, just one wish, she'd have granted herself a pencil skirt and a face full of makeup. This was so *not* a good test of her mettle. "N-no problem. I live upstairs. I'm Nicole DaSilva."

The girl beamed. "I'm Daniella. *Noah* and I stayed back so he could finish my kitten tatt!"

Nicole felt legitimately sick. "Great, so uh, what's the problem?

She looked at Noah, but he was staring at the computer, refusing to meet her gaze.

"I need to pay by card," Daniella said. "I didn't bring any cash even though I know *Noah* likes it better that way."

The way she said his name made Nicole want to dive into a vat of battery acid. She bit the insides of her cheeks. "It's okay, either I'll get the machine working or we can arrange a wire transfer."

"Great!"

She moved to the counter and Noah stepped aside. The tension emanating from his big body was palpable. Was he embarrassed he'd called her to help? Or was he awkward because Daniella was making googly eyes at him and saying his name weird? Feeling slightly better, she restarted the payment program and reconnected the studio account to the PayWave device.

"Is it okay if we run through your client details?" she asked Daniella.

The younger woman beamed. "Oh, *Noah* has all that stuff already."

"*Here.*" Noah shoved a post-it note at her. It read; *Daniella Bright, 3" x4" tortoiseshell kitten. Five-hour session. $700.*

Below that, scribbled in different handwriting, was a mobile number followed by a love heart. Nicole stared at it. It stared at her. Her vision greyed at the edges.

"So, I'm thinking we should go to Garden State," Daniella said. "They do *amazing* espresso martinis."

Noah grunted.

"Okay, grumpy! You pick the place!"

The silence that followed was as thick as custard. Nicole typed in Daniella's details as loudly as she could, trying to break it. She could feel Noah watching her. Was he noting the lack of makeup? The hollows under her eyes, the scar on her chin? And why did she care? He sucked. First, he'd asked her out and now he was going for a drink with this... *alleged person* who was nice and also the worst person Nicole had ever met. She held her hand out to Daniella Bright. "Can I have your card, please?"

"Oh, sure!"

Daniella's fingernails were a velvet purple. The colour would have looked horrible on Nicole, brought out the blue in her veins, her spider fingers. But maybe that was what Noah liked, purple nails and kitten tattoos. As she swiped her card and told Daniella to punch in her pin, she made her decision. She was moving away from Melbourne and getting rid of her tattoo. Screw Sam and Tabby, they'd left her in this mess. Screw her dad, he'd started this mess. And most of all, screw Noah, the flaky, van-driving, probably bikie-being jerk. They could all go do one.

The machine pinged its authorisation. "It looks like it's worked," she said. "Do you need a receipt?"

Daniella looked across at Noah. "Um, no?"

"Okay, well..." Nicole raised her eyebrows at Noah, *You deal with this.*

He jerked to life, like a robotic giant. "You want to book another session while you're here?"

Daniella tucked a strand of hair behind her ear. "Um yeah. But I'll call when I know my work hours."

"Right," Noah said.

"Right." Daniella's gaze flicked to the door. "So... you have my number?"

Nicole looked at the post-it note. What would happen if she just... put it in her mouth and ate it?

"Yeah, I've got it," Noah said. "I'll walk you out."

"Great!" A relieved-looking Daniella waved at her. "Thanks, Nicole!"

Nicole nodded. It was that or say the supremely unfair 'please stop coming here.'

Noah hustled his client out of the door and Nicole stood behind the counter, waiting so she could leave without seeing them talking or kissing or whatever awful thing was happening out the front of her dad's studio. She closed her eyes and thought of her perfect future. Now she'd decided she was leaving Melbourne, she could transfer to Sydney? No, that was where The Rangers lived. Tasmania? Too small.

Paris? Her heart jumped; she'd always wanted to live in Paris. A tattoo removal and then Paris? Was that where her perfect future lay? The door opened and Noah strode by without a sideways glance. "Sorry about that. You can head back upstairs."

Nicole gaped at him. Oh, she could head back upstairs, could she? He was sorry, was he? Anger, hot and lovely, ignited her jealousy like a match through kerosene. She marched after him, catching him as he reached his tattoo room. His music was still playing, a rap song with ugly words and a pretty music-box beat. "What are you doing?"

Noah's expression was flat. "Cleaning my machine."

"Not that. You and your client. You asked for her number."

"And?"

"Do you have any idea how unprofessional this is?"

Noah's jaw flexed. "You need to go home."

"Don't tell me what to do!" Nicole was aware her voice was rising, knew she sounded mildly insane, but she didn't care. "You can't act like this place is your live-action Tinder. It makes us look like perverts!"

"It's just a drink."

"It's not! It's my sister's reputation!"

"Sammy doesn't give a fuck. You know she's 'dated' a few clients herself."

He tried to shake off her hold, but Nicole clung on, ignoring the heat pulsating through her palms. "Not lately. Not now she owns the business. You know it's not just her reputation you're ruining, it's my dad's as well."

"Don't talk to me about your old man."

She felt a thrill of genuine fear. He was angry, but that was good. She was finally getting to him after all these weeks of being gotten to. "He's my dad, I can talk about him if I want to. What's your problem anyway? First Kelly, now Daniella. Is it that hard for you to find women to sleep with outside the studio?"

He leaned down, eyes bright with something she couldn't define. Not anger. Not irritation. "You jealous, Nikki?"

"No!"

There was a beat. Noah's lips curled into a smile and Nicole yanked on his hand like it was a church bell. "I'm not! You're just selfish and confusing!"

"Oh yeah?"

"Yes! You say we can't sleep together, then you make me touch your cock. You ignore me all morning, then you ask me to lunch. You act like you're so dangerous to be with then you hit on some barely legal—"

Noah's hands clasped her waist, lifting her into the air like she was nothing. She screamed, more out of shock than anything. "What are you—"

He clapped a warm hand to her mouth. "You'll see."

Noah had crossed the floor in one massive stride and laid her on his leather tattooing chair. Leather that was still warm from Daniella's body. Offended, she tried to get up, and he pressed a big arm across her chest and shoulders.

"What do you think you're doing?" She gripped his arm and pulled but he was like graffiti-covered concrete. "Let me go!"

"I don't think I will. You've got a problem, Nikki."

"Yeah, you!" She struggled against his hold, but even as she moved, she knew she'd be disappointed if he let go. He didn't. His forearm bore down, pinning her to the chair. "You're all shook up. Vibrating. You're stressed and it's making you act like a bitch."

"How *dare* you—"

"Sammy called you a bitch. Right after she took your phone and laptop. You're driving her and Tabby spare. You're manic. You can't sleep or sit still. No one knows what to do with you."

Her heart was pounding, a dry, sweet prickle in her mouth. "Do you?"

It came out softer than she wanted, more of a plea than a challenge.

Noah's eyes were bright with that sharp, unknowable energy that split her open when they first met. "Yeah."

"You're lying."

His expression turned hard and ugly as a gargoyle. "We'll fucking see."

He ran his hand along her stomach and into the hem of her shorts. She whimpered. She knew she should be fighting, but her body was soft as wet sugar.

He shoved his hand down her shorts and into her cotton underwear, not toying, not playing. His fingers cupped her... there, sliding through the disgusting slipperiness she hadn't known she had.

"Nice," he muttered. "Now hold still."

And a finger, an impossibly thick finger slid deep, pushing her sensitive walls apart. Sensation blasted through her like the music in a horror film. Nicole screamed and jolted upright. "Noah! Please?"

"Fuckin' relax." He pushed her back onto the chair. "You'll get it. This won't take long. You're so fuckin' on edge."

He pulsed inside her and his fingers made the most embarrassing slippery noises. Nicole screamed, this time because it felt so humiliatingly *good*. She didn't want to be seen like this, to be touched like this by a man who just thought she needed relief and was going on a date with a pretty twenty-two-year-old.

"I told you to relax." Noah's fingers slipped out of her and he tugged, circled around, and *tugged* on her clit. "Relax and pay attention."

She shrieked as pleasure sizzled through her. "Noah!"

"Yeah, that's it." His fingers slipped down again, pumping into her cunt. Nicole screamed a third time, this time because she was scared she'd wake up alone in her bed with her pillow between her knees.

"Concentrate," Noah snarled. "Feel me fucking your tight little pussy. You like that, don't you? You like getting fucked?"

"Yes!" she screamed, arching her lower back so hard it ached. "Yes! I don't want it to stop."

"It won't." Noah adjusted his arm so that her fingers were trapped under it. She felt more pinned than ever, yet still sure it was going to end. Even as her cunt swelled and the rough thrust of Noah's fingers felt a hundred times bigger. Even as her nipples hardened and her toes curled, she knew it wasn't going to happen no matter how much pleasure he force-fed her. "Let me go! I can't do it!"

Noah pressed his face against hers. "Too fuckin' bad. You're gonna get it."

Her cunt throbbed hard, a circle gripping tighter, tighter, tighter. "No!"

"Yes. You love it too much. You're gonna come like the dirty little girl you are."

She recalled her fantasy, being naked and spread open on a dirty mattress. Noah the biker between her legs, taking what he wanted from her. She was so wet and bad, of course she'd come. What other purpose did she have?

"That's it," Noah said. "That's a good girl. Give in."

"More names," she gasped. "Meaner!"

He didn't miss a beat. "Come, you filthy slut. Come, then you can suck my fingers while I fuck your pussy raw."

Nicole felt the swell of something flawless between her legs, like a diamond being born. She could hear herself crying out, but it was a stranger's voice. The real her was inside vibrating with joy.

She could smell herself in the air, the sweet musk of lost control. She laughed, enjoying the freedom to not care about it or anything.

Noah straightened, slipping his hand from her underwear. Nicole's shorts snapped back into place, as though nothing had ever happened. She looked up and saw him wipe his hand on his jeans. "That what you needed?"

"I…"

He stared down at her like an expectant dentist—clearly not caring he'd just made her orgasm harder than any man she'd been with before. "Yeah?"

"I need to go."

She stood on her rubbery legs, needing to be somewhere away from the salt smell and pounding rock music and *him*. She rushed out of the room, pulling the door closed behind her.

"Yeah, that seems about right," he said right before it shut.

7

Noah's earliest memory was of the clubroom. He was playing with a screwdriver, trying to push a nail back into the dusty floor. He pushed too hard and the screwdriver cut his hand open. A thick slug of burgundy blood had oozed out and he'd opened his mouth to scream and then he bit his cheeks instead.

Bikers didn't like kids. They might love their own, but as a concept 'kids' didn't rank high. They couldn't follow orders or ride a bike; they couldn't do anything but cry, shit and sleep.

Noah didn't know how old he was when he cut his hand on the screwdriver. Four? Five? Not at kinder, because he could draw by then and the nail came before the pencils. The clubhouse was his daycare, tools were his toys, the naked women on the walls were his babysitters. His dad was in the other room laughing in a way that was almost as scary as yelling. No one wanted him there. He'd tried to stay quiet, stay out of the way.

Then the pencils.

He didn't know who gave them to him. A little red box just appeared one day. He'd picked them up, pressed them hard against his fingers and he'd been born. He didn't know any other way to put it. Paper became his life's mission, shopping receipts, electricity bills, phone books and magazines—finding blank spaces and filling them with the pictures in his head.

He had another memory, almost as clear as finding the pencils. He was lying on the floor, drawing on a phone book when his dad sat beside him. He smelled like sweat and what Noah would later realise was whiskey.

"Like drawing, don't you, mate?"

He must have said yes because his dad's next words came in clear as a bell. "Good. Stick with it and you'll be tattooing the boys in no time."

Baby Noah was sick with excitement. He didn't know what tattoos were, but he understood being useful for The Rangers. He understood not being a pain in the ass.

He stopped sketching dragons and forests and kings and drew The Rangers patch. He drew it until he could draw it in his sleep. His dad stuck the pictures on the club walls.

"When are you getting him a machine, Harry?" other bikies asked.

"Soon as he's old enough not to fuck it up."

It was the summer of 1999 when his old man showed him the black and silver machine.

"Take it home, work out how to use it. Nobby'll show you the ropes next week, but I want you to have a handle on it by then."

Noah nodded, the earth shifting the way he did when he saw that red box of pencils. "I'm gonna do the patches?"

"Yup, but you better not ink yourself or I'll kick your head in. I don't need more reasons for your mum to get the cops onto me."

But two days later he'd given himself a Ranger helmet on the inside of his left arm. His dad didn't kick his head in, he gave him a beer.

"You're a Ranger now," he'd said, and Noah's dumb thirteen-year-old heart had almost burst with pride.

NOAH WOKE up five minutes before his alarm went off. That was standard, as was the hard-on throbbing between his legs. The dull unease was new. Especially without an alcohol fug in his mouth or the burned taste buds that said he'd smoked a full deck the night before. For a second he lay there, unsure what his problem was. The answer came in a hot wave—Nicole on her back, around his fingers, squealing and moaning and…

"Fuck."

He'd finger-fucked Nicole on his chair. His boss' twin. His mentor's daughter. The recently separated accountant and tight ass he'd been hard for since day one. He'd told himself he'd never go there and he'd failed. Now he was due at a staff meeting with her in less than an hour. He closed his eyes against the morning light, replaying the way Nicole looked arching back into his chair, thrashing as she came. She'd been sopping wet, so small it was like she'd never been fucked before. He wrapped a palm around his throbbing dick and gave it a slow pull. She was so goddamn needy for it. Maybe she didn't like that about herself, but she was. The things he could do to that tight little—

"Nuh." Noah yanked his hand away from his dick. Not happening. Didn't happen last night, wasn't going to happen today. He picked up his pack of Bennies and stuck one in his mouth. Not the best habit, but what was the point of owning your place if you couldn't smoke in bed?

He took a deep drag on his cigarette. He'd thought—hoped— some of Nicole's appeal was the sexy librarian thing, but last night she'd been barefoot and barefaced, and he'd almost had a heart attack when she showed up to help him with the pay system. Shame he couldn't say anything good or nice or even constructive to her. Shame he'd let her get all jealous over Daniella, enjoyed it, then made her come in his tattoo room so their situation was more fucked up than ever. His gut cramped, sending sharp pangs burrowing into his chest like eels. This dumbfuck infatuation was going to kill him. He ashed into his bedside mug and got up. He pulled on a RCVC t-shirt and jeans and headed downstairs, a fresh Benson already between his teeth. Paula was sitting at the kitchen table, her knees pulled up to her chest as she watched something on her phone. She looked a little bizarre, with her teenage body language and fifty-something face.

"Morning," she said. "Coffee?"

He shook his head. "Meeting. What are you doing today?"

"I've got a bakery shift at one, *Dad*. I promise I won't nick any of your smokes while you're out. God, you don't stop, do you?"

It often occurred to him that Paula was the only person in the world who thought he was chatty or overprotective. That made sense, but it was still a strange thing. "I'm heading off. I'll see you later tonight."

"Whatever," she said, returning to her video. "I'm going out tomorrow night, by the way. Around seven."

Her high, determined tone made him turn. "Shredder?"

"No. AA."

Noah took in her flush, the way her fingers twisted at her phone. "Seriously?"

"Yes! God!"

"Okay. I'll see you at home at nine then."

She lifted her chin. "Fine."

"How'd you sleep?"

Paula shrugged. "How about you?"

He'd slept like dogshit, but he couldn't say it without her pressing for why. "Alright. See you later."

Paula pointed to the leather jacket waiting on the kitchen bench. "It's cold outside. You gonna wear it today?"

Noah suppressed a wince. "You didn't have to give it to me."

"You've been letting me stay with you for free, it's the least I can do."

"Alright." He walked over to the jacket and slung it on feeling like a viper trapped in another snake's skin. Paula smiled. "It looks great. How's it feel?"

"Fine," he lied. He'd take it off as soon as he could, leave it at work. It didn't have patches or buckles, but it didn't need them. It was a Rangers' jacket, her ex-husband's. Something he never wanted to wear again.

He left praying Paula meant what she was saying about AA. He didn't need more drama, and no one stirred up more drama than bikies.

He set off on foot down Vandal Street, irritatingly warm and, as always, thinking about Nicole. They'd messed around now. Did that mean they were free to explore the thing between them? He doubted it. Nicole was a nester. Once the dust from her breakup settled, she'd pick out pictures for Bumble or eHarmony or wherever girls like her looked for guys who weren't him. Anyone could see Nicole DaSilva had a life template and the spot marked 'husband' sure as fuck wasn't Newcomb sized.

Husband. Noah snorted as he lit the cigarette between his teeth. He had some fucking nerve even thinking the word, considering he had no money, a criminal record and a pending vasectomy. He needed to get his head out of his ass and leave Nicole alone. She'd sort her own life out eventually, then she'd be gone. Time would sand his feelings down to nothing and in the meantime there were cigarettes, looking out for Paula, and painting. He'd buy a new canvas tonight. He'd stopped when Paula showed up and started calling him 'Picasso,' but who gave a shit? He needed the distraction.

"Hey man, could I have a ciggie?"

The asker was a scraggly guy in his twenties, no jacket despite the morning air. His old man spoke in his ear, *'Piss off, freeloader.'*

Noah handed the guy a cigarette and his lighter.

The guy grinned. "Thanks man. I'll give you one someday."

Noah doubted it, but that wasn't the point. The point was, not giving what you could afford to give was shitty. Edgar showed him that. In the club, anything you had was for you first, The Rangers second and no one else. But why? He wasn't going to run out of cigarettes.

We all belong to the world, Edgar said. *And we all owe the world.*

He flicked his butt into the street bin outside Silver Daughters. Belonging to the world was one thing, belonging to people was a whole other game. He'd trusted Edgar and he liked his daughters, but he didn't want to join another gang. He felt the way he did about Nicole, but didn't want her turning those gorgeous, life-template eyes onto his shoddy excuse for an existence. Best case scenario, she'd ride his cock until Sam found out, or her guilt would keep her away.

He reached Silver Daughters studio and paused, stretching out both sides of his neck, making them crack before he headed around back to the DaSilva's house for the meeting.

The smell of pancakes hit him as soon as he opened the door and his stomach flipped over. Nicole was here; only she would have made pancakes. He toed off his boots, noting Gil's flashy sneakers. Probably already pestering Nicole for sugar-free syrup. That was good. The more people, the less he'd have to talk.

"Noelle! The Big No!" Tabby bounded toward him, her red skinny jeans and huge green hat clashing with her colourful tattoos. "I need a minute of your time, good sir."

Sidestepping her clearly wasn't an option, so he allowed Tabby to lead him into the cramped laundry room and shut the door. "What's up?"

"Oh, you know, the sun, the Dow Jones. Cool jacket BTW."

Fuck, he'd forgotten about the jacket. He'd shrug it off, but Tabby would read into that. "What do you want?"

"Have you taken any steps toward fulfilling my request? Actually, false question, I know you drove Nix home after her party. Don't ask me how I know."

"I wasn't going—"

"I tracked her phone. And your phone. I'm tracking both your phones. The Find My Friend app has unleashed a whole new world of phone tracking, and I am its emperor."

Noah rubbed a hand over his eyes. This fucking week. These *sisters*. "Stop tracking my phone."

He moved for the door, but Tabby blocked him. "Not so fast. You and Nix haven't smashed. Or if you did, it took all of the two seconds you were parked in our street."

Noah shook his head. He shouldn't have started smoking so early, this was going to be a bitch of a morning. "Leave it, Tabby."

She lifted her chin. "The window's closing."

He frowned, not wanting to encourage Tabby to keep talking, but needing to know what she meant.

Tabby grinned, pleased with herself. "Nix is beginning to doubt herself. No solid moves to call off the wedding and she and Fuckface Magee were on the phone for an hour last night. No yelling either, they were actually having a *conversation*."

A hollowness entered Noah's head. So that was how Nicole had spent her night after he'd fingered her? Talking to her ex? He'd eased her sexual pressure and she'd used her clarity of mind to reopen negotiations? Well that was just fucking fine. Not like he had any claim. Not like he wasn't going to take Daniella to Garden State and fuck her seven ways from Sunday afterward.

"Not my problem," he told Tabby. "Get out of the way."

But in the manner of all DaSilvas, she didn't budge an inch. "You know he cheated on her, right? Aaron? She found condom wrappers in his suit jacket. He was doing some chick from work behind Nix's back."

That halted his escape. He stared at Tabby. She wasn't smiling anymore. "He broke her heart, man, but she stayed with him. He laid the 'it was a mistake, but we need to have more sex' guilt trip on her and she bit the bullet."

Noah forcibly loosened his fists. "Why are you telling me this?"

She gave him a look. "Stop dicking around and do what you know you need to do."

She whirled around and left the laundry in a kaleidoscope of colour. Noah leaned against the washing machine, his head a slow-motion car crash. Nicole, cheated on?

Where he was from, cheating was a fact of life. A guy fucked whoever he felt like fucking at parties, clubhouses and barbecues.

The wives and girlfriends took it in their stride, or pretended to because that was the life. You shacked up with a biker, you understood men who lived outside the rules didn't make an exception for monogamy. His old man had a dozen girlfriends while he was growing up, brought them to parties and to his mum's place without a lick of shame. But that was biker land. The DaSilva girls had been raised on love and equality by a dad who adored the shit out of them. So how the fuck had Nicole ended up in the same relationship model as his mum—wearing the blame for her partner's bullshit?

For the first time in his life, he was pissed at Edgar. How had he let Nikki stay in that position? Why hadn't he tried harder? Made it clear what she was worth? She'd been so desperate in his tattooing chair. So sure he'd lose interest, or it wouldn't work. She needed affection, security, fucking adoration and no one, not even Sam or Tabby, seemed to realise how much. If that wasn't Edgar's fault, whose was it?

He heard Gil laugh and realised he needed to move before he was accused of hiding, probably by Tabby to cover her tracks. He eased the laundry door open and headed for the kitchen.

Everyone was seated at the dining table. Sam and Scott were holding hands, and Tabby was showing Gil something on her phone. Nicole stood over them, passing out pancakes. She had lilac shadows under her eyes. He felt a stab of irritation. Why wasn't anyone helping her?

"Hey," he said. "Need any more plates?"

Nicole looked up at him, and for the briefest second, he thought she was going to smile, then her gaze dropped to his chest. A crease appeared between her eyebrows and her face changed. She looked panicky, almost terrified.

"What's—"

"Hey man," Gil said. "Nice jacket."

Noah looked down, then back at Nicole's wide, wondering eyes, and it clicked. She knew. It had finally happened. The hairs on his neck lifted in a salute to how fucked he was.

Sam patted the seat beside her. "C'mon, Noah, take a seat."

He sat, firefighting the panic spreading through him. When did she find out? Had she told anyone? She couldn't have; Sam would have confronted him, Tabby and Gil would have wanted details. Nicole handed him a plate of pancakes and he took them without a word, wanting to stand and kiss her until he pulled everything she knew about his father out of her mouth.

Sam beamed at him. She was always smiling these days, a side-effect of the Brit sitting by her elbow. Still, he doubted there would be many smiles once Nicole dropped her bombshell. "How was the rest of your shift? You send Daniella out, okay?"

"Yeah, no problems."

"Daniella's cute," Tabby said, forever the shit-stirrer. "She single?"

"Time to start," Nicole said loudly. "Sam, can you give us a manager run-through?"

Sam saluted her twin and stood up. "Okay, so it's not been a bad week in terms of productivity, but..."

Noah tried to listen, but it was impossible. How had she figured it out? Had she found his record, or was it just news articles and pictures of his old man? Those things people Googled every now and again?

He shovelled pancakes in his mouth as Nicole took them through her agenda; advertising, finance, general upkeep and the schedule for the next week.

"Is there anything anyone would like to discuss?" she asked.

Yeah, can you not tell everyone my dad's a bikie? he thought, but he kept his mouth shut.

"Great," she said. "Meeting adjourned."

Gil leaned back in his chair. "Fuckin' finally. Good pancakes, Nikki."

Noah contemplated pushing him over but thought better of it.

Scott gave a soft round of applause. "You run a tight ship, Nicole. I don't think I've gone to a meeting that good that ran under forty minutes."

Nicole smiled. "I went to a seminar last year about the Gorman four-point structure. That's what I use."

"I've heard of that!" Scott said enthusiastically. "Where did you take it?"

Sam caught his eye and grinned, as if to say, 'Look at these nerds.' Noah tried to smile back, but in his mind, she was shouting 'I can't *believe* you never told me you were a bikie, you cunt!'

"Coming downstairs?" she asked.

He shook his head. "Gotta talk to Nicole."

"About?"

He thought fast. "The pay system. I had trouble with it last night."

Sam rolled her eyes. "It's a pain in the arse, isn't it? But Nix wants to keep a tight fist around the finances."

"Why?" Gil asked. "There a problem?"

"Not right now, but Nix thinks we lost a chunk of change sometime during the last year. She wants to find it."

Gil rubbed a hand through his hair. "What if Edgar took it to fund his little retreat into nowhere?"

Sam shrugged. "He might have."

Noah scowled at Gil. "He didn't."

"How do you know? No one knows where Eddie is or why he left."

"I just know."

"How?"

Noah gritted his teeth. "You got Franco booked at eight, don't you?"

"Yes," Gil huffed. He stood. "See you pricks later."

He slouched off, his baggy hoodie and swooshed hair giving him the profile of a sulky teen. One down, three to go. Noah hung around as Scott, Sam, and Nicole chatted, trying to look like he wanted to be there. He was about to give up on a moment with Nicole when Tabby clocked him. "Oi, Sam, I found a log that looks like a dragon outside. Come see it."

She then frogmarched her older sister and Scott outside, dropping him a huge wink he chose to ignore.

Nicole immediately headed for the kitchen, pulling pink rubber gloves out from under the sink. He strode after her, feeling like a bull in a china shop. "You shouldn't do that. You cooked."

She whirled around. "So, who's going to do it?"

Noah held out his hands.

She looked at him in disbelief. "Seriously?"

"Seriously." He tugged the gloves away and pulled them on. They were tight, but they fit. He gently nudged her away from the sink and plunged his hands into the soapy water.

"Did you learn to wash dishes in The Rangers?" Nicole asked, her blue eyes hard as glass.

He didn't reply. Couldn't. Hearing that name come out of her mouth was a sock in the gut. "How long have you known?"

"A couple of days. Do they know?"

"Who?"

She gestured to the doorway. "Sam and Tabby and the others?"

He shook his head.

"What about my dad?"

He turned back to the plates, scrubbing the syrup from a chipped dinner plate and placing it in the drying rack.

"Noah?"

"I'm not talking about this here."

"Then where—"

"My place. Come over and we can talk."

There was a pause. "Is this about sleeping with me?" Nicole's tongue snuck across her lower lip and it was so cute, he smiled. It felt like clay cracking.

"You're the one who wants it, Nikki."

"I do not! You're the one who… did that to me last night."

"Because you were begging for it. Because you wouldn't have left me alone until you got it."

He turned in time to see her going a furious red. "Don't be a… dick." The word came out jerky, as though her swearing reflex was rusted over. It was fucking adorable. "Don't," she hissed. "Don't think that I'm cute."

He couldn't help it, he stepped forward and cupped a gloved, soapy hand to her cheek. Nicole's mouth turned up, her gorgeous blue eyes closing, and he did what he'd wanted to do for weeks, months, forever. He kissed her, and everything went quiet as a velvet sunset. She tasted like the first shot of whiskey, sweet and smooth, burning all the way down. His cock turned to steel against his thigh and he pulled her closer, pressing her slender, shivering body against his and feeling it soften. She liked this, being held like this and god, he liked it, too. He still wanted to throw her down and fuck her but this soft, slow-moving bliss was something else.

Something clattered downstairs and Nicole shoved him away. "We can't! We shouldn't! Not again!"

She sounded so panicky, he laughed for what felt like the first time in ages. "Sorry, Nikki."

"Stop calling me Nikki!"

"Sorry, *Nicole*."

"Screw you." From the hot way she was looking up at him, he knew she wanted him to kiss her again. Normally he'd oblige but her sisters were way too fucking close. "My place?"

She glanced nervously at the doorway. "Tonight?"

He thought of Paula and her mystery meeting. "Tomorrow. I'll have the place to myself."

Her eyes narrowed. "Do you live with—"

"I have a roommate. Sort of. I'll explain tomorrow."

"Oh my god, fine," she said, then hesitated. "Are you going to meet up with Daniella?"

Jesus Christ, she was cute. "You still jealous?"

"No," she said, practically green. She still had soap bubbles in her hair. He brushed them away, chest throbbing like he had a big internal bruise. "I'm not interested in Daniella."

"What about Kelly?" she shot back. "Or any of the other girls you're sleeping with?"

Unbidden, the truth came out of his mouth. "I'm only interested in one girl. She's tall and pretty and she doesn't know what she wants."

Nicole's brows drew together, and he didn't know if she was going to hit him, kiss him or cry. He held his breath and the front door creaked open, Tabby and Sam's voices floating in.

Nicole took a step back, her hands on her hips. "Text me your address. I'll see you tomorrow."

She turned and strutted away, heels clicking on the hardwood floor. Noah felt that psychic lifting of hairs. None of his problems were solved and bigger ones were looming but right now he couldn't bring himself to care. He turned back to the sink and kept washing.

8

What did you wear to an interview with a possible biker? Pantsuit? Too formal. Tracksuit shorts? Too casual. Heels and a pencil skirt? Too work-y. And too sexy. Noah might get even more of the wrong idea.

Nicole had laid out every piece of clothing she owned, sure that if she could just figure out what to wear, everything would take care of itself. The problem was, most of her stuff was still hanging in her walk-in wardrobe in Adelaide. She could borrow something from Sam. Dressing in her black skinny jeans and docs mig,ht make her feel a little tougher, and Noah wasn't attracted to—

Nicole froze. How had she not considered this before? She whirled around and picked up her phone. Opening the notes app, she typed another question:

34. Do you, or have you ever wanted to sleep with Sam? If so, am I a consolation prize now she's with Scott?

She nodded grimly and locked her phone. Whatever happened this evening, she was going to ask Noah everything she wanted to know, which, as of now, was thirty-four separate things.

She held up a baggy Panda t-shirt she'd brought to clean in. This would do. It would remind her she was going to him as a detective, as a journalist, as Miss freaking Fisher. She was not—*not!*—going to sleep with him. She put on the T-shirt and an old pair of denim shorts. Her phone vibrated, and she looked down, expecting to see Noah's address. It was a text from Aaron. *'Call me.'*

Her finger hovered over the little phone icon, then she moved it away. They would have to talk eventually, but not right now. She needed her wits about her. Even though she and Aaron were over, and her sisters weren't entitled to every detail of her life, she felt guilty about the kiss she and Noah shared in the kitchen. It was strange to feel guiltier about that, than him giving her an orgasm in his tattooing chair. But that had been panicked and purely sexual, the kiss on the other hand... it came loaded with implications.

Nicole cupped the back of her neck, echoing the way he'd held her. The numbing bliss of it all had to be an exaggeration. It just couldn't have felt that good. She stroked her palm across her right breast, feeling her nipple harden. He'd been so controlled, so comfortable giving her pleasure. She'd never been with a man who needed so little reassurance to make her feel good...

Sam pushed open her door. "Knock, Knock. What are you up to?"

Nicole tore her hands away from herself. "Nothing!"

"Are you doing yourself standing up?"

"No! God, you're so gross!"

Sam raised her hands. "It's not an accusation. There's nothing wrong with doing yourself."

Nicole shoved her feet into her runners. "I know! I got the same speech when we were kids."

"Yeah, that was brilliant of dad, wasn't it? Girls never get told they should knock out a few solo runs before they have sex and it's fucked."

Nicole didn't say anything. She'd done time in therapy, dissecting what it meant to be a prude in a family of 'live and let live' hippies. Two years and five thousand dollars to learn what she already knew —her mother's abandonment and Greyson's carelessness had left her terrified of sex. And being terrified of sex was twenty times harder when you were surrounded by people who talked about sex as though it was Monopoly or something. But that was her problem, not something she had a right to burden the Tinder-happy population with.

She tied her laces in triple knots. "Do you need something?" she asked Sam.

"Nah, Scott and I are getting Vietnamese, do you want anything?"

"No thanks, I'm going out."

Sam eyed her t-shirt and shorts. "Where?"

"Coffee with Amberley," Nicole lied. "From school, remember?"

"No," Sam said with the apathy she had for everyone they went to school with. "Are you wearing makeup?"

Nicole touched her cheek. "No. Why, is it noticeable? Does it look bad?"

"No. I'm just surprised. I haven't seen you go out without makeup since..." Sam made a face. "Your whole adult life? And most of your teen years?"

"It hasn't been that long."

"Yeah, maybe," Sam said, clearly not believing her. "What gives?"

"I'm just trying to be more relaxed about the way I look."

The pride in Sam's face was equal parts endearing and offensive. Was she really such a basket case? God, Sam didn't even know she'd been debating lip injections. Or her plans to get rid of her tattoo. Nicole tugged her sleeve over her watch strap. "Okay, I should get going."

"To see Amberley?"

Nicole couldn't meet her twin's eyes. "Yeah."

Sam frowned. "Nix, are you up to something?"

Nicole hesitated. She could tell her sister she was going to see Noah, but that would mean unloading everything that had happened, and her suspicion Noah was a bikie. She loved Sam, but she got mad first and asked questions later—as her boyfriend could attest. When they were kids, Scott had accidentally gotten on Sam's bad side, and she'd built a website to auction off his virginity.

Her phone vibrated, and this time, she knew it was Noah texting her his address. Her stomach squirmed like live snakes. "I'm not up to anything," she told Sam. "Can I please borrow your car?"

"Sure." Sam still had a funny look on her face. "Are you sure you're okay?"

"Definitely. See you later."

Once she was safely in Sam's car, Nicole checked the text. Noah's address was 313 Sherbet Street, Brunswick. She typed the address into Google Maps and waited as it calculated the time it would take to drive there—one minute. Noah lived two streets over. How did none of them know that? She growled and opened the driver's side door before realising it would make Sam incredibly suspicious if she didn't drive. Gritting her teeth, she started the engine.

His place was an inoffensive two-story brick, not so different from her house. The garden surprised her with its pink and yellow roses and smooth green grass. Maybe he was renting off one of those old Italian guys who still showed up every week to mow? Or it was a decoy because the house was full of goat skulls and inflatable sex dolls...

She killed the ignition, rubbing her sweaty palms on her thighs. This would be over in an hour. She'd ask Noah her questions then get the heck out. She shoved the car door open and headed up the front path with what she hoped was an authoritative-yet-relaxed expression. It felt like her cheeks were set in concrete. She rapped on his door. There was no answer. She knocked harder. "Hello? It's Nicole. DaSilva. From work."

God, why was she always saying ridiculous things around Noah? Why couldn't she be quiet like he was? It made people give you way more intelligence credit. She heard footsteps pound toward her and swallowed, trying to rehydrate her tongue. Her whole body felt like it had dried out.

Noah opened the door. As always, he was bigger than she remembered, tall and wide as a wall. The green of his eyes seemed darker, too, moss on a Nordic mountain. He looked at her, seeing in the way only he seemed to see her. Through and beyond in the way that made her face feel like a disguise. "Hey, Nikki."

"Hey." She tugged at the sleeves of her hoodie. "Nice garden."

A curl of his lip. "You find the place okay?"

"Ha-ha. I can't believe you live so close to the studio. You could have said something."

"Where's the fun in that?"

"Hmph."

He stepped aside, showing her a long cream-coloured hallway. Music was playing from somewhere, that thudding rap Noah liked. Trap music, maybe? Tabby would know.

"Coming inside?" he asked.

"If I did, where would I go?"

"Down the hall and to the left. We'll have a drink in the kitchen."

She licked her cracked lips. "Okay."

Noah Newcomb's house was not only free of dead goats but *nice*. As clean as her house, with the most gorgeous art on the walls. She stopped to examine a painting of a quince tree luxuriating in the afternoon sun, and Noah cleared his throat.

She kept moving, turning left into the sweetest little kitchen she'd ever seen, with a big wooden counter top and herb pots everywhere. "Okay. Who owns this place?"

"Me." Noah strode toward the fancy stainless-steel fridge. "Pinot okay?"

"Sure. Did your house come furnished?"

He grinned. "You were expecting deer heads and grease on the walls, weren't you?"

"Umm...?"

He pulled a green wine bottle from the fridge. "Not my style."

"How did this become your style?"

"If you grew up where I did, you'd like nice things, too."

It was easily the most personal thing he'd ever told her. Nicole was bursting to ask for details, but sensed the time wasn't right. She scanned the kitchen, taking in the shelves of brightly-coloured cookbooks and the pretty lighting. It was still bizarre to think this house was Noah's.

"When did you move in?"

"Three years ago," he said, collecting glasses from a kitchen cabinet. "Me and your dad fixed it up on weekends."

So, her dad had been here. She felt an unexpected throb of homesickness. Not for the house a couple of streets away, but her father. "That doesn't surprise me. Dad loves fixing up houses. We used to want to get him on one of those renovation shows."

"He would have hated it."

She smiled, struck by how weird it was that the stranger getting her a drink knew her dad so well. "How did you..."

The painting hanging over the dining table stopped her in her tracks. She moved closer to study the canvas. A tiny ship bobbed at the base of an enormous cliff, indigo waves surging around it, gushing veils of pearly foam. She wasn't as artistically talented as the rest of her family, but she knew this was a beauty. The brushwork was flawless and the colours... you could practically feel the churning pressure of the sea, the frailty of the boat as it teetered on the verge of capsize.

"Who did this?"

No answer. She turned to see Noah pulling the cork from the pinot bottle, caution etched across his handsome-ugly face.

"It's yours! You paint?"

Noah poured a huge quantity of pinot into a single wine glass. "Want ice?"

"That quince tree in the hall, that's yours too, isn't it? Are they all yours? They're amazing! Who taught you? Why doesn't anyone else know you paint?"

Noah brought the glass over. He gestured for her to sit below the painting and she did. He sat across from her and she noticed his cheeks were ruddy. Was he embarrassed? God, maybe he was. She accepted the wine and took a panic swallow. It was good, crisp and applish. "Thanks. And sorry for asking a million questions, but your work is *beautiful*."

The red on Noah's cheeks darkened. "Thanks."

"How long have you been painting?"

He shrugged. "Couple years?"

"Did my dad teach you?"

Noah smiled. "Nah. He bought me my first set of brushes, though."

Again, she wasn't surprised. If there was one thing her dad liked more than tea and renovations, it was helping people find what they were good at. She glanced at the seascape. "I knew you're a great tattooist, but these should be in galleries. You should be famous."

Noah shook his head. "I don't want to sell them."

"Why not? Do you only want to paint for the love of it or something?"

A pained expression crossed his face. "It's... complicated."

More complicated than being a bikie's son?

He had to be referring to his family history. The thought of asking him about his father, the bail jumper, sent prickles down her spine. Nervous, she took another sip of her wine. It occurred to her that Noah had *pinot* in his house. "Do you drink white?"

"No."

"Then why do you have it?"

A corner of his mouth lifted. "For you. I figured you'd be nervous."

"I'm not nervous!"

Noah raised a brow.

"Okay, so maybe I'm a little nervous. Can you blame me?"

"Nope. That's what the wine's for."

"Thanks," she said and took a pointed sip. She was barely half a glass in but she already felt a little drunk on nerves and revelations. She squinted at her wine. "We should discuss things. I have a list of questions, you know. Thirty-four of them."

"Oh yeah?"

"Yeah. About bikers and money and tattooing and lots of things."

Noah shifted forward. The chair creaked ominously, but he didn't seem to notice. "Did you really wanna talk?"

"Yes?"

He stared intently at her. "Look at me and say it."

She tried, but the minute she met his gaze, heat flared in her middle. She buried her face in her wine. "I can't. But I do want to talk."

"Nikki, it's okay to be uncomfortable being alone with me."

She shouldn't have liked the nickname, but she did. She liked the nickname and she liked the reassurance that came with it. "I'm not uncomfortable, I just don't know what to do."

"Do you need to know?"

It was a strange question, like a riddle. Did she need to know what to do? "Yes. Otherwise, how would I make decisions about what comes next?"

Noah didn't say anything, but she could feel him thinking about the answer. She could ask what it was, but she had a feeling she didn't want to know. Instead, she sipped her wine until she emptied the glass.

"More?"

"Do you want me to be drunk?"

"I want you to be comfortable. Do you want to be drunk?"

"A little bit," she admitted. "I think I need to be for things to progress. Not heaps drunk, just… tipsy."

A small smile. "So get tipsy."

"Isn't that going to be annoying for you? Waiting for me to get drunk enough to say things?"

He shrugged his massive shoulders. "I've got nowhere to be."

So, he refilled her glass and she drank. She drank and studied the ocean painting above him and thought about sex and love. Noah watched her, refilling her glass when she came close to the bottom. When she'd had almost three, her brain was buzzing as well as other, less savoury places.

His eyes, she thought. *They're like jade in the afternoon sun. And he lets me be quiet. He doesn't fill up the silences because that's easier. He just lets it all be. That's so attractive. He's so attractive.*

It was the first time she let herself admit it without a guilt chaser. She smiled at Noah, and he smiled back. Then he reached out and brushed his hand against hers. Electricity zapped through her. She

CUSTOMER RECEIPT

The Shakespeare Gift Shop
Henley Street , Stratford upon Avon , CV37 6QW
17/02/2025 12:45:34
RECEIPT NO.: 1939
MID: XXX44094   TID: XXXX8862
AID: A0000000031010
Visa Prepaid
XXXXXXXXXXXX0814
PAN SEQ NO. : 00

SALE :   GBP14.00
TOTAL :   GBP14.00

PLEASE DEBIT MY ACCOUNT
NO CARDHOLDER VERIFICATION
CONTACTLESS
PLEASE KEEP THIS RECEIPT FOR YOUR RECORD
AUTH CODE:878661

let it thrum for a second and then pulled away. "I don't know why I want you. It doesn't make sense."

He nodded, but something in the composition of his face changed.

Nicole could have slapped herself. "I mean, you're not my usual type. You're attractive, obviously."

Noah's brows shot up.

"I mean, you must know that. Heaps of women are into you."

He said nothing.

"Seriously," she said, feeling like an idiot. "You're huge, and you're stoic, which falls into that whole, you know, alpha thing. And you're covered in tattoos, and most of them are nice even though they're old —which isn't a diss; sleeves just all used to be horrible. Oh, and your eyes are pretty. Or handsome, or whatever it is you say when a man has pretty eyes."

The silence that followed this word-vomit was deafening. Nicole pressed her fingers to her face, and when she had the courage to peer through them, Noah smiled a pirate smile at her. "Alpha?"

"Shut up!"

"And huge?"

She swatted his arm. "Stop it!"

"Pretty eyes?"

"Leave me alone!"

"Would you say I'm the most alpha?"

Nicole covered her face again. "Please don't be mean to me. I'm really vulnerable right now, in your mysterious house with all your nice things."

He said nothing and when she resurfaced, he wasn't smiling. Instead, his gaze was hot, something like determination. Only determination didn't usually make her feel like her clothes were too tight. "What?"

Noah flicked the rim of her wine glass, making it ting. "Let's talk about what's gonna happen once you finish this."

"What do you want to happen?"

He leaned forward, a scrap of setting sun highlighting the hard planes of his face. "I want to take you to bed."

Nicole looked at her glass, wishing he could be cruder. If he was a pig, it would be easier to pretend her desire was something he was making her feel.

"That not something you want?"

"No, I mean yes." She swallowed, her throat as tight as a lock. "I want that—to be with you that way. But I'm so bad at all of this. I'm sure I'm going to ruin it. Or we won't work together, and I'll have taken this big risk for nothing."

"Nikki..."

She looked down at the table. "Please don't tell me I'm overreacting."

"Never." There was a hard ring in his voice. "Look at me."

Reluctantly she glanced up at his eyes.

"You're not overreacting," he said. "Come here."

"Where?"

He patted his thighs. Nicole hesitated, then stood and moved toward him. Noah grabbed her thighs and lifted, arranging her so she was sitting across his legs. He was warm beneath his clothes, his thighs, and chest rock hard. He curled an arm around her back, and Nicole leaned in, breathing his smoke and cedar scent.

Noah's hand smoothed across her back. "What do you like, Nikki?"

"In bed?"

"Yeah."

He must have meant limits and safe words and stuff. All the grown-up, one-night-stand talk she'd swerved by never having sex outside relationships. "I want to use condoms."

"I... sure." He leaned back to look at her, his brow furrowed. "Anything else?"

Nicole racked her brain for bases she might have missed. "You can be, you know, rough or whatever, but please don't hurt me, like pull my hair super hard or give me bruises. And please don't go near my butt. I've never done that and... not the first time."

Her words were meshing together like melted wax, but that was from nerves, not wine. In fact, the wine was probably the only thing that could ever inspire her to say such a thing out loud. That and Noah's hand stroking her back in firm hard circles.

"Swearing?" he asked.

"Excuse me?"

"I know you don't like it at work, what about bed?"

"I... what do you want to say?"

"Fucking, cunt, pussy, cock," he said as though reeling off a list of colours. "Whatever I want. They a problem?"

How did she feel about it? In the warm afternoon air, sitting at his dining table, it made her feel a lot of things; nervous, embarrassed, humiliated... but mostly because she'd always hated swearing, but the thought of Noah saying the c-word while he was inside her made her thighs clench. "Do you want to call me dirty names again? Like you did in your chair?"

His gaze flicked sideways. "Yeah, but that was a bit of a mess. We don't have to go there again."

She realised he was nervous, a little convinced she was going to change her mind and bail. That made her feel better for some reason. "What if I want to go there?"

Noah dipped his head, and she knew he was hiding a smile.

"You're allowed to want me," she said, feeling prickly. "I like that you want me."

Those unearthly eyes snapped up to meet her. "Do you?"

It was a fair question. The attraction had been there since day one, and she'd resented it, hated it, and was now giving into it. But did she like it?

"I... yes. I like that you want me. It makes me feel very..." She wanted to say 'overwhelmed', but that wasn't right. "*Different.*"

"Good-different?"

She nodded.

"I can live with that."

He wrapped his arms around her, creating a warm gate across her lower back. Nicole pressed her head into his shoulder and tried to relax. How would the sex start? Would he carry her to his bedroom? Were they going to do it in his kitchen?

Noah shifted, bending so his mouth was beside her ear. "You want to hear a story?"

"About what?"

"Places bad men go to have a good time."

The world around her seemed to be vanishing, narrowing into a single space. She shifted closer to Noah, needing his warmth. "Okay."

"Sometimes when we needed to blow off steam, we'd hire out a club, put all our own people behind the bar. Have a party. Do you know what I'm saying, Nikki?"

She nodded, scared to speak and break the veil of intimacy between them.

"Word would get out pretty quickly. Guys tried to buy their way in. Girls'd do whatever it took to get through the door. Can you see them lining up outside?"

She nodded because she could. It would look like Emerald Bar last Saturday, only darker, and the girls would be wearing even less clothing.

"It'll be a big place. Packed from top to bottom. Can you see that, baby?"

Nicole closed her eyes and saw big rooms lit with neon lights, half-naked women carrying trays, and big, menacing man shadows. The music in Noah's kitchen seemed louder, perfect for the scene. "Is this party real?"

Noah's fingers traced across her collarbone. "It's real right now. It's a big loud party and there's pills and empties on every table and people fucking in the corners."

A chorus of moans took up in her mind, like in porn. "What am I doing there?"

"You came with your friend," Noah said, instantly solving the problem she'd had when attempting her own fantasy bikie scenario. "She's off fucking a guy in the bathroom, you're all alone."

She closed her eyes, seeing herself sitting on a couch alone, wanting it and fearing attention. "Are you there?"

"Yes."

She could see him, bigger and scarier than the other men in the club. Women watching him, talking to him. He was important, even she could see that.

Noah sat back and tucked a finger under her chin. "Hey."

"Hi," she said, opening her eyes. She felt shyer than she could have believed possible.

Noah didn't seem to be suffering from the same stage fright. His hand slid lower to cup her breast. "Name?"

Nicole couldn't breathe; the offence of it, the insult of it, was turning her on almost as much as the touch. "Nicole. Can you please not grab me?"

The corner of his mouth tipped up. "This is my place." The subtext was 'I can do whatever I like.'

As though to prove it, his finger and thumb slid to a close around her nipple. Nicole shuddered, shifting against his thighs. "Please..."

"Yeah?" He bent his head to nuzzle her neck, his stubble grazing her skin.

"People are watching."

"Yeah."

Noah unzipped her hoodie and tugged it off, his hard hands running the length of her arms.

"We don't know each other."

"Doesn't matter." He tugged at the bottom of her t-shirt, and she raised her arms so he could pull it off. Her black bra was revealed, in all its basic glory, but Noah stared like it was a sequinned Simone Pérèle.

"What?"

"Your body..." He shook his head. "We're done talking."

She opened her mouth to protest, just on principle, but he bent forward and kissed her, gripping her hair to keep her from moving away. This was nothing like the kiss in her kitchen. It was hard and uncompromising, even a little mean. She moaned into his mouth and rocked against him, the hard fork of her jeans rubbing against her swollen pussy.

Noah's hands slid around her back, and—pang—her bra was open. Impressive. She shrugged her arms forward, but as the material tumbled down her forearms, shyness re-grasped. She folded an arm across her hard pink nipples.

"None of that." Noah tugged at her wrist, but she wouldn't re-expose herself. She needed to be in a bed, in a dark room. She needed this to be more normal. "Can we go somewhere else?"

"Okay."

He reached beneath her and lifted her into the air. He headed back up the hallway and paused at what had to be his bedroom door. "Ready?"

No, but that was different from not wanting him. She nodded, and he opened the door and carried her inside.

9

Noah's room was spartan, little more than a huge bed and a chest of drawers. She could see there were more paintings on the walls, but she couldn't make them out. His smell was everywhere, earth and tobacco. He lay her on his sheets, and she shifted into them, trying to warm them up.

She could hear her breathing, fast and shallow.

"Look at me."

She did, though Noah's face was half-hidden in shadow. Without the bright glow of his eyes, he looked coarse and unattractive. "Take your clothes off. All of them. Shoes, too."

Oh God, she was wearing her runners in his bed. She toed off her shoes and struggled out of her jean shorts. Despite their age, the waistband was tight, and she had to writhe in his sheets, her bare boobs jiggling, as she forced them down her legs. She felt like an idiot. Noah had done such a good job of setting the mood, and she was trashing it.

When she finally kicked her shorts away, she tucked both thumbs into her panty-line. She pulled her underwear away from her body, arching her back and biting her lip. It was a pose that had always gotten good results from Aaron.

The bed sank as Noah stuck his knees in it. "Knock that shit off."

"Sorry," she said, mortified. "I told you, I'm not good at sexy."

"It's not that. Don't pretend. If I wanted to fuck a porn star, I'd pay for it." He loomed over her, an angry shadow. "I want to fuck you. You know why?"

"No," she lied. He wanted to unwrap and corrupt her, be the guy who showed her how good sex could be. What other advantage did she have over the Kellys and Daniellas of this world?

He shifted, settling on top of her, one knee on either side of her hips. "You want dick more than any girl I've ever met."

The answer was so shocking, so unexpected that Nicole was legitimately offended. "*Excuse me*?"

"You think you're better than it, don't you, baby? You think you're better than sex?"

"No," Nicole said hotly. "But I don't want... *that* more than anyone else."

Noah gripped her wrists, pulling them above her head. "You calling me a liar?"

"No."

"Good." He bent his head and wet heat encapsulated her left nipple. She cried out, her hips rising to press against his. Noah pressed back without hesitation. She could feel him beneath his jeans, hard as iron. She imagined it sliding deep inside her and an involuntary whimper escaped. Noah laughed, moving back so that she ground against thin air. "Not horny at all, are you? Not desperate for a fuck?"

"Shut up!" she said, from some pocket of fury she hadn't known she had.

He nipped her ear, firm enough that she gasped.

"You listen to me now. You think you're so good, so pure, better than all us animals who fuck. You're wrong. You're the kind who needs to be touched every day. And I'll prove it to you, right in this room, you hear me?"

Nicole wanted to tell him he was stupid and gross and wrong, but it wasn't as strong as her curiosity. Did he know her better than she did? Than her boyfriends did? Was he talking rubbish or was he about to make a fool of her? He already had, she realised. He was a big, mean man who washed dishes painted masterpieces and bought her white wine. He refused to stay where she wanted him to.

"I said, 'You hear me?'"

A shiver wove its way down her spine. She was trapped between Noah's soft sheets and his hard body. The world was dark and quiet around them—they might have been the only two people in the world. "Yes. I hear you."

"Good." He nipped her ear. "From here on out you're gonna shut your mouth and feel, and I don't want to see any of this pretend pouting bullshit. I don't need you to play Barbie doll for me. You want to get fucked and you will. Just take it."

She nodded, her need like a physical pain.

A flash of teeth. "You're gonna love it, but you really want me to stop, you say my full name, okay? You know it?"

"Noah Harold Newcomb."

His hands loosened around her wrists and the air between them changed. It was the 'Harold', she realised. He didn't know she knew his middle name, his father's name. She felt the unspoken things rise between them and was sure he was about to get off her, but then he leaned forward and bit her earlobe again. "That's right. Now, tell me you want to get fucked."

She nodded, relieved and aroused.

"Say it."

She closed her eyes. "I want you."

"Close enough." Noah sat back on her hips. "How long's it been?"

Since she had sex? Nicole cast back. Maybe six weeks? No, more like eight? God, when was the last time she and Aaron had slept together?

A hard tug on her nipple. "Just say it."

"Um, a few months, I think."

She felt him smile, heard it in his voice when he said, "Good. Now lie back."

Nicole obliged, keeping her hands over her head and her thighs together. He shut the door and the room became even darker. She snuggled back into Noah's sheets enjoying the warm and softness of the cloth. She'd never imagined him owning nice sheets—but she'd never imagined a lot of things about him.

She could hear him taking off his clothes, but the darkness swallowed the view. She wondered if he was into doing it with the lights off, or if the darkness was for her benefit. She did like it. Aaron always wanted the lights on and the curtains opened. He'd drag her to the mirror as often as he could. She got used to being exposed but she never liked looking at herself during sex, no matter how many body positivity articles she read.

Noah grasped her hips and climbed on top of her again, higher than before. His bare hips bracketed her stomach and his cock fell along her chest, almost to her chin. The hairy drag of his testicles on her belly was so strange, she squealed. "What are you doing?"

Noah tapped her cheek. "No talking."

"But—"

"It's what I want, Nikki."

He cupped her tits, stroking her nipples with his rough thumbs. Nicole moaned, a tugging sensation drawing her belly tight. It didn't seem right that she could enjoy herself while he was sitting on her like this, his skin so hot and hairy, his cock so smooth and long. On the other hand, it was so bizarre, it was hard to place it against any of her other sexual encounters. That was weirdly freeing.

Noah pinched her nipples and she whimpered.

"Like that?"

She shook her head.

"Okay, little liar. Hold still." Noah bundled her breasts together, closing them around the smooth heat of his cock. "Open your mouth. Wide as you can."

She parted her lips, stretching her jaw. Then, operating on an instinct she didn't understand, she tilted her chin and slid out her tongue. The tip of his cock was thick and clean. She lapped, tasting salt. Noah hissed and his fingers tweaked her nipples. "That's it, dirty girl, keep licking."

He slid forward, rubbing his cock between her breasts, his scrotum dragging across her chest, and a hot humiliation swamped her. What kind of girl was she, to let him do this? She couldn't even *say* what he was doing to her, it was too gross.

"Lick," Noah grunted. "More tongue."

Nicole pressed her chin to her sternum and licked him as he pushed his cock between her breasts. It wasn't an easy manoeuvre. She had to keep her neck bent and he was moving so fast she had to lick even faster but as she did it, she found a rhythm and it became easier.

"Good girl," Noah tugged her left nipple. "Deeper. Show me you love it."

I will, she thought. She didn't love it, but she didn't hate it either. The awkwardness she'd felt was seeping away and she was lying in warm sheets, in the dark, making Noah feel good, and all she had to do was lick his penis as he slid between her breasts. He was heavy, but he wasn't putting all his weight on her. It wasn't uncomfortable and she knew uncomfortable; waxing and high heels and eyelash extensions and control underwear, and Bikram yoga and long meetings and early mornings and late nights were uncomfortable. Life was uncomfortable. This was kind of... *delicious*.

She lay back, concentrating on the small tweaks and tugs on her nipples, feeling the corresponding tug between her legs. She was horny, she realised. She was so horny it was like a pleasurable headache. If she wasn't terrified of taking things further, she'd have asked him to screw her, but instead she just licked and felt and enjoyed. At least until he stopped, removing the hand on her right breast. She bent forward and took the head of his cock in her mouth. It was as big as a fleshy golf ball and she bobbed as much as she could, twirling her tongue around the flared head.

"Fuck," Noah groaned, but he settled on top of her again.

Nicole let a squeak of impatience escape her mouth and he laughed.

"You want me to tell you you're a good girl for trying so hard?"

Noah tugged her right nipple, wrapping her breasts around him again. "I'm not going to. I know you love this."

He spat, the sound as ugly as what they were doing. She heard him slick his saliva along the base of his cock, felt him swipe it in the valley between her breasts. Heat swelled between her legs and she felt herself dampen as effectively as Noah had slicked her breasts. She moaned, dismayed with herself.

"What's wrong?"

"You're disgusting! You're on top of me and you're not even touching me and—"

"You like it?"

"No!"

But they both knew she was lying. Noah laughed and fucked her faster, sliding the head of his cock into her mouth. Nicole closed her eyes, listening to the slick sounds, feeling the ache in her jaw and the rub of his genitals. She imagined how it would look if someone came into the room. How they'd see a big, muscly tattooed man fucking her tits and her licking his cock and whimpering as though he was doing her a favour. Heat speared her middle. She was aching, swollen with wetness. She reached down to touch herself, but Noah was in the way. She shifted, missing a lick so that Noah's cock brushed her chin.

"Keep it up, Nikki."

Nicole tried. She bent forward and tried, but she was light-headed, and her jaw was throbbing. She was moaning, exactly as desperate as Noah had accused her of being, but she didn't care. "Noah…"

"Yeah, baby?"

"I need… I just, please?"

"You need more?"

Of course, he couldn't just let her have more. "Yes! Yes, please yes! More."

Noah turned, gripping her underwear and pulling it tight against her labia. It parted her lips and molded the cotton around her swollen clit. She screamed at the sudden stimulation. "What are you—"

"Shut up and lick my cock."

Noah pulled her panties up from the back so that they stretched up her ass, turning her cotton hipsters into a high-waisted thong.

"See what you can do with that," he said and kept right on fucking her tits.

Nicole was furious, but doing or saying something required concentration she didn't have. Her cunt was throbbing and her underwear was like a harness, holding her in place, stimulating her overstimulated body.

Noah spat again. This time wetness splashed onto her nipple, slicking her right breast. Noah spread it across her. She imagined him finishing on her, on her nipples and face. He could do it if he wanted, come on her, and if he did…

Noah gripped her hair. "Suck my cock, Nikki."

Filthy, she thought. *So, so filthy.*

But she licked, and though she wasn't one of those girls who could get off with Kegel exercises or tight jeans, she could hear herself crying out as she rubbed hard against her panties. She sounded crazed, desperate, the kind of girl who ruined pornography because she was just too loud. Too eager. She was going to come, she realised with giddy exhilaration. She was that girl.

Nicole turned her head away to avoid sucking Noah. He gripped her cheek, shoving her back into line, but she shook her head. "Can you go faster? Like, use me?"

He could have laughed at her total hypocrisy, instead he urged her mouth back onto his cock. "You do this, I'll do the rest."

She sucked him fast and eager as he pulled hard at her nipples. Her orgasm was crushing her insides, making wetness flow through her. Noah's body kept her pinned to the mattress and she kicked her legs, arching uselessly against him.

"That's it," she heard him say. "That's it, you filthy girl, come."

And she did, she arched back and let the rough rub of her underwear guide her to orgasm. It was more relief than pleasure to feel the gold pulsing through her. She closed her eyes and sighed, twitching a little with aftershocks.

Noah climbed off and she breathed deep into her chest, happy as a kitten in the sun. "I just came."

"Glad to hear it." His response was so casual, mortification curled icy tendrils through her middle. He hadn't even finished and here she was, practically falling asleep.

She opened her eyes. "I'm so sorry, can I do something for you?"

"You just did. Don't apologise."

"What should we do now?"

He grabbed her waist, turning her onto her belly. "This."

"What's this?" Nicole asked, wanting to be helpful.

"Just go where I put you."

He hauled her onto all fours, pulling her knees back and pushing her forearms down. Nicole felt like an opposable joints Karate Barbie, being moved into different fighting poses. Noah pulled her underwear down and she felt her labia part. Embarrassed, she tried to cover her wetness, but he slapped her ass. "Don't move."

He got off the bed and she heard a drawer open, a crinkly packet torn open. It was about to happen. Her heart contracted. Noah would be her fourth. A square, tabletop number. The bed heaved under Noah's weight. God, they were about to have sex. What if his penis didn't fit? It had felt massive between her boobs and Aaron always said she was small. What if it hurt? Noah ran a hand over her back and she almost jumped a mile. "Sorry!"

"It's okay, just take it easy. Breathe."

She breathed, feeling tight and inflexible.

"Arch your back."

She did and he brushed a thumb down her crack, and she started. All the heat she'd felt before had vanished, her stupid anti-eroticism had struck again.

Don't worry about it, an unfriendly Sam said. *Just get it over with.*

Yeah, and put your hand back when he's going inside you, whispered paranoid Tabby. *Make sure the condom's still on.*

Noah stiffened behind her. Could he tell she no longer wanted it? How? She hadn't done anything. Before she could tell him to keep going, he shifted to the side, lying beside her. He wrapped his fist around his cock, a shadowy tower. "Climb on."

"Ex... cuse me?"

"Get up here and ride. It's not rocket science."

"But—"

He sat up and gripped her hair. "You still want it hard?"

Nicole's cunt contracted, her nipples re-tightened. Suddenly it was like she hadn't just come in her own underwear; it was like she'd never been satisfied at all. She clasped his hand, feeling hair over rough skin. "*Yes.*"

"Then do what you're told."

"I can't." Her voice was a high whine, so put on she might as well have said 'Make me, daddy.'

His hand tightened in her hair. "Ride me or I'll drag you outside and fuck you in my front yard. Okay?"

She shuddered. "Yes."

Noah let go and she climbed on top of him. It was like straddling a living statue, or maybe a huge Clydesdale horse. She had to spread her knees wide to touch the bed. Breathing fast, she wrapped her hand around the base of his cock, angling so it was where it needed to be. His skin was so warm, it was almost hot. "Noah..."

His hands caressed her hips. "You okay?"

"Yes," she said, reassured that he was there and he still cared, at least enough to ask if she was okay. She pressed herself back against the head and it slid in with ease. She rocked, gently flexing and contracting. He was wide, wider than anyone she'd ever been with and as she sank lower, the pressure between her legs built until it was just a few shades away from pain. She breathed out. "Has anyone ever told you you're big. Like... in a bad way?"

"No," Noah said, amused. "Is that what you're doing?"

"Kind of. I mean, it's good, but it's a lot." She shifted around a little, embarrassed. "Can you... with the bossiness again?"

A soft chuckle. "Demand you take my dick?"

"It helps! It's like, when your trainer tells you to do five more push-ups. You want to do it; you just need the motivation."

"Take your word for it." Noah sat up and gripped her jaw roughly. "You want to get fucked, Nikki?"

Nicole closed her eyes. "Yes."

"Then sit on me, you little whore."

Nicole moved without thinking, raising herself up on her heels and grasping his shaft with her left hand. She bounced, finding it was easier to sink down this way. She had more control and while it ached, there was no pain. She was about three quarters down, and highly pleased with herself, when Noah let out a moan. "Fuck, you feel good."

She paused, startled. "I'm glad?"

"Forgot you were fucking me?"

"No! A bit. I guess I just focused on taking you."

His hands closed around her ass, pulling her deeper onto him. "Take some more."

Nicole bounced a little harder, glad he couldn't see her smile. She was having sex with Noah and he *liked it*. She found her rhythm, pressing forward and back and as she moved, a prickling heat spread through her lower body. "Oh my god."

"Yeah," he said, gripping her ass. "Tell me."

"You're so big." It was such a cliché, but it was the truth, there was just more of him, so deep inside her it was like she'd never had sex before.

"Yeah." He pumped up into her, making her nerve endings burn and her fingers curl into fists. "Harder. Fuck yourself harder."

Oh, she liked that. She liked that she was fucking herself on him, the idea of using him the way a needy, horny girl used a toy. She moved faster, the prickling now a fire in her midsection.

Noah tugged at her right nipple. "You missed getting fucked?"

She nodded.

"What was that?" Noah pulled her nipple harder, making her cry out.

"Yes, I missed it."

"Of course you did." He released her nipple, his fingertips trailing down her abdomen. He spread his palm across her lower belly, stroking his thumb across her clit. She jolted, missing a stroke with her hips.

"Don't like that?"

She nodded. Then shook her head.

He laughed. "You like it a bit too much, huh? I'll keep it up then. Fuck me faster."

She tried, but her thigh twanged and she sank onto her knees. "I'm sorry, I can't."

Noah made a small noise of impatience and hoisted her off him as though she weighed nothing. He tossed her beside him on her stomach and the bed bounced as he got behind her. "Put a hand between your legs."

Nicole shoved her right palm between her thighs. She was so swollen, she could barely cup herself.

Noah gripped her ass, hauling her backward. "Don't just lie there, diddle your clit."

God he's such an arsehole, Nicole thought. *He's an arsehole and the things he says are so gross and—*

She gave herself a tentative stroke and almost passed out from the sensation.

"Exactly," Noah snarled. "Now keep it up, fuck yourself."

"I can't—ohhh!"

His cock slid inside her, almost knocking her fingers out of the way. Noah grunted, gripping her hips as though they were handlebars. "Rub yourself off or I'll stick it between your tits again."

Disgusting, she thought happily, playing with herself. *So, so disgusting.*

She rubbed fast and light, trying not to overwhelm herself, but it was no use. It was so much deeper this way. So much harder and faster than she'd managed on her heels. He drove himself inside her, his balls slapping her rubbing hand, and the ugliness of it made her arousal surge like a forest fire.

"Noah!"

Noah's hands were splayed wide on her hips, wrapping them, crushing them. "Yeah?"

But she was saying his name just to say it, picturing how they looked together, him big and tattooed riding her body. It would look bad, like a wolf tearing apart a lamb.

Noah sucked air through his teeth. "That's it, clench that pussy."

Nicole pulled her inner muscles, trying to obey, but he was so deep inside her, pumping so hard, it was difficult to tell what was going on except she was getting hotter and wetter and it was almost painful to keep petting her clit.

"Fuck, *Nikki*."

"Don't call me that!"

She was rewarded with a slap on her backside. "Shut the fuck up."

"And what if I don't?"

His movement slowed and she exhaled, dizzy at her own daring. What would he do next? Where would this go? Was she about to get choked or tied up or properly spanked?

Bring it, a stranger's voice thought. *Show me how bad it gets.*

Noah bent forward, his sweaty body pressed along her spine. "You want it that way, huh?"

"What way?"

"You know." His hand closed over her lower face and he shoved two fingers in her mouth. He thrust deep inside her, his hips banging into her ass and his fingers slid deeper, making her choke a little. He was everywhere, all over her, sweating and grinding and pushing himself inside her. She gagged, arching her back and pumping her hips.

"Nowhere to run. Nowhere to hide. Keep touching yourself, slut."

Nicole's head was thrumming. She rubbed her clit, feeling him at both ends. Her moan came out as a pathetic gargle.

"That's it," Noah crooned. "Come like the filth you are."

And she did. As he said those horrible things, her fingers pressed hard on her clit and she throbbed, vibrating with pleasure that went up and up and out.

"Nghhhh," she moaned around his fingers. "Plggghs?"

She was begging, though for what, she didn't know. Her orgasm was throbbing in bright white rings, but she needed something else. Something more.

"Easy." Noah's hard belly lifted off her as he knelt upright. His hands closed around her hips and he fucked into her, so hard it was like he was trying to ruin her. He was silent, his breathing in slow bursts. He muttered something she couldn't hear.

"Wh-what?" she asked as he drove deep inside her. But he only groaned, he was lost in his own world now and she had the sense she was outside him. Experiencing, not participating. She closed her eyes, wanting to stay in the moment, to not take his distraction so personally.

Noah bucked, once, twice and then he held himself inside her. He made a low, guttural sound as though he was furious. "Jesus Christ."

Nicole rubbed her face into his sheets, a little stunned it was all over. He was still stuck inside her. Should she say something? Aaron used to just pull out and head for the bathroom. This was uncharted territory.

"You okay?" Noah's voice was different, deeper, lazier. He sounded like a ten-day pleasure cruise.

She smiled. "Yes, are you?"

"Great." He patted her ass and withdrew. She collapsed onto the mattress, and heard him get heavily to his feet. It was over, they were done.

"You want water?" he called.

"No thank you."

Noah padded to the door, opened it and left without another word.

Nicole wrapped her arms around herself, hating the fact she wished he'd held her. She'd just had filthy, horrible, wonderful sex. Why did it have to mean more than that? Why couldn't it just be what it was?

She lay there listening, wondering what he was doing. Peeing? Ditching the condom? She sat up, wondering if she should try to find the light and get dressed or stay and make small talk. God, this was all so awkward, how did her sisters do this? How did anyone do this?

Her mind slid to Aaron, how he'd feel if he knew what she'd done. He'd *despise* her. She could almost see his brow furrowing in disgust. *'Is that what it takes? A bikie choking you while he calls you every name under the sun?'*

She felt a shallow pang of shame, but it was swallowed up by a wave of vindication.

Screw you, Aaron, she thought giddily. *It was good. I came. And I am sexy.*

Noah's bedroom door banged open. Nicole pulled her hands from her eyes and saw her new lover in black briefs. Silhouetted by the light of the doorway, he looked superhero-eqsue.

"You good?" he asked, holding out a glass of water.

"Yes," she said, accepting the glass. The cold water unstuck her throat and she felt a little less rattled, though she wished she was wearing more clothes. "Thanks."

Noah sat beside her, flicking on a beside lamp. Nicole blinked and turned to look at Noah. When she saw him, she did a double take. She'd felt his whole body—its warmth, its hardness, its heft, but she hadn't seen his bare skin beyond his arms. It was a little overwhelming. He was covered in bright, gorgeous tattoos and he was cut. That was the only word she could think of. His body was all heavy muscle and bone. He looked like the cover of a men's health magazine.

"Something wrong?" Noah asked, a smug smile tugging at the corner of his mouth.

"Do you work out?"

He grinned. "Yeah."

"At the gym?"

He shook his head. "I do weights here. And I run."

"Really?" She knew she sounded silly, but it was just too strange to imagine Noah jogging through the Brunswick reserve like her and Sam. "Do you run after work?"

"At night mostly. You do yoga, yeah?"

"Sometimes. I should do it more." She examined the tattoo on Noah's lower belly—a huge brown and gold eagle flying toward a bound man, its razor claws extended. The man looked grim, his muscled body heavily scarred. With a jolt, she realised it was her dad's work—familiar as the Old McDonald song.

"Prometheus," she said, and touched Noah's stomach. His skin was warm and tense, like a muscly hot water bottle. He flinched and she pulled away. "God, I'm sorry. That's so rude."

Noah clasped her hand and returned it to his skin. Electricity coursed up her fingers and when she looked at him, her breath caught in her throat. It was so strange, those pretty eyes in that uncompromising face. And now she and Noah had slept together. Been inside each other. She felt naked, more naked than her bare skin suggested. Unable to hold his gaze, she looked at the eagle tattoo. "My dad did this?"

"Yeah."

She traced the eagle with a fingertip, wondering what they'd talked about while her dad tattooed. Art? Music? Her sisters? *Her?* God, she hoped not. There was a curling banner beside the eagle. She moved her head, trying to read the words.

"Sic Semper Tyrranis," Noah said.

"What does it mean?"

He hesitated, and Nicole realised, with a throb of horror, it could be some bikie motto. "Never mind, you don't have to tell me."

"Thus always to tyrants."

"Huh?"

"That's what it means."

"And is that... meaningful to you?"

"It's a long story."

Nicole had no idea what to say to that and it was clear Noah didn't want to elaborate. The silence grew between them like moss and she needed to say something to break it. She looked around and her gaze fell on the stack of fantasy novels beside his bed, their covers black and silver, crimson and eggplant purple. "Why do you like fantasy novels?"

"I just do."

Well, that was a good start. She tried again. "Do you read a lot of them?"

"Couple a week."

"There are that many?"

He gave a small huff. "Yeah."

Silence. More damnable silence.

"Do you read?" There was noticeable strain in Noah's voice, as though every word of small talk cost a day of his life. Which was especially strange, considering he'd just done such filthy things to her in complete relaxation.

Nicole attempted a smile. "I don't read as much as I want to. I'm halfway through *Nine Perfect Strangers* but I'm too busy to finish it."

He gave a small huff.

"What?"

"You're not too busy. You just don't know how to do anything unproductive."

Her face stung with embarrassment, but then the perfect comeback line swelled in her mouth like a liquid bead. "I just slept with you, didn't I?"

There was a pause. Nicole's stomach plummeted.

"I'm sorry, that was mean."

Noah's mouth twitched and then he laughed. It transformed him. Suddenly, his heavy face was alive, a knotted tree swaying in the breeze, an old steam train rushing through the countryside. He wasn't handsome, but he was *beautiful*.

"You gonna bill me?" he asked. "For taking up your time?"

His face was still bright with laughter and his voice was different, too. Like an Oboe she'd once heard being played on a frosty London street. "I could put it in my Google Calendar under 'exercise?'"

He grinned. "Not bad."

She leaned across, instinctively wanting to kiss him. She held back just in time, a lump rising in her throat. Stupid thoughts. Stupid feelings. "Why don't you call me Nix like everyone else?" she demanded.

"It's too hard. You need something soft. Pretty."

He said it so easily, like it was nothing. The silence swelled again, but it wasn't uncomfortable. She had the feeling he was waiting, letting her decide what to do next. She thought of her questions, but she didn't want to ask them. So what did she want? Her stomach growled and the idea of dinner rose. Maybe they could order food and eat under his gorgeous painting. She could drink the rest of the wine and they could talk about her dad and the studio and maybe even The Rangers. And, because she wasn't trying to impress him and he never said anything about anything to anyone, she could suggest fried chicken. Almost childishly excited, she opened her mouth and a loud ringing filled the air.

Noah looked at the chest of drawers where a phone was vibrating brightly. "I'm sorry, I've gotta..."

"Go ahead."

He rose and picked it up. "You okay?"

A woman's voice, high and panicky. Nicole couldn't hear what she was saying, but she sounded upset. Noah was silent, listening intently, then after a few seconds he stood up. "Be there soon."

He straightened his neck, letting the phone fall onto the bed. Nicole saw the word 'Paula' turn grey as the call disconnected. Her heart fell stupidly, embarrassingly far. "Who's Paula?"

Noah stooped, picking up a pair of jeans. "My housemate. She needs my help with—another long story." Noah rubbed his forehead. "Look, I wouldn't normally do this but...."

Her heart sank. "You need me to leave?"

"No, you can stay if you want, but I have to go."

"Oh, okay." Nicole was amazed at how chirpy she sounded. "I'll get dressed."

"No rush. You can have a shower if you want?"

Ah yes, all the spit and the sex and general grossness of her body. She looked at her hands, willing herself not to cry or cover up. To hold on for as long as it took for him to leave.

Noah knelt on the bed. "We'll talk soon."

"Okay," she said with all the fake brightness she could muster.

Noah's lips pulled tight and he stood, picking a t-shirt off the floor. "The door locks from the inside. Let yourself out whenever you're ready."

And he left. Nicole listened to his footsteps.

Come back. Don't let that be it.

His front door slammed, and she chewed the insides of her mouth trying not to cry. The shame hit her like a punch, deep and hard in her chest.

Slut.

She was such a slut. Her pussy twinged with a psychosomatic fear she'd almost forgotten.

You slept with a biker. A stranger. Maybe a cheater—who was that girl on the phone? He doesn't care about you, he's just used you. You barely checked the condom; he could have taken it off. He could have given you something.

Tears prickled at the corners of her eyes but she refused to blink and let them spill. Her brain could do what it wanted to, but she wasn't going to let herself regret this. It was just sex, followed by an awkward goodbye. This was how single people lived. This was how Noah operated.

"Get dressed," she said aloud. "Get dressed and go get chicken on your own. This is not a big deal."

It felt that way though. Like a big deal. She had the gnawing feeling she'd done something stupid. Not the sex, but the penetration. She'd let Noah in and she hadn't meant to and the resulting helplessness was awful. She stood and flicked the bedroom light on and gasped. Four stunning paintings hung over his bed. They showed the moon in various stages of waxing and waning, reflected in a garbage strewn lake. The surrounds were subtly different in each; greener, then ruddier then splashed with snow, then covered in flowers. Animals crept in shadows, kangaroos and native mice and possums, and in the furthest, a feral cat. They were the seasons, she realised, the collision of man and nature. Looking at them hurt her chest. It stole her thoughts clean away from the sex she'd just had.

"Noah, who are you?" she asked the paintings, the room, the universe.

There was no answer.

10

Parking on Sydney Road was a bitch even when he wasn't jumpy about Paula. Noah pulled into a fifteen-minute zone, praying he'd be in and out fast enough to avoid a ticket. He got out and walked as fast as he could without attracting attention, hoping Paula had managed to get to the front of the Brunswick RSL on her own.

No such luck. She was in the corner of the sandstone building, but Shredder was standing over her, talking in a way that suggested a quiet disagreement. Paula was nodding, smiling; you'd have to spot the way the end of her cigarette was quivering to know how scared she was.

Then why'd she fucking call him? What are we doing here?

Questions for later. Noah squared his shoulders and strode toward the unhappy couple. Paula's eyes lit up. "Hey! You made it."

"Let's go," he said, avoiding her eyes. "Van's in a tow away."

He hadn't expected ignoring him to work, but it was still disappointing when Shredder caught his gaze. His face split into an ugly grin, showing yellow teeth and steel fillings. "Junior! Been a while!"

He was fatter than Noah remembered him but the sneer was the same. So was the anvil tattoo he'd put on Shredder's neck five years ago. He felt a flush of fondness for his work before his internal shutters went down, sectioning off the parts of himself he'd die before he let Shredder see.

"We're leaving," he told Paula. "Got your bag?"

She nodded, but Shredder took her arm. "Not so fast. Let's head back in and have a drink. Catch up. There's a lot of things I'd like to know, Junior. Where you been living? How you been working since you turned your back on us?"

Noah ignored him, taking Paula's other arm. She shook off her ex-husband and came willingly, but her triumphant smile was as unpleasant as Shredder's sneer. This was supposed to be over. Yet here he was, mediating another drunk confrontation between a bikie and his missus.

"Heard from your old man?" Shredder said. "Seen him?"

If Noah had it his way, he'd never have seen him. He'd have come out of the womb and into a Harold Newcomb-free world. He tightened his grip on Paula's arm, lengthened his stride.

"Oi!" Shredder bawled. "Turning your back like I didn't half fuckin' raise you. Come back here!"

Passers-by stared but Noah refused to make eye-contact. His blood was burning, the rage that never went away churned through him like magma. 'Never gone, only dead', The Rangers said, but he'd been gone. At least, he had until Paula found him. He'd given her a chance and she'd dragged Shredder, fucking *Shredder,* back into his life. He clenched his teeth, refusing to let anger take the wheel.

Breathe, Edgar used to say, and he breathed. He breathed like a fucking bull as he marched Paula up the street, his skin prickling for the punch that might be coming.

"You fucking dog!" Shredder yelled. "You ungrateful little shit."

He relaxed a little at that. If Shredder was yelling, there wouldn't be fighting.

"He's pissed," Paula said. "He won't chase us. He wasn't that bad anyway. Just too drunk for any fun."

He didn't smile. After everything Shredder had done, she'd called him, gone out with him, and now she was making his excuses again.

For the first time in years he reached for the mantra that saved him when he thought he'd never untangle himself from The Rangers. *Things do change.* He repeated it to himself as he unlocked his van and opened the passenger door. *Things do change, things do change, it seems like shit stays the same but it changes, you just have to wait long enough.*

Paula flicked her cigarette and climbed into the van. "I'm sorry about calling you. I didn't tell Shredder where we live though."

"Seat belt."

She rolled her eyes and buckled herself in. "I swear, he doesn't know where I'm staying. That's why he got angry. He thought he had a root coming, but I wouldn't fuck him again. I promise. I just wanted to know how things are at home."

Noah nodded, but he didn't believe her. She'd called Shredder, *seen him again,* and in doing that, she'd re-tied the thread that existed between her and The Rangers. That was a fuck of a hard thread to cut, and just like drinking, a relapse made you vulnerable to total collapse. He wanted to ask why she'd done it, but he knew why. Because she was lonely, because things back home were good once. Because she missed the life.

Paula had called him four months ago, so drunk and upset he could barely hear what she was saying. Through sobs, he worked out Shredder had locked her in the house before leaving on a week-long trip to Perth, taking her wallet and phone with him—a long term punishment for flirting with one of the new blokes at the club; the short term being a cut lip and a fractured wrist. Paula had broken a window, hitchhiked to a friend's and gotten his number from one of his ex-girlfriends—Noah never found out which.

"You're the only one who's ever gotten out," she'd said. "Help me."

He'd always liked Paula; she was loud and funny and switched on. She was also trapped almost every way a woman could be trapped. He'd left for Sydney that afternoon, brought her back to his place and helped her find a job. He knew he was taking a risk, Shredder was not the kind of guy who took theft, and helping his wife leave him would be seen as theft, lying down. But he owed Paula the same chance

Edgar had given him. A stable place where a second chance could take root.

Only, it hadn't taken root. Nostalgia had pulled Paula past the bruises and bad times and back into her ex-husband's orbit. Now Shredder, and who knew how many other Ranger assholes, were in Melbourne, sniffing around his new life, threatening to fuck up everything the way only bikies could.

Noah looked across at his housemate, a sulky fifty-something teenager, pissed at how her night had gone. He didn't think she'd hold out much longer. As Shredder's woman, she'd had status, community, access to money, and drugs. No matter how shitty life got, it made sense in a way living with him didn't. But that was no reason to ditch the new for the familiar. Things changed and they could change for the better. Edgar taught him that.

"You shouldn't go back," he said. "You know what's there."

She lifted her chin. "What's there?"

Petty rivalries, violence in every shade of red, black, and blue, never painting, never reading, only tattooing the ugliest shit on the ugliest men, having his old man's heel crushed into his neck every day of his life. "A world of bullshit."

Paula laughed like she wished what he said was funny. "Don't be a drama queen."

"Fine, but if you're gonna keep seeing him, you can't stay with me."

"You chucking me out?"

"No, I'm warning you. I've got a life here and I don't need Shredder or any of the boys around fucking it up."

Paula's upper lip curled. "It's none of your business who I see or what I do!"

"It is when it's Rangers."

"Why? I told you, I didn't say where we live."

"Don't play dumb. I'm being honest with you, be honest with me. You know they can figure it out and now I've picked you up, Shredder's got every reason to try."

"So? They don't give a shit where you are. You've been gone for years, the club's moved on."

She said it defiantly, as though it might hurt.

Noah's hands tightened on the wheel. "They'll give a shit that I helped you ditch Shredder. They'll give a shit if they find out I'm tattooing."

"Why would they—"

"They're the ones who trained me up. Paid for my machine. Got me my reputation."

"So?"

He didn't answer. Paula wasn't in the mood to listen. She was going to keep picking fights, talking herself into calling Shredder for reassurance and he'd be damned if he helped her do that. He wasn't angry anymore, instead a powdery exhaustion was setting in like concrete dust. Why was it so easy to repaint the past with rose-tinted homesickness?

He still felt it sometimes, that longing to ink patches into sun-damaged skin, to ride behind his old man, to go to parties like the one he'd described to Nikki.

Nikki...

Paula's situation had driven thoughts of her clean away, but now they were back with a vengeance. The van hit a red light and Noah closed his eyes, remembering the look of pained excitement as he fucked Nicole's perfect little tits.

Jesus fucking Christ, that *sex*.

He'd never fucked like that before. As though the world would end if he didn't blow her mind. He'd been so blindsided, so horny, he'd barely known what to do with himself or her. They needed more time, *all the time.*

Paula flicked his arm. "Green light, go!"

"Shit." He opened his eyes and accelerated to catch up to the Suzuki in front of him.

"Worried about Shredder?"

But he wasn't. Thoughts of Shredder and Nicole didn't seem able to coexist in his head. His mind was back in his bedroom, feeling her skin, listening to her moan. He'd only been gone forty minutes; could she still be at his place?

She wasn't. Sam's car was gone from the front of his house when they got there. Feeling even more lethargic, he parked the van, wondering if this was payback for all the times he'd wished one night stands would evaporate. His music was still playing inside. A$AP Rocky, LSD. God, the way she'd felt around him, tight as silk and wet as rain. Could he call her and ask her to come back? He'd sound desperate, but fuck it, he *was* desperate. Seeing Shredder had wrung him dry and Nicole's body was the only thing he could think of that would take him from a three to a ten. He wouldn't be selfish. He'd give her everything she wanted in the sack, eat her pussy, make her come as much as she wanted. They were so fucking good together—surely, she'd felt that? Surely once wouldn't be enough for her either? He wandered to the kitchen, debating whether to call. Paula followed.

"Hello, hello." She pointed to the pinot on the table. "Since when do you drink white?"

Noah smiled, remembering how Nicole had chugged half the bottle before she could look him in the eyes and admit she wanted to fuck.

Paula laughed. "I know that stupid look. You had a girl over, didn't you? Is she *pretty*? Do you *love her*?"

Irritation prickled the back of his neck. He collected the glass and poured the remaining wine down the sink before placing it in the dishwasher. He thought of Nicole's mouth, the oak-y sweetness on lips so small and soft and eager they belonged to a fairy tale princess. All of her was like a fairy tale princess. She looked like one of the elves from the not-sexual fantasies he'd had before his hormones hit overdrive. Fantasies where he, the best knight in the kingdom, saved Tolkien's elf princesses and received invitations to go to their bed chambers and do things he didn't understand.

When he'd first seen Nicole, it felt like someone opened a door to one of those fantasies and let the elf princess come to him. He'd stared at her, confused by how clear she was, this woman built from his daydreams about Liv Tyler and Terry Brooks novels. Then he'd noticed her gaze skimming his tats, the distrust in her blue eyes, and he'd remembered this wasn't a world where chubby little bikie brats got their wishes fulfilled. The elf princess was Sam's twin and she didn't like, trust, or want a bar of his ex-con ass.

Or so he'd thought.

He *had* slept with her, the elf princess. And no amount of nostalgia was going to make the memories of fucking Nicole to an orgasm any glossier than they already were. He headed for the hall, some stupid part of him hoping she was still there, naked in his sheets.

"Sleep well!" Paula called. "We'll talk about this girl tomorrow."

Noah didn't say anything. He felt shitty about it, but he doubted he could talk to her about anything without letting his resentment spill out, much less Nicole. After all, if Paula hadn't been out re-confirming her ex was a prick, he might have still been in bed with the girl of his literal dreams. His bedroom was cool, the smell of sex not gone from the air. He lay on his sheets and replayed what he and Nikki had done from start to finish.

What had she told him when he gave her a lift home from the bar? That she wasn't sexy. What horseshit. In the beginning, she'd been stiff; playing sexy for an invisible camera. But once she relaxed it was hotter than a bonfire. She'd fucked like it was a revelation, her eyes closed, her lips curling into a secret smile. When she said she wasn't sexy, she must have meant she didn't *feel* sexy, and whose fucking fault was that?

Noah reached for his smokes, placing one between his lips and lighting up. Everyone had a map of how to fuck—where it started and what to do. He'd bet his tattooing hand Nicole's was designed around her ex. That dickhead must have liked her posing like a model in a skin magazine, helping him act out his favourite pornos. Well, he could go fuck himself. He was old news. He'd made Nicole feel sexy and if he had half a chance, he'd do it again.

He lay there, smoking and recalling Nicole's body—the tight pink of her nipples, the splash of black hair on her pubic bone, the red flower of her cunt. He didn't do portraits, but he'd give every dollar he had to paint her naked. He'd have her on his bed, smiling that just-fucked smile, the afternoon sun turning her skin to moonbeams. He'd paint her and then maybe she'd see she was beautiful.

He'd made a study of Nicole over the past few weeks and barely a day passed when someone, usually a male client, told her she had beautiful hair, pretty eyes, a gorgeous figure. The smile she gave in response was bright and empty. "Oh, thank you! Thanks so much!"

It was white noise. She didn't think she was beautiful, so it didn't matter. And maybe it didn't, she'd given no signs she wanted him playing some pseudo boyfriend role in her life, soothing her nerves and painting her naked like that guy in fuckin' Titanic. What she needed from him wasn't sloppy compliments. It was dick.

He could show her the ugly side of sex; that was what she wanted, after all. And if they opened painful places, maybe he could slice them wide and bleed her clean. An ugly metaphor, but pretty people could be ugly. That was what he'd tried to show her. Sex could be ugly. The good things in life weren't all beautiful. She was, though. The best-looking woman he'd ever slept with. Noah drew deeply on his cigarette. He wasn't sure what was next for him and Nicole, but he was sure he'd find out. The energy that had brought them together wasn't going to fade after one admittedly stellar fuck.

NICOLE WASN'T in the office the next morning. Neither Sam, nor Tabby seemed surprised by this, but Noah couldn't ask why without showing his hand. He kept his head down, literally, filling in a black-work angel he was tattooing onto Ferdinand's thigh. He was a brick-layer whose daughter died in a car crash. His soft sniffs and gentle questions kept Noah's focus razor-sharp. When they were done, it was another story. He had an hour-long break to drink coffee and smoke and wonder where the fuck she was. His next client, a vet from Preston, cancelled on him—annoying, but she agreed to pay half his hourly fee. Now with even more time on his hands, Noah settled himself at reception and tried to read *Destiny's Dawn*.

He failed miserably. Every time the door opened, every time someone *walked past*, he looked up, his adrenaline spiking. Didn't help that he'd slept like shit. He'd had the same fucked up dream over and over— Nicole naked in the doorway of The Rangers clubhouse. He ran to pull her away, and she turned to silver water between his fingers. Didn't take a genius to join the metaphysical dots on that one.

The tiger doorbell roared, alerting him to a new client. Not Nicole; worse than Nicole.

"Heya!" Daniella's lipstick matched her pink mini-dress perfectly, and unless he was mistaken, there was a sharpness beneath the pep.

Alarmed, Noah tried to think if they'd arranged to meet and came up blank. "Hey. I don't have you in today, do I?"

"No, I just wanted to see you." Her smile was hard as varnish. "You didn't answer my text about drinks."

Fuck, she was right. The message had come a few hours after he'd finger-fucked Nicole in his tattooing chair, and he'd read without seeing, forgotten it existed until now. "Sorry."

"No problem," she said, though her smile remained hard. "Are we still on for drinks?"

Noah rubbed the back of his neck. *No time like the fucking present, son.* "I, uh, don't think that's a good idea. Sorry."

Daniella's smile vanished. "Why?"

"I just..."

"Come on, tell me. I can take it."

The hardness in her voice surprised him. He opened his mouth, and the truth came out. "I'm interested in someone else."

Daniella looked like a girl who'd just missed her bus. "Is it that woman who helped us with the card-swipe thingy?"

Noah did a double-take. "Yeah, Nikki. How'd you know?"

"I could just tell." She didn't sound hostile, just a little down.

He wanted to stay silent, god, how he wanted to stay silent, but he knew he owed her. "I wasn't trying to fuck you around when I said yes to drinks, but things changed, and yeah..."

"I get it." Daniella hoisted her bag higher on her shoulder. "Good luck."

"Yeah. Don't let this stop you asking guys out. It's fucking ballsy."

Daniella's smile returned, only this time it was warm. "Thanks. Well, follow my example with Nikki, and hopefully, you'll have good news when I come in for my next tattoo."

"Yeah, maybe—"

The tiger doorbell roared, and as though she'd been summoned by the use of her nickname, Nicole DaSilva stepped into the studio. She was done up like he'd never seen her done up; black leather skirt, tight black top, her hair pulled into a glossy black pile on her head. He'd never seen her in black before. It made her skin look snow white, and her blue eyes and red lipstick pop like fireworks. She looked like a dominatrix. Or a supermodel dressed up as a dominatrix for a weird fashion thing.

He gaped, and out of the corner of his eye, he saw Daniella doing the same thing. He had no idea where the girl who'd drunk his wine and moaned in his bed had gone. Maybe this Nicole had eaten her.

"Hey," he said. "Where you been?"

"Around." She headed for the hallway, her heels clicking like dominoes.

"Nice to see you again," Daniella said.

Nicole flashed her a tight smile. "You too. Have such a fun time going out with Noah. I hear he's a real dark horse." She disappeared up the hall, heels snapping on the hardwood floor.

Daniella raised her eyebrows. "Looks like you've got work to do."

"Yeah," he said, because yelling 'It's not what it fuckin' looks like, okay? I was doing the opposite of that!' wasn't an option. "Have a good day."

"You too." She grinned. "Dark horse."

Noah was going to kill someone. Something. After he got Nicole to explain what the fuck was going on.

He waited until Daniella was gone to head up the hall. Gil, Tabby, and Sam were all with clients, their music playing over the burr of their tattooing machines. Nicole had shut Edgar's office door. He knocked, but she didn't say anything.

Well, fuck that. He pushed the door open and his heart kicked inward—she was so fucking pretty. Why was she so pretty? How was this fair? "Hey."

She didn't look up from the computer. "Can I help you?"

"Yeah, you can tell me why you look like Morticia Adams."

That got her to make eye contact, albeit eye contact as frosty as the arctic tundra. "I had an appointment."

"At a haunted house?"

Her smile was saccharine sweet. "A laser clinic."

He looked at her wrist, the diamond watch covering what he knew was beneath, and his mouth damn near fell open. "You're getting your dad's work taken off?"

"No, I'm having a tattoo I don't want removed."

"Why the hell would you do that?"

"Because it's my body, and I can do what I want with it."

"Right." Heat rose in the back of his neck. "And what you want is to get rid of the tattoo your whole family shares?"

Red bloomed in Nicole's cheeks. "I was eighteen when I got it. I wasn't ready. I didn't know what it would mean."

"And what does it mean?"

She turned her head, refusing to look at him.

Noah couldn't believe this; what the hell was going on with her?

"Do you have anything else you want to say?" Her tone was calm, but the colour on her cheeks was high. She was upset, or anxious, or something, she just didn't know how to let it out.

He leaned in close. "I can't tell you what to do, but I can tell you what I tell all the cleanskins—if you think getting a tattoo is gonna make you a different person, you're wrong. Taking one off is the exact same thing."

Nicole kept her eyes on the screen. "Maybe that's what you tell the cleanskins, but you know as well as I do that sometimes tattoos are more than just tattoos."

"So what does that mean? You want to get rid of your family history? Where you came from?"

She said nothing.

He touched her shoulder and found her skin ice cold. "Your sisters know what you're planning, Nikki?"

"No." Her voice was wavering. "But it's not up to them. I don't like it anymore. I don't want to be that girl anymore."

"What girl?"

She blinked, shedding two fat tears. Her eyes were so blue today, he was surprised the water was clear. He'd expected it to be sapphire.

"Nikki, talk to me."

She shook her head. "You wouldn't understand. You're exactly like them. Sam and Tabby and Dad and everyone else that comes in here."

He couldn't help smiling a little at that. "I thought you'd know better than anyone that I'm not like everyone else that comes in here."

Her ruby mouth curved upward. "Maybe not *exactly* like everyone else."

"Not even close. But seriously, are you okay? You're a ball of nerves right now, baby."

The endearment slipped out without his conscious choice, but it didn't feel wrong. Neither did the fact she turned and wrapped her arms around him. It felt like pulling on a hoodie on a cold morning, like the first cigarette of the day. He rubbed his hand along her back, trying to warm her.

"Noah?"

"Yeah," he said, sure she was ready to talk. But when she pulled away, she was looking at him differently, her pupils wide, her lips parted like a gift.

"I want you to touch me. Right now."

If it was anywhere but Edgar's office, with anyone but Nicole, he'd have fucking gone for it, but it didn't feel right. "Bad idea."

"You're not supposed to care about that."

She could have meant his attitude in bed, but the twist in her mouth said she meant The Rangers, his history, his reputation as a piece of shit bikie. He thought of Shredder and shook his head. "Don't put me in that box, Nicole. You don't like it and neither do I."

She brushed a hand over his chest, her citrusy perfume tickling his nose. "You must like it a little bit, you dirty talked me about it last night."

The memories sent a throb running down the length of his cock. "You're upset."

"So?" She leaned in, her lips promising oblivion and bright red after-effects. "I want to do it again, rougher this time."

"No, you don't."

Her hand slid around his waist, sending sparks up his back. "I do. I need you, Noah."

And he was done for. The idea of her needing him was so electric it might have been a stimulant released into his arm. Outside, Sam's music pounded, Chvrches with tattoo machines thrumming beneath it. His choice felt like no choice at all. He bent his head and kissed her. Her mouth was cool and eager. He tasted her lipstick and it made his dick hard. "Nikki."

Her hands slid down his stomach, tugging at the button on his jeans. "Yes?"

He gripped her wrists. "Not so fast."

"But I need it."

It. Not him. *It.* She said she wanted him, but really she wanted escape from whatever was fucking with her head. It shouldn't have stung, but it did. He kissed her harder, trying to get inside, but she was holding back. Not faking, but not showing. He needed more. That real girl in his bed who'd told him what she liked.

He nudged her backward, easing her back into her office chair. She sat down, pressing her palms to his thighs. "Do you want me to go down on you?"

Fucking *if only*. "Nah, put your hands on the armrests."

"Why?"

"Because if you don't, I'm gonna tell the whole studio you came while I was fucking your tits."

She blanched. "You will not."

He opened the door and cleared his throat for effect.

Nicole clutched his thighs like a drowning kitten. "Okay! I'll do it!"

"So do it," he said, shutting the door. "Hands on the armrests."

She did it and he reached across her, grabbing the roll of electrical tape on the desk. He pulled out a length, reveling in the sharp tearing sound.

"You can't tape me!"

"That's exactly what I'm going to do."

"This top is expensive."

"I'll buy you a new one."

She hesitated. "What if... what if someone walks in?"

"I'll make sure they don't."

"Noah, you just can't, okay?"

"Okay." He circled the tape over her tits, making sure it bound tight enough to squeeze. For the first time since she'd walked through the door, Nicole looked like the girl sitting in his kitchen. She stared at the tape, and pressed her legs together. Turned on, but unwilling to admit it. Too fucking bad. She wanted 'it' so bad, she'd get it the way he wanted to give it. He looped the tape around her a few more times, until he was sure she wouldn't be able to jerk away. She was breathing hard, red spots back on her cheeks. He turned the chair so she was facing him. "So."

"So, what?"

He nudged her heels apart with his foot, spreading her legs as much as her tight skirt would allow. "How do you feel?"

"I..." The blush on her cheeks darkened. "What are you going to do to me?"

"What I feel like doing." Noah flicked off the lights, plunging them into semi-darkness. Nicole didn't say anything but he could practically hear her relief at not being observed. He unzipped his jeans and pulled out his cock, maneuvering until it was comfortable. He was already hard but gave himself a couple of rough strokes.

"What are you doing?" she whispered.

"You know what I'm doing." With her free hand, he cupped the nape of her neck. "Still want to suck it?"

"Yes… but it'll be hard in the chair."

"Won't be easy," he agreed. He smoothed his hand up her neck and into her silky hair. "But you'll try hard for me, won't you?"

She shuddered slightly beneath his touch. "Yes."

"Open your mouth."

He felt her jaw fall open. She really was going to do it. He hovered a moment, contemplating putting himself between her lips, feeling the hot suck of her mouth for the first time. But that was what she expected him to do. He knelt, feeling for the hem of her skirt in the dark. Once he touched the soft leather, he rolled it up her legs.

Nicole jerked in the chair. "What are you doing?"

He could smell her now, hot and tangy. His mouth watered, and he shoved her skirt higher, forcing it up her thighs. "What I feel like doing."

She jerked again, kicking her legs. "No!"

He paused. "You don't like head?"

"No! I mean, yes. Sometimes. But I haven't had a shower today and—"

He'd heard enough. He reached up her thighs, hooked his thumbs into her underwear, and tugged. God, he'd been thinking about doing this for fucking ever…

She squirmed in her chair. "Please, Noah, I'm all sweaty from the skirt. It's too gross."

The word sparked actual anger in him. Gross? What about her tight, silk-skinned pussy was gross? And even if it was sweaty, who gave a flying fuck? Sweat was salt, and this was sex. It wasn't always pretty, and it didn't fucking matter. He leaned back, trying to find her gaze in the dark. "How about you shut up and let me eat your gorgeous pussy, Nicole? How about that?"

A short, heated silence.

"Fine. Just do it then."

He could hear her promising herself she wouldn't like it. Wouldn't come. He'd fucking see about that. He spread her legs, and seeing all that silky skin, couldn't help rubbing his face along her thigh. His stubble rasped against her and she gasped softly. Following her lead, he rubbed her again.

She made more delicious noises. "You said you were going to go down on me..."

He grinned to himself and gently bit her thigh. She wanted to play, she could wait a little longer. He continued his game, kissing and licking her thighs, getting closer and closer to the heat of her cunt.

After a few seconds, Nicole was panting, shifting in the chair. "Noah?"

"Yeah, baby?"

"Sleep with me. Right now."

"No condom."

"I don't care."

There was an edge in her voice. He could feel recklessness pulsating out of her, the need to make some big fucking mistake. He'd been an idiot to push her. She'd come in dressed like a BDSM porn star and he hadn't seen that she was out for blood. The appeal of being the one to take her in this state, fuck her raw and make her come was undeniable, but he wasn't that big an asshole. "No."

He bent his head, intending to give her what she needed, but she squirmed away. "I mean it... fuck me."

The curse came out strained, unnatural. She was trying to be something she wasn't again, some girl who could have casual sex and not feel anything. Noah's gut tightened. Was this because of Daniella? Or because he'd left last night without making sure she was okay? "Nikki..."

"Don't! Don't call me that. Just... fuck me. Do it, please? If we don't do it now, we'll never do it again."

She meant it. Her words had that hard ring of truth. She was bound, but she was issuing ultimatums like a queen on her throne. He hesitated, not knowing what to do.

A loud knock almost startled him out of his skin.

So Steady

"Nix?" Sam called, and the warmth of her tone said she had no idea what was going on.

Nicole stared at him, her eyes wide and panicky. "Yeah?"

"Is Noah in there?"

Logically, he knew that if Sam was aware of what was going on, she'd have kicked the door down like Terminator. Holding that in his mind, he stood, quietly tucking away his cock. "What's up?"

"Jonah, your next guy's here."

"Thanks. Out in a minute."

"Cool." Sam paused. "What are you guys talking about?"

"The pay system," they said at the same time, then cringed at how fake that sounded. There was another pause.

"Whatever," Sam said. "Just get your ass out here, I'm up to my elbows in it right now."

They listened as Sam's boots stomped away and breathed a shared sigh of relief. Noah flicked the lights back on and saw Nicole looked horror-struck. She'd strained against the tape, pulling it so tight it was cutting into her shoulders and breasts. "Oh, baby—"

"Don't," she said. "Let me out."

He grabbed a pair of scissors from the desk and cut her free. She tore the rest away herself, tugging her skirt down her thighs. "You need to go."

"Nikki..."

"Please don't call me that," she said, her voice wavering once more. "I'm fine, that was fine. You're a good lover and a nice person, but I don't want to talk about it or anything else. Please just go."

With Jonah waiting and Sam close, he didn't have time to protest. He kissed her cheek. "Come see me."

She turned away, rubbing the watch that hid her tattoo. God, removing her tattoo felt like a bad omen, although everything felt like a bad omen right now. He headed down the hall, a fresh headache pounding behind his eyes.

11

"Aren't our pups the cutest fucking pups in the world?"

Nicole, crouched over Miles, had to disagree. She had a plastic bag wrapped over her hand and she was bracing herself to collect his crap. Lilah and Poppy, the other two puppies she was walking, were taking advantage of her proximity to lick the heck out of her face. "Can you help me?"

"You've got it," Tabby said comfortably. "Why don't you just leave it, anyway? It'll fertilize the grass."

"That's not how fertilizer works!"

"Oh, come on. No one'll know it's us."

"You're a horrible person."

Tabby grinned. "Yeah."

The two of them were walking the six half-cocker spaniel, half-Rottweiler dogs Tabby had rescued from euthanization. They were only supposed to be at Silver Daughters until they were old enough for adoption, but all six had been weaned —yet, no one, particularly Tabby, was making any effort to find them new homes. They were becoming a disturbingly regular part of life at the studio; even their dad's cat, Midnight, barely hissed at them anymore. Nicole collected Miles' poo in the bag and dropped it in the bin. Rubbing her hand against her bare thigh, she asked, "When are you going to sell the pups?"

"When they're ready."

"They're beyond ready. We can't have six full-sized dogs running through the house and studio."

Tabby covered Specter's ears with her hands. "Not in front of the kids!"

"They're fully grown dogs now. They chew everything, they eat a bag of dog food a day, and they leave hair *everywhere*."

"It's not too bad. Besides, Morgan's already been adopted, remember?"

"Yes. By Scott. Who feels so guilty about leaving her alone in his apartment she still lives with us."

Tabby looked up at the sky and shrugged, the 'live and let live' gesture so reminiscent of their dad, Nicole's chest ached. "Well, whatever. Hey, where do you think Dad is?"

"Dunno. I miss him, though."

She did, too. Things made sense when he was around, running Silver Daughters, calling her every week with updates on her sisters. She'd felt distant enough to breathe, and connected enough to love them at the same time. Now she had no idea what she was doing. Suddenly, loneliness burst through the plastic wrap she'd stretched over herself since she and Noah almost hooked up in the office.

Where was Edgar DaSilva? Why couldn't he come back? If her dad was here, things wouldn't have had to change. She exhaled, willing the pain to fade into a manageable ache. It was stupid to feel lonely on a walk with her sister and six puppies. Self-indulgent. As for Noah, why did she even care that they'd slept together? It didn't mean anything. He was an ex-bikie who was all up her butt about getting her tattoo removed. He didn't get her at all.

Nicole swiped a hand over her sweaty forehead, streaking her hand with brown. She'd changed out of the black leather and into pink shorts, but she hadn't washed her face. Now she was melting NARS all over herself.

"Nix?" Tabby's voice sounded like it was coming from far away. "You all right?"

God, couldn't she hold it together for a single walk? She was such an idiot. "I'm fine."

"You don't seem fine. Are you thinking about the missing money?"

No, although that was another reason to feel like an idiot. She'd been at Silver Daughters for weeks and found nothing to explain the hole in their finances.

"I'm fine," she repeated. "Let's keep moving, it's hot."

They made their way to the Carlton Gardens, Tabby skipping, Nicole fighting tears beneath her sunglasses. When they reached the lawn, Tabby knelt to release the dogs from their leads. Nicole knew she should stop her; the gardens weren't a dog park, but she was too weary to stand in the way of her younger sister's boundless energy.

Her phone buzzed. She pulled it out of her pocket and saw Beverly Dean had sent her a Facebook message.

> *Hi lovely, I hope I'm not overstepping the mark here, but is everything okay? No one's heard from you in a while! Let me know if anything's wrong! xx*

"Oh, god," she groaned.

"What?" Tabby asked, unclipping a yelping Morgan.

"Beverly's asking if I'm okay. I think she and the girls know something's wrong."

Tabby looked quizzical. "You haven't told your Adelaide friends about the big splitsville yet?"

"I'm waiting for the right time."

"And when will that be, exactly?"

Nicole didn't say anything. She unlocked her phone, deleted the messenger app, and switched the whole thing off for good measure. It wasn't a long-term strategy, but she needed a moment—an hour and a single afternoon—to think.

And who knew? Maybe once she turned her phone back on, her

friends would have forgotten about her, Aaron might have cancelled the wedding himself, and her boss might have given her a transfer to Paris, and the missing money would be back in Silver Daughters' bank account, and Noah would have moved to Japan to go down on Japanese women while they were tied to their dad's office chairs. Maybe everything might sort itself out.

Lilah, her favourite puppy, rubbed against her leg. Nicole bent over and stroked her velvet head. The dogs might be inconvenient, but really, was there anything better than puppies? A car honked loudly from the nearby road, and she straightened up to see a silver Toyota full of dudes clapping, presumably at her ass. "Oh, God."

"Oi, lads." Tabby flipped them off like she'd been trained to do it. "Your turn now! Show me where you piss from!"

Nicole tensed, but the guys just wound up their windows and rolled past. Tabby lowered her middle finger. "Typical. No banter in them at all. Fucking plebs."

Nicole pressed a hand to her chest in a misguided attempt to slow her heartbeat. "You shouldn't antagonize guys like that."

"They shouldn't drive around honking at butts. Anyway, who cares? They're gone, and we're in a park." She resumed unclipping the puppies. Nicole shook her head. Sam raged; Nicole stewed, but Tabby's anger flicked in and out like a switchblade. She cut and then retracted to a persona as sunny as their father's.

"How do you do it?" she asked her little sister. "Why are you so happy?"

"Beautiful day, six pups. What could be better?"

Exactly what she'd been trying to convince herself of without any of the sincerity. She spotted something on Tabby's lapel—the pink cat brooch their dad had sent her in his only correspondence. The one she'd been holding when she and Noah had their first kiss. She nudged Tabby's shoulder. "Hey, that's my cat pin!"

"You never wear it."

"That's not the point. Dad gave it to me!"

"Fair." Tabby bundled the dog leads in her left hand and reached for the pin.

"No!" The thought of touching the cat brooch filled Nicole with an inexplicable panic. "You keep it. Just give it back when you're done."

"Will do! Cheers, bruv."

Lilah continued to rub herself against her shin. Nicole gave her a little push. "Go play with your brothers and sisters."

Lilah gave a small whine, then trotted away, her coat gleaming in the sun.

"She's Noah's favourite," Tabby said. "He's always picking her up when he thinks I'm not looking."

"Really?"

"Uh-huh."

Nicole imagined Noah cuddling Lilah and felt a flush ripple across her skin. She looked over, but Tabby was safely absorbed in her phone. She fanned herself. "Instagram?"

"Tobes. We're meeting up tonight to discuss how to wash all six puppies at once."

Asking why they were attempting such a thing, or how Toby fit into this situation, was unnecessary. Toby's parents had bred the puppies, though they'd planned to kill them once they discovered they were mutts. He and Tabby had rescued them, sharing the bulk of their care ever since. Though Nicole doubted the puppies were the thing keeping Toby around. "What's going on with the two of you?"

Tabby shoved her phone in her pocket. "Nothing. We just hang out."

"He's very good-looking."

She shrugged. "He's too basic for me to go to town on."

Well, there was no denying that. Tabby's tastes had always run to the extreme—face tats, hardcore goths, guys who thought Bigfoot was real. Weirdos. Nicole's least favourite had been a pro skateboarder with a forked tongue. Just thinking about it made her shudder. "Maybe basic might suit you? Something different?"

Tabby rolled her eyes. "Yeah, maybe you should keep your attention on Lilah, she's eating that guy's copy of… is that *Paradise Lost*? Wow. What an edgester."

Nicole followed her sister's gaze and saw Lilah heckling a guy reading on the lawn. He was laughing as he tried to pull his book from her teeth, but she was still mortified. "Oh my god, stop her!"

"You stop her." Tabby shoved her side. "She likes you best! Also, I have to go get the others back. They're raising public ire."

Tabby pointed to where the other five puppies were rushing across the lawn like a horde of black and gold wildebeest.

"Oh my god."

"Don't worry about it. Just go get Lilah."

Nicole was already sprinting toward the book guy. "I will!"

As she got closer, she saw the guy tussling with Lilah was polo shirt preppy. She hoped he wouldn't be a jerk. "Lilah," she called. "Come here!"

Lilah glanced over, her teeth still latched onto *Paradise Lost*.

The guy looked up at her, revealing laughing blue eyes. "She yours?"

"My sister's." Nicole patted her thighs. "Come on, Lilah! Come here!"

With a last shake of *Paradise Lost*, Lilah released the book and trotted over, looking pleased with herself. Nicole picked her up and tucked her under her arm. "Sorry about that."

The guy stood, the sunlight glinting on his close-cropped hair. "She's super cute."

"Thanks," Nicole said, flustered by his handsomeness. "She's a brat."

"Who doesn't love a brat?" He walked toward her, and she realised he wasn't as tall as Noah. Though why that had even occurred to her was ridiculous.

He held out a golden brown, tattoo-free hand. "I'm Davis."

Nicole shook his hand, careful not to drop Lilah. "Nicole."

"So Lilah belongs to your sister?"

"Kind of. It's a long story." She gestured to Tabby who was running in circles around the park, five puppies in tow. She looked as she was—a nutcase. Davis followed their progress across the park, looking amused. "Bit of a free spirit?"

"That's one way of putting it."

He laughed comfortably. "Family. You can't pick them, can you?"

"No. Both my sisters and my dad are all a bit... Pippy Longstocking. I'm the odd one out."

Davis' smile widened. "Maybe it's a good thing. No offense to your sister, but you're stunning. And you seem a lot less nuts."

"Oh!" she said, not surprised exactly, but taken aback.

It's only okay when I say my sisters are insane, she thought. Then she realised Tabby had released six mutts into a public park. "Yeah, my family doesn't have much of a filter."

Davis chuckled. He was closer again; she could see the dimple in his tanned chin, a freckle on his right cheek. "So, if we fall in love, we'll have a killer story to tell our grandchildren."

She smiled on autopilot, thrown by the conversational about-face. She'd known he was flirting, but *grandchildren*? "It would be a good story."

He nodded. "Is there any chance I could get your number?"

"Ooh, I um..."

Dammit, she'd forgotten all the excuse lines she'd given out before 'fiancé' had been enough.

"I don't want to come on too strong," he said quickly. "Are you seeing someone?"

She recalled the feel of Noah between her legs. *'How about you shut up and let me eat your gorgeous pussy, Nicole?'*

"Oh, um, no. I'm not."

"So, can I have your number?"

She stalled, confused by her own confusion. Why shouldn't she give him her number? She was single, and he was handsome and tanned and owned an Apple Watch and had just indicated he was serious enough about relationships to want grandchildren—unlike a certain bikie, who'd abandoned her in his bed after two seconds of awkward small talk.

Do it, the Sam in her head demanded. *Give him your number. Why not? Seize the carp!*

Brushing aside that her twin didn't know about Noah; didn't

know a lot of what she was thinking right now, Nicole chose to agree. "Okay, sure."

Davis looked relieved. "Great. Do you have your phone on you?"

"It's flat," she lied. If she turned it on now, there was no way her problems had been magically solved. "Do you have a pen?"

"I do." Davis patted his jeans and pulled out a blue biro, then he handed her *Paradise Lost*. "Write it on the inside cover."

"Oh, I don't want to ruin your book!"

He flashed her a smile. "You won't. You'll be improving it."

She scribbled down her number without looking. In her mind's eye, she was seeing Noah's hands, patterned from wrist to knuckle with tattoos; the same hands that painted those beautiful paintings. Why did this feel like a betrayal? They didn't mean anything to each other. Neither did she and Davis, but at least she knew he wasn't a bikie. At least he wouldn't lecture her if she got her tattoos removed. She handed him his book and pen and smiled as wide as she could. "Can I ask you something?"

"Anything."

"Do you have any tattoos?"

He laughed, an easy open laugh. "No, I don't. Is that a problem?"

No.

Yes.

Nausea roiled through her like a rising tide and Lilah squirmed, trying to escape her tightening grasp. She kept her smile steady, relaxing her hold around the puppy. "Not at all. Okay, I should go get my sister. Nice to meet you."

"You, too," Davis said with a small frown. He patted *Paradise Lost*. "I'll call you later."

"Great!" Nicole lied, walking away as quickly as she could, relieved to put distance between herself and Davis. She found Tabby under an oak tree, all five puppies piled on her chest. "We need to go."

Tabby squinted up at her. "Did you give that prep-meister your number?"

"Maybe. I mean, yes. It was a panic move. He said the puppy meeting would be a good story for our grandkids."

Tabby snorted. "What a douche."

She stood, brushing the bark from her dress, and Nicole wondered why she'd called him a douche. She pressed on the word like it was a lemon half.

It's douchy because it's insincere. Because Davis doesn't know you and talking about grandkids is presumptuous. It's also a little bit scary that a stranger could say something so intimate.

Then, like a key slipping into a greased lock, she could see why Tabby and Sam hated Aaron so much. He'd always been polite, at least at first, but he was always saying big, flowery things, giving her expensive gifts, and saying romantic stuff too soon. And he'd always dropped little barbs, the way Davis had. Calling Tabby nuts, watching her run through the park with such obvious, 'glad I don't know her', superiority.

She thought about her number, scrawled into his book. She hadn't wanted to give it to him, so why had she? Just because he said she was stunning? Because he had an Apple Watch? Or was it—nausea stabbed at her insides—because he didn't have tattoos?

"Did you ask old mate why he was reading *Paradise Lost?*" Tabby asked.

"No. Have you read it?"

"Yeah."

That wasn't surprising. Tabby was a stealth genius. She'd read most of the classics in high school, devouring the kind of fat Russian novels that Nicole felt drained just glancing at. "What did you think of it?"

"Thematically interesting," Tabby said, vaguely. "Paradise Lost was the theme of Sam's Ink the Night competition. Weird coincidence, huh?"

"Yeah." Nicole suppressed a weird burp. "I guess."

"That was the night Scott and Sam hooked up." Tabby twiddled her pink kitten badge. "Maybe it's a sign. Maybe Davis is your next boyfriend."

Nicole sank to her knees on the dry grass, mouth dry, head spinning. Her nausea was in her throat like a slimy ocean, but when she coughed, nothing came out.

"Shit!" Tabby pounded her on the back like she was choking. "Nix, are you okay?"

"I'm fine," she said, easing Lilah onto the grass. "I'm just dizzy."

She pressed her face in her hands, trying to see through the thoughts swamping her brain. Noah, her DaSilva tattoo, Davis, Aaron, her boyfriends, her future; it was all swimming like dirty clothes inside a spin cycle.

"Do you want me to get you some water?" Tabby asked, sounding scared.

"No." She stood up, feeling weirdly steady despite her stumble. She didn't know much, but she knew where she needed to go. She held out the dog leashes to Tabby. "Can you take the pups home without me?"

"Of course." Tabby's forehead was creasing with worry. "So you're okay? Do you need me to get you some Hydrolyte?"

"No, I just need to go somewhere by myself. It's important."

Tabby took the leashes. "Call me in an hour," she said as Nicole ran toward the edge of the park. "Do it, or I'll track your phone!"

Noah's house was thirty minutes away by foot. By the time she reached his street, her makeup was dripping down her face, stinging her eyes. She knew she must look horrible, but she didn't care. She was so scared of losing the diamond clarity she'd found in the gardens before she saw him. He was her end point. He'd be able to tell her what to do.

When she reached his door and knocked, she found it locked. That was weirdly offensive, as though he should have known she was coming and been waiting in the front yard. She banged on the wood. "Noah? Are you there?"

A hideous possibility occurred to her—he and Daniella in bed together, his gorgeously tattooed body working against her smooth, tan one. Jealousy cramped her stomach... or maybe it was a stitch? For the first time, she wondered what the hell she was doing here.

She turned to leave, and the door swung open. There was Noah, not having sex with Daniella. At least not if his fully clothed body and grumpy expression were any indication. He saw her and his face changed, lifted maybe. Brightened. He opened his mouth, but she didn't let him get the first word.

"Do you believe in destiny?"

A line appeared between his dark brows. Nicole pointed at it. "Don't. I know I'm acting like my dad. Or Tabby. But don't pay attention to that. Just answer the question."

"Do I believe in destiny?and "

"Yes."

He stared at her a moment. Birds chirped, insects hummed. "I don't know."

It wasn't what she wanted to hear, but it felt honest, and the honesty kept her talking. "I was in the park, and I met my next boyfriend."

Noah's jaw hardened.

"Not like that!" Nicole said quickly. "But also, totally like that. He's the next one. He's my next boyfriend that's exactly like all my other boyfriends. I know it like I know all the songs to *High School Musical*, even though I don't want to."

Noah's brow furrowed, and Nicole wasn't sure whether it was because he hated the movie or her being there.

She drew a deep breath. "I don't want what I want. It's just momentum."

"What is?"

"My life. It's just a collection of things I can't stop doing over and over."

"Right." He looked at her hard. "So what *do* you want?"

It was a valid question, but she didn't have a ready answer. It felt like the first thing she'd ever been asked. She rubbed the stitch in her side, listening to Noah's music thudding down through the hall.

"Any second now...?"

She stared at her dusty Nikes. "I don't know. I just wanted to come and see you."

"Why?"

"Because…" Her bravery floundered. Could she really say this?

"Nikki?"

The nickname jolted like an electric shock. She opened her mouth. "Because you don't treat me like anyone else you don't baby me. And I need your help."

His brows lifted. "With what?"

"It's kind of a long story, but I promise it's not a sex thing."

The corner of Noah's mouth quirked. "Your face is covered in black shit."

"Oh no." Nicole reached up and confirmed her mascara, shadow, and liner were smeared around her eye socket. "Can I use your bathroom?"

Noah shook his head… not *no*. More like he couldn't believe what was happening. He was still smiling. "Sure."

12

Noah watched Nicole walk up his hallway. For the first time since he'd known her, she looked like a mess. There was a line of sweat down her back, her hair was a tangle, and she was rubbing at her face, smearing her already smeared makeup.

Do you believe in destiny?

How had she known he'd been lying on his couch wondering the same thing? Paula was missing. He'd found a note on the kitchen table saying she'd gone to see Shredder. Her phone was off and when he'd called her work, they'd told him she hadn't showed up for her shift. Her second chance was over, and now he was wondering if it had ever started. She'd been hurt so fucking badly, but her heart had stayed even when her body left.

It felt like a sign. He liked his life in Melbourne, but he was treading water. He hadn't had a girlfriend since The Rangers, no close friends, except Sam, who didn't know shit about his past, and Edgar, who'd gone on hiatus. House aside, he had no roots to anything and no plans to lay any down. He'd thought he was done with groups, clubs, families—but maybe he was just holding the door open for The Rangers? Was the club a riptide he kept swimming away from when his fate was to drown? He dreamed about it sometimes. Going back. Would he call Shredder one day asking to pick up where he left off?

"Do you have any more pinot?" Nicole asked, turning to reveal the kabuki mask that was her made-up face.

Noah struggled not to laugh. "Nah."

Her mouth turned down, and she looked so much like a sad clown, he had to bite the insides of his cheeks.

"Got something stronger if you want it?"

"Vodka?"

"Whiskey."

She grimaced. "Yes, please."

He collected the bottle from the lounge room and poured a splash into a couple of water glasses. Nicole examined her face in his stainless-steel toaster and yelped. "You must think I'm crazy for coming over like this?"

"I don't." Not true, but he was glad she'd come over all the same. He handed her a glass. "Here."

"Thanks." She held up her whiskey. "To um... 'destiny' is a bit pretentious, isn't it?"

He smiled. "To destiny."

They tapped glasses, and she threw back her whiskey in one. "Urgh. It tastes like a bushfire."

"You're not wrong." Noah took a small sip. He'd had a couple before she'd gotten here, and if things went the way he hoped, he needed to stay sharp.

"So..." Nicole toed his kitchen floor with her sneaker. "I need your help with something personal."

Noah frowned. Did she mean sex? Weird way to phrase it if it was. Also, she didn't need to run from the park with her makeup all over the place to get at his dick.

Nicole laughed, and despite the clown makeup, or maybe because of it, she looked stunning. He watched, feeling like someone was folding warm metal over his chest, binding him.

"What?"

"You think I'm here for sex, don't you?"

"Aren't you?"

"No! I mean, maybe." She ducked her head, still smiling, and the metal pulled tighter. Too tight for comfort.

He drank some more whiskey. It burned away a little of the stupid sensation. "So, what's up?"

"Okay, I'll tell you. But before I tell you, we need to have the talk."

"The talk?" His heart hammered. Did she mean that talk when girls tried to find out how serious you were about them? Was she... were *they*...?

"I mean we haven't had a single serious conversation about The Rangers. How ridiculous is that?"

Of course. Of. Fucking. Course. Feeling stupid, Noah jerked his head to his living room. "Sit down?"

"Sure."

He topped up their glasses and led her to the couch. Nicole sat delicately on the right-hand cushion, crossing her ankles, and fixed him with an alert smile. If it wasn't for the strong smell of sweat and the mascara streaks, she could have been interviewing him for *60 Minutes*. Noah bit back another smile. "So, shoot."

"Are you a biker?"

"No."

"But you used to be?"

He sighed. "You know who my dad is?"

"Harold Newcomb."

God, he hated hearing her say that name. "Yeah."

"And? What about him?"

Fuck, he didn't want to have this conversation, but what else could he do? She was waiting expectantly, clearly willing to hang on until he gave her an answer. He scratched at his stubble. "I was never not gonna be a Ranger. It's like getting baptized when you're a baby. You didn't ask for it, it's just what happens."

Nicole nodded. "But you left?"

"Yeah."

"You didn't like being a bikie?"

He licked his lips, wanting to be honest but not wanting to scare her and send her running. "It's not as easy to explain as that. I grew up in the club; it's all I knew."

"So, you *did* like it?"

"Parts of it."

"What parts?"

Noah considered how truthful he could be without freaking her out. "It's like being Keith Richards' kid. Or how I guess that'd be. Everyone knew who I was, I had all this cash and I could do whatever I wanted. Girls'd see me and…" Noah cleared his throat. "Doesn't matter."

Nicole raised her eyebrows. "Go on?"

Fuck. "Never mind. It was okay, is all I'm saying, until…"

"What?"

He shook his head. "Can't."

"Yes, you can, just open your mouth and talk."

"I'm not much of a talker."

"Reeeeaally?"

"Sarcasm." He wagged a finger in mock disapproval. "Beneath you."

"Can I ask why you don't want to talk about why you left The Rangers, or is that the same thing?"

She was like one of the DaSilva puppies with a sock. But, unlike when people usually pumped him for information about his past, Noah didn't mind so much. It was Nikki, after all. He drank the last of his whiskey. "It's the same thing. All that loyalty bullshit tangled up in my head."

And there was the shame, the crashing grey-waved embarrassment of having been that man, and at the same time, missing that man. Of feeling so fucking weak for still letting the life fuck with his head after all these years of freedom.

Nicole was looking at him strange; her eyes wide, her mouth parted.

For a second, he was confused, and then his mood lifted. "You're into it, aren't you? The gang thing gets you horny?"

"No!" she said, unconvincing as fuck.

"It's okay to wanna fuck me cause I used to be a bikie."

She leaned over and slapped his arm. "I'm not attracted to you because you're a bikie!"

"Used to be." A pause. "We can pretend I'm still one if you want."

"It's not like that!" she wailed.

"I don't have a bike anymore, but I could borrow Gil's. Take you for a ride?"

She pushed him in his chest. "Stop teasing me! I mean it!"

He leaned backward, laughing and loving that he was laughing. "Easy, sweetheart. I'm a bikie, ya know?"

"Stop it!" she shoved him again, and he caught her around the waist and pulled her close.

"Or what?"

She glared at him. "I'll bite you. I'm a good biter. Just ask Sam."

"I'd rather find out for myself." When she didn't smile, he bent closer. "It's okay. We don't choose what does it for us."

He'd meant to make her feel better, but she stiffened. "Is that how you feel about me? That you wouldn't choose to be attracted to me if you could?"

Her face was challenging. She wanted him to brush the question off or stay quiet, but he sensed how much she wanted to know the answer. For the first time it occurred to him that she might have doubts. Insecurities. That was ridiculous, but why else would she ask? "You're gorgeous, Nikki. It's not hard to want you."

"But you wouldn't if you had a choice?"

He frowned. "You know we don't go together. You said it yourself."

"Because I'm uptight? Or because you're a biker?"

"Ex-biker."

"Ex-biker. I guess I want to know why you're interested in me. You could have other girls, Daniella. Kelly. I just don't know why…"

Why you want me.

He could hear the question as clearly as if she'd said it aloud. He opened his mouth and the tightness closed in, a metal snake. No. No words. No talking. Not without tearing his guts open so wide, he'd die. He cleared his throat. "You said you needed my help. What with?"

Nicole blanched. "I was wondering if I could borrow your van tomorrow."

Noah frowned. "What for?"

"I need to drive to Adelaide and get my things. My clothes and my computer, all my photo albums and old diaries. All the important stuff. I'll pay for petrol and a service if you're due. I just need my stuff back."

Noah's heart gave a hard squeeze. "Does that mean you're moving to Melbourne?"

His poker face must be going to shit because Nicole was suddenly wary. "I don't know, but after that thing in the park, I know I'm done waiting for things to sort themselves out. I want my life to be different and I need to take a step in a different direction. I think this is it."

"Isn't there someone you could hire to get your shit?"

"Aaron won't give anyone a key. He says it's a security thing."

Noah snorted.

"Yeah, he's just holding my stuff ransom. I need to go get it myself while he's at work. Avoid all the drama."

"What if he's changed the locks?"

"I'll break a window."

Noah raised his brows.

"It's my house, too! Legally, he can't do anything."

Maybe not, but the legality of her breaking in wouldn't mean her ex wouldn't flip his shit, and what if he came home early? Found her while she was still in town? "You gonna head up there with Sam or Tabby?"

"God, no. They'll want to confront him, or egg his car, or put dildos in the letterbox. I can't worry about myself and them at the same time."

She had a point. Noah could just see them stirring up shit and acting like they were doing Nikki a favour. But the idea of her making the twelve-hour journey solo twanged at his insides. He changed tack. "Have you ever driven a van?"

"No, but how hard could it be? It's just a big car."

"No, it isn't. Look, you shouldn't go on your own."

She looked up at him. "What are you saying?"

What *was* he saying? There was an obvious answer, but that was out of left field. For one thing, he'd need to cancel his Saturday clients, lie to Sam, leave his house alone while Paula was still in possession of keys—

"I'll take you," he said. "To Adelaide. I'll drive."

Nicole blinked. "You don't have to do that."

"I know, but I will."

She looked apprehensive.

"I won't confront your ex. I won't get out of the van if you don't want me to."

"Really?"

"Course." He knew a lot of ways to intimidate idiots that didn't involve leaving a van. "When do you want to leave tomorrow?"

Nicole chewed her lower lip. "Early? I want this to be done."

"Okay, I'll have to tell Sam I won't be in."

"Don't do that, she can't know we're going away together!"

The panic in Nicole's voice was unflattering as hell, but it made sense. "She doesn't have to know. I've only got two clients. I'll tell her they both pulled out. Rare, but it happens. And even if we're both missing, she won't think we're together, will she?"

Part of him hoped she'd say yes—that she'd told her sister what they'd done, asked her opinion on what to do next, but Nicole shook her head. "No, she won't think we're together."

Another pang of unfounded irritation. He shoved it aside. "So then we'll head out without a problem. What are you gonna tell Sam and Tabby?"

Nicole's shoulders crept up to her ears. "I don't know. That I need some space, I guess. I was thinking of staying the night at a hotel tomorrow. Break up the drive a bit."

The air between them changed. Noah found it harder to keep looking her in the eyes. What came next? Did he say he'd pay for the rooms? Bring the condoms? All he could think about were scratchy sheets and Nicole's silky skin, hours and hours to see what their bodies could do.

"We don't have to... together. We can get separate beds?"

"Right. That what you want?"

Nicole looked up at the ceiling, her fingers drumming against her glass. "I don't know. It's hard to know what I want right now."

They'd circled back to the point she'd arrived with—the attraction they couldn't get away from. He closed his eyes, wanting to say it —I want you—and knowing he didn't have the capacity. He moved closer, feeling that crackle that came whenever they stepped into each other's orbits, hoping she could feel, too.

"Noah, you can ignore this if you want to, but do you... like me?"

There was something in her voice now, a breathiness that made him want to take bites out of her skin. *Isn't it obvious?* he wanted to say, but that wasn't right. He nodded.

"Really?" Delight overtook her features, making her so pretty, it hurt. The sensation unstuck something inside him.

"Liked you the moment I saw you."

"That day in the studio? But I was such a bitch!"

He shrugged. "You didn't like the look of me, but you were honest about it. Your instincts were right, anyway. I'm scum."

She swatted him again. "No, you're not, and I wasn't thinking that when I first saw you. I was thinking..." Her shoulders crept toward her ears.

He grinned. "What?"

"I didn't expect you to be so much."

He felt that right in his chest. He knew exactly what she meant. He reached out, pressed his hand into her lower back. She came to him easily and when he bent down, she closed her eyes, tilting her lips to him. Kissing her wasn't like kissing anyone else. It was like returning to a place you loved. The beach. The forests. His heart was thumping in his ears, his chest; every inch of his skin. This girl, *this fucking girl.* He wrapped his arms around her back. Her skin was too cold, her body vibrating as though it was thriving on energy alone. He wanted to touch her all over, but it wasn't sexual exactly. He wanted to feed her; give her what she needed to be okay again. But as he closed himself around her, she shifted, pulling away.

"Sorry," she said, her eyes glistening. "But you see what I mean, right? You're too much. *We're* too much."

Noah didn't know what to say. He could feel her about to leave and knew he wouldn't be able to stop her.

"I should go," she said right on cue. "Tabby will be wondering where I am."

"Okay. We still on for tomorrow?"

"Of course." She straightened the hem of her t-shirt. "I'll, um, pack my bags, come over in the morning?"

"Sure. Text me the time."

Nicole nodded, then rocked on her toes like a diver hesitating on the springboard.

The back of his neck prickled. "Just go if you want. Don't worry about me."

But she didn't turn and leave. Instead, she rushed forward and kissed him on the cheek. "Thank you so much, Noah. I like you and yes… thank you and bye!"

Then she turned on her heels and rushed away as swiftly as she'd come. Noah pressed a hand to his cheek, replaying the rosebud brush of her mouth.

Jesus Christ, he was fucked.

13

The sun was kissing the horizon as Nicole snuck down the hallway. She was barefoot for maximum quietude, hugging her overnight bag to her chest. She passed Sam's room where Scott Sanderson's snores were audible even through the wood. She tiptoed past Tabby's door, praying none of the puppies would wake up and start howling. One foot in front of the other, easing her way across the floorboards, when her bag swung into the walls.

"Fuck," she said, then gasped at herself for swearing. She must be all jacked up on pre-adventure adrenaline.

Tabby cleared her throat. "Who's there?"

"Me," Nicole whispered. "Sorry, I'm just... talk later."

She left before Tabby could fully wake up and ask or accuse her of anything. The front door creaked, painfully loud in the quiet. Holding her breath, she slipped through the smallest possible crack and into the cool morning air. She'd made it.

Nicole slung her bag over her left shoulder, feeling absurdly pleased with herself. The morning was bright, promising. She crossed the street, wondering if Noah was up and about or if he was still lying in the bed where he'd screwed her brains out. Her stomach turned in a strange little spiral.

Stop it, she chided herself. *This isn't about that. He's doing you a favor.*

And she wasn't wearing makeup... though she had shaved, smoothed toning SPF primer over her face, and spritzed herself with Miss Dior. But that didn't count. They were going to spend hours and hours in the car, smelling nice was just polite. She'd blown her chances with the '*do me... no wait, stop... keep going... stop... wait... keep going.*' Not to mention showing up at his house asking about destiny and whether he liked her. She shuddered at the memory. What was next—asking him to hold her hand and walk around Brunswick Shopping Center? She needed to be much, much more grown-up about this situation, and she would be. But as she walked the frost-lashed streets, she decided to let herself be excited about going on a road trip with him for as long as it lasted. Let a good thing be a good thing.

Noah wasn't still in bed. She spotted him from up the street, moving things around in the back of his van. The sight of him made her chest contract. She paused, unsure how to approach, but he turned and caught sight of her. "You escaped."

She smiled. "Barely."

"The dogs catch you?"

"Tabby."

His quiet laugh made her knees feel like spaghetti. He hardly made a sound, but his shoulders shook and his face made that fascinating shift from stern to beautiful.

"What now?" she said, her voice far too high.

"Gimmie your bag."

She handed it over and he eased it into the back of the van and closed the door. "Let's go."

"Sure, can I use your bathroom first?" She didn't need to go, but she did want to see that quince painting again. And the ocean one.

Noah blanched. "Can you wait until we're on the road?"

He sounded odd. Edgy.

"Is everything okay?"

"Yeah, we should just get going."

It was hard to believe him. Nicole scanned the surroundings, looking for whatever had shifted his mood so suddenly. Was he hiding some girl he didn't want her to see? She caught sight of his front door, saw the black marks that had been smudged across it. "Oh my god, what happened?"

Noah swore. "Get in the van, Nikki."

But she walked toward the door, squinting, trying to work out what the smudges were—soot? Garbage? When it clicked, she felt like an idiot. It was spray paint; someone had tagged Noah's house. She turned her head to the side, trying to work out what the biggest graffiti scrawl said. When she did, she gasped from the sheer ugliness of it. Horrified, she whirled on Noah. "Who did this?"

He rubbed his forehead so hard it was like he was trying to smudge his hand tattoos. "Get in the van."

"Stop saying that and talk to me. Are you in trouble? Is it the...?" She couldn't bring herself to say 'The Rangers', and that was just, as well. At the mere implication, Noah opened his eyes.

"I'm not talking about it here." He opened the passenger door, his jaw set, his pupils like pinpricks. Nicole was about to comply when she noticed his windows, or rather, the lack of them. All four frames had been taped up.

"Did you get robbed?"

He sighed. "What do you think?"

He was utterly serious, but Nicole had the strangest urge to mess with him. Which was weird because she never felt like messing with anyone. She put her hands on her hips. "What if it was me? What if I did it?"

There was a short pause. Noah glanced at the sky, shaking his head as though asking God why this was happening. Nicole could tell he was trying not to smile.

"I *could* have done it," she said. "I'm mysterious."

"Sure," he said, but the warmth had returned to his voice. "C'mon, Nikki, I mean it. Let's get out of here."

Despite her joke, silence fell when Noah got behind the wheel. Nicole couldn't understand it, sure someone had written 'dog cunt' on his door, but he hadn't been mad when she showed up. He'd been mad when she noticed it. He'd been trying to protect her or something. They travelled across the empty streets of Brunswick and toward the city without a word. She wanted to ask him if he knew the way to Adelaide—he didn't have his phone open on a GPS app—but thought that might insult his biker heritage.

They crossed the Bolte Bridge and Nicole had to bite her tongue to keep from talking about how pretty it was. The sun was climbing steadily, washing the Melbourne's CBD in golden light. The skyscrapers always looked so clean and colourful from this angle, framed against a periwinkle blue sky. She looked out at the concrete flats of South Warf, the gleaming Rialto tower, and spotted the Estrada building where Scott and Toby worked.

"Nice view."

Nicole turned, delighted. "It is nice! My dad used to drive us across the bridge just to see the city from here. I love it!"

Too enthusiastic. Noah's smiled dimmed. He didn't reply and she didn't press, turning her attention back to the view, the van purring around them like a four-wheel motorcycle. Noah drove well, keeping a reasonable distance between the van and other cars. She thought of Aaron stop-starting and swearing and tailgating anyone he thought had wronged him. Being in the car with Noah was soothing, like having a personal bodyguard.

She looked across at his profile and wondered if he'd find that idea offensive. Maybe, but he didn't have to know. He could be her bodyguard in her head, ready to protect her from Aaron and Sam and Tabby and her old friends and her old life. But her tongue didn't seem content to keep the idea to herself. "Do they have bodyguards in bikie gangs?"

She braced for irritation, but Noah didn't seem offended by the question. "Sometimes, if a big boss knows someone's out to get him."

"Or her." Nicole paused. "Are there female bikies?"

Noah shook his head.

"Is that sexist that women can't be bikies? Should we aspire to be bikies? If there were female bikies, would the world be a better place?"

He snorted. "Probably not."

Camera Obscura's French Navy came on the radio, and Nicole tapped her fingers to the fluttery beat. There were so many things to say, but as they sped along, she didn't feel like saying them. It was relaxing, moving fast but sitting still. Her breathing felt deep and medicinal. Was it Noah's presence beside her? Or was she just happy to be gone?

To her surprise, Noah broke the silence. "How're you feeling?"

"Good," she said. "I've never run away from home before. It's kind of exciting."

Noah did the little head-shake that said he was amused against his better judgment. "Glad to help."

"Did you ever run away from home?"

His features twisted, and she realised that was a pretty loaded question.

"Sorry, you don't have to answer."

"I know," he said, eyes on the road. "I did, it just doesn't feel like it sometimes."

She wanted to ask what he meant but decided it could wait. She and Noah had hours to get to know each other, after all. For the first time ever, she was on a trip without willing herself to already be at the destination.

They barrelled along the freeway for twenty minutes when Noah unexpectedly slowed, pulling into a small petrol station and coffee place.

"What's happening?" she asked.

"You said you needed the bathroom?"

"Oh! That was just an excuse to see your paintings again."

A smile tugged at the corner of his mouth. "Then I guess let's just get a coffee."

He pulled up next to the drive-through box and wound down the window. "One large latte, one medium decaf latte, and four almond croissants."

"Sure thing!" came the crackly response. *"Drive through."*

Nicole wanted to thank him, but she was so baffled he knew her coffee, she couldn't get the words out. They drove to the delivery window. Noah paid, handing her a bag of still-warm croissants and a takeaway coffee, wedging his own cup between his knees.

This is the smell! she realised. The warm, spicy smell she'd been unable to make out. It was almond pastries. "How often do you come here?"

"A lot." He gestured for the croissants and she handed him a flaky pastry, wiping her hands on a napkin so she wouldn't lick her fingers.

"Two are for you," Noah said, mouth full of croissant. "Eat one."

"I'm not hungry."

Her stomach growled angrily but she ignored it. Simple sugars aged your skin. They gave you cellulite, and stimulated your hunger, so you were starving twenty minutes after you finished a doughnut. Why hadn't she made a miso bowl or cut up some carrots—

A big hand poked her side. "Nikki, it's a fucking *croissant*."

Something in the way he said it, like he was passing down one of life's great truths, made her snort with laughter. "Can you read minds?"

"I don't need to read minds," he said drily. "It's all there on your face. Eat before I eat it for you."

He'd already finished his first one and had reached over to take a second, so it wasn't an idle threat. She pulled a pastry from the bag. It smelt like heaven. She paused, trying to take in the moment, then she bit down. The croissant was gorgeous; crisp on the outside and buttery in the middle. It was hard not to cram the rest into her mouth.

"Good?"

"Yes," Nicole said with all the dignity she could muster. She shredded a piece off, took the lid off her coffee and dipped the piece of pastry inside. "Thank you."

"Anytime. Your dad does that, too."

"What?"

Noah's smile was soft. "Dunks the croissants. Used to whenever I bought him one."

"Oh."

The thought of her dad and Noah eating together gave her food extra sweetness. She thought about it as they drove back out onto the road, happy she could eat quietly without worrying Noah would get offended. When she was done, she swept the crumbs into the empty bag. The van felt cosier, sweet smelling and comfortable. High on freedom, caffeine, and sugar, she stretched her arms and legs.

"Happy?" Noah asked.

"Yes, thanks to you."

He ducked his head. "No problem."

Nicole yawned and then the words came unbidden, *dog cunt*. Brunswick wasn't known for its crime. She was positive the trashing of his house had something to do with The Rangers. There was still so much she didn't know about Noah's past. Full and alert, she decided to go for it. "What was it like? Growing up a biker?"

A muscle flickered in Noah's jaw "Shitty."

"In what way?"

Nothing.

Nicole felt like a dick. "I'm sorry. I'll stop asking."

He shook his head. "You don't have to do that."

"But you look angry."

"That's just my face."

"Not all the time. Not when you're talking to me."

As though to prove her point, he smiled. Then he scrubbed a hand across his forehead. "Look, what do you want to know?"

Nicole had a million questions, but she decided to go with the practical. "Are you still involved with The Rangers?"

"No."

"Not even on a casual, Snapchat-every-now-and-again basis?"

His gaze was fixed on the road. "No."

"Then what's the deal with your house? The spray paint and the windows?" Silence swelled between them, making her tetchy. "You said I could ask!"

More silence. She could feel his anger. It was making his face harder, clenching his knuckles on the wheel. A thrill of fear ran down her spine. How had she forgotten that she didn't know anything about Noah except that he did tattoos and had a criminal background? That they were practically strangers?

"Noah…" She sounded weak, afraid. She tried again. "I didn't mean to make you angry, but if you're going to be like this, I want to go back to Melbourne."

Noah's gaze cut across at her and for a moment she was sure he was going to yell, then he grimaced. "I'm sorry."

"Pardon?"

"I'm sorry for going cold on you. Wasn't fair. I told you, you could ask."

Nicole blinked at him. No frills. No attempt to justify his behaviour. No demand for her to forgive him. Getting an apology like that was weird. "Thank you."

"Do you still want to head to Adelaide?"

She looked out at the fields rushing past. It would feel so deflating to go home without getting her things. "Yes, please."

But she didn't ask him anything else. She got out her phone and worked on the group email she planned to send to her boss and all her friends explaining her failed engagement and plans to return to Melbourne. Kim Petras sang about Hillside Boys as she added and deleted sentences, wondering whether to say Aaron had cheated, or if that would make her seem bitter.

"Nikki?"

She started a little at being addressed. "Yes?"

"I don't know who did the windows and doors, but I'm pretty sure it was my housemate's ex. Or someone my housemate's ex paid off."

"Your housemate who needed your help after we…?"

Noah smirked, then his smile faltered. "Yeah, Paula. She's the wife of one of my dad's bikie mates."

Nicole pictured a sexy bikie blonde with big hair and heaps of tattoos. Nausea rose in her chest. "Are you…?"

Noah shook his head. "She's older; early fifties. More like a mum to me than anything else. She called me up, said she wanted to get out of the club's orbit, so I let her move in for a bit. But it looks like she and Shredder have gotten back together."

"Shredder?"

"Nice name, huh?"

Nicole shook her head. "Why would she wreck your house after you helped her?"

"Shredder wouldn't have seen it as helping." He turned to look at her. "I'd have helped you either way, but I'm glad to be getting out of the state for a couple of days."

"Oh, well, I'm glad to help." Nicole bit her lip, remembering what he'd said about it not feeling like he'd run away from home. "Do you miss being in The Rangers?"

Noah kept his eyes on the road. "I'd be lying if I said no."

Nicole twisted the hem of her t-shirt. Ever since he'd admitted he'd been in a bikie gang, she'd stopped being so scared of him, but it was unsettling to know he wanted to go back. For the first time, she wondered what he'd done while he was a member, and realised she must seem so *naïve* to him. A suburban girl whose only crime had been stealing a toffee cup from the school fete when she was nine.

"But it was bullshit," Noah said. "Every bikie gang goes on about brotherhood and loyalty, but that's bullshit. It's about money and scaring the shit out of people so you can do whatever you want. It's ISIS without the politics."

Nicole blinked, trying to process his outburst. "So, The Rangers are involved in criminal stuff? I did some research and it said not all biker gangs are. Some are just about riding bikes, and the cops drum up charges against them because of the stigma."

Noah's laughter was cold. "The Rangers are crooks to their back teeth, Nikki. And I'd bet my legs the others are, too. It's a cover, saying you're 'bike enthusiasts.' The stigma's there for a reason."

His voice had changed, become harder and more ocker. Nicole felt a creep of nerves at being in such a close space with him. She looked at the paper bag, reminding herself she knew Noah; her dad knew Noah. "What did you do in The Rangers?"

"All kinds of shit."

"Was it… like a regular job? Like nine to five?"

"Nah, for most guys, it's an after-hours thing. They do their own work during the day. But like I said, boss's son. I got patched in when I was sixteen."

If she hadn't read *Blood in the Gears*, Nicole would have had no idea what he was talking about, but she understood he'd been made a full member of The Rangers. "You were so young!"

He grinned as though she was as woefully naïve as she suspected he found her. And she was. She'd grown up in such a bubble, finding out that real, dangerous bikers existed was a bit like finding out Hugh Jackman was actually Wolverine.

"So you were involved in…?"

An ugly smile. "Everything, Nikki. Fuckin' everything. Drugs, driving sawn off shotguns up north, paying off cops. Everything. But mostly, I did the tattoos."

"The patches?"

"And anything else the crew wanted. I had a lot of work."

She nodded, trying to absorb what he was saying. She looked across and saw the spider web on his elbow. Her heart pulsed hard. "Did you go to jail?"

He nodded, barely inclining his head. "Ten months."

Nicole tried to absorb this. It wasn't *shocking*, exactly… more surreal. "What did you…?"

"Aggravated assault."

"Oh." Nicole had subconsciously hoped it was drugs or theft or a non-violent crime, but if she was honest with herself, she'd suspected it was something like this. Noah's menace wasn't artificial—she'd known that from day one. He was hard in a way she'd never seen in another man. She remembered the paintings hanging in his house. How could one man contain such contradictions?

"Do you want to know what happened?"

No, but if she didn't hear it, her imagination would fill in the gaps, probably making it ten times worse. "Okay."

"I kicked the shit out of one of our guys for talking to the cops.

Dad's idea. He thought I was young enough to get away with a suspended sentence." He snorted. "I was young enough to believe that bullshit and that's about it. Barely left the guy's house before I was arrested."

Nicole could barely swallow. She kept her eyes locked on the road, the grey tarmac, the rushing white lines. "How old were you?"

"Twenty-one."

Nicole pictured herself at twenty-one, living at home, finishing her last year at uni, trying to eat less fried chicken. "How was jail?"

He shrugged and, perhaps remembering he'd agreed to discuss his past, added, "Boring."

"You didn't get beaten up or anything?"

"Nah, people knew who I was."

Of course, men would hardly have been lining up to take a swing at the son of a biker boss. She tried to imagine Noah behind bars and found it surprisingly easy; he'd have had a rounder face, less tattoos, adult muscles beginning to drape themselves over his arms and chest. She smiled, imagining him doing push-ups and chin-ups in his cell, then remembered how he'd got there—assaulting someone for talking to the police. She glanced sideways at his profile and squirmed at how bluntly, viscerally, attracted to him she was. What did that say about her? About both of them?

Maybe he sensed her discomfort because he added, "I regret it. All the ugly shit I did."

"Do you? Even though you miss being in the club?"

"Yeah, I don't miss the life, I miss feeling like..." He broke off with a shake of his shoulders. Nicole was reminded of a duck, ruffling its feathers after a fight. She waited, trusting him to speak.

Noah sighed. "It sounds like horseshit, but before I got locked up, I didn't know any better. Everything that went on at the club was normal to me. Then I got locked up and realised none of that loyalty, blood oath, brotherhood shit mattered. I was responsible for my life and I didn't fucking like my life. So, I changed it."

Nicole opened her mouth to say something then closed it.

"You think I'm scum, don't you?"

"No! No, I promise, it's just confusing."

"What's confusing?"

She exhaled, trying to loosen her chest. If she'd learned anything from spending time with Noah, it was that there was no point in softening your words. "I like you and I'm attracted to you, but what you did is scary and I have no idea what to think about it."

"Sure."

Silence fell, breathing like a living thing. Had she said the wrong thing? Had she utterly screwed this up?

It doesn't matter, Sam reminded her. *It was the truth. You're not judging him, but you're allowed to be unsure.*

Ten minutes passed and she started to feel the after-effects of the coffee. She fought the sensation for another half-hour, but when it became clear Noah wasn't going to say anything or stop the car for some unrelated reason, she cleared her throat. "I have to go to the bathroom. For real this time."

"I'll pull over at the next place."

Five minutes later they pulled into a petrol station, this one shiny-new and plastered with ads for Snickers and energy drinks.

"I'm gonna fill up," Noah said without looking at her. "Want anything?"

"I'm good," she said, making a beeline for the bathroom. She performed her ablutions, then stood in front of the mirror, finger-combing her hair. Despite her lack of makeup, she looked okay. Better than okay. Her eyes were bright and there was a glow to her cheeks that had nothing to do with the CC cream.

"Stop it," she told her reflection. "He's an ex-biker. He's been to *jail.*"

But that seemed abstract, blurry in the face of the man who'd bought her coffee. Did it matter that Noah had an ugly past if he regretted it?

No, but she knew her forgiveness was motivated less by compassion and more by the fact that he'd made her orgasm so hard her brain had melted. Was she one of those women who got suckered in by a charming criminal? Became complicit in his dodgy behaviour without even knowing it?

Dad liked him, she reminded herself. *Dad liked him, and Sam trusts him, and he paints like an angel. And he's driving you to Adelaide to help you move—*

And to get away from a bikie-wife who may or may not have spray painted the c-word on his house. So how broken are those ties?

Valid questions, but not ones she could answer. She'd have to wait, give Noah the benefit of the doubt. Trust. She washed her hands in a way she wished she could wash her mind and left the bathroom. She paused as she passed the petrol station counter and grabbed a couple of bottles of water, beef jerky, and salt and vinegar chips. The attendant looked at her strangely. "Doubling up?"

Nicole frowned. "Um, I guess so?"

Was this some new kind of slang? She'd have to ask Tabby. She walked outside to see Noah already inside the van.

"Hey," she said as she climbed inside. "I got water and snacks and stuff."

Noah's brow furrowed.

"What? Are you not hungry?"

He pointed at the inner console where she saw two bottles of water, a packet of beef jerky and salt and vinegar chips.

"Oh!" Nicole said. "Doubling up! That's what that meant!"

She beamed, and to her surprise, Noah beamed back. Truly. His face broke wide and the skin around his eyes crinkled, and he was so handsome, she felt dizzy. Before she could say anything he leaned in and kissed her, hot and hard. Her surprise evaporated. She clutched the back of his neck and pulled him in closer, relishing his warmth, the short bristles of his hair. When they broke apart, her head was spinning. "What was that for?"

"Do I need a reason?"

"No, but I'd like one."

"Okay, how about you're fucking beautiful?"

He said it hard, like a challenge, watching to see how she'd respond.

There was pleasure, yes, but a million write-offs hovered. Was he just trying to get on her good side to keep her from asking about The Rangers? Was he just trying to get laid? Was she as beautiful as Daniella in his eyes? What about Kelly? He could say this to everyone because she wasn't, couldn't be, had never been beau—

"*Nikki*." Noah's green gaze bore into hers. "It's a fucking croissant."

And she laughed again. Laughed the way he'd smiled when he saw her carrying the doubled up snacks. He was right. It was just an effing compliment. Why couldn't she just eat it? Believe him? She swallowed. "Thank you. I'm glad you think I'm beautiful. I think you're—"

But he'd put a knee into the console and kissed her again. She moved closer to him, feeling the salt and vinegar chips crunch beneath her and not caring one bit. His mouth was needy, crushing against hers like he had an urgent message to give with his tongue. They kissed for a long time. Nicole's spine hurt from the awkward position, but she didn't stop and neither did Noah. Some part of her knew she was being ridiculous, but the reality of it couldn't touch her. Not when he was. She kissed him back without thinking, without breathing. Her body was so tight it felt like she could break.

And maybe it would be good to break? Break and see what comes next.

A horn blared behind them and they broke apart. A bald guy in a Ford Fiesta flipped them off. They were blocking the pump. Chuckling, Noah released the handbrake and drove away, waving a lazy apology to the man.

Nicole moaned and buried her face in her hands. "How old are we?"

"Old enough that we can make out at a petrol station." Noah grabbed her hand in his warmer one. "You okay?"

Nicole looked at their joined hands. Hers pale and thin, his big and scarred and covered with gothic-looking tattooed tendrils. They were nothing alike, but it felt good to touch him.

Trust, Nicole thought. "Yeah, I'm okay. Can we keep going?"

14

Nicole's neighbourhood was about what Noah expected; neat brick houses, bright white fences, green grass despite the sweltering heat. A place for young professionals to rear their two-point-five children and aim for the upper echelons. A place where the likes of him were as welcome as antibiotic resistant gonorrhoea. Nicole was twisting her fingers in her lap. She'd fallen silent in the last hour, fiddling with her phone and staring out the window. He'd thought about saying something, but he'd already asked if she was okay—to which she said 'fine' in a high boiling kettle voice—what else was there?

"Noah?"

His hopes skyrocketed. "Yeah?"

"I know we talked about it but you don't have to come inside with me. I can just go in by myself." She said it quickly, as though he might *want* to see the evidence of her life with another man.

"No problem."

She kept staring out of the window, curling her fingers so tight, her knuckles were white. He saw himself reaching over and taking her hand, forcing her to stop self-flagellating, and talk to him. His palm tingled. He could do it. He counted down; five, four, three—

"We're up on the left." Nicole said. "Number twenty-seven."

Fucking perfect. Noah slowed down, looking for twenty-seven. His eyes locked on a two-story slice of middle class. "That it?"

Nicole wasn't listening. She craned her neck, looking around. "Oh, thank God. Aaron's car isn't here. He mustn't be home."

Noah felt a thrum of disappointment. It'd be easier this way, but he'd been nursing a couple of dumbshit confrontation fantasies. Mostly of shoving Nicole's ex through a window while making it clear he'd fucked his fiancée into multiple orgasms. He parked at the curb and pulled out his cigarettes. "I'll wait here. Call if you need me."

"Sure." Nicole's brows drew together. "You haven't smoked the whole drive."

"You don't like it."

Her smile drilled a hole in his chest. "Thanks, Noah, for driving and the croissants and talking to me. It's been great."

The heat in his chest tried to turn itself into words, but then his brain jammed. He nodded, stuck a cigarette in his mouth and felt like a fucking idiot.

Nicole pushed the passenger door open. "Okay, I'm going to head in."

He watched her walk up her garden path, her watch flashing in the sun, the one that covered her tattoo. He realised he'd never actually *seen* Nicole's daisy tattoo. He had the sudden urge to follow her, convince her to pull the watch off her wrist, see the pretty lines inked into her delicate skin. He could picture what it would look like— Edgar, Sam, and Tabby had the same daisy chain on their left wrists —but he wanted to *know*.

He closed his eyes. What would he ink on her, if he had the chance? The answer came at once—the ocean beneath an apricot sunset. He'd put it on her right wrist, wrapping around the delicate web of navy veins, the whole thing smaller than a book of matches. Pretty, feminine, perfect. He opened his glove compartment and pulled out his notepad and biro. The design wasn't complicated. The beauty would come into the kiss of colours; cerulean and lilac water, ruby skies and butterscotch sunlight. He wasn't competent in the watercolour style of tattooing, but compared to painting, how hard could it be? He made a brief list of the inks he'd need and then paused, cigarette hanging from his lip.

What the fuck was he doing? Drawing out this tattoo like it was going to happen? Like Nicole didn't want to get rid of the ink she had? He threw the notepad back in the glove compartment, beyond embarrassed at himself.

Don't forget why you're here. He'd told himself that over and over while he was driving, but some dipshit part of him refused to get the message. It was time to sit himself down for a little talk. It was time to Make Some Things Clear. "Newcomb. You fuckin' idiot. Don't go telling yourself you're in love with her."

A response came in the form of an indignant head-rush. Who knew if you were in love with someone or not?

"I mean it. What do you and Nicole DaSilva have in common?"

Sex. They both liked... pancakes?

"Exactly. Look at yourself."

He flipped down the mirror and studied his face, and Harold Newcomb stared back with his mother's fish-green eyes.

"Do you look like her next boyfriend? Do you think she wants people to see you two together?"

Sick of looking at himself, he flipped the mirror back up and scanned his arms, examining the black roses, bloody axes, charred bones and brick-toothed dwarves, Cthulhu's tentacles and snapping dragons.

"She wants kids. You think she wants to have your kids?"

He saw himself walking toward school gates to pick up a perfect black-haired, blue-eyed kid, the other parents locking their car doors as he passed. In the social media age, it'd take about twenty minutes for motivated mums and dads to find out who he was. Who he'd been.

"Daddy, why is everyone scared of you?"

And Nicole's disappointment. Her stress. Her regret in procreating with someone who looked like a professional bail jumper. A heaviness settled in his gut, dousing the fire that ignited when he was planning the watercolour tattoo. Who the fuck did he think he was kidding?

He got out of the van, needing to move, to get out of his own head. He paced the footpath, smoking and searching for something else to think about when Nicole burst out of the house. Her face was bunched up, her eyes rimmed red. He flicked his cigarette onto the asphalt and stomped it. "You okay? He in there?"

"No!"

There was an odd ring to her voice. She doubled over and he realised she was laughing. Deep belly laughter. "What's going on?"

"Come look!"

"I…"

She ran up to him and grabbed his hand. "You *have* to come look."

He followed her to the house and into her snow-white hallway. The place smelled strange, a flowery freshness undercut with something vaguely familiar. There was a picture on the sideboard—Nicole in a tight white dress with her arms around a guy in a suit. He had a long neck, curly hair and a distinctly cuntlike aura. Noah wasn't one of those guys who hated white collars on principle, but this guy looked like a cunt. The way he gripped Nicole's hip rubbed him the wrong way. Like he thought he owned her.

You don't, Noah told the image. *You were an ungrateful fuck and she's leaving you.*

She led him into a poshly decorated living room and he realised what it was at once—old party stank; flat beer, old wine, stale chips and meat fat. The source wasn't hard to find; the coffee table was heaving with garbage. Cheese rinds, greasy sausages and strawberry stubs were all slowly rotting on expensive flower-patterned plates. "What the fuck?"

Nicole giggled. "Aaron's been entertaining, but that's not the worst part. The worst part is *this*."

She tugged him around a corner and inside a flash-looking kitchen, or he imagined it was flash in normal circumstances. Right now it was more putrid than the living room. Plates were piled on the marble countertop and every glass in the house appeared to be piled on the sink. The bin was overflowing, spilling food packaging everywhere. A crusty chicken carcass lay in the sink and a huge peach-smelling candle had melted all over the kitchen bench, giving the trash a disgusting faux-sweetness. Noah had a solid stomach, but right then he was close to heaving. "Your ex is fuckin' foul."

"You haven't even seen the *piece de resistance*." She moved around the bench and pointed to a wine glass. "Look."

Noah leaned forward and saw a black and gold square stuffed inside the lipstick-dotted glass. "Is that a—"

"Condom wrapper? Yes. And if you look over here..."

She directed his gaze to a plate covered in shepherd's pie guts. He turned his head sideways and started to laugh. He couldn't help it. It was that or puke. "Oh, *fuck off*."

"I know!" Nicole was giggling hard and fast, a chipmunk on speed. "I always knew he was gross but that's—"

"Disgusting."

His revulsion only made her laugh harder. She threw back her blue-black hair and lost herself to giggles. He watched as she gripped the kitchen bench for support. Her hand was so close to the used condom, he couldn't stand it. He strode over and picked her up.

"Where. Are. You. Going?" Nicole gasped, her body convulsing in his arms.

"Leaving. Right now."

He carried her out of the house, placed her beside his van. She was still laughing and he had to wait a whole minute before asking, "How you feeling?"

Nicole wiped her eyes. "Good. Happy."

"Seriously?"

"Seriously. I can't think of a better metaphor for Aaron than what's in there." She waved at the house. "That's what he's like, all this nice stuff covered in..."

"Shit?"

She grinned. "Yes. But I was the only one who ever saw it, and I never had any proof to show anyone. Even myself. After he did something mean I'd question my judgment because I *know* I can be uptight and oversensitive. I never believed that he could be the problem because he always looks so good and knows what to say."

She gave a giddy, guilty laugh. Noah stayed silent. It was that or asking for her ex's car registration and calling in some old favours. Risk his good behaviour bond for the first time in years.

She was looking at him, waiting for him to say something. He needed to talk, but he had no idea how to put across the knotty tangle of his feelings in a way that made sense. This was the stuff of paintings; aubergine for anger, aquamarine for relief, rose gold because she was rose gold.

Her ex had been a dumb cunt to buy her a silver watch. She wasn't silver, just like she wasn't uptight or oversensitive. She was warm and bright, supple and strong. She glowed from the inside. She was rose gold. He opened his mouth and choked. Again. He cleared his throat. "What now? You want to get your stuff?"

Nicole blinked. "Oh, um, yeah. Sure."

Idiot. He was an idiot. What the fuck was wrong with him? She was pouring her heart out and all he could do was nothing. Worse than nothing. Change the subject. But then what did he expect? He looked back at the house. "Where do you wanna start?"

"Upstairs, I guess." Nicole pressed her lips together. "Oh no...."

"What?"

"I just realised I didn't bring anything to take my stuff in. God, I'm stupid."

Thank fuck, a chance to redeem himself. "I've got boxes."

"You, *what?*"

"I brought boxes. I had a few lying around the house because of—"

"Thank you! Thank you! Thank you!" Nicole ran at him and threw herself into his arms. It was quite a jump; for a second she clung to him like a koala. He dropped his cigarettes to stop her from slipping. "Nikki."

"Sorry," she said, still hugging him hard. "You're just so, so nice."

Christ, she even smelled like rose gold, like fresh bread and sunshine. His heart started going like a bass guitar. "They're fucking boxes."

"No, it's more than that."

Then she kissed him like it was nothing. Bliss numbed his brain. He cupped the back of her head and tasted rose gold, felt it welling up in his own chest, like maybe he had it in him, too.

"I'm so attracted to you," she mumbled, but he didn't reply. He didn't need to talk when he could show, and he could show her right now. He was just starting to get some tongue happening when he heard a car pulling up nearby.

Nicole tore her mouth from his. "Oh no."

They both looked at the driver, but it wasn't her ex. A middle-aged woman pulled up next door and was staring at them through her windscreen.

"Who's that?"

A blush spread across Nicole's cheeks. "Mrs Harris."

"She looks pissed."

"We are making out in public."

"Private property."

"I don't think she appreciates the distinction."

Nicole shifted and, reluctantly, Noah let go of her ass, letting her slip back onto her feet. "Want me to get the boxes out?"

"Yes, please."

They headed back into the house. He trailed Nicole through her kitchen, holding a box, breathing through his mouth to escape the smell. Nicole avoided the mess as best she could as she collected a crystal clock, a ballerina figurine, and a space-age potato peeler.

"It's the best one I've ever found," she explained when she caught him looking at her funny. "No way can Aaron keep it."

"No objection here."

He waited for her to collect more things, but Nicole clapped her hands. "Okay, that's all for this floor, should we head upstairs?"

"You sure you don't want the plates or glasses or anything?"

"No, he can keep it all. They're disgusting."

He frowned. Despite the grot, they looked expensive and he'd bet his left nut Aaron hadn't picked out or paid for them. "I can wash them while you do upstairs?"

She stared at him, her eyes so wide, there was more white than blue. "You'd do that?"

"I don't *want* to do it."

"But you would. You'd wash all this gross stuff for me?"

"Uh, yeah?"

Pink stained her cheeks and the way she was looking at him made him wish he wasn't holding the box. "You're not gonna jump again? I might break your clock."

She smiled but her eyes were bright. "I'm going to go upstairs and empty out my wardrobe. Can you meet me with a new box?"

"Sure. I'll have a smoke and head up."

He headed outside and saw Nicole's blonde neighbour was still in her car. She got out when she saw him, unlocking the doors so two kids burst from the back, shrieking and shouting.

"Come and get your things," she called. The kids ignored her, rushing over to the fence.

"Who's that?" one asked, loud enough to let him know he could answer himself. Noah opened his mouth but blonde mum beat him to it.

"Kids, get away from the fence!"

"But, Mum!"

"I mean it!"

She hustled her brood away from him and if looks could give cancer, she'd be a bigger health risk than durries. He gave her a wave, hoping to smooth things over, and pure fear washed over her features. She practically shoved her kids into the house, casting terrified looks behind her the whole time.

"Fuck."

He'd been in Brunswick too long, he'd forgotten how white bread the burbs could be. Probably thought he was Nicole's bad news sidepiece. Mrs Harris' curtains twitched. He sighed and lit up, thoughts of the condom crusted plate flashing through his mind. He bet Mrs Harris smiled and waved when she saw Nicole's ex. It wasn't fair.

Yeah, he had tats and a criminal record, but he'd never left a used dinger on a plate.

He smoked his cigarette to the filter, waiting for Mrs Harris to quit spying on him. She didn't. Either that or her curtains were full of mice. He had a feeling if he didn't get out of her eye line soon, the cops would be called.

"Welcome to the neighbourhood," he muttered, flicking his butt on the lawn and heading to the van. He grabbed another box and headed inside and up the stairs. The off-white carpet was dotted with crumbs and streaks of black polish. God, Nicole's ex was one feral asshole.

"Hey," Nicole called. "I'm almost done!"

He followed the sound of her voice, nudging the furthest door from the staircase open. Nicole was standing over the bed arranging glittering dresses inside what looked like a big sports bag. "I forgot I had this! Helpful, huh?"

Noah grunted, taking in her old bedroom. It wasn't too bad. There were hardly any personal touches. If it wasn't covered in coffee cups, dirty clothes, and electronic cords, it would have looked like a hotel room. "Your ex been redecorating in here, too?"

"Yeah, sorry. He's so gross." Nicole sounded satisfied. "Why didn't he hire a cleaner? He can afford it."

But Noah had known men with her ex's attitude his whole life. The kind who wouldn't wipe his arse if he could get his missus to do it. "Too lazy."

"True," Nicole said cheerfully. "But that's not my problem anymore."

There was a small painting hanging over the dresser. He put down the empty box and examined it. It was an owl flying into a snowstorm. It was a pretty thing, the snow fluffy owl was cruel-beaked and proud. The brushwork around the wings was a bit sloppy, but there was life there. Beauty.

Nicole got up and stood beside him. "I got it at a charity auction and I just fell in love with it."

"It's good."

"I was worried you'd think it's tacky."

"Why?"

"Because you have such good taste." She hesitated. "And because Aaron thought it was tacky."

"I don't think Aaron's in a position to call anything tacky ever again."

She laughed; a high, happy laugh, and he saw rose gold. She was so sweet, so fucking lovely. They looked at each other for a beat too long and Nicole cleared her throat. "I've filled the bag, could you maybe take it downstairs and I'll start on the box?"

"No problem."

I can't, he thought, *descending the grimy stairs. I can't fuck her in her ex's bed. That'd make me as big a prick as he is.*

But he was hard against his thigh, his head full of how she'd looked and felt the first and last time they'd fucked. Even the sight of Mrs Harris posted behind her curtains wasn't enough to put him off. If anything, it made him want to do it more. Fuck this uptight crusty house and this uptight crusty neighbourhood, if she was down, he was down.

When he returned to Nicole's bedroom, sex didn't seem to be on her mind. She was deep in a dresser drawer, piling old receipts on the floor.

"I should have filed this ages ago," she muttered. "I can claim loads of stuff in here."

"There something else I can do?"

"No, I'm almost done. See what I did with Aaron's stuff?"

Noah looked around. A big pile of clothes, books, the duvet and bedsheets, and a tonne of miscellaneous trash had been humped into the far corner of the room. "Wanna burn it?"

She laughed. "Kind of, but it's not worth it. Aaron'll just think I did it because I still love him, and I don't need that."

He watched her pile the receipts into a shoebox, around a pair of sparkly heels. "They're sexy."

"Oh! Thanks! I've never had a guy be nice about my shoes before."

He nodded, hating her ex some more. "Want me to take the boxes out to the car?"

"I guess, but I have no idea where I'll put all my clothes and stuff in Brunswick. With all three of us home, there's hardly any space."

"What about at my place? It's not far from yours and I've got a spare bedroom now Paula's gone."

She beamed at him. "Oh, that would be amazing! Thank you."

There was another hot moment, both staring, neither of them talking. A bolt shot through him—her nipples were pushing against her t-shirt. His hands became loose fists. He wanted to suck them more than he wanted his next cigarette, his next breath. She stood, a little unsteady on her feet, and pulled out one of the top dresser drawers, walking to her bed.

"I've kind of forgotten what's in here, actually." She upturned the drawer and colourful stripes spilled across the mattress. "Oh, um..."

She'd just tipped a rainbow of lingerie onto the bed; silk thongs, garter belts and bras. Filmy, frothy shit that would look incredible on her. She glanced up at him, a flash of faux-shocked eyes. She was hoping he'd do something about it. Well, she'd come to the right place. In this pretty, ugly house full of expensive bullshit and filth, he was going to fuck her like they just invented fucking.

Nicole was gathering up her tiny panties like autumn leaves. He didn't remember crossing the room, it happened like a cutaway in a movie. One minute he was near the door, the next he'd snatched her up. She tilted her mouth to him, offering, and he took it without question. The kiss was like melting into springtime snow. "I like all that silky shit."

Nicole's lips were red with kissing. She looked more like an elf princess than ever. "Really?"

"If I could take my hands off you, I'd ask you to try them on."

She kissed him again. Her mouth was hungry, desperate, demanding to be taken out of her head and into pleasure. For the second time that day, he conceded. Only this time he didn't have the willpower to play games. He grabbed her ass and hauled her up against him. She moaned, wrapping her legs around his back. "Noah."

God, the way she said his name in that bratty, urgent whine. He cupped her right tit, pinching her nipple. "Yes, baby?"

The blue of her eyes shrank as her pupils blew outward. "Do me again, please? Do me like you did before?"

The longing in her voice made his cock throb. She wanted to fuck him in her ex's bedroom. The dirtiness of the request transmuted his fear that he was exactly what was spray-painted on his front door. What was the point of being a big, ugly bastard who scared people if you didn't occasionally get a transgressive fuck out of it?

"What was it like before?" he asked.

"Hard. Mean."

A sinking sensation. Concrete. Swamp water. It shouldn't have been so shitty—knowing she felt about him the way he did. That the thrill factor, and the fact he owned a van were the only reasons they were here. But it was, and it pissed him off.

"Noah?"

He turned Nicole around and pushed her into her rainbow lingerie. "I can do whatever I want. You'd better do what I want, too."

"I will." She slid out of her shorts to expose a soft blue thong that framed her ass like a dream. "Please hurry—he might come home."

He reached down, yanking off Nicole's t-shirt and unsnapping her bra.

"Noah!"

He pulled his t-shirt over his head. "Get your panties off now."

She pulled down her underwear, exposing the perfect peach slice of her pussy. She was wet. The smell of her called to him in a way that made him dizzy. He unbuttoned his jeans, dropping them to the floor, and pulled his cock from his briefs. He was fully hard and a single stroke had him pushed to the edge.

"Noah?"

"Yeah, baby?" He reached between Nicole's legs. She was soaked, and when he slid his fingers inside her, she shrieked like a whirlwind. "Want more?"

She nodded frantically.

"Okay," he said, grabbing a handful of the ass that had been tormenting him all day. All summer. "You'll get your fast fuck, but because I want it, not because of your ex. You've got some fuckin' nerve talking about him while I've got my hands on you."

"I'm sorry, but Aaron—oh!"

He spanked her. Not at full-force, but not gentle either. He spanked her again on the right side, eliciting a half-aroused, half-humiliated scream.

"What are you doing?"

He pushed his fingers through her hair, bunching the silken strands like rope. "You mention that cunt while I'm touching you, you'll get it twice as hard. Understood?"

She nodded, spreading her legs wider, clearly so horny, she'd agree to anything. He reached for his jeans and his wallet when he saw something that changed his mind. She was still wearing the watch, that silver fucking watch. "Gimmie your left hand."

She raised it at once, watch flashing in the afternoon sun. He turned her wrist over and flicked the catch.

"What are you doing?"

He pulled the watch away. "It's his. You're not wearing it while I fuck you."

The watch slid away like a dead snake. He tossed it into the pile of her ex's shit and looked for her tattoo. He couldn't see it. Nicole had snatched her hand away, covering her wrist with her other hand. "You've already fucked me with the watch on."

"You think that's helpful?" Noah spanked her again. "You're done, Nikki. He's fucking history. Get rid of your tattoo, buy another watch to cover it up, just don't wear his shit while I fuck you."

She turned to face him, her cheeks as red as her ass. "Why do you even care?"

A thousand answers hovered; he ignored all of them. "Spread your legs."

She did what she was told, arching her back. Her right hand was still cupping her wrist though, concealing the daisy chain. Fine, let her have her secrets.

He reached for his jeans. His blood felt hot, too hot. Too long had passed since they'd done this. He'd wanted to eat her out, show her he could do more than fuck fast and hard. He slid two fingers inside her and she rode him like a cowgirl, pumping back on his fingers. Blood pounded in his ears and cock. He pushed up into her, his mind blank, his body beyond ready.

"Do me, Noah. Please?"

He worked his fingers inside her but she shook her head.

"Your cock. Please?"

Fuck, she was so goddamn needy. He wasn't going to give in.

"Please?" she said again. "Please?"

His head spinning, he pulled away from her. He gave himself a second to admire her, long-legged and bent over, before lowering his mouth to her cunt. He'd make her come that way, grinding on his face the way she had on his fingers.

Nicole reached back, grabbed his shoulder. "No."

"Don't want your pussy licked?"

She pulled him closer. Her pussy pressed up against his bare cock and she smiled. "I want you to do it like last time."

The memories almost had him bite through his tongue. He reached for his jeans and swore. "No condom."

He'd considered slipping one into his pocket but that felt fucking presumptuous. Now they were screwed. "Do you have any?"

"No." Disappointment blazed across her face and then her eyes narrowed. Her small, cool hand wrapped around his cock. "Noah...?"

Stupid. Bad idea. The date of his vasectomy loomed before his eyes. This was exactly why he needed one, situations like this. "Can't fuck you raw."

"I know," she said, sounding tortured.

But despite their agreement, the head of his cock was rubbing up against her slit, toying with what they shouldn't do. He reached down, guiding her movements. She moaned whenever he brushed her clit, clutching his shoulders. The streaks on her cheeks looked like war paint, her mouth was red as blood.

"Please," she moaned. "Please?"

He *never*... he *shouldn't*... but this was Nicole DaSilva begging for dick. What the fuck was he supposed to do? He slid his cock to her opening, his brain buzzing, his mind on nothing but how she'd feel around him. He spit in his palm and slicked it along the length of his cock. "You want it?"

"Yes. *Please.*"

There was no subtlety in what came next. He shoved his cock inside her like a soldier planting a flag, showing what he owned, what he'd fought for. She gasped as he stretched her wide, arching her back, trying to get more. "Noah... you're so *big*."

He gritted his teeth. She felt like heaven, and her saying stuff like that was only going to end it way too early. He needed her to make less noise. He picked up his t-shirt and pulled the opening over her head.

"What are you doing?" Her voice was muffled, but he could hear her excitement as he covered her face. "Keep quiet. Keep quiet and get fucked."

She whimpered, pushing back on his cock. He bound the t-shirt around her chin in a loose knot she could tear off if she needed to get free. Her moan made a fucking animal out of him. He pushed deep, gripping like he never wanted to let go. He knew it couldn't get her off, but he couldn't slow down. They needed more time for that. More time and a room that wasn't the place she used to fuck her ex. The thought got him so pissed, he spanked her already reddened ass. "Say my name."

She shuddered, her cunt tightening around him. "Noah!"

He'd semi-gagged her but now all he wanted was hear her talk. "Louder."

"Noah!"

He fucked her for a furious minute, watching her writhe and grind against him, breathing hard against his t-shirt.

"Feel good?"

She nodded, his t-shirt swaying around her face.

"Tell me it feels good. Tell me it's the best you've ever had."

"It's the best, it feels so, so good."

But it wasn't the same, having her parrot his own words back to him. He slid out, patting her hips. "Get on all fours."

She obliged at once. "Noah...?"

"You want me?"

She nodded frantically and his smile became something altogether soppy because it was part brag and all revelation. Somehow, in fucking her bareback with a t-shirt on her head, he finally understood she was into this as much as he was. His chest throbbed, touched in some indefinable way and he gritted his teeth. "Close your eyes and take my dick. I want you to come."

He knelt behind her, sliding deep inside her cunt. He fucked her as slow as he could without busting, dragging himself in and out—thinking about football, about Monet. Even, when she drew tight and slippery around him, The Rangers.

"Noah," she whispered. "Noah..."

God, it was fucking corkscrews not to come. "Yeah, baby?"

She whined, tossing her hips and pressing back against him.

"Gonna finish?"

She nodded, making his t-shirt slip so her beautiful hair was suddenly loose around her shoulders.

"So come," he snarled, fucking her fast. "Say my name while you do it."

He drove inside her, watching, feeling. She came screaming his name, her hands raking the carpet and when she was done, she laughed, shaking all over. "Noah..."

"Hold on." He was now so close it hurt. He closed his eyes and pressed deep, feeling the pressure pulling him down. In seconds, heat was burning through him and he collapsed onto her, breathing like he'd run a marathon. "Jesus."

Nicole's hands reached behind her and smoothed his sides, cool as a bathroom floor. "Good?"

He nodded, burying his face in her sweet-smelling hair.

She giggled. "Are you going to move again?"

"Maybe..." Realising he was crushing her, he rose onto his palms. "You okay?"

She looked over her shoulder and beamed at him, then her expression changed so fast, it was almost funny. Her nostrils flared, her mouth flattened. "Oh no..."

"What? What is it?"

She cupped a hand between her legs. "We... without a condom."

Jesus. This was why you never did what he'd just gone and fucking done. "I'm sorry, Nikki—"

"Don't be," she whispered. "I told you to do it."

"If you're worried about getting pregnant..." He had no idea how to finish that statement. *I make great toast? I'll pay if you want to get rid of it? I wouldn't mind being tied to you like that, Nikki.*

The doorbell cut him off before he could say anything stupid, ringing loudly somewhere beneath them. He froze. "Who's—"

"I have no idea." Nicole whipped his t-shirt off, looking terrified. "It can't be Aaron, he wouldn't knock."

That obvious fact got his heart going again. "Maybe a salesperson or something?"

"I'm not sure." Still pale, Nicole stood, pulling his t-shirt over her head. It fell almost to her knees, a baggy black dress. She grabbed the box of tissues off the side table and swiped one between her legs. Then, to his irritation, she ran to the pile of Aaron's shit, extracted her watch, and snapped it over her tattoo. "Stay here. I'll see who it is."

Before he could say anything, she was padding down the stairs. He considered going after her, thought better of it, and slumped back on the floor, utterly wrecked. He listened, female voices drifting up toward him. He couldn't make out what they were saying. His head *was* pounding. Had he just barebacked Nicole in her ex-fiancé's bedroom? He didn't want to be proud of it, but some caveman part of him was beating his chest and telling him to wipe his dick on Aaron's pillow.

Nicole returned a few minutes later, looking mortified. "Oh my gosh..."

He sat up. "Everything okay?"

She pressed her hands to her mouth, avoiding his eyes. "Yes, it was Mrs Harris."

"What did she want?"

"She thought... well..." Nicole giggled and he felt his mood lift. She was happy. That meant everything, no matter how bad, was okay.

"She thought I was robbing the place?"

"Basically." Nicole giggled. "Sorry, it's just funny. She's such a prude and when she saw I answered the door, her eyebrows shot up her forehead. She asked me if I was comfortable being alone with you."

"What'd you say?"

She gestured at his t-shirt. "I don't think I had to say anything."

He laughed, feeling like a boulder had been rolled off his chest. "She knew you were fucking the robber?"

"You're not a robber!" Nicole looked offended on his behalf and it was so sweet, he had to hold her. He reached forward, grabbing her legs and pulling her onto his chest. She went down willingly, mock-pounding at his chest and shoulders. "Let me go."

"No," he said, kissing her cheek. "I'm not done stealing from you."

She turned her serious navy eyes onto him. "You're not stealing from me, I *want* you to take things from me, and I'm sorry about before. I'm on the pill, I'm not worried about getting pregnant, it's just..."

"Yeah?"

She kissed him, light and soft. "I like sleeping with you."

It was a compliment, but not what he wanted to hear. As she bent to kiss him again, he realised he was fucked. He was in love with Nicole. Stupidly in love, and all the talking-to's in the world weren't going to change that.

Fuck.

15

Nicole turned and looked up at the house. Strange how once upon a time it had been her dream, the place where her real life would begin.

"Anything else?" Noah asked.

He'd been weirdly formal since they'd gotten up from the floor. A way to let her know she shouldn't get serious, maybe? Or perhaps he was just bored. She rubbed her palm on her shorts, trying to rid herself of the itchiness that had sprung there.

Stop it, she told herself. *Just because he isn't all over you doesn't mean he's given you something. And he hasn't given you something. And if he has, it doesn't matter. But he hasn't. Because he told you he got tested three months ago and he always uses protection.*

Somewhere in her mind, Sam cackled. *Yeah, because no dude has ever said that and not meant it.*

"Shut up," she whispered.

"Sorry?"

God, that was all she needed—for Noah to think she talked to herself, or more specifically, her sisters in her mind. She turned on him with a TV host smile. "I think we're all good! Thanks so much!"

"Uh, sure," he said, eyebrows raised. "So, we done?"

"I think so." She looked at the house once more. The carcass of her old life. All she had to do was lock the front door, leave her key in the letterbox and it would be done. Why did that feel so anticlimactic?

"You want a minute?"

He meant alone, possibly to cry or do whatever it was heartbroken people did, but she *wasn't* heartbroken. While she was packing her last box upstairs, she'd allowed herself to imagine staying, pulling her things out of the boxes, and resuming her life with Aaron.

That had been heartbreaking. She'd cried into her winter coats. Despite the unprotected sex, her unresolved life, and her unknown relationship to the man beside her, she'd known the only way was forward. The decision to leave felt good. Strong and light, like Plexiglas. She was determined not to question it.

She smiled at Noah. "I'm fine. Do you want to get some dinner?"

"Uh... yeah? Around here? Or... where d'you wanna go?" It was cute to see him off balance, this man who'd screwed her on her bedroom floor. Ex-bedroom floor.

"I was thinking about The Lighthouse. They do amazing salt and pepper crab."

"Crab?"

"I feel like celebrating."

He smiled then, one of those slow smiles that made her insides feel like sugar dissolving into warm milk. "Sure, let's get crab."

"Great!" She realised she was wearing cotton shorts. "I might go inside and change, if that's okay?"

"No problem." He gestured to his black t-shirt and jeans. "As long as you don't mind that all I have is this."

"That's fine." She raced around to the back of the van and grabbed the sports bag she'd filled with dresses. She hesitated, then grabbed the shoebox with the heels he'd called sexy. Why not? "I won't be long."

He smiled, pulling his cigarettes from his pocket. "Take your time, I'll be here."

He's lovely, Nicole thought, heading back to the house. *He should stop smoking though. Maybe I can give him that Allan Carr book Bethany read. She hasn't smoked for eighteen months—*

She stopped in the doorway, horrified. She and Noah were about to go out for dinner, the first thing between them that could remotely be called a date, and here she was, plotting a way to change him *in her ex-fiancé's house.*

"Get a grip," she told herself, heading into the lounge to change into her stretchy black fishtail dress. It was a little glam, but she wanted to look pretty.

For Noah? Maybe, but also for her future life. She'd escaped the momentum of her past. Surely that warranted some sparkles.

She pulled off her bra and then, remembering the dress's clinginess, her underwear. They were damp from what she and Noah had done. Her nerves fizzed and she reminded herself it was unlikely that anything bad had happened.

But not impossible, Sam said.

I don't want to think about that.

She tugged on her Jimmy Choos, wiggling her toes so they settled in the narrow fit. She and Sam had long toes—*proof of our primate ancestors,* Tabby always said. There was a bottle of Miss Dior in the sports bag, so she spritzed herself. She finger-combed her hair, regretting her makeup was miles away in Melbourne. She considered going upstairs and having a good rummage for stray foundation samples, but the sun was dipping and the last thing she wanted was a confrontation with Aaron.

She collected her discarded clothes and was about to shove them in her bag when she realised she didn't want to. Whenever she wore them, she'd think of being here, in the middle of Aaron's filth.

She had her nice dresses and her owl painting; she didn't want anything else. Using the cups and plates would only remind her of her failed engagement—and the condom. She looked at the front door where Noah was waiting, smoking, thinking his Noah thoughts. Her lips curled into a smile.

I'm lucky, she realised. *Aaron is the unlucky one.*

Her heart racing, she walked to the foul-smelling kitchen and pulled the magnetic notepad and pen off the fridge. She scrawled as fast as she could.

Goodbye, Aaron, I'm going to have nightmares about the condom but it made going through with this so much easier. I'll have a solicitor call about the house.
Good luck, Nicole

She stuck the notepad back on the fridge, and her watch flashed in the lowlights. Her gut contracted.

She could keep it. It wasn't her engagement ring, it was a nice Cartier watch. Sam and Tabby would let her get away with it. Noah didn't like it, but he couldn't tell her what to do. It was the same thing as getting rid of her tattoo—her choice. She let her hand fall back to her side, the watch feeling heavy as a shackle. She wished Noah had broken it. Thrown it on the floor and crushed it under his feet. He was an ex-biker who'd been to jail, if he hated the watch so much, why hadn't he destroyed it?

Because he's a good person, you idiot. He's not going to curb stomp your eight thousand dollar watch.

She rocked on her toes, trying to think of another way. She glanced at her front door, picturing Noah leaning by the van, smoking. If she ended everything, many possibilities would have room to breathe, to test their strength.

What do you think? she asked her internal sisters.

Do it fast, Sam said.

Like a band-aid, Tabby added.

It came off with the flick of her thumbnail. She cupped it in her hands like pirate treasure. She held it up to the light and watched the diamonds glitter.

"Goodbye," she said, kissing its face. "Thank you for being such a good watch. It wasn't your fault. You didn't ask to be a metaphor."

She draped it carefully over Aaron's used condom, feeling a hundred kilograms lighter.

The sun was setting as she strode outside, but it seemed extra-bright, as though it was supercharging itself. Noah stared at her, smoke curling from his mouth. At first, she thought he'd noticed the lack of watch, then she remembered she was wearing a tight, showy dress and heels. "Like it?"

He nodded, his green eyes narrowed. "C'mere."

She walked toward him, and because she was embarrassed, she did a little turn. He rubbed his jaw. "You…"

"Yes?"

"Never mind." He pressed his non-cigarette hand to her waist, pulling her close. "I'd kiss you, but I'm pretty sure your neighbour's watching."

"She's not my neighbour anymore."

His lips were on hers before she'd barely finished the sentence. Kissing her like something out of a movie. He smelled like sweat and he tasted like cigarettes, and Nicole was certain her ex-neighbours were all watching from their windows, but it didn't matter. When he pulled away, his green eyes were blazing, but she liked that he didn't say anything. That they could keep whatever was between them out of language and inside sensation.

"Should we go?" she asked, slipping her hand into his.

"Sure, hang on a sec." He crushed his cigarette into the bottom of his shoe and flicked it onto her—Aaron's—front lawn, where she noticed several butts were already lying like discarded bullet shells.

"Noah!"

His expression was deadpan. "What?"

She shook her head, unable to stop smiling. "Take me to dinner, please."

He opened the passenger door to the van and, feeling oddly like a princess, she got in. "Thank you."

"Sur…" He faltered, looking, for the first time since she'd known him, shocked. "You're not wearing your—"

"I know. Don't say anything. I'm raw and I might cry."

"Fucking hell, Nikki—"

"I mean it, don't talk!" But she laughed because it was so ridiculous to have to tell Noah Newcomb, the living wall, not to talk.

He leaned in and kissed her, soft and sweet on the mouth. "I won't talk."

"Don't," she warned as he pulled away. "Still don't say anything."

He didn't, but there was a smile on his face as he headed around to the driver's side of the van.

She directed him to The Lighthouse by memory. It was her favourite restaurant in Adelaide. She was always trying to drag Aaron, her friends, and colleagues there. It was, she reflected, probably the only thing she was going to really miss about the city.

"What kind of food do you like?" she asked Noah. "I know you have burgers all the time at work, but do you like Italian, or Indian, or Mexican?"

He smiled a little. "Sussing me for future date potential?"

Nicole felt herself flush. "No, just curious."

"S'alright. Thai's probably my favourite. You?"

Nicole almost said her automatic response—sushi—then realised she wasn't at work or with friends or on a first date. Noah knew her family, which meant he'd probably already heard about her nugget obsession. "Fried chicken."

His grin confirmed he had already known that.

"Tabby?"

He shook his head. "Sam. She told me this story about the two of you. You were sixteen and you'd gotten someone's brother to buy you a box of wine and..."

"No!" Nicole pressed her hands to her ears. "Stop!"

"... and you drank about half of it on your roof because your dad was downstairs running a silent mediation workshop..."

"Stop!"

"And then you decided you had to go to McDonalds, or you'd die—"

"It was KFC, thanks very much."

Noah cackled. "The dirty bird."

Nicole put her thumbs in her ears again.

"And then you ate twenty-six nuggets?"

"Twenty-eight," she said with all the dignity she could muster.

Noah laughed. He laughed and laughed and banged the steering wheel.

"Are you done?" she said, trying and failing not to smile.

"Almost." He rubbed his eyes. "The impressive part was you didn't throw up afterward."

"It was sheer spite, Sam said I was going to, so I didn't. I felt sick for a week, though."

Noah gave a loud, contented sigh. "Great story."

She rolled her eyes. "Thanks. What about you? What's your worst teenage drinking story?"

He glanced across at her and she knew she'd trodden on a landmine. While she was staining her teeth burgundy with boxed wine, he'd been a fully patched member of a bikie gang. She doubted his worst drinking story was one he wanted to tell. Or one she wanted to hear.

"Sorry."

"S'okay." His eyes were fixed on the road. The air between them had crystalized slightly.

Nicole cast around for a different subject. "Do you cook? Like dinner?"

His smile returned. "Yeah."

"Really? What do you make?"

He shrugged. "Stir-fries, curry. I do pretty good lasagne."

"Really?" She was amazed. She hadn't expected him to say yes, let alone mention lasagne. "Who taught you to cook? Your mum?"

His mouth twisted and she could have slapped herself. She'd just stepped on the same 'Noah's family was heavily involved in a bikie gang, he did not have a conventional childhood' landmine again.

"Forget it. I don't know why I said that. My mum didn't teach me to cook. She left when we were little, but even when she was home, she never made anything. Dad cooked."

She could feel Noah watching her and she kept her eyes on the road.

"I taught myself to cook," he said. "I had to."

Something in his voice tugged at her heart like a balloon string. "Because no one cooked for you?"

"Because I had scurvy."

"*What?*"

He smiled. "I had scurvy. Like what pirates get."

"What? How?"

"We only had toast at home; pizza, and fish and chips at the clubhouse. When I was twelve, all my teeth started coming loose and I had a headache all the time. I went to the doctor and he told me I had scurvy."

Nicole gasped. "No!"

He grinned and extended his left forearm toward her. She saw the tattoo that took up the greatest part of the skin was a mottled black pirate ship. "Secret's out."

"What did you do?"

"Doctor told me to eat vegetables, so I did. Raw 'til I figured out how to cook them. Wasn't too hard."

Nicole couldn't smile, she was still too horrified. "What did your parents say?"

"Mum wasn't much of a mum. Dad wasn't much of a dad. They didn't give it much thought. In fairness, they didn't look after themselves any better than they looked after me."

"Did *they* have scurvy?"

He gave a funny little laugh. "Nah. Everyone in the clubhouse was into Coronas. I guess the lemon slices saved 'em."

Nicole shuddered, then felt ashamed. She'd drunkenly eaten more than two dozen nuggets, who was she to judge anyone? "I guess I'm glad you didn't all have scurvy."

Noah smiled. "They're not together. My parents. They split when I was fifteen."

"I'm sorry."

He inclined his head, though it was clear he didn't consider the event a tragedy. He didn't seem eager to discuss it further, and for once, Nicole understood. There were few things she hated, like talking about her runaway mother. She pointed to the traffic lights. "It's the next left from here. Down by the water."

A heat warmed her right thigh. Noah had put his hand on her leg. She glanced at him, but his eyes were on the road. Nicole wanted to cry then, not because she was sad, but because the hot weight of his hands soothed her in ways that didn't make sense. They travelled the rest of the way in silence, Noah's palm on her leg. Nicole watched the world whir past, the quiet in her brain so luxurious, she was disappointed when they finally got to The Lighthouse. Noah pulled into the car park and turned off the engine. They stayed sitting, watching the sunset stain the ocean like a painter's daydream.

Noah's hand tightened on her thigh. "Stunning."

"I love the ocean."

"Not what I meant."

Nicole ducked her head. His compliments were still a little jarring, especially since she wasn't wearing makeup. "The painting over your kitchen table is as beautiful as the view here."

"Nah."

"I mean it!"

Noah's smile was kindly. "Thanks, baby, but there's no chance. Art can't ever come close to life. It's too bright and big and you can feel the energy pulsing through every part of it. All I can do is reflect it, talk about how magic it is. A good painting's a sunbeam in a box; the real world is the whole fucking sun."

Nicole didn't think she'd ever heard him say something so heartfelt. Or long. She stared out at the ocean and realised he was right, the world was alive, shifting and melting in a way a painting couldn't. His were beautiful though. The most beautiful paintings she'd ever seen.

"Ready for food?" she asked.

"Yup." But he made no move to undo his seatbelt, instead staring at the restaurant, a big glowing white Tudor building. "We're a long way from KFC."

She smiled. "We are, but that's not a bad thing. Want to go in?"

"Do you?"

There was a little too much emphasis on his words for it to be a throwaway question. He was asking something else, about her, about them.

Nicole smiled. "Yes. I want to have dinner with you in The Lighthouse."

He raised their joined hands to his mouth, but he didn't kiss the back of her palm. He kissed the daisy chain her dad had tattooed into her wrist when she was eighteen. Nicole's heart blew out to twice its normal size. "You like it?"

He opened his mouth, but nothing came out. He shook his head, gave her hand a final squeeze and opened the driver-side door. Nicole watched him go, wondering what it was that he kept trying and failing to say.

She'd told Noah he wouldn't look out of place, but once they were inside it was clear her Nostradamus skills were a little off. The hostess, Debbie, gave him the kind of side-eye that said she'd already punched the first two zeroes of the emergency number into her phone.

"You here for work, Nicole?" she asked.

Nicole squirmed a little, knowing the easiest thing was to say yes. Debbie knew Aaron. Answering her question meant saying a lot more than she'd intended. She looked at Noah, his expression blank, and her first thought was that he wouldn't care if she said 'yes.' Then she remembered how he'd looked in the van, how rude Mrs Harris had been, how he hadn't chosen to grow up in a bikie club, or be hugely tall or get scurvy. She took his hand, that warm, rough lifeline that had brought her to Adelaide. "Here for fun, actually. Can we please have a table for two?"

Debbie's face was smooth as cream. "Sure."

But Nicole was sure she was mentally adding 'if you insist.'

"I'm sorry," she said when they were seated. "Debbie shouldn't be so snotty to you."

"Doesn't matter. Want champagne?"

"I... yes."

And he told the waiter rushing up behind her to bring them a bottle of Moet like it wasn't anything. And when it arrived he didn't look remotely out of place holding a long-stemmed glass. In their upscale surroundings, his size and tattoos had taken on a rebellious glamour. He might have been a football player relaxing in the off season with his overdressed girlfriend. She noticed a few women watching him with mixed curiosity and attraction and felt a prickle of jealousy.

He's mine, she thought, *we just had sex on my ex-bedroom floor.*

"Toast?" Noah asked, his green eyes glinting as though he knew what was on her mind.

"Sure, go ahead."

"To you," he said, tapping his glass to hers. "And your tattoo."

Nicole looked down and was shocked to see the daisy chain looped around her wrist. She'd grown to... not hate it, but *resent it*. Resent its hippy-dippy prettiness, the way it made her a girl with tattoos who wasn't remotely as cool as her sisters. For the first time she looked at it and thought maybe it suited her. She tapped her champagne glass to his and they both drank. Their waitress returned and Noah ordered them both deep fried, soft shell crab.

"That's a bit old school, ordering for your date," Nicole teased.

"You wanted something else?"

She didn't, but she stuck her tongue out at him anyway. A thought occurred to her. "Oh my god, it's getting late and we haven't booked a hotel yet."

Noah said nothing, but the look he gave her made her feel like her skin was on fire.

"I guess there's, um, lots of places in town," she corrected. "It can't be that hard to find one. We can look after this."

He nodded, his gaze like gleaming jade.

Nicole drank deeply from her glass, tasting nothing. A hotel room, a big blank bed where she and Noah could explore the hungry thing between them. Their waiter brought warm brown bread and a big dab of salted butter. She ate, letting the richness wash across her tongue.

Noah watched her. "Christ, it's hard not to look at your mouth."

"So stop staring and eat!"

He smiled and did just that. Conversation between them flowed as quickly as the wine. They talked about the sports they'd played in school—football for him, netball for her.

"We're so heterosexual," Nicole said. Noah laughed.

When their waiter slid her crab in front of her, she saw the young man clocking her daisy chain. She nodded and Nicole knew what he was thinking; that she and the big tattooed guy shared a common thread after all.

And we do.

The wine she'd drunk bubbled inside her. She could have sworn she saw the same brightness in Noah. And here they were, eating a nice meal in a nice restaurant, talking and smiling, ignoring the heat that would have them tearing their clothes off later. Nicole looked down at her daisy tattoo and dredged up some of Sam's courage. "There's something real between us, isn't there?"

Silence, but when she looked up, Noah nodded, his mouth tight.

"Can you... maybe say that? I'm sorry, it just feels like maybe you don't mean it."

Noah put down his knife and fork. "Nikki, if this goes places, you gotta know that..."

"You can't talk about personal stuff?"

He inclined his head.

"Why?"

"Million different reasons." He shook his head like he was getting rid of a cobweb. "Remember how you asked why I don't show my paintings?"

"Yes."

"This is the same thing. It's not that I don't want to, it's just..."

"Painful?"

Noah nodded.

"Okay." Nicole licked her lips, thinking around the dilemma. "But you've told me a little about your past. You've told me I'm beautiful."

"That's just facts."

"Shh, please be serious."

"I am," he said, picking up his cutlery. "I just don't know if I can say what you need."

Nicole picked up her own knife and fork and they ate for a while. Her crab was puffy and delicious. She'd eaten almost half when Noah spoke. "You seem happy."

She looked up to see he wasn't eating, just staring at his plate.

"I am."

Noah nodded slowly, then cleared his throat. "Anything to do with me?"

She felt like her heart was going to burst, because in that moment a stone-grey cloud rolled back and she could see it. A future between the two of them.

"Everything to do with you," she said. "You know what you make me feel?"

A raised brow.

"Steady."

The brow rose even higher.

"It's a good thing," she said, abandoning her knife and fork and reaching out to touch his hands. "For ages, as long as I can remember, I've been up and down and up and down all the time. I want everything to be perfect and I try so hard to make it that way, sometimes I feel like I'm about to collapse. But being with you never makes me feel like that. You make me feel like I have my feet on the ground." She laughed as she realised the contradiction in her words. "Not when I think about your past, but when I'm with you, here and now, I feel so steady."

Noah stared down at their hands. "That's a good thing?"

"Totally. If I was dizzy and stupidly nervous, I'd be sure it was just infatuation, but it feels like there's something else here. On my end anyway."

Self-conscious, she sat back, tucking her hands into her lap like she was interviewing for a dream job. And maybe she was.

Noah looked up, knocking her sideways with his strange, contradictory beauty. "You saying you're not infatuated with me?"

"No," she said primly. "I said it's more than that."

"Good." He picked up his knife and fork. "It's more than that for me, too. Eat your crab."

Nicole hesitated, wanting more reassurance and knowing it wasn't something she could or should ask for. She picked up a crab leg and crunched. "Control freak."

"You'll find out what makes me a control freak after."

Heat swirled through her and she chewed on autopilot, wondering if she'd be able to swallow another bite with so many butterflies in her stomach. She contemplated putting the rest in Tupperware, and if the crab would survive until Melbourne, when Noah pulled out his phone, swearing when he saw the name flashing up. Silver Daughters Ink.

"You got your phone on?" he asked.

She felt a stab of panic. "No, I turned it off so Tabby wouldn't track my phone. Why? Do you think Sam and Tabby know we're together?"

"Looks like it. I never get work calls this late." His forehead furrowed. "I've got a heap of messages; I didn't notice them coming in."

"From who?"

"Tabby. Paula." He swore under his breath again.

"What? What do they say?"

She knew she should keep her voice down but she had a bad feeling, and being drip-fed bad news wasn't helping.

"It looks like your ex called."

"Shit."

"Yeah and, uh…"

Noah's face took on a strange pallor, as though his human colouring was being sucked out with a straw. He stared down at his phone as though he couldn't believe his eyes.

"Noah?"

"We need to go," he said, standing up. "Right now."

One look at his eyes and she knew there was no question of staying. She'd be getting her crab to go after all. She stood up, thinking wildly of what could be wrong. "What happened? Is anyone hurt?"

"Yeah, Paula. My housemate. It's a long fucking—look, let's just go, okay?"

And he walked toward the register at the far end of the restaurant without another word, leaving Nicole in the dregs of what she'd thought would be a night to remember forever.

I'm pretty sure it will, a nervous Tabby told her.

Hold tight, Nix.

But for once the voice of her sisters wasn't the slightest bit comforting.

16

"Are you okay?"

He nodded curtly. "Yeah."

Frustration licked its way up Nicole's wrists. She didn't want to be demanding, but they'd been in the car for twenty minutes. He'd smoked two cigarettes and said exactly nothing. She wanted to switch on her phone and call *everyone* but would have felt patronizing, like asking a child to read a picture book, getting impatient when they struggled with words, and snatching it out of their hands so you could tell *them* about the rainbow fish. Still, she couldn't wait forever.

"Noah," she said in her best accountant voice. "What did the messages say?"

He shook his head. Not like he was saying no, but like he didn't know where to start. He wasn't speeding, but he was sitting right on the speed limit, his hand groping for his cigarettes.

"We can start small. Paula, your old housemate's involved?"

"Yeah."

"And Tabby and Sam met her?"

He stuck the smoke in his mouth and ignited. "Yup."

God, she wasn't seeing the connection on this one. "How and why is that a bad thing?"

"I don't know how to get it out, Nikki. It's a fuckin' mess."

"It's okay." She touched Noah's thigh. He tensed then relaxed or at least grew less stiff. She groped around for a change of subject. Something that would calm him down and reinforce the connection they had to one another. "You know how I didn't like you calling me Nikki at first?"

"Yeah?"

"That's because my mum used to call me Kitty. After she left, I made sure no one called me that anymore. I know 'Nikki' doesn't exactly sound like 'Kitty', but it's the same ballpark."

"I can stop."

She smiled at him. "No, I think it was just a reflex. Besides, my mum's been gone for twenty-two years. She doesn't have a right to nicknames."

She could feel him staring at her and fought the urge to say something conciliatory, the way she did whenever her friends asked about the mother-shaped hole in her life. Talking about Deborah DaSilva always filled her with the most uncomfortable rage. She wanted him to see it. To know she wasn't, *couldn't*, judge.

She met Noah's eyes, saw tension roiling below the surface. "Can you please tell me?"

His jaw tightened. "Paula went to Silver Daughters this afternoon, her and Shredder."

"What happened?"

"I don't know. She's got issues with drinking. Drugs. Tabby's text said she was pissed, screaming and making a scene." He sounded rough, torn open. "She told them about me. Told them everything."

"You mean The Rangers?"

"And that I've been locked up. And whatever the fuck else Paula decided to let loose." His cheeks looked grey beneath the stubble. "Tabby wasn't happy, and she said Sam's furious."

She squeezed his leg. "She'll get over it. She had to find out sometime. At least it's over, right?"

But he continued to stare blank-eyed at the road. Nicole listened as some of her most precious possessions sloshed around in the back of the van. She remembered her watch and Aaron's condom. Sleeping with Noah on her old bedroom floor. A floating sense of unreality washed over her. The day felt three long and two wide, and they were still seven hours from Melbourne. It wasn't close to being over.

"Where's Paula now?" When Noah didn't reply, she squeezed his leg. "Noah?"

"Dunno. That's why we needed to leave." An ugly smile twisted his mouth. "What are we gonna say about us?"

Nicole blinked at him. "Pardon?"

"Sam and Tabby know we've driven to Adelaide together."

"How?"

"Your ex called Tabby. Told her and Sam we fucked in his bedroom."

Nicole gasped. "How does he know about that? We didn't use... there wouldn't be any *evidence*."

A ghost of a smile. "Dunno, I'd imagine he had a conversation with your neighbour."

Of course, Mrs Harris had watched them kissing, seen her in Noah's t-shirt. Probably tripped over herself to tell Aaron. She covered her face, as though she could hide from her sisters and Aaron, what they now knew. "That gossipy b!"

"Yeah, genie's out of the bottle now. Tabby says Sam's pissed."

"But she isn't?"

Noah grimaced. "She was kinda hoping for something like this."

"What do you mean?"

He shifted uncomfortably in his seat. "She came up to me after you got dumped. Told me to... you know. Help you get over it."

Nicole felt like screaming. After her cathartic escape from Aaron's house and their dream dinner, she'd been on top of the world—all ready for a fresh start. But the night had taken on the momentum of a runaway train. "She told you to sleep with me?"

"Yeah. Said it'd get you to stop chasing your ex. But, Nikki, I swear that's not why I—"

"Please be quiet," she screeched. "I need to think about things!"

Nicole pressed her fingernails into her cheeks, denting her skin. It wasn't the worst thing in the world that her sisters knew about her and Noah—but it wasn't fair. They'd slept together twice and hadn't had a single real date. She was supposed to figure this out before Sam and Tabby could weigh in with their Muppet balcony opinions.

"Do you want kids?"

Her mind on seven different things, she didn't even think. "Of course."

"How many?"

"Three."

"All girls?"

"I don't mind, as long as they're all healt..." She stared at Noah. "Why?"

"Because I don't want them."

Nicole felt like toddler Tabby had sunk her fists into her stomach, the way she did when she used to feed her. "Why?"

He gave her a hard smile. "Because the world's fucked."

"But by that logic, no one should do anything."

He shook his head, the subtext clearly that she didn't have a clue.

"Shut up!" she said, though he hadn't spoken. "Are you just scared you're going to be like your dad?"

Noah's fake smile vanished. "Don't talk like you know me."

"Well I do!"

"Is that what you think?"

"Yes! I've seen you being nice to sad customers and playing with the puppies, and you looked after Sam when my dad left and slept on the visitors couch after Greg Sanderson tried to burn our house down."

"So?"

"So, you're a nice guy!" she snapped. "You're nice and you take care of people, and you don't have to be a dad if you don't want to, but if it's just because you're scared of being like your dad, then you're a big pussy!"

The word rang around the car like an echo. Noah laughed a short but undeniably authentic laugh. "You okay, Nikki?"

Not anymore. Now her heart was pounding, and her forehead was sweaty, and she didn't know where to look. She rubbed her palms on her skirt, her mouth slicking with saliva.

"Nicole?" Noah barked. "What's happening?"

I'm having a panic attack, you melon, she thought, but she couldn't say it. Panic was gathering like an acid ball in her stomach, and though she tried to stop it, the worst memory rose like a corpse. Crying in the doctor's office, alone because she couldn't tell Sam or her dad or anyone where she was, and the doctor's fake smile. *"You don't need to cry, it's common. Antibiotics'll clear it right up."*

"Really?" she'd asked between sobs.

"Unless there's permanent damage to your uterus. Then there can be complications with your fertility."

And then she'd cried and cried and cried because she'd always wanted to be a mother and now she wouldn't be, because of stupid, pointless sex with stupid, pointless Greyson, who licked her ears and couldn't make her come.

"You just need to be more careful," the doctor had said, rolling her eyes.

"But I am careful," she'd said. "I'm always, always careful. Always! I look after my little sister and I cook dinner and… and I was *school captain!*"

And then the doctor had laughed, a high giggle, and Nicole's walls had turned grey and collapsed in like molding papier-mâché. Noah's voice was like heavy waves crashing over her brain. Saying things she couldn't make out. She'd had unprotected sex with him. How could she have done that? Put herself at risk the same way, *worse* than the same way.

The van slowed and she heard the *tack, tack, tack* of the indicator coming on. She shook her head, remembering the hours they had left to travel. "We can't stop."

But they were already parked. Noah flicked the hazard lights on and took her hand. "Nikki."

The van swam back into focus. "Sorry."

"Don't be sorry. What's wrong?"

"I can't..." Her panic mixed with molten embarrassment and acid tears burned the backs of her eyes.

"You can. Say it."

And maybe it was the stress of the day, but she was suddenly, furiously sick of carrying the secret she'd kept locked inside her for nine years. "I had chlamydia when I was nineteen. My high school boyfriend, Greyson, gave it to me."

The silence burned like dry ice.

"He told me he was safe. He never got tested, though. I started feeling weird down there and I went to the doctors and they told me it was *that*. Then when I got upset, she was so, so mean to me. I can't believe how mean she was, and for no reason. I was just this terrified kid who'd only slept with two people."

"Nikki..."

"Please don't? I know this has nothing to do with right now, but sometimes I get stressed and then I think about it and I just... break a little."

A big hand smoothed over her hair. "Nikki, it's okay. STD's happen, they're not the end of the world."

Shame washed over her in a hot wave. "It shouldn't have happened! It was *disgusting*. And the way the doctor looked at me, like I was just the dirtiest girl."

"You're not dirty." He hesitated. "In that way. You can be dirty in the good ways."

She laughed, then felt utterly ridiculous. "I'm sorry about freaking out. Like we don't have enough to deal with."

"It's okay." He rubbed a thumb over her cheek. "Is this because of what we did together?"

"Probably. I shouldn't have told you to do it without a condom. I'm never that reckless. I never do anything wrong."

A soft laugh. "Maybe that's part of the problem. You never let yourself have any fun and then it all builds up and you binge."

"Maybe," she sniffed. "Sorry for freaking out."

"Stop saying sorry. You don't have anything to be sorry about. And I promise, to the best of my knowledge, I'm clean. I always use condoms."

It should have been reassuring, but it just reminded her of all the other lovers he'd had, women who weren't so childishly paranoid about sex. She yawned, wanting nothing more than to curl up and sleep forever.

"Have you ever talked to anyone about this, Nikki? Your dad? Your sisters?"

She shook her head.

"It must have eaten you alive."

It had. She'd stayed up late for weeks, months, crying and making promises. A month later, a different, nicer doctor said she was clean, but the damage had been done. She'd had nightmares, felt phantom itches, froze with terror whenever Greyson went down on her. And there was Sam and Tabby, dating and sleeping with strangers and giggling about sex like it didn't have terrifying consequences. Like it was just *fun*.

"I was so lonely," she told Noah. "And I knew Sam and Tabby would have supported me, but I was just so mad at them for not getting something when I did. When they slept with a million more people than me. I couldn't say anything."

"Is that why you went to Adelaide?"

She went to say 'no', but the word caught in her throat. She remembered what she'd said to Noah, a million years ago this morning, *'I've never run away from home before.'* She snorted.

"What?"

"Just thinking about what a hypocrite I am." She swiped a wrist across her eyes. "We should get going. Get back to Melbourne and sort everything out."

"That can wait until you're feeling better."

"I'm fine!" She scrubbed her face with her palms. "Sorry, I think I've cried in front of you more than I've ever cried in front of anyone."

"Stop fuckin' saying sorry."

"Or what?"

Noah leaned in, his smell and his hardness so close, it made her dizzy. He kissed her, lightly, sweetly, then sat back, jerking his thumb behind him. "Get in there."

"What?"

He turned off the engine, opened his door and climbed out. Nicole scrambled after him. He was standing at the back of the van, shoving boxes out of the way.

"What are you doing?"

He seized her by the waist and laid her down in the back of the van, on top of what felt and smelt like a beach towel. "Noah!"

He climbed in after her, his weight shifting the van downward. "Pull your dress up."

"What?"

He made an impatient sound and gripped the hem of her silvery stretchy dress.

"Noah, are you trying to *have sex with me*? By the side of the road? In a van?"

"Nope."

"Then wh—"

"I'm gonna eat your pussy."

"No!" She pressed her hands to her thighs, holding the dress down. "Noah, that's my worst fear, that's my biggest trigger, a guy putting his mouth there. I don't—"

"Too fuckin' bad. I want it."

"I know what you're doing, but I don't want to play 'bad man' right now. What if someone sees?"

"The windows are tinted, and even if they pull over, you can just yank your dress back down. You're telling me you haven't thought about it? Me, making you come like that?"

"Yes, but—"

He gripped her hips and hauled her back down toward him. "You want to make this hard, Nikki?"

"What would that involve?"

In an instant she was lifted, turned and placed on his thighs. He hauled up the hem of her dress and laid a swift, blistering slap on her ass.

"Oww!"

"You gonna let me eat you out?"

"It's too gross!"

He spanked her again. "You're fuckin' crazy."

"Oh, that's original, calling a woman—oww!" She was angry, but she was also laughing, hysterically, yes *crazily*. It felt so hot it was almost too much, but it felt good. Cathartic.

"You're. Fucking. Gorgeous." He spanked her after every word. "Anyone'd. Want to. Eat you. Out. Get it through. Your. Head."

Nicole gasped. The pain was sharper now, flicking between her ass cheeks, heating her. She could picture it now, his mouth on her clit, making her melt into him. "Noah?"

"You want it now?"

She nodded.

"Good." He turned her onto her back and knelt down, burying his face between her legs. She screamed, the sensation so sharp that it almost hurt. Then he licked her and everything went butter-soft and hazy. God, it wasn't sharp at all, it was *amazing*.

"Noah..."

He removed his face from between her legs. Even in the darkness, she could tell he was smug. "Like it?"

She gripped his head and pressed it back down.

He laughed as he went back to work, flicking and stroking and making her pulse like a strobe light. She'd had this before, but it had hurt. Noah just touched her, warm and wet and lovely. Her midriff tightened. God, it was happening already. She was going to finish so quickly. She felt herself tip up, squeezing exquisitely as Noah's tongue ran the length of her pussy. Then a thought came.

She was sitting in the doctor's office, crying and itching and wanting to die. That was her body; that was her, dirty, dirty, dirty. She squeezed her eyes shut, feeling the shame anew, Noah's tongue like an eel against her labia. Then the memory shifted, went sideways. Noah burst into the room, big and covered in tats and smelling of smoke. He stood between her and the doctor, glowering at the shocked-looking woman.

"There's no need to act like that," he told the doctor. "She's just a kid. She's done nothing wrong."

He turned to her then, held out a big hand. "Come on, Nikki."

And he led her from the doctor's office. He'd taken her to get her antibiotics and ice cream. Then he'd kissed her and told her that the two weeks they had to wait until she could have sex would be like foreplay, because it was no big deal.

Nicole snapped back into the present, her thighs tight around Noah's head. The pleasure was rushing through her, rising like a tide. It didn't so much circumvent her panic, as rush over it, like a wave crushing a sandcastle. Sex was complicated, but it was wonderful. She moaned, her head banging back against the bottom of the van. "Noah!"

He continued to lap, even softer than before so that her body shuddered. "You like that, baby?"

"Yes." A car rushed past, so fast and close that it rocked the van. Nicole smiled. "I can't believe that just happened."

He sat up then lay beside her, not touching, but close. They lay there a while, her heart racing, her skin prickling with goosebumps in the cooling air.

"That was nice."

He made an affirmative grunting noise, his arm wrapping around her.

"Can I... do anything for you?"

"Nah, I'm good."

"I like the way you touch me." She could hear the delicate note in her voice. Like wind chimes. Only she didn't know why it was there. Was she hopeful or trying to put distance between them? She had no idea, only that she needed him to say something. But he stayed quiet. Separate.

That's how he is, she reminded herself.

She remembered imagining he'd come into the doctor's and rescued her. Her face went hot as fire. What right did she have to lean on him like that, even in her memories? She thought of the stresses they had waiting for them at home and a jolt of panic hit her, making her insides churn. "Should we get going?"

"Probably."

She felt what he was about to say before he said it, a burst of adrenaline in her mouth, a tightening of her leg muscles.

"You're something else, Nikki. You're lovely."

The rough sincerity in his voice only made it worse.

"But?"

"But, I'm not the guy."

"What does that mean?"

"I'm not the guy you marry and have three kids with."

Her chest splintered just a little. In the quiet of the van, Nicole could almost believe she'd heard it happen. "Does that mean we shouldn't sleep together anymore?"

A soft, strained laugh. "You're gonna have to fill me in on that one."

"Why?"

A beat.

"Because I'll have you for as long as you'll have me. But this isn't going to be more than what it is now."

Another hairline fracture, the splitting of something delicate and lovely that lived deep inside her and between them both. "What is it now?"

There was a silence, and she must have developed a sixth sense for Noah's silences because this one was slippery and cold-blooded as a snake. She couldn't stand it.

"Can you please take me home?"

He was silent a second, maybe surprised, maybe just thinking. Then he sat up. "Of course."

17

It was three in the morning when they reached Brunswick. Noah's eyes burned and his back ached, but he wasn't tired. He'd been chain smoking, but the adrenaline would have been enough on his own. He'd tried to call Paula on their last petrol stop, but she'd hung up on him. He couldn't stop himself from imagining his house destroyed, burned down, overrun with scumbags. Beside him, Nicole sat bolt upright, her eyes glassy.

"Almost there," he said, and she nodded like a porcelain doll come to life.

They pulled up outside Silver Daughters and he saw the studio lights were on. His stomach contracted. He'd expected Sam and Tabby would have gone to bed by now. Nicole unbuckled her belt, a dreamy look on her face. She drifted out of the van and toward the door of the studio like a sleepwalker. Noah watched her go, wanting to reverse and head to his place and knowing that'd only make things worse. He reached for his cigarettes and remembered he'd smoked the last an hour ago.

"Fuck it." He pushed open the driver side door and followed Nicole into Silver Daughters. The tiger doorbell roared as he stepped inside the familiar building, but he couldn't see Nicole, only a grim-faced Tabby, looking unusually washed out in an oversized white hoodie.

"Where's…?"

"Nicole? In bed. Stay here, Sam's coming."

It was strange how different she looked when she wasn't smiling, her heart-shaped face appeared older and—he felt stupid for thinking it—mean. There was something strange in her face, neither Edgar, nor the twins. Her mother, maybe, that mysterious, reckless woman he'd never met.

He heard footsteps overhead and guessed it was Nicole in her high heels, getting ready for bed. He remembered how she'd looked sitting across from him in the restaurant and his insides ached. Still, he was glad she wasn't going to be here for this. That she'd get some sleep.

The door at the back of the studio creaked open and the six half-spaniel puppies burst in. They rushed around his heels in a black and gold surge. He bent down to pet them, and Lilah latched onto his finger. She was his favourite, cuddly and mischievous and in total awe of Nicole. He stroked her soft head as Sam's battered Doc Martens entered his line of vision.

"Hey, Noah."

If Tabby looked mean, Sam looked off balance. She was pale and her eyes were red-rimmed and puffy. Noah wouldn't have thought he could feel more like a shit-heel, but he did. "Sammy…"

She shook her head. "I can't believe everything that's happened tonight."

"I'm sorry about Paula. Did she do any damage?"

To his shock, Sam's eyes filled with tears. "I wish she had. That would have been easier to deal with."

"What do you mean?"

Tabby glared at him. "Are you serious right now?"

Yes? No? Noah gritted his teeth. "Look, I'm half dead from driving, and after everything that went down, I don't get what the problem actually is. What's wrong?"

Sam looked to Tabby—a bad sign. Noah had never known her to defer power like that.

Tabby straightened up. "Okay, so here's what happened—we're at work, minding our own business, wondering where Nicole is but not *super* worried. Then I take a call from Aaron, who's giving birth to the world's biggest cow because his neighbour said some tattooed guy had sex with his fiancée on his bedroom floor."

"Ex-fiancée."

For the briefest moment it looked like Tabby might smile, but the light in her eyes vanished as soon as it came. "Ex-fiancé. Anyway, I hung up, a bit pissed you and Nix snuck off without telling us, but whatever. Then this woman comes in reeking of Aldi vodka and demanding to see Sam."

Noah looked at Sam, who nodded. "She was a mess, drunk. And this guy was waiting for her out front; he was fucking scary."

Shredder. Noah shook his head. "I'm sorry."

"For what?" Tabby asked in a mock jovial tone. "Siccing your crazy roommate on us, or never mentioning that thing where you're a bikie who's done time for assault?"

"I'm not in The Rangers anymore."

"But you used to be? And you've been to jail? And your dad's Harry Newcomb, the bail-jumping psychopath murderer?"

He felt anger hardening his features and took a deep breath, trying to keep his temper under control. This was his fault; he'd kept the information from them and now he was paying the price. "Yeah."

Sam shook her head. "Why didn't you tell me? I've known you for *years*."

"Your dad knew."

Sam and Tabby exchanged glances.

"Dad knew everything?" Sam demanded. "Your father and jail and everything?"

He could hear the hurt in her voice, the betrayal. "I didn't mean to tell him. The way we met, it was just... relevant."

"You met at the pub," Sam said. "Dad asked you about your tattoos and you had a few drinks and he offered you a job."

That was the story. The one Edgar had told her after she got home from the tattooing expo in Vegas to find him taking up tattoo room two.

"Yeah, that's not exactly how it happened."

Sam's face fell. "What do you mean?"

"What I said."

Tabby's eyes narrowed. "Oh, fuck this."

She walked around the register so she was standing in front of him and poked him in the stomach. "You need to be forth-fucking-coming from here on out, or we'll call the cops."

As always, the word 'cops' made his sac tighten. Didn't matter that it had been years since he'd done something arrest-worthy. "Why the fuck would you call the cops?"

Tabby set her jaw like a Hollywood tough guy. "Paula told us you owed her money. Actually, she said you owed some guy called 'Shredder' money."

Jesus, those amoral assholes. "She's lying. I don't owe him or anyone else shit."

"That's not what Paula said. She said you were in for about twenty grand. Something about your 'education?' What was that? Filing off your fingerprints and giving you an illegal firearm so you could rob petrol stations?"

Noah's brain throbbed. "They mean training me to tattoo when I was a kid, but—"

"You learned to ink with The Rangers?" Sam interrupted. She looked horrified and he knew why. To her, tattooing was an expression of love, creativity, *good*. He was sure that to her, learning the trade by drilling patches on the backs and arms of bikies was sacrilege. But what could he say? No, he hadn't?

"Yeah, I did, but that wasn't my choice."

He could see neither sister believed him. Why would they? Yesterday he'd been their mate and today he was an ex-con with a murderous bikie for a dad.

"So, Paula," Tabby said. "We tried to calm her down while we called you, but you and Nix weren't picking up."

Because they'd been on their way to that fancy restaurant. It felt like another life now, Nicole beaming across from him in her pretty dress...

"And when we told her you weren't answering, she freaked out again and started yelling about how if she didn't get her money from you, she was gonna get it off us because she'd heard we almost got our place burned down and she knew people who'd do it properly."

Sam let out a low animal moan and he wanted to sink through the floor. He kept thinking this situation couldn't get any worse, but it seemed bottomless.

He held up his hands. "I know this sounds cheap, but I don't think she meant it. She was drunk, and she and Shredder don't have any pull around here. But if you want to call the cops, you can. Call them right now."

"I don't think you want us to call the cops, man." Tabby's voice could have cut steel.

"Why?"

"Because after Paula left, I had a brainwave. I went into Dad's office and looked over Nix's spreadsheets."

"And?"

"Nix guessed we'd lost around fifty thousand in the past eighteen months, but she couldn't see where the money had gone. All our supplies are invoiced, all our client payments checked out. She was starting to think Dad took the money."

"He didn't."

Tabby gave him an icy smile. "Glad we agree."

"So, what did you find?" he asked. He knew he should sit back, let her talk in her own time, but the sooner she got it out, the sooner he could prove he had nothing to do with whatever she'd decided he was guilty of.

"I found that you're the person who's been stealing from us."

"How?"

Bad idea, asking a question. He should have just said no, but he was so fucking confused. Sam and Tabby looked at him like he'd crawled out a drain.

Tabby gestured to the cash register. "You've been taking cash out of the till, then fiddling with your hours on BackBooks so the daily totals add up."

Noah's heart contracted. How could she think that? He barely knew how to use BackBooks—the online client roster, at the best of times. "I haven't."

"No? Then why does BackBooks show you've been logging in at the end of the day and reducing your hours?"

"Why the fuck would I do that?"

"I already told you," Tabby snarled. "You've been taking cash out of the fucking till. If you didn't bump off a couple hours, we'd notice the money was missing right away."

"How would that work? BackBooks doesn't handle the money, I'd just be making myself look like shit!"

"No, because you figured out BackBooks data doesn't affect the payroll system. You must have been pissed when Nix updated the software and fucked up your little racket. Is that why you fucked her when you said you wouldn't? To figure out if she was onto you?"

Noah's head was swimming. "I've never stolen a fuckin' cent from this place! And you *wanted* me to hook up with Nicole."

"What?"

Tabby ignored Sam. "That was before I knew you were a fucking bikie. How do you not see how guilty you look? Paula says you owe money; we've been missing money. You don't want to fuck Nicole, she puts in a new pay system that undercuts your scam and suddenly you're trying to isolate her. Take her interstate without any of us knowing about it."

"That's not... that's a fuckin' coincidence!"

Tabby laughed, a high, slightly hysterical laugh. "Well, isn't that a coincidence! I thought it was fucking dodgy that you didn't have social media, but I thought, 'Oh, well, Dad trusts him, Sam trusts him, he probably isn't a dodgy cunt.' And this whole time you've been lying to us. Stealing from us."

"I haven't!"

"You haven't been lying to us?"

"No," he said and realised that was a lie.

"You don't even see what a shitbag you are. Get the fuck out of here before I sic the cops on you."

Noah felt like he was wearing a mask. That neither Sam nor Tabby could see him anymore. He stepped forward, wanting them to see him, and Sam wrapped a protective arm over her sister's shoulder. Dragged her backward. His stomach dropped. She was scared of him. Sam, his old friend, the closest thing he had to a sister, was wearing the 'don't frighten the bikie' look. "Sammy, you know me. You know I wouldn't—"

"Please go."

"But—"

"I mean it, please just go. We can talk about this later or something. Just go."

Noah looked upstairs. Nicole was up there, could he wake her up and have her explain... what? That he'd gone down on her in his van? Told her he'd never be able to give her what she needed?

He shook his head, confused by how years of stability, steady employment, keeping to himself had gone to shit. He looked at Sam until she met his gaze. "I haven't been stealing from you and your dad."

She closed her eyes. "Just go."

"But when... when can I come back?"

He sounded pathetic, like a little kid dropped off at the supermarket while his mum bought a bag of meth, but Silver Daughters was his home. Surely Sam understood that?

Tabby pulled away from her big sister. "We don't know what to do. We're going to look over the finances with Nix tomorrow. We'll call you when we decide if we should go to the cops."

He saw the resignation on Sam's face and it was like a thunderbolt struck him. "You're gonna fire me?"

Sam nodded, fresh tears filling her eyes. Tabby's face was stonier than ever. "Are you going to make this hard for Nix?"

He looked upstairs to where Nicole was no doubt sleeping off their insanely long day, tucked up like a fairy tale princess, long black hair on pink pillows. "Nah."

"You mean it?"

The roaring in his head was so loud it was like he had seashells clapped over his ears. "We all know I'm not good enough for her."

Sam opened her mouth and snapped it closed. He knew she'd been about to say some reflexive friend thing about how he was good enough. Suddenly the backs of his eyes were hot and tight as the hood of a car. Fucking hell. He refused to blink, letting his eyeballs burn. He pulled his keys from his pocket and walked to the register. Sam and Tabby walked backward, like he was carrying a force field that repelled people. His chest tight, he slapped the keys on the counter.

"Hold onto these. Nikki's stuff is still in the back, anyway."

Sam frowned. "How will you get home?"

Noah was suddenly exhausted, wrung out like an old sponge. This had been the longest twenty-four hours of his life and he wasn't even done spilling his guts. "I live a couple of streets over."

The hurt in her eyes was lemon juice in every one of his self-inflicted wounds. "Sorry. About that, and everything else."

And he left before he could fuck up anything else.

Outside, the air was warm and close. He felt dirty; his mouth thick. He headed for home, aware that Paula and Shredder could be waiting and unable to give a single fuck. As he walked, he thought about the night he'd met Edgar.

He'd told himself he'd gone to Melbourne to drink and see old mates, but if he took a step backward, another motive became clear. He hadn't tattooed in weeks, hadn't painted or sketched. He kept picking up his phone, his thumb hovering over his dad's number, over Shredder's number, Magger's number. He was talking himself back into it. The life. He'd been in the city for a week when it rained in a way that felt like the sky had opened. He'd gone to the pub and drank until he was pushed out into the slippery darkness. Getting kicked out wasn't a problem... until he realised he'd lost his wallet and phone. Head full of hard music, he walked in the direction of nothing, seeing spirals. Then his foot connected with a jutting footpath crack and he slipped over, bashing his head. It didn't hurt, but when he touched his face, black blood mixed in with the rainwater. He sat on the wet asphalt, waiting for something. Anything.

To this day he had no idea what Edgar was doing on the street in the early hours of the morning—collecting mushrooms? Dancing in the rain? He just seemed to appear in his leather hat and jeans, smiling at him in that calm, sad way. "Need a hand?"

He did. So, Noah had let him hoist him to his feet with hands that were surprisingly strong for such a slim guy.

Edgar pointed to his left shoulder. "That a Persian manticore?"

"Mmm," he said, trying not to sound like a fuckin' mess.

Then Ed had looked him over, as though he was seeing him for the first time. "You tattoo."

It wasn't a question, which didn't make any sense. Noah stared at him, wondering if he was a hallucination brought on by weeks of running his willpower down to zero. "Used t'tattoo. Not'ne'more. Not frages."

"But you're still an artist."

Another not-question. Noah had frowned, his face so heavy it felt like it had been set in cement. "Who are you?"

"Edgar DaSilva. I own a studio over the way."

He held out his hand and Noah shook it, his head sick and spinning, half convinced the man was an illusion. "A tattoo studio?"

"Yes."

"Coincidence."

Edgar had smiled. "I don't believe in coincidences. Want a coffee?"

Noah had followed Edgar back to his place, climbing the back stairs with one hand hard on the rail. His head was throbbing, his mouth tasted like bile. The house was a neat little box full of wood firelight and polished copper wind chimes. And colours. Periwinkle curtains, forest green rugs, fuchsia cushions, and sorbet yellow lampshades. He turned on the spot, staring at the colours like he'd never seen them before, because that's how it felt.

"My daughters," Edgar said, holding up a silver-framed photo.

Noah had struggled to get his drunk eyes to focus on the picture. Eventually, his vision cleared, and he saw three black-haired girls in school uniforms.

"What're their names?"

"Samantha, Tabitha, and Nicole."

"Nicole'za good name," he said, because it was. There was a girl in a book called that, or maybe it was a movie?

Edgar pointed at the girl on the far right. "Samantha's in Las Vegas at a convention. Tabby's doing... something in Johannesburg, and Nicole's in Adelaide. She works in finance."

Noah stared at pretty Nicole. Her bright blue eyes made him feel woozy. "Can I sit down?"

"Of course. I'll get you a coffee and we can have a chat."

"No," he tried to say, but the tenderness in Edgar's voice slipped between his ribs like a knife. He didn't remember the next few hours of conversation, but they must have talked, and he must have said a lot because when he woke on the couch the next morning, Ed knew his name, his heritage, and his whole family history.

"Sorry," Noah said.

"Nothing to be sorry for, mate."

Over a breakfast of bacon and blistering black coffee, Edgar offered him a job in his studio. "Part-time at first, trial basis and everything, but if you're as good as you look, we'll put you on full time."

"You don't want that," Noah told him. "I don't want that. I need to head back to Sydney."

Edgar put down his ceramic mug. "You don't need to head anywhere. We both know what you'll do if you go back to Sydney. Choose something else."

"Why?"

"Because you've got the rest of existence to be dead," Edgar said calmly. "Wake the fuck up and be alive."

Something about that got him, like a bullet from a sniper's gun. He'd cried, sharp and sudden, like a little kid. It was humiliating, but it tore down the last of his resistance. He accepted Edgar's hankie and took the job.

He thought it'd be a disaster, but it wasn't. With the machine in his hand, easing ink under skin, he felt like he'd come home. He met Sam and they got along. When she looked at him, she didn't see a criminal, just a guy with tattoos who didn't like talking. That was Edgar's magic, his protection. He'd built something in Melbourne these last five years and now it was crumbling around him.

"Fuck," he muttered, patting his pockets for cigarettes that weren't there. "Fuck, fuck, fuck."

When he reached his street, he could see his front door was wide open. Paula and Shredder. Question was, were they still there? The answer was no. What was there was a complete annihilation. The inside of his house made the mess Nicole's ex had left look like a couple of chocolate wrappers. The dining table was broken. The couches turned over and the cushions slashed. The legs of every chair he owned were splintered and every glass, jar, cup, and plate had been smashed. But none of that mattered, what mattered were that his paintings, every last one, had been stacked into the fireplace and set on fire.

18

Nicole woke with a dry mouth and a bad feeling. She blinked, trying to get her thoughts in order. Her dreams had been strange; Noah in black robes urging her onto her knees to confess her sins. Weird sex stuff had ensued. She held up her wrist to check the time and at the sight of her bare wrist, it all came flooding back—Noah, the van, their round trip from Adelaide, coming home so tired, she could barely walk. She sat bolt upright, listening hard. She could hear people talking. Sam and a guy. Noah? She pulled her pink Adidas shorts over her still damp underwear and headed for the kitchen. She was near the doorway when her heart dropped. The man talking wasn't Noah, it was Gil. "You need to go to the cops. I'll call them if you want. He can't get away with this."

Nicole stepped into the morning sunshine. "Who can't get away with what?"

Sam and Gil exchanged glances.

"Does she know?" Gil asked.

"Know what?" Nicole said. "What's going on? Where's Tabby? Where's Noah?"

"I... just... come here." Sam stood and steered her toward the dining table. "Do you want a cup of tea?"

"I want to know what's going on. Why do we need to call the cops?"

There was a loaded silence.

"What?" Nicole snapped. "Is this about Noah's housemate? Because I think we should give him a chance to deal with the situation before we go running to the cops."

It felt weird to be arguing *against* going to the police. All her life, *she* was the one who wanted to call the law when things went wrong, while Sam shouted about police corruption and Tabby hid whatever drugs she had on hand. Sam rubbed her lower lip. "Nix, I know you and Noah have a thing going, but there's something you don't—"

"What?" Gil laughed. "You've been fucking Noah?"

Both she and Sam glared at him. Gil mock-shivered. "Twin chills."

Nicole didn't have time for this. "Is this about Noah being an ex-bikie? Because I know you must be upset that he didn't tell you, but that's no reason—"

"It's not that," Sam interrupted. "He's been stealing money. That's how we got so deep in the hole before you showed up."

Nicole felt like she had a paper jam in her brain. "What? How do you know that?"

She hated Sam's look of sympathy, as though she was about to say something that would break her heart. "Noah's been reducing his hours on the computer and stealing cash out of the till."

"No, he hasn't!" She wasn't defending Noah out of loyalty. The idea of him grifting from the till was as ridiculous as if Sam said he'd killed someone with a candlestick.

Her twin's moo-cow look of compassion didn't budge. "Tabby's got a better read on the facts than I do, but his login's been used almost every night around closing time to change his hours. And Gil was saying he's always telling clients to pay cash if they can."

Gil nodded vigorously. "I swear I've seen him lurking by the till after hours. Sam needs to sack him. Call him up and tell him to stay away before he rallies his bikie mates and breaks in or something."

Nicole scowled at him. "Is there a gas leak in here? Noah wouldn't do that. He wouldn't do anything like what you're saying."

"Don't blame yourself for not spotting it," Sam said, missing the point. "It was easy for Tabby to find proof because she had an idea of what to look for."

"Because Noah's a criminal," Gil added. "He's been to jail. Plus, that Paula bird told Sam he owed her money."

"No, he doesn't," Nicole said, feeling like a broken record. "He gave Paula a place to stay while she was trying to leave The Rangers. Now she's back with her ex, who's the Sergeant at Arms. Are you going to believe her over Noah? The guy you've worked with for years?"

Gil leaned on the back of a chair. He had sweat circles under his arms. "That's what he told you. Face it, none of us knows what he's like, Nikki."

"I did! And don't call me Nikki!"

Gil took a panicky step backward. "Sorry. Jesus."

Sam walked over, rubbed a circle on her back. "Hey, calm down, okay? I know this is hard—"

"It's not hard! You're not listening!"

She remembered the words spray-painted on Noah's door. *Dog cunt.* He'd said she wouldn't understand, and she hadn't. She hadn't understood that in telling Sam and Gil and the rest of them that he was an ex-bikie, he'd have friends—people who'd known him for years—so ready to believe he was scum.

She shrugged off her sister's hand, stepped back so she could look at her and Gil. "Noah became a Ranger because his dad ran the club, but he *left* on his own, way before he met any of us. Why would he throw in a life of crime just to steal out of our cash register?"

Sam's face tightened. "Why don't you ask him? He's the one who lied to us."

"He didn't lie! He just didn't tell the truth, and with the way you lot are all carrying on, can you blame him?"

She knew she sounded shrill and accusing, and doing so was undermining her credibility, but she didn't care. Noah wasn't a dog c-word and he wasn't a thief, and she was going to yell at her sister until she believed it.

"Okay, Nix." Sam's cheeks were red, a dangerous sign. "So, he shouldn't have told me he's an ex-bikie with a record? Even when I became his boss?"

"If you'll remember, *I* told you I thought he'd been to jail the moment I met him. He's got a spider web tattoo."

"So?"

"So, you're not an idiot. You knew he looked dodgy and he wouldn't tell you where he lived or talk about his past, and you just rolled with it. Now you're acting all... *butthurt* because, wow, shocking news, he's got a history and he used to be dodgy. Like geez, what a twist? Who could have known?"

Her twin's jaw jutted, and Nicole balled her hands into fists. She and Sam rarely fought, but when they did, it was always a knockdown, drag 'em out. If Sam went for her hair, she was going to knee her right in the groin.

"I might go!" Gil said, backing away from the dining table as though it might burst into flame.

As though on cue, Tabby burst into the room, her blue eyes shining. "Are we having a fight about Noah?"

"No," Sam hissed.

"Yes, but you don't need to be so excited about it," Nicole snapped.

"Woot!" Tabby pulled off her olive-green army jacket. "Let's air some emotional wounds! Springer style!"

Gil practically ran to the door. "I'll be downstairs if you need me!"

Tabby raised her fists, posing like a 1920s boxer. "So where are we at, accusation-wise?"

"Go away," Nicole said.

"Don't tell her to go away, she can stay if she wants," Sam snarled. "I can't believe you fucked Noah. You fucked him and now you're trying to defend him even though he's been stealing from us. You don't even know him!"

Nicole forced a laugh because she knew it would drive her twin batshit. "So, this is about who knows Noah better, is it?"

"That's not my point!"

"You're getting angry like that's your point," Tabby piped in.

"Shut up," Sam snarled.

"Don't tell her to shut up." Nicole turned to Tabby. "You're such a shit-stirrer, why can't you just butt out?"

Tabby raised her hands. "I'm just trying to help! Money stuff aside, I don't care that you fucked Noah."

"Of course you don't! According to him, you took him aside and told him to seduce me."

Tabby scowled. "I have never used the word 'seduce' in my life and you know it. Anyway, what's your point? You saying you didn't like it?"

A hot ringing in her ears. She ran toward Tabby, intending to push her, punch her; make her take it back, but her sister ran away, cackling.

"What the hell?" Sam screamed. "Who *are* you fuckin' people?"

"Your sisters," Tabby said cheerfully. "Why are you so cut about Nix banging Noah? It was always going to happen. They have more chemistry than… somewhere with a lot of microscopes."

Sam bared her teeth.

"A high school science wing! Anyway, if I'd known Noah had that much bad boy cred, I wouldn't have made it happen. Fucking a bikie is taking it a bit far."

"He's not a bikie," Nicole snapped, lunging for her. "And you didn't make it happen."

"I sort of did," Tabby said, dancing away. "And you have to admit, Paula showing up here with a Sergeant at Arms, asking for money means Noah's probably still tapped into the dodgy bikie scene."

"'Probably' isn't evidence," Nicole snapped. "He's known Paula for a long time. He was trying to give her a second chance outside The Rangers, like the one Dad gave him."

Tabby's brow wrinkled. "Dad?"

"Yes. Dad knew about Noah being in The Rangers."

"I know," Tabby said. "Noah told us last night."

Nicole gaped at her. "And you didn't stop to think that maybe that's more evidence that he's not a petty criminal, and using his computer login isn't the smoking gun you think it is? Unless you've found more compelling evidence to back up your stupid accusation?"

Tabby looked up at the ceiling. "Well..."

Sam pounded her fist into her palm. "Can we shut the fuck up about the money for a few seconds and discuss why Noah didn't tell me he's been to jail?"

Nicole rounded on her, theatrically rolling her eyes. "Why didn't you ask? He would have told you if you did. Except you didn't ask, because you were happy living in ignorance."

"I wasn't!"

"You were. You've got this thing where you don't want to dig up anyone else's dirty little past because then they might go digging up yours."

Tabby gave a loud fake gasp. "Ooh savage call! Absolute savage!"

Sam's face contorted in rage. "You're so fucking perfect, aren't you, Miss Clenched Asshole?"

"My butthole is relaxed, thanks."

"Like fuck it is. Where do you get off judging me when your life is a museum?"

"What's that suppo—"

"Aaron. The house. The watch. The way you mince around panicking about what everyone thinks about you all the time. You're a conservative think-tanks idea of a sex robot."

Nicole faked a laugh. "Oh, nice! Did you steal that one from John Oliver?"

Sam's upper lip curled—she hated being accused of inauthenticity. That was the thing about sisters, about family; you knew the make and model of all their buttons.

"Okay, how's this for a call. I know about your tattoo."

Nicole was genuinely nonplussed. "What?"

"Your tattoo. I know you want it lasered off. I saw your search history."

Tabby's gasp was real as the rising sun. "Nix, you're not! You *can't*. What would Dad say?"

Buttons, Nicole thought. *Family know where all the buttons are.* "I'm not getting the daisy chain off."

"So, someone else went to your laser consultation, did they?" Sam snarled. "I called, you know, pretended to be you. You went in this week."

"But I haven't booked in for the laser!"

"You will," Sam said. "You don't want it. You never wanted it."

"Yes, I did!" Nicole looked at Tabby and saw she was crying. Her own eyes filled with tears. "It's just a lot, sometimes. Tabby, *please don't cry.*"

She moved toward her baby sister to hug her, but Sam stepped into her path. "You might as well get rid of it. Not like it means anything to you, Little Miss Perfect."

"Of course, it means something! And I'm not perfect."

Sam laughed. Even Tabby smiled through her tears.

"You are perfect," Sam said, and she didn't even sound that angry anymore. Just amused. Just smug. "You're a Barbie gone wrong. Banging Noah's the spiciest thing you've ever done."

Anger popped in Nicole's ears like firecrackers. She rushed forward and pushed her twin in the chest. "Fuck you."

As always, saying the f-word felt strange, slippery and exhilarating. Sam gaped at her.

"That's right! Fuck you. Fuck both of you. You have no idea what I'm like. I let you talk in my head, and you don't even have the slightest idea. Noah has a better idea than you. Noah treats me like I'm a real person, and my own fucking twin doesn't!"

She tried to shove Sam again, but her twin grabbed her arms. "What are you talking about?"

Nicole struggled to get free. "I'm not Little Miss Perfect. I had chlamydia. I had an STD. I had a dirty vagina, and I'm not. Fucking. Perfect!"

Silence. Outside a bird chirruped and traffic roared. Nicole pressed her hands to her cheeks, feeling a near-religious sense of relief. It wasn't enjoyable, but it was something. She felt like she might keel over from how *something* it was.

"When... when was this?" Sam whispered.

"When I was nineteen."

"And who...?"

"Greyson. He gave it to me."

Her twin's mouth fell open. "That long ago? When you were still at home? Oh, Nix..."

Sam took a step toward her, but it was her turn to back away. "Don't you fucking 'Nix' me after what you just said."

She'd wanted Sam to look hurt or contrite, but her face crumbled like a sandcastle. Big tears welled in her eyes. To her left, Tabby was white as a ghost. "Why didn't you say anything?"

"I don't know." Nicole took a steadying breath. "Actually, it was because you both act like I'm boring and perfect. You always have. And whenever I do anything that isn't boring and perfect, you make fun of me. Like I'm not allowed to exist outside the idea you have of me."

She looked from Tabby to her twin. "You always call me when things are wrong, expecting me to fix your problems, but you want to make fun of me, too. You want to tease me because you're so bad and I'm so good and it wasn't until I met Noah—"

Just saying his name made her heart convulse. She shook her head, unable to finish the thought. "I'm not who you think I am. I wish I was, but I'm not. Sorry. But also, fuck you."

"Nix..." Sam extended a hand, but Nicole took a step back.

"I'm going downstairs to find out what happened to the money. If anyone comes near Dad's office in the next ten hours, I'll freak the fuck out."

And she turned on her heel and left.

SAM HAD A POINT. Not about her being Little Miss Perfect, but that it was easier to track the loss of income when you knew what to look for. She scanned the cash deposits Silver Daughters Ink had made at the bank for the past three years. Eighteen months ago, there was a noticeable decline. About six hundred less per week. When she checked BackBooks, their staff register, this was indeed the time Noah's login was used to shave hours off his weekly work roster. And this had indeed thrown off the studio's totals, concealing the wads of cash that were vanishing from the till.

Neat. Not particularly clever, but neat.

So who in the f-word had done it?

Sam and Gil thought she was being naïve, no doubt the cops would feel the same way if they were brought in to assess the situation. Bikie works in tattoo parlour. Bikie's login is used to conceal theft in tattoo parlour. Bikie committed the theft in tattoo parlour.

Neat. Not particularly clever, but neat.

Only it f-wording wasn't. This wasn't about her attraction, or crush, or whatever you wanted to call her bone-deep longing to hold Noah's hand once more. This was about the fact that Noah skimming thousands from their till made no gosh-darn *sense*. He *was* an ex-bikie, which meant that if he wanted fast and easy money, he could sell drugs, or hire himself out as muscle, or tattoo patches onto bikies in his beautiful, highly sought-after style. He could do real crimes. *Blood in the Gears* crimes. This sneaky shoplifting just... *wasn't his f-wording MO!*

But the money had gone missing at Silver Daughters Ink. That was undeniable. She'd come to Melbourne because it was undeniable. And the cash skimming was the most convincing reason as to where it had gone that she'd been able to find in months. But what no one else had considered was that a thief using Noah's client login to change their hours was way more logical than Noah incriminating himself in such a boneheaded way. As she read and re-read bank statements and daily rosters, Nicole became convinced it wasn't an accident. Someone was framing Noah, or at least exploiting the fact that he was the dodgiest-looking person at SDI.

But how to prove it wasn't him? Cash was hard to trace, and shuffling the hours had kept the thief out of sight for almost two years, even as the losses crippled the business.

Who'd done it? Who'd taken the money?

Not Sam. She was the worst actress in the world, and she'd been devastated when Silver Daughters nudged bankruptcy. Not Tabby. She'd been in Bondi until a couple of months ago. Not her dad. The karmic implications of stealing money and blaming it on someone else would have killed him before he'd taken a single note.

There was Scott's dad. He'd tried to burn their studio down, and he'd wanted their business gone for years. For a second it seemed utterly plausible, then Nicole realised sneaking in every week to take small amounts of cash out of the till and frame Noah Newcomb was an incredibly convoluted revenge plot for a guy who'd hurled Molotov cocktails at their building. No, this wasn't about revenge. It was theft, pure and simple. The common blight of the small business. The reason she'd told her dad to update their financial software every year because employees...

She wanted to pinch herself. She wanted to slap herself. She wanted to go back in time and pinch and slap every day for two years. She knew who it was. She knew who the dog c-word was.

Gil had been in her house just this morning, talking about how Noah was a criminal, saying they needed to go to the cops. She stood up, needing to move as more details spilled into her brain like hot honey. Gil was a divorced father of three who wore Supreme t-shirts and Stone Island jogging pants. Gil had a Gucci watch that cost more than the one she'd left with Aaron. Gil was always bitching about child support payments, but Tabby teased him about his boots, express ordered from Kanye West's Yeezy line. She imagined Gil sliding a few fifties out of the register and the image was as vivid as any HD movie.

"Oh my God," she whispered. "Oh my God."

She paced her dad's office, turning the revelation over in her head like an explosive device. It had no cracks, no scratches; it was utterly perfect with just one problem—proof.

"No cameras," she said, sitting back down at her dad's desk. "No cameras, and he wasn't stupid enough to use his own login or change his own hours. He must know about Noah's history, or maybe he just thought he'd look innocent in comparison."

He was right. Nicole remembered his insistence that they called the cops, and flushed with anger. Yeah, he'd love that. Next to an ex-bikie with a record, he'd look like butter wouldn't melt in his sly little mouth. He was nervous this morning, Nicole realised— talking a lot, sweating buckets. He knew the jig was nearly up. His defense relied on everyone assuming Noah was guilty, but he must know that was risky; Sam and Noah were old friends, and now he knew Nicole had slept with him. What if he panicked? Called the cops himself and tried to pass it off as a citizen's arrest kind of thing?

"Noah!"

She jumped to her feet again. She'd left her phone upstairs. After flouncing off, she hadn't wanted to go back and collect it, but she needed to call Noah and tell him what was happening, or maybe Gil so she could confront him, or maybe the police, but to explain that they couldn't trust a man called Gil, or maybe—

A knock at the door. Three fast ones and three slow ones.

"Go away, Tabby! I can't deal with you right now!"

"I can't," Tabby said. "I feel so terrible I'm glued to the ground outside the office and the only way to unglue me is with forgiveness."

Nicole could hear the puppies, sniffing and scratching and rubbing against the door. Could hear a watery note in her baby sister's voice. The sister she used to feed and dress and read Winnie the Pooh to. "I've got work to do."

"I know, but I have to tell you I'm sorry. I'm a dick and so is Sam. We're bullshit sisters. We're judgmental assholes, and we both want to say you can get rid of your tattoo if you want to. It won't change anything. It's just ink. Family is more important than ink. Even in this family."

Nicole bit her lip, trying not to let the animalistic howls tearing at her windpipe come out.

"Nix, can I come in?" Tabby pleaded. "I want to give you a hug."

Nicole pressed her hands into her hair. "Okay, but first I have to tell you something and I need you to listen to me."

"Anything! Fire away! I'm all ears. Say it. Whatever you want to say, just say it. Fire away!"

She smiled, she couldn't help herself. Then she remembered the missing money and panic licked up her throat once more. "Gil took the money. He used Noah's login to shave his hours. He's spent all Dad's money on fancy runners and his stupid fancy gym and—and *tracksuit pants for idiot teenagers!*"

There was a pause.

"Gil?" Tabby asked, but not like she didn't believe her. Like she was scared it was too good to be true.

Nicole flung open the office door and the puppies burst in, yelping and rubbing against her ankles like a velvet stampede. "It was him. I can fucking *feel it*."

Tabby smiled. She was holding Nicole's favourite mug. "I like it when you say the f-word."

"Thanks." Nicole took the tea and drank, trying to drown her panic.

"Gil," Tabby said slowly. "He does have a lot of stuff; all the clothes and that Fat Boy, but he said his aunt died and left him some money. It could just be a coincidence?"

Nicole smiled and Tabby smiled back, and she knew they were both thinking the same thing—about their dad saying what he'd said a million different times—'I don't believe in coincidences.'

"Gil," Tabby repeated. "But how are we gonna prove it?"

Nicole felt her smile fade as the immensity of their challenge re-reared its ugly head. "I don't know. Cash is so hard to trace and we don't have cameras."

"We should tell Sam about your theory. Three heads are better than one." Tabby lifted the office phone. "I'll call her."

"No!" Nicole snatched the receiver from her. "She doesn't want to talk to me right now. Not after what I said."

"I told you, she's sorry about all that."

"What if saying sorry is just a strategy to lure me upstairs and punch me in the face?"

Tabby rubbed her chin. "I won't deny Sam is capable of some crazy shit, but she wouldn't do that. She's making you a pie."

Nicole froze. "An apology pie?"

"Yeah, mint chocolate. Your fave."

The backs of Nicole's eyes burned. Her twin wasn't great with words or feelings, but her pies were magnificent. Better than apologies really, because you could eat them. She wiped her eyes. "Okay, let's go upstairs. But I don't want anyone to mention me sleeping with Noah. It's not important right now. We need to focus on the problem, which is Gil."

Tabby grinned and wrapped her arm around her waist. "Sure, though once we clear Noah's—well not *good name*, semi-good name, maybe—can we discuss the possibility of him becoming our brother in law?"

Nicole shook her head, sadness welling like a little pool at her center. "He said he's not the right guy for me. He doesn't want kids."

"Ah, that's a load of shit," Tabby said comfortably. "He'll cave in."

"Thanks, Tabby, that's what I always wanted, a partner who caves." She was being sarcastic, but she did feel oddly better as they headed for the back door.

"Sorry Greyson gave you the clap, by the way," Tabby said. "What a shit cunt."

"Yeah." Shame at the memory of that bright, awful experience flickered through, but it didn't sting as much as she thought it would. A small miracle on a day full of bullshit. She flicked Tabby's ear. "The clap is gonorrhoea. I had chlamydia."

"Like the koalas?"

"I guess." A burst of defiance flared through her and she grabbed the tail of the comet. "You know, it's common. Chlamydia. One in five people get it."

Tabby considered this. "I can't say that's a good thing, but I do know you have nothing to be ashamed about. Also, you're way better than one in five people. You're like… one in five billion people."

Nicole didn't say anything because she wanted to stop crying for at least a thirty-minute period, but she hugged her sister closer as they headed upstairs to Sam and her pie, the puppies surging around them like living water.

19

Stasis was never Noah's thing. Fitz, the road captain of The Rangers, used to call him Recovery for the way he bounced back after hangovers. It could have been nature, nurture, or both, but shit just didn't seem to stick to him the way it did to other people. And when it did, it never seemed to be for long. Easy come, easy go. Or so he fucking thought.

It had been twenty-four hours since he'd left his van at the DaSilva house. He couldn't eat, still hadn't slept, hadn't showered. He couldn't get out of bed and that didn't make sense because, again, he wasn't sleeping. He was just lying there staring at the ceiling, feeling stupidly grateful that Shredder hadn't slashed his mattress or taken a shit in his sheets. He wondered if that was Paula's influence, some warped kind of parting gift.

All in all, he'd rather have his paintings.

He'd assumed he'd get up when the nicotine cravings kicked in, but as the day wore on, it became clear that wasn't going to work. He wasn't thirsty, he didn't need the bathroom. His human instincts seemed to have abandoned him.

Nicole would have made it better, but that was a dead end. By now her sisters would have spoken to her and she'd think he was a thieving asshole, too. He'd never get to kiss her, or fuck her, or take her out for dinner. He wouldn't work another shift at Silver Daughters, or have another beer with Sam. His life in Melbourne was done. If he was smart, he'd get out of town before he found himself in front of the cops explaining that yeah, he'd once kicked the shit out of someone for a bikie gang and gone to jail for it, but he wasn't a bad guy.

He didn't have the energy to leave, though. Not one bit.

As the afternoon sun faded, an itch spread through his hands and legs. He wasn't antsy enough to get up, but he knew he'd have to do it soon—at least to shower. His vasectomy appointment was due to kick off at nine. He'd have to go to that. If he didn't, he'd lose his deposit. It was one thing to lie around like a corpse not eating, drinking, or smoking. It was another to let a ball sac clinic steal two hundred bucks.

He was turning on his side, wondering what Edgar was doing, when he heard a hard knock at the door. Who the fuck was that? Couldn't be Shredder; he wouldn't fucking knock. The cops? He didn't move. If they had a warrant to arrest him, they could force their way in. It wasn't like it mattered anyway.

"Noah!" called a woman. "Open up."

The voice was familiar. Someone he'd fucked? Did he have an outstanding date? They weren't in for a good time, if that was the case. He doubted he'd be able to get a hard-on for anyone that wasn't Nicole for at least a year, and even after that, he'd probably think of her.

"I know you're there, you big dildo," called the woman. "Come to the door or I'll murder you!"

"Tabby!" a man scolded, and the mystery was solved.

Noah rubbed at his right eye, his exhaustion doubling over on itself. He thought about Newton's first law of motion; that an object at rest would stay at rest unless it was compelled to change that state by an external force. He'd been hoping the force would be getting the snip. He wasn't in the mood to deal with Tabitha DaSilva.

There was another knock, this one harder, more authoritarian.

"Noah, if you're there, we'd like to speak with you." It was a second man, his voice clear and British. Scott Sanderson, Sam's boyfriend. Jesus, they'd sent a whole crew to deal with him. He swung his feet out of bed, feeling heavy and useless.

"Coming." His voice was rusty with disuse. It made him sound exactly like his old man. He swallowed a couple of times. "Hang on a second."

"Excellent!" Tabby said. "Everyone look concerned but not *too* concerned."

"Shh."

Noah rolled his eyes. "What do you guys want?"

"Just to talk," Scott Sanderson said, calm as a police negotiator. "Could you please come to the door?"

Noah bent and picked up a relatively clean t-shirt. "I will if you stop talking like I've got C4 strapped to my chest."

"Fair enough."

He dressed quickly, a little worried the lethargy would seize and bring him back to bed. He cracked his neck on both sides before heading to the door and turning the lock. Tabby stood before him in puffy green pants and a red crop top. She was flanked by Scott and a mate of Scott's whose name he couldn't remember.

Tabby's jaw dropped. "Whoa. You look... interesting."

Noah's mood blackened. He'd gone a day without food or soap, but he wasn't a fucking leper. "What are you doing here?"

Tabby opened her mouth, but Scott stepped in front of her. "Apologising, first of all."

Not what he'd been expecting. "Apologise for what?"

"For the accusations that were leveled against you," Scott said, in pure lawyerese. "Sam regrets not giving you the time and space to defend yourself."

"Same," Tabby called from behind him. "I regret it, too."

Relief unlocked his chest and he breathed deep for what felt like the first time in days. "Sam's sorry?"

"Yeah." Scott gave him a small smile. "She's still pissed you didn't tell her about yourself, but she'll get past that."

"I..." Noah frowned. "How the fuck do you know where I live?"

Scott tugged at his collar. "Well..."

Tabby popped out from behind him. "Phone tracking. Come on, man, you know I do that."

Scott closed his eyes. "Timing, Tabby."

"What? He deserves to know." She smiled at him. "Want to know how Nix is?"

God, just hearing her name was like swallowing a shot of Tabasco. He looked away, actually catching the tall kid's eye. He cast around for his name and landed on *Toby*. Fucking weird that he was here.

Scott cleared his throat. "So, that's not the only reason we're here. Can we please come inside and talk?"

Noah looked over his shoulder and saw, unsurprisingly, his place was exactly as fucked-up as Paula and Shredder had left it. "I've got some... maintenance shit happening right now. What's there to talk about?"

Scott grimaced. "We think Gil is the one stealing from Silver Daughters."

"Huh?" he said, sounding stupid, feeling stupid. "You think it was *Gil*?"

"We *know* it was Gil," Tabby said.

"No, we don't." Scott met Noah's gaze. "Can we come in?"

Noah let them in, his mind spinning a hundred and eighty degrees. Gil? Fuckin' Gil with his hard boiled eggs and turkey steaks? His dumbass kids clothes? How could it have been him? He'd have noticed. He'd have *stopped him.*

"Wow, this place is fucked." Tabby sounded delighted. "What happened? Did the dog-cunt people do this?"

Noah ignored her. "How do you know it was Gil?" he asked Scott.

Scott pulled a piece of paper from his suit pocket and handed it to him. It was a bank statement with many of the dates and amounts highlighted. "What am I looking at?"

"Silver Daughters' cash deposits from eighteen months ago."

Scott pointed to a deposit of two thousand dollars. "Here. This is when the totals drop. The week before it was two thousand, five hundred. We think that's when he started skimming the till."

Noah's heart sank. "That's not evidence."

"What if I told you that was the week Gil joined his new gym." It wasn't Tabby or Scott who spoke, but the tall kid, Toby. Noah stared at him, taking in the cookie-cutter blue shirt and neatly combed hair.

"How'd you know that?"

"He called the gym and found out," Tabby said. "And he got the owner to tell him that Gil's been paying in cash."

Noah stared at him. "Seriously?"

The kid hunched his shoulders. "Yeah, I guessed he wasn't depositing the money because if he was, he could get in trouble with the tax office, so I narrowed down the places where he might be spending it. I got lucky."

Tabby flicked his shoulder. "It wasn't lucky, it was fucking genius."

Toby flushed scarlet.

"Do we know anyone else who might have a record of Gil spending cash with them?" Noah asked.

"I called a couple of big brand shops in the CBD," Scott said. "Places Sam and Tabby could remember Gil mentioning. An assistant at Incu knew who Gil was, but he said he hasn't been in for a while."

No, he wouldn't have been. He looked at Scott. "Has the skimming slowed down since Nikki got here?"

"Stopped as far as we can tell."

Noah nodded, furious but trying to keep it at bay. He needed to think. "So, it adds up, but we've got no proof?"

"Pretty much."

He screwed up his face. "What about the gym? Do they have any of Gil's money on hand?"

"No, the guy who runs the place didn't want us poking around his finances."

Tabby gave Toby a glowing look. "He didn't even want to talk to us, but Toby freaked him out. Told him that if he was helping Gil launder the cash, he could be culpable when we went to the police. That got him to talk."

Noah grinned at the kid. "You'd make a good lawyer."

"Or a pilot," Tabby said cheerfully. "Or a doctor. Or an engineer."

"But he's my assistant," Scott said. "No poaching."

Toby ducked his head, clearly uncomfortable with the flattery. "Guys..."

Noah leaned against his kitchen wall, trying to see the bigger picture. "Okay, Gil's been robbing SDI blind. What now?"

Everyone's smiles faded.

Scott tugged at the collar of his shirt. "That's why we came. We need to think of something fast. Gil called Sam last night and told her he's got a job offer in Sydney. He's quitting."

"No." He hadn't meant it to come out so hard, but Tabby and Toby took a step backward.

Scott spread his fingers. "It's okay. Nicole told him he has to give two weeks' notice, or he'll be in breach of his contract. He's still here; he's coming in on Monday."

He inhaled, expanding his deflated lungs. Nikki had saved them, found a feather-light way to buy them more time. Of course, she had. He kept breathing, kept thinking. So Gil had stolen from Sam and made Nicole work a million hours trying to figure out why their family business was failing. Gil had robbed them blind and he was going to leave, lumping Edgar's daughters with the mess he'd made. Why hadn't he guessed this? Stopped this?

In his head, he heard Gil defend himself. *It wasn't personal, man, I just wasn't making enough to make ends meet.*

Maybe he'd phrase it differently in the flesh, but Noah was sure he wouldn't apologise and he sure as fuck wouldn't give back what he'd taken.

"Wow," Tabby said. "You look scary. Are you thinking bikie thoughts?"

Noah looked at Scott. "You gonna go talk to him?"

Scott's tight smile said he was thinking the same things he was. "Perhaps. Sam wouldn't like it, though."

And neither would Nicole, but looking at Scott, he could see they agreed—the girls didn't have to know. Not if things played out the way he, and he suspected Scott, wanted them to play out.

"His kids aren't home," Scott said. "They'll be with their mother until next week."

"Useful information."

"I thought so."

Noah patted his pockets for his cigarettes and remembered he was out. He'd have to fix that before they saw Gil. "I know his address, should we go over there now?"

"I don't see why not."

"Hang on," Tabby said loudly. "I thought the plan was to go to the cops?"

"The cops won't be able to do anything with what we have," Scott said. "Not before Gil goes interstate and makes it twenty times harder to investigate, let alone prosecute him for what he did."

And even if we found proof, Noah thought, *the courts run slower than mud. It'd be months before Sam's saw a cent from Gil, maybe years. She'd have to spend thousands on a solicitor and a shit judge could still fuck her over.*

"How much?" he asked.

"Huh?" Scott said.

"How much did Gil take?"

"Almost eighty thousand dollars."

Noah could see some of his rage reflected in Scott's eyes. "So, we talk to him."

"By 'talk' do you mean 'break his kneecaps?'" Tabby asked. "Are you going to make him give you money or you'll kick his ass?"

Noah didn't say anything. He wasn't sure if Scott intended for her to come with them or not. All in all, he'd prefer not. It wasn't a girl thing; Tabby was a loose cannon of the highest order and a situation like this one needed zero of that. And if he was honest, he was still stinging from the way she'd come at him about the bikie thing. He knew she'd apologised, but they'd been friends and she'd been so fucking quick to believe he was scum.

"Holy shit," Tabby stage whispered. "It is *on*! Should I go back to the house and get my balaclava?"

"You're not coming," Toby and Scott said at the same time.

Tabby turned to the kid. "Why the fuck not?"

"Because you need to stay at the house and make sure Sam and Nicole don't get suspicious," Toby said.

Tabby scowled. "That's a fake job to get me out of the way."

The kid didn't deny it. He was standing taller than before and his expression reminded Noah of a teacher, the kind you couldn't fuck with.

"I want to see Noah doling out vigilante justice," Tabby said. "And I'm useful in these situations, remember when I tasered Scott's dad?" She turned to Scott. "Sorry for tasering your dad."

Scott shrugged. "He deserved it. But you shouldn't come with us to Gil's."

"Why?"

Toby put a hand on her shoulder. "This is going to be intense and you're not the best person to have around when things are intense."

"But—" Tabby snapped her mouth shut. She looked furious, but Noah could see she wasn't going to push harder.

"Tab, please don't be mad," Toby said. "I'll wash the puppies for the next six months."

"Whatever," Tabby said. "I'm heading home. Good luck with your OG bikie shit, I guess."

She turned on her heel and marched away, the swishing sound of her pants undercutting her furious exit. When his graffitied door slammed shut, Toby winced. "She's never gonna forgive me for this."

"You did the right thing," Noah said. "She's a liability."

Toby looked miserable. "I was just worried she'd get hurt. I couldn't handle that."

"How long you been together?" Noah asked, mildly curious. As far as he knew, Tabby had never had a serious boyfriend.

Toby's expression became even more miserable. "We're not together."

An awkward silence fell.

"So..." Scott said. "What now?"

"We sit down and discuss this." Noah clapped his hands together hard, then cringed. He'd just echoed his dad opening a chapter meeting. "Let's just sit down."

"Sit down where?"

Noah looked around his fucked up kitchen, every chair broken, the floor covered in splintered glass. "Pub?"

20

Noah looked in the rear-view and saw Toby gnawing a fingernail. "You don't have to come if you don't want. Two'll be enough."

Toby shook his head. "I can handle it."

"You're nervous as fuck," Scott said, his feet tapping up a symphony on the floor and a thin sheen of sweat on his brow.

Noah readjusted his grip on the wheel. He didn't blame them for being nervous, but he hoped they'd pull themselves together by the time they got to Gil's. The little prick wasn't dangerous, but this was a dicey, borderline illegal situation where a million things could go wrong. For the first time in years, he racked his mind for old memories. Helpful shit.

"Best shakedown's a quick shakedown," his dad had said some half-forgotten summer afternoon. "Quick, and you keep your mouth shut."

Yarrow had said something about a tyre iron, and his old man laughed. "You come in that hard, they'll run out the back door. Call the pigs. You need to sound reasonable. Half the effort and better results."

"Stay quiet," he told Toby and Scott. "We're not here to chat about what he did and how we know. We say what we need to say and take it from there."

Toby nodded, as though to prove he could keep quiet.

Scott rubbed his sweaty forehead. "Did you do this sort of thing for your father?"

He kept his eyes on the road. "Not as much as you'd think. They've got guys to do what we're about to do."

"Punishers?" That came from Toby.

Noah bit back a smile. "Sons of Anarchy?"

The young man flushed.

"How'd you join The Rangers?" Scott asked.

Now the cat was out of the bag, Noah knew he should get used to being asked about it, that he owed answers and explanations, but right now it felt like Scott was trying to start shit. "Why'd you want to know?"

Scott didn't look remotely ruffled. "Curiosity, mostly."

Hard to argue with that, especially on the way to a shakedown as he gave tips straight out of Harold Newcomb's mouth.

"My old man was the president of the mother chapter. I was recruited before I was ever recruited."

"Did you like being a bikie?"

"I didn't like it or not like it. It was all I knew."

"So, why'd you leave?"

Noah had no interest in answering that. He tugged a cigarette out of the pack he'd pulled from the machine in the Edinburgh Castle. As he did, he glanced at the back of the van, the empty spaces where Nikki's boxes and bags had been laid out just last night.

"Nicole got her stuff okay?" he asked, but Scott didn't say anything. It was clear he wasn't going to until he answered his question. Noah gritted his teeth. "We're almost at Gil's, we don't have time to get into my memoirs."

More silence. It proved they'd been listening to him, though that was more annoying than anything. He wondered what Nicole would say if she was here.

Not so nice the other way, is it?

No, it wasn't.

So, what are you going to do about it?

What could he fucking do? He drummed the steering wheel, echoing Scott's foot tapping. "I left 'cos I couldn't breathe."

"Can you be a little more specific?"

This fucking guy. He lit up, tasting the prickle of tobacco. It felt almost new after his break and it eased the snarl in his chest. It still felt like a fist would come crashing across the back of his head if he talked about it. But maybe that meant he should. Burn that old loyalty and the shame underneath it. "I wanted to tattoo full-time, but I wasn't gonna get the hours while I was under my old man's thumb. Which was where I was staying unless I wanted to do something about it. So, I left."

"And now you can say you left a bikie gang because of creative differences."

Noah didn't want to smile, but he couldn't help it. "Pretty much."

"I'm sorry if I sounded aggressive," Scott said in a different, more amiable voice. "The news just took us all by surprise."

The smile faded from his face. "You think I'm still connected? That I'm a risk?"

"Not necessarily, but Sam and I have realised we don't know much about you. So, we don't know if you're a risk and I think that concern is higher, now you and Nicole…"

Noah's head pounded with nicotine and sudden, bright-hot fury. "Me and Nicole, what? You think I'm gonna hurt her?"

"I don't mean it that way." Scott's voice was calm. "It's clear you care for each other, but like I said; we don't know you as well as we thought we did. We're going to need some time and a little fucking reassurance, Noah. And if you can't talk about your past with transparency or warn us before something like what happened with your ex-roommate happens again, Sam and I are going to have a hard time supporting your relationship."

The worry in Scott's voice was the only thing keeping Noah from pulling over and punching him in the mouth, because he'd rather fucking die than expose Nicole to The Rangers. That was why he'd stayed away, told her she couldn't paste him into her storybook future even though it was killing him.

"Noah?" Scott asked.

"I'd never hurt Nikki."

"I know that," Scott said, and he sounded like he meant it. "She defended you. About stealing the money. She never believed you took it. She had a fight with Sam about it, then she went off and figured out Gil was skimming the cash."

Noah felt a key slide between his ribs and open a place he didn't want opened. At least not right now. He turned and met Scott's gaze squarely. "After this, I'll sit down with you and Sammy and tell you whatever you want to know, but we're less than five from Gil's and I need to focus."

Scott settled back into his seat, looking pleased. "Sure. We okay?"

Noah took Sam's boyfriend in, studied him like he was about to tattoo his upper arm, or paint his portrait. His milky skin made him look closer to twenty-three than thirty, but his eyes were calm. That said he was comfortable in his own skin, aware of limits. He'd never considered being mates with Scott, but maybe that could change, now he didn't have anything to hide. "Yeah, we're okay. Smoke?"

Scott shook his head. "Quit after university. Only have them when I'm drinking these days."

"Maybe we should get a drink after this?" Toby said. "If it all goes well."

Noah was going to say that sounded like a good idea, but Gil's street came up sooner than he expected. He hit the indicator. "We're almost there."

The car fell silent and nerves he hadn't expected to feel twisted in his belly. Gil's place was exactly how Noah remembered it—a squat brick flat with a dying lawn and skeletal lemon trees.

"Shit place," Toby said.

He and Scott laughed and some of the tension in the van dissolved.

"Maybe he hasn't stolen enough of Sam's money to upgrade," Scott said. "Should we get going?"

Noah ground his cigarette into the ashtray. "Yep. No sense hanging around."

They got out of the van. Scott was sweating again and Toby practically walked to the gate on his tiptoes. Noah's nerves twisted harder. He headed for the front door, Scott, and Toby in his wake.

We're tall, he reminded himself. *Bigger than Gil even with all the heavy lifting shit he's been doing, and we don't need to kick the shit out of him, we just need to get the job done. With a bit of luck, this'll be last time I do something like this.*

He rapped on the door, not too hard, not too insistent. There was a faint clatter inside the house. Toby made a noise like a dog toy getting stepped on. "He's here."

"Breathe," Noah warned. "Relax and stand tall."

He followed his own advice, straightening up, squaring his shoulders. He could feel Scott and Toby following suit. Footsteps padded toward the door, then it swung open.

"Hey..." Gil's unshaven cheeks sagged. "What are you doing here?"

Noah smiled, sliding his foot between the door and the jamb. Clichés were clichés for a reason. "Afternoon."

Gil looked wildly from him to Scott to Toby. "I... hey, how's it going?"

"Not bad. Can we come in?"

Without waiting for an answer, Noah moved forward. For a second it looked like Gil wasn't going to get out of the way, but he stepped aside. "Sure. Got beers in the kitchen."

Noah headed down the hall and paused at Gil's living room. It smelled faintly of weed and baby vomit, and it was full of boxes. Most were taped shut, but the ones that were open were full of clothes and kitchen stuff. He turned to look at Gil, who was the colour of an old sports sock.

"Going somewhere?"

He swung his arms, seemingly lost for words. Scott and Toby were doing what they were told—standing behind Gil, triangulating him between their bodies so that if he ran he'd have to move through them.

"What's happening?" Gil blurted out. "Is the studio in trouble or something?"

Noah folded his arms across his chest. "You've been stealing from Sam. Skimming out of the till for more than a year."

Gil's face was a pantomime of shock, eyes wide, mouth open. "That's fucked! You're the one who was stealing!"

God, what a fucking rat. What a cowardly little bastard. How hadn't he seen it before? Hadn't he run away when Scott's dad had tried to burn Silver Daughters down? Wasn't he always bitching about what the world owed him, while being as mediocre a father, friend, and employee as possible? "We've got proof, Gil. You've been paying your gym membership in cash. Eric, the guy who runs the place, gave us some of the notes you used. They match the ones Sam got from the bank a month ago."

It was all bullshit, but it was useful bullshit, meant to cut Gil's whining at the knees, get a confession out of him if they could. It worked like a charm. He collapsed like a sandcastle onto the dirty carpet. "Noah, mate, I didn't mean it, things were tight, and I needed the cash, but I swear I didn't mean to hurt the business. I swear it wasn't a year, it was..."

Noah looked around at Toby. His phone was in his hand, filming everything Gil said. Shitty evidence, but good insurance.

"... my ex wants to send the kids to St Martins and—"

"I don't give a fuck," Noah said, because he knew Gil would go on all night if they let him. "We're not here for excuses, we're here so you can make amends."

Gil took his hands away from his face, all sobbing and shaking instantly melting away. "What do you mean?"

Noah smiled, walked over to the nearest box and sifted through it. It was mostly mens shirts. He picked one up and read the label. Eton. He picked up another one. Givenchy. He didn't know much about fashion, but they looked and felt expensive. Gil watched him, his expression rat-like. He didn't like him touching his precious shirts.

That was too fucking bad. Noah turned and handed Toby the box. "In the back. Pack it properly, we're gonna need the space."

"What the fuck?" Gil put a foot to the ground, about to stand.

Noah put a hand on his shoulder, keeping him down. "I told you already, we're here so you can make amends."

"But that's my stuff!"

"And who paid for that stuff?"

"I did!" Gil tried to get to his feet, but Noah pressed hard on his shoulder. His skin was damp beneath his t-shirt. He'd hit the panic stage.

"Calm down."

But Gil twisted like a rat in a trap, turning to look at Scott. "Mate, you're not gonna go along with this, are you?"

To his credit, Scott's gaze stayed ice cold and he said nothing.

"Hey Scott," Noah said. "How much money has this prick taken from Sam? Seventy thousand?"

"Closer to eighty."

Noah whistled. "That's a lot of shirts." He shook Gil's shoulder. "Are you telling us you're in a position to pay us out eighty grand right now? Today?"

"I...."

"Cash or transfer—we're not fussy. We'll even round it down to seventy, if that's easier?"

Gil flinched. "I can pay you back, just give me some time!"

"We don't want to give you time. And even if we did, you're not coming near Silver Daughters again."

"So, what do you want?"

He smiled. That was the fucking question to ask. "Money. But since you don't have that, we're gonna go through your house, take everything of value we can find, and call it even. Sound fair?"

Gil's eyes bulged. "You can't fucking do that!"

"Not normally, no," Noah agreed. "But you stole eighty grand and a lot of people would say you can't do that, so swings and roundabouts."

Noah felt Gil swallow. "What if I go to the cops?"

Noah tightened his grip on Gil's shoulder, feeling the bones and muscle shift. "You want to think hard before you say something like that again."

Gil lowered his head, saying nothing.

Toby reappeared in the hallway and Noah jerked his head at a packed Corona box by the door. "What's in there?"

Toby used his keys to slit open the tape and flipped the box open. "Sneakers. Fancy ones."

"Take them out to the van."

Gil shuddered, but still he said nothing. Noah checked his phone. They'd been there five minutes; they needed to move faster. He caught Scott's eye. "Can you have a look around?"

Scott nodded and headed for the back of the house. He emerged a minute later with an armful of puffy jackets. "These are all Moncler."

"I don't know what that means."

"They're about eight hundred each."

Noah grinned. "Chuck them in the van. We've got towels down."

"Sure." Scott's dark eyes fell on Gil. "You okay?"

Noah squeezed Gil's shoulder. "Am I okay?"

Gil nodded and Scott headed outside. When the door clicked shut, Gil looked up at him, genuine tears filling his eyes. "You can't do this, man. I'll pay you back. When I get up to Sydney, I'll send the money to you every week!"

Toby came back before Noah could answer. "What now?" he asked. Despite his earlier protests, Noah got the impression he was enjoying himself.

"Just keep grabbing boxes. Leave any kid shit you find, but everything else is fair game. Get Scott to help you with the TV."

"What!?"

Noah ignored Gil. "Fill up the van. If we have to do two trips, we do two trips."

Toby gave him a salute, grabbed another box and left. Once he was gone, Gil shoved his hand. Caught off guard, Noah lost his grip and Gil stood up, squaring his shoulders. Anger buzzed in his eyes.

Easy, Noah thought, ignoring the alarm ringing through his body. *Easy.*

Gil glanced at the hallway and his body tensed to run. Noah lunged, grabbing for Gil's upper arm. He gripped and twisted like clockwork, forcing his ex-colleague back onto his knees.

"Sorry," Gil wailed. "I'm sorry."

"Shut the fuck up." He crouched low so he and Gil were face to face. Gil's eyes were wide, his breath had the cheesy smell of chocolate protein powder. Noah felt a dizzy sense of Deja vu. He was twenty-one, high on coke and his old man's approval, making some slimy, weak fuck pay for what he'd done.

He tightened his grip, making Gil cry out, and then he saw Nicole in his mind, smiling across at him in the car. He loosened his hold, letting Gil slump onto all fours. "Stop fighting it, you're fucking done."

"I've got kids," he wailed. "I've got kids."

"Edgar has kids. Three daughters you fucked over because you had to have as much brand shit as possible. Don't act like you did what you did for your kids. It's fuckin' pathetic."

"Noah?" Scott had returned. He was studying the scene with a coolness that increased Noah's respect for him tenfold. "Is this necessary?"

"'Fraid so," Noah said. "We should head out pretty soon."

Scott nodded. "Where's your motorbike?" he asked Gil.

"What?" Gil struggled against his hold, kicking out. "You can't take my bike, you prick."

Noah twisted his arm a little harder, keeping him in place. "If we were pricks, we'd take your car as well as your bike. I'll get it later, Scott. You see what else is around."

Sam's boyfriend nodded and headed back to what Noah assumed was Gil's bedroom.

"You and Sam don't have shit on me," Gil hissed. "I could get you locked up for what you're doing, you bikie piece of shit."

"Maybe." Noah leaned in close. "But if I go away, it won't be for more than a few months, and what do you think I'll do when I get out?"

Gil made a noise like a mouse being stepped on. "You wouldn't..."

"I will. Even if it lands me back in jail for ten years, I will. I'll break your arm and if I do it right, you'll never ink again. Is your Fat Boy worth that? Are all the shoes and bullshit jackets?"

Gil looked away, but not before Noah saw the panic in his eyes. He was scum, but he was an artist. He'd felt a tattoo pouring out of him like liquid gold. Losing that was a death sentence that'd kill him for the rest of his days.

The acrid smell of Gil's sweat filled his nose. It made Noah want to gag but he leaned in even closer. "Take the easy choice. Let us get what we came for and move on."

"I knew you were with The Rangers, man. I Googled you a year ago and I never told anyone."

Noah laughed. "Don't appeal to my better nature. If you knew what I was, you should have known not to steal from Sam and try to pin it on me."

Gil snapped his mouth shut, his eyes darting around as he thought of the next tack to take. Noah realised he was doing what he'd warned Scott and Toby not to do—talking too much, letting Gil think this was a debate and not a shakedown. He stood, rubbing his hands on his jeans to get rid of Gil's sweat. "I've said all I want to say. What'll it be? You gonna let us get on with it?"

Gil gnawed at his lower lip. "If I let you get on with it, Sam won't go to the cops?"

"Nope."

"And you won't stop me leaving for Sydney?"

"Why the fuck would we want you here?"

Gil looked at the carpet as if searching for the Hail Mary pass, then his shoulders slumped. "Take what you want."

"Including the bike?"

He nodded, his eyes watering at the edges again.

"Good," Noah said. "Go get me the keys."

Ten minutes later the van was packed to capacity with clothes, electronics and a couple boxes of tattooing ink that had come straight out of Silver Daughters storeroom. When Toby found them, Gil had gone white as a sheet. After that, he'd practically helped them pack the van.

"I'm sorry," he said as Scott slid in the last box. "I mean it. I'm sorry about everything."

Scott looked at him like he was an unwashed urinal. "Sod off. Ready to go, Toby?"

Toby, who'd been arranging Gil's chains and rings into a shoebox, nodded, still taking his vow of silence seriously. He tucked the shoebox under his arm and climbed into the passenger seat.

"Okay," Scott said, slamming the back of the van shut. "Just two more things."

He turned to Gil and tapped his wrist. With a look of utter misery, Gil unbuckled his Gucci watch and handed it over.

"Thanks," Scott said carelessly. "And you'll call VicRoads tomorrow and transfer your bike into Sam's name?"

Gil nodded, ashen faced.

"Wonderful."

Like Toby, Noah had a feeling Scott was enjoying himself, but why not? Everything had gone well, it looked like they'd be going for that victory drink, after all.

"Are you ready to head back to Sam's?" Scott asked, gesturing to Gil's Fat Boy.

Noah took in the glossy black machine, his mood hovering between lust and fear. He hadn't ridden in years, let alone to where Nicole was, full of questions and expectations and a bright, colourful future. He wasn't ready. Not for any of it.

"Noah?"

Noah walked over to the bike and sat astride the leather seat. The sensation of metal against his thighs was like a homecoming. It had been years and years and years, but it was so fucking *familiar*.

"You sure you know how to ride that thing?" Scott asked.

Noah looked across and realised he was joking. He grinned. "Pretty sure."

He kicked the stand out of the way and turned the engine over. It roared like a pet tiger. He fought to keep the smile off his face. He turned to Gil, who looked like someone had punched him in the back of the head. "We're done here. Head back inside."

Gil opened his mouth, then closed it. Then he walked away, hands in his jean pockets. Noah watched him go, wondering how expensive they were. Maybe they should have taken them?

"I think we can leave him the clothes on his back," Scott said, reading his mind. "We did well."

"Yeah, you and Toby handled yourselves just fine."

Scott smiled sheepishly. "I went a bit Sanford experiment, didn't I?"

"You got the job done, that's all that matters. See you at Silver Daughters."

"Wait one sec. You know Nicole's there, right? That she'll want to see you."

Noah's gut tightened. "What's your point?"

"That she'll be able to see you. You know, be close to you. In the flesh, as it were."

"Huh?"

Scott winced. "You're going to make me say it, aren't you? Jesus, you'd think this would be easier than robbing a man..."

"The fuck are you talking about?"

He sighed. "Okay, no offence, but you look like shit and you smell worse. And that was fine while you were freaking Gil out, but I don't think Nicole will appreciate it. Especially if you're going to convince her that she should overlook all this bikie business and whatever the fuck you said to her last night, and be your girlfriend, or old lady, or whatever it is you want to call it."

"Oh." Noah looked down at himself, seeing his stained t-shirt and patchy jeans anew. He could only imagine the state of his teeth and stubble. "Yeah, I should shower."

Scott looked relieved. "And shave. And change your clothes. Give your entrance a less authentic biker feel."

"Yeah, okay. Message received."

Noah revved the engine. He'd have to be quick getting home; Gil's helmet didn't fit and he didn't want to get busted for riding without one. He didn't want to get busted for anything ever again. "See you soon."

Scott shoved his hands in his pockets. "One more thing?"

"What?"

"Thanks for what you did for us. For Sam. I didn't think we'd see a penny from Gil, and I know we don't have eighty grand's worth of things, but at least he didn't get away with it. And that's thanks to you."

"Oh." He found himself wishing for Gil's helmet so he wouldn't have to look Scott in the face. "Yeah, no worries."

Scott nodded, clearly as uncomfortable as he was. "Right, well, if things go well with Nicole, well, then... welcome to the family, I suppose."

He turned and strode to the van, looking profoundly awkward. Noah grinned. He had a feeling he'd be giving Scott shit about this someday. It was a good feeling to have. He revved the bike, feeling like he'd just been handed the keys to another life. Maybe he had. He needed to get home, shower, and get to Silver Daughters. Open the lock.

21

John Mayer crooned about the nature of gravity as Nicole stared out of her bedroom window. She didn't believe Tabby's half-assed claim the boys were playing golf. They didn't need to take Noah's van to play freaking golf—they'd gone to confront Gil. She didn't know why the idea made her so nervous—it wasn't like Gil was dangerous. It just seemed like such a reckless thing for Scott and Toby to do.

"Was it Noah's idea?" she asked Tabby, but she'd just covered her ears and shouted 'lalalalalalalala' until Nicole gave up. A typical Tabitha DaSilva victory.

All she'd wanted to know was if he was okay. He hadn't answered any of her calls or messages. His being gone shouldn't have changed anything, it had been less than two days, but she ached. She missed him. Everything seemed more unstable without him around, crowding out tattoo room two, reading his books at the front desk, sitting at Monday meeting, saying nothing and eating everything. Last night she'd dreamt he was her priest again, cupping the back of her neck and forcing her to her knees. If she never slept with him again it would be the single biggest non-death tragedy of her life.

Hello? A bit of focus, please? mind-Sam snapped.

Nicole forced her gaze back to her laptop and re-read her draft email.

Hello all,
Due a change in our personal circumstances, Aaron and I are no longer getting married. I've decided to move back to Melbourne to spend more time with my family. I'll be contacting people individually to sort out loose ends, but for now, I'd just like to say thank you for all you've done for me, Nicole DaSilva

In the 'to' box was her boss, her Adelaide friends, wedding providers and any and all relevant parties she could think of. The message was hokey and a bit 'politician forced to retire', what with the bit about spending more time with her family, but it was the truth. She was done trying to make the narrative of what happened with Aaron compelling and tasteful and mutually blameless. It was time to let the train go off the tracks and see where the damage fell.

Besides, it was only a formality. From the messages she'd been getting, Aaron was telling everyone in Adelaide she cheated on him with Noah. Sam wanted to mail him a king brown snake, but Nicole told her about the plate condom and, once they were both done laughing, agreed they didn't need any more of his pettiness in their lives.

She re-read the email again, her mouth bone dry. Telling everyone was the right decision, but she wasn't sure about moving to Melbourne. Now the mysterious money pit problem was solved, she had no real reason to stay.

Except Noah.

He was the fishing hook that would keep her tethered to home. If she left, the line would stretch out behind her for miles and miles, reminding her that no one had made her feel like he did. Calm and excited at once. Sexy without having to try.

And he liked her, she knew that, he just didn't think he could be the man she deserved. But why shouldn't she stay and prove to him that he was? Did she have to wrangle a commitment to a ring and three kids before they went on a real date, or saw a movie, or tried tying each other up? Did she have to have a plan perfectly in place to enjoy what was between them?

Give me three months, she imagined telling him. *Give me three months of dating and then say you don't think you're the guy for me.*

She stood up, needing something to do. Something else to think about. She paced over to her old bookshelf, scanning the novels that were as familiar as her sisters' faces—*Charlotte's Web, A Chinese Cinderella, A Series of Unfortunate Events,* the *Twilight* series. God she'd loved those books when she was thirteen. She moved closer, tracing the black and red spine of *New Moon.* Something was nagging at her. She pulled the book off the shelf and opened it to a random page. Bella was contemplating a dangerous cliff dive in order to see Edward in her mind. What had triggered her memory? It wasn't the cliff diving, or the Volturi stuff...

"Holy shit, this fucking email." Sam strode in, talking like they were already mid-conversation. "Nix, this Russian guy wants to fly me to Thailand to give him an axolotl tattoo! And he's offering ten grand! For one weekend! And a holiday! That'll put a dent in what that fuckstick stole from us, huh?"

"Ah... Yes?"

"You're damn right, yes!" Sam raised a victorious fist to the ceiling. "Tabby was saying we should break out dad's incense. Have a cleanse. Symbolic, you know."

"Um, sure. Smudge away."

"Great." Her twin paused. "You're not re-reading *Twilight,* are you?"

Nicole closed the book. "No. Wait, why can't I re-read *Twilight?*"

"Because it's pus."

"It's not!"

"It is. Pure white and green pus."

Nicole made a face. "They're YA novels for teenage girls. Besides, *you* read them."

"I also read *Cleo* magazine and got a bunch of weird ideas about what to do during sex. And just because I read the Twilight books didn't mean I *liked* them. I wanted every character to get the black lung and die. Especially that giant vampire edgelord."

"Mmm." It was true Sam hadn't been particularly generous to the series. She had been forever telling girls at school that Edward was a sexual predator and sending them links to videos of people burning the books in metal bins. But Nicole hadn't cared about Sam's opinion and anyway, she didn't like Edward, she liked—

"Who was the guy you were all boned up about?" Sam asked. "That abs dickhead? Jason?"

Nicole's cheeks went hot. "Jacob."

"That's right! The werewolf that lady-drip puts in the friendzone. That was incredible! I gave you so much shit about his sadboy mooning and his fake gang. Man, he was the first mildly bad boy..." Sam paused. "Holy shit. Wait... Holy. *Shit*."

"Don't," Nicole begged. "Please?"

But it was already too late, Sam doubled over, her hands on her knees, so choked up she was laughing without making a noise, her whole body shaking.

"Stop," Nicole said. "Noah isn't—"

"Noah is your Jacob," Sam gasped. "Oh my god, Noah is your Jacob!"

Nicole ran at her, intending to slap her before she could tell Tabby and escalate this whole situation, but she screamed like an eight-year-old and ran from the room. "Tabby! Tabby, come quick!"

"What?" Tabby yelled. "I'm trying to fucking meditate!"

Sam hammered on her bedroom door. "Noah is Nix's Jacob. He's her *Jacob*!"

"That doesn't make sense, you crazy moll."

"It does if you pay attention. It's *Twilight*. Nix always had a massive wide-on for the werewolf motorbike guy. We thought it was weird she wanted to fuck Noah, but it isn't. He's the motorbike guy! He's Jacob!"

There was a short silence, in which Nicole hoped both her sisters had died.

"Oh my god!" Tabby gasped. "You're right!"

Nicole screamed her frustration. "Stop talking about me like I'm not here!"

"You look like Bella," Tabby shouted. "Your life is Twilight!"

Nicole could hear her running down the hallway, Sam and the puppies in hot pursuit. They sounded like the stampede that killed Mufasa. She ran to the door and held it closed. "Don't come in here—"

Both her sisters burst into the room, pulling her away from the door and crash-tackling her back onto her bed.

"Get off," she screamed as the puppies jumped up to join them, stepping on her hair and arms and faces.

Tabby bit her arm. "You loved Jacob. You loved Jacob and now you love Noah. Your life is *Twilight,* nah, nah, nah, nah, nah, naaaah."

"Bella ends up... with... Edward," Nicole panted, trying and failing to extract herself from her sisters or the mounds of puppy flesh.

"Yeah, but he's not what you wanted," Sam said, digging her long fingers into her side. "You wanted Bella to marry Jacob and now you're the Bella!"

"You just said Bella is a lady-drip!"

"Yeah, but you're fine."

She glared at her twin. "Thanks."

"No probs."

"I can't believe how synchronistic this is," Tabby said, raising Lilah high in the air. "Noah's in a gang like Jacob, he has tattoos and a motorbike like Jacob. And he abs, at least that's what it felt like when I gave him a hug. What is his actual muscle situation? He cut?"

Nicole shoved her sister away with such force, she managed to get her away from her. "Stop it! Noah and I aren't a couple, we haven't been on a date, nothing between us has been sorted out."

"Yet," Sam and Tabby said at once.

"Yet," she agreed. "But it might not."

"But it might," Tabby said. "I have faith in the universe."

So do I, Nicole thought, then she punched her little sister on the shoulder. "I do not look like Bella."

"It's a compliment! Kristen Stewart's banging!"

Sam knelt up, looking out of the bedroom window. "Yeah, so I think the universe is doing its thing ahead of schedule."

"Why? What can you see?" Nicole asked.

Sam smiled. "Come look."

She stood and saw a guy on a motorbike parked by the curb, his heavy arms were flexed, his shaved head bent against the sun. Her heart squeezed tight, sending bright flutters down her body. "Did you know he was coming?"

"No, but he's here."

Tabby appeared at her elbow. "And he's not even wearing a helmet. So badass."

"It's not safe."

"Fuck safety. Go down there."

Nicole chewed her lip. "Do you think I should?"

Sam and Tabby nodded.

"But I'm not dressed! I didn't want to jinx seeing Noah by wearing nice clothes, but now he's here and I'm in my pyjamas!"

"So, change!" Sam picked up her pink cotton dress. "Put this on! Tabby, find her sandals!"

With her sisters' help, Nicole whipped off her pjs and put on the dress, dragging the comb Tabby found through her hair and applying Sam's chapstick.

"You look great," Sam said, shoving her out of the door. "Good luck. And don't worry, I'll stop Tabby from yelling shit out of the window."

"Thanks." But she didn't head for the stairs, instead she held her twin's gaze. The mirror she was born looking into. "Sammy... do you think this will work? Me and Noah? Really?"

Sam didn't smile. She didn't roll her eyes. She seemed to take her question as seriously as she'd asked it.

"I knew you were crushed out on each other," she said slowly. "But I didn't think anything would come of it. Noah's so closed off, I didn't think you could handle that."

Nicole's heart sank. "Oh."

Sam shrugged. "But I clearly don't know shit. I didn't know that Gil was stealing from me and I didn't clock Noah for a crook, but you did. You see shit I don't, so without turning it back on you, I think you're the best person to decide if Noah can be what you want in a partner."

Nicole nodded. "He said he doesn't want to be a dad."

"That doesn't mean he won't want to have kids with *you*." Sam smiled. "People do change, Nix."

"But—"

Sam held up her hand. "You asked me what I think, and here it is—when you're around, Noah's paying attention. He's there for you in a way he was never there for me or Tabby or even dad."

"Oh, Sammy, I'm sure that's not true."

"I'm not being self-pitying," she said loudly. "But Scott showed me being loved is about being seen, and you and Noah see each other. In ways we just don't, and we're fucking twins. So the takeaway on my end is you should give it a shot. Also, he's your Jacob. That's very clear to me now."

"Great, thanks." Nicole pinched her side and they both laughed, then they hugged.

"I love you," Sam whispered. "I'm proud of you."

The backs of Nicole's eyes prickled. "I love you, too. I'm so glad I came home."

"He's coming to the door," Tabby shrieked. "What are you cunts waiting for? Are you trying to make me lose my fucking mind?"

Nicole let go of Sam. "See you soon."

"Always."

And she flew down the stairs toward him, not thinking, just feeling. But maybe she should have been thinking, because when she opened the door, she did the most Bella Swan thing possible, she tripped over the front doorstep and hit her chin on the wooden steps.

Noah swore, crouched so their eyes were level. "Nikki! Are you okay?"

"No." Her right knee and chin were throbbing, but her pride hurt the worst. "I can't believe I fell again. Sam didn't see, did she?"

Noah's silence said that she had, and Nicole was sure she could hear giggling from behind and above her. She stood up, brushing her burning palms against her dress. "So, you were with Scott and Toby, right? You went to see Gil?"

"Nikki..." He shook his head. "I didn't come here to talk about Gil."

"Are you sure, because isn't that his motorbike?"

"Maybe. Look, do you think I could get a kiss before we get into that?" He was grinning and she wanted to be mad at him, but the relief that coursed through her at the sight of him just felt too good.

She smiled, betraying her ego. "Maybe."

"Close enough." He pulled her close, but they didn't kiss. They swayed together slowly, drinking each other in.

"I'm sorry about... everything," he said.

"You don't have to be sorry."

"I do. I never gave you the full picture and you had faith in me when the shit hit the fan with Paula and Gil, anyway."

"Of course, I did. Noah, I *want you*. I want *us*."

She hadn't meant to say it so desperately, so *earnestly*, but it came tumbling out, as uncensored as her teenage crush on the fictional werewolf, Jacob Black. Before Greyson, before the horrible doctor's office, before she gave up on feelings and put her faith in The Plan. And it felt good to be that vulnerable. That wide open.

Noah's arms tightened around her like steel bands. "I still don't know how to be with you the way you want."

"You don't need to! We'll just take it a day at a time for a bit. Figure it out. There's no rush."

He looked at her with his insanely green eyes. "You mean that? You can give me some time?"

"Yes," Nicole said without hesitation. "All the time."

"I still don't know how I'll go talking about everything. Not just about you, but about heaps of shit. That's why I never showed anyone my..." He looked around, as though searching for witnesses. "My paintings."

"Because it makes you feel vulnerable?"

He shuddered. "See, even hearing you say that makes me wanna leave the state."

"The word is cringe. It makes you want to *cringe*. And you're going to have to get over that because your paintings are beautiful and a condition of us going out together is that I want to show them to people. Sam, at least. And Tabby."

Noah looked at the sky. "Yeah, that might be a problem."

"Why?"

"Long story."

Nicole pressed a palm to his lovely mouth. "Has anyone ever told you that you talk too much?"

He smirked, pulling back and biting her fingers. "You might. One day. If I can figure out how to tell you how I feel."

She smiled, eyes burning with unshed tears. "I missed you."

He ducked his head. "You don't have to. I'm not going anywhere." Noah bent his head, his mouth close to hers. "I can't say it yet, but I… and you. Get it?"

She nodded furiously and for the first time in a long time, it felt like everything might be o—

"Kiss! Fuckin' kiss!" Tabby's head was sticking out of her bedroom window. When they looked at her, she shook her fist at them. "Kiss, you plebs! I'm sick of waiting!"

Sam appeared and put Tabby in a headlock. "Sorry, I tried to hold her back but she's stronger than she looks. Hey, Noah."

Noah raised a hand, a flush weaving down his neck.

Gosh, he's adorable. Nicole raised her middle finger to her sisters. "Get out of here."

They didn't budge. They stood in the window as they stood in her mind, watching, ready to cast their loving, snappy judgment. She sighed and turned to Noah. "You can put me down if you want to. They're going to keep watching us until we—"

He kissed her, his mouth as warm and hot as the sun on her back. Sam and Tabby cheered above them, and as Noah's arms tightened around her, Nicole felt really, truly, temporarily perfect.

22

Five and a half months later

"Fuck!" Noah pulled his thumb away from the barbecue, examining the bright red line he'd just singed into his skin. He sucked it, irritated.

"Oh no, civilian casualty!" Tabby dumped the salad she was carrying on the table and came over to inspect his burn. "Want me to take over?"

Noah glared at her. "No one's taking over."

Tabby threw up her hands. "I'm just offering to help. You know, Nix already fucks you, you don't have to impress her."

"Aren't you single?"

"Aren't the sausages burning?"

Noah returned his attention to the barbecue. Tabby was fucking with him, the sausages looked fine, browning nicely, although maybe that was just on the outside? Who the fuck knew what was going on inside them...

Tabby patted him on the back. "Don't stress. Dad burned everything to shit and we never complained."

Noah nodded, then remembered his ongoing effort to verbally respond whenever anyone talked to him. "Thanks."

"No probs." Tabby tipped her purple snapback at him. "Like my hat?"

He squinted. "Is that one of Gil's?"

"Sure is."

"Shouldn't it have gone up in the sale?"

"It wasn't a sale; it was a boutique lifestyle experience."

Noah rolled his eyes. Tabby had taken the wheel in pawning off Gil's things, posing in the clothes and auctioning them off two at a time, claiming she was doing a Marie Kondo cleanout. That made no fucking sense considering it was all men's clothes, but it worked. The returns had been twice what Nikki had predicted. Nowhere near eighty grand, but combined with the sale of the Fat Boy, it went a long way toward filling the money pit Gil had dug for them.

Tabby pulled the hat off her head and showed him the lining. "I couldn't have sold the hat. It's a fake. See?"

He couldn't see shit but he trusted Tabby's judgment. "Huh."

"Yep, ole Gil wasn't as classy as he made out."

"He never made out classy." It felt like too long since he'd turned a sausage, so he turned a sausage. He'd forgiven Tabby for believing he was a bikie. As Nicole pointed out, her little sisters' anger had been about not tweaking his secret as much as anything else. Tabby liked to be the one with all the information and solutions. He wondered if Toby had figured that out yet.

"Any word on what Gil's up to?" Tabby asked.

"Nah, far as I can tell he's not inking right now."

Tabby gave him a hard look. "Would that be because someone by the name of N. Newcomb called the places where Gil was tattooing and told the owners he's got light fingers and expensive taste?"

Noah turned another sausage, feeling fully justified in staying quiet.

Toby walked toward them carrying a big stack of plates. "Sam wants to know if you're ready for the chicken?"

"Jesus, I don't know."

Noah studied the barbecue, panic rising. In the months that Nicole had slipped into his heart, his feelings had changed. Or more accurately, the *way* he felt changed. Art used to be the only thing that got under his skin, now he *felt* the little stuff. When Nicole didn't call, he got nervous. When he inked an important piece, his nerves pounded. When Lilah got an ear infection and had to get a white cone around her head, he felt so fucking bad for her, he bought her a whole bag of chicken necks. It was fucking unnerving, feeling so much shit, but it was worth it. He was painting like a fucking virtuoso and he got Nicole in his bed every night.

Yesterday she'd turned to him, sweat glossing her perfect breasts, and moaned, "How is it always *so good*?"

"Um, Noah?" Toby said. "The chicken?"

He shook his head, snapping back into the moment. "Bring it out. Not like this situation can get any more fucked."

"Sure."

He expected Tabby to say something, but she wasn't listening. She was opening a cider she'd pulled from nowhere and staring at Toby's ass. He wanted to call her out, but he knew she'd deny looking. No one knew what her and Toby's deal was.

"Should we be worried?" Nikki had asked him a week ago. "Tabby might destroy him. She does that, you know, and Toby's so *nice*."

Noah told her not to worry. He had a feeling Toby's niceness had limits. And even if it didn't, caring less about what other people were doing was something his girl was trying to work on. She was doing great at it, too, and whenever she slipped up and tried to over-control herself or others, he spanked her. It seemed to be working for them.

As though summoned by his thoughts, Nicole walked toward him, her smile like a punch to the chest.

"How are things going out here?" she asked.

"They'd be better without the audience."

"Quit your bitching," Tabby said distractedly. "The snags are burning."

Nikki poked her sister. "No, they're not."

She stood on her tiptoes to kiss him, slipping her cool little tongue into his mouth. She was fucking fire, his girl. Last night, she'd screamed so loud while he was bending her over, it was lucky no one called the cops. Their kiss deepened and he nipped her lower lip, reminding her of what a dirty little thing she was.

He'd been right, she came to him when she was too horny to think straight and he fucked her back to concentration. A job he'd happily do forever.

Nikki backed away, flushing and smoothing her sundress. "It's a beautiful evening."

"Yeah," Noah said. "You're here."

Tabby made a face. "Pukeasaurus Rex. I'm going inside."

She left and Noah turned the sausages because someone had to.

Nicole looked around the yard, bouncing on her toes. "I hope everyone has a good time tonight."

"Who gives a shit if they don't?"

She laughed and slipped her arm around his waist. "They're my family, I have to give a shit."

"No, you don't. It was Sam's idea to have a DaSilva barbecue."

"But they're my crazy aunts and uncles, too! And I haven't seen any of them since the mistletoe disaster of '08."

"So, if they act up tonight, you can just shaft them for another decade."

She smiled, but then her expression turned serious again. "Do you think it's weird that we're about to have this big family event when my dad's still missing, and Sam and Tabby are walking tattoo factories and I'm a recovering control freak?"

God, she was fucking delightful. He kissed her forehead. "Yep, because it's exactly like what we talked about."

"We talk about things?"

"Sarcasm." He clipped her with the tongs. "We talk about how things don't have to be perfect to be good, remember? Or that's the bullshit you pulled out when you sent my fuckin' painting to that art cunt."

"Esteemed gallery owner," Nicole corrected. "And I did that because it's a crime to keep your paintings locked in your house like children you're ashamed of. The world needs to see what you can do, and stop cringing. You're not allowed to cringe, it's an insult to everyone who's dreamed of painting the way you do."

Noah turned another sausage, trying to swallow the supernova that had opened in his throat.

"Anyway," Nicole said, holding up her right wrist. "I've already atoned for my paint-stealing sins, remember?"

"How could I forget?"

A few weeks ago, they'd been in the studio, listening to Sticky Fingers and waiting for it to hit five so they could go out for an early dinner when she'd turned to him. "I've figured out how I can apologise for trying to show the world your immense talent."

"Oh yeah?"

"I want you to tattoo me."

He'd refused, told her it wasn't necessary, that she didn't need to prove how she felt about him or apologise. But she'd insisted, begged even. Then she'd told him that she loved him and after months of mental paper jams, it had come out. "I love you, too, Nikki."

And she'd held up her wrist. "Prove it."

Nicole dropped her arm back to her side and looked around. "I should go help Sam with the punch. Be back soon."

"Sure," he said and watched her leave, noting she'd sat in mustard or something and there was a yellow stain on the back of her pretty white dress. He opened his mouth to tell her about it, but Tabby slashed a hand across her throat. "It's payback for throwing out my old Barbie playhouse. Tell her and I'll slap the fuck out of you."

Noah rolled his eyes and returned his attention to the barbecue, though he couldn't stop smiling.

This was life, he realised. Filth and wholesomeness living side by side, crossing over and flipping back. There wasn't anything purely pure or perfectly bad, they were colours melting together like they did in the sunset he'd tattooed into Nicole's right wrist.

He looked up and saw Sam and Nikki laughing about something, their faces full of identical excitement. He was sure they were talking about Nikki's new project. His girl was handling Silver Daughters finances and setting up a freelance accounting business, yet she'd still found the time to launch a women's sexual health initiative. The Pink Party scheduled group visits to STD clinics, followed by high tea, mini golf or spa packages.

"I aim to make getting tested for STD's a routine experience for women," Nicole had written on the home page of the website Tabby built her. *"With proper education and the support of her peers, I hope all women can live healthy, more well-rounded lives, without the fear of being stigmatized for having sex. Shame has no role to play in a woman's bedroom (unless she's into that!)"*

Nicole DaSilva. Sometimes he questioned how he'd ever understood the world before she came into his life. Had he really just rattled around thinking nothing could change and everything was already doomed?

Scott arrived, carrying the chicken he was supposed to cook. "How're the sausages?"

Noah shrugged. "I'm doing my best."

"And that's all anyone can ask. Get you a beer?"

"Yesterday."

Scott returned with a Pale Ale and Noah gulped gratefully. He was considering the chicken—did he need to oil the hotplate? Was that a thing?—when his phone buzzed.

The back of his neck buzzed and, somehow, he knew who it was. He looked around carefully, making sure no one was in hearing distance, then turned his back and answered. "Hey, Ed."

"G'day, Noah."

Edgar's voice was slow and calm. It sounded like it was vibrating on a different frequency from the plane their bodies occupied, and it probably was. "How are things?"

"I can't talk," Noah said. "We're having a barbecue."

"Ah," Edgar said comfortably. "How are the girls?"

Noah looked at them; Sam laughing at Scott, Tabby draining the last of her cider can, Nicole fussing around with plastic cups. "About the same."

"I doubt that."

He was right, but Noah didn't say so. He was already paranoid someone would notice what he was doing and ask who was on the phone. "Are you coming home?"

"Too soon to tell, mate."

Noah rolled his eyes. "Eddie, I know I promised not to tell, but it's almost been a fucking year."

"But the girls are doing better without me."

It wasn't a question. Edgar sounded as sure as the sphinx.

"Maybe, but I know they miss you and I'm not sure how much longer I can keep this to myself. Especially now Nikki and I are…"

"In love," Edgar said with satisfaction.

When Noah had called to let him know they were dating—five months into their relationship—Edgar hadn't sounded the least bit surprised. In fact, if he didn't know better, Noah would have said he'd expected it to happen.

"You should think about coming home," he repeated, though he knew he wouldn't sway Edgar. In his own, sea-salt-and-wind-chimes way, he was more stubborn than all three of his daughters.

"We'll see," his former mentor said with clockwork predictability. "Take care of them for me, won't you?"

"I'll do my best, but you should write to them again. And maybe something less fucking cryptic this time?"

He laughed. "We'll see about that, too. I'll let you go, mate, love you."

And he hung up, leaving Noah standing at his barbecue with his family, the burden of knowledge just a little bit heavier. As it always was when Edgar called. He turned around to continue laying out the sweet and sour chicken wings and found Toby staring at him, his hands full of raw steaks, his handsome face blank. "Were you on the phone with Tabby's dad? Do you know where he is?"

And maybe it was just bad luck, or maybe it was his practice of replying whenever someone asked him something, but Noah didn't even think to keep quiet. "Yeah. Don't tell anyone."

Reflexively, Toby turned to look back at the party, at the laughing DaSilva sisters.

"Oh, man," he said. "Oh, this isn't okay."

"Hope you're good at keeping secrets."

"I'm not."

"Then you'd better learn fast." Noah clapped his hands hard, just like his old man used to. "D'you know how long you're supposed to cook chicken?"

The End

ABOUT THE AUTHOR

Eve Dangerfield's novels have been described as 'genre-defying,' 'insanely hot' and 'the defibrillator contemporary romance needs right now' and not just by those who might need bone marrow one day... OTHER PEOPLE! She lives in Melbourne with her beautiful family and can generally be found making a mess.

ALSO BY EVE DANGERFIELD

The Daddy Dearest series

Act Your Age

Not Your Shoe Size

The Playing For Love series

Begin Again Again

Return All

First and Forever

Back Into It

The Silver Daughters Ink Series

So Wild

So Steady

So Hectic

The Snow White Series

Velvet Cruelty

Silk Malice

Lace Vengeance

Bound to Sin (3x1)

The Beyond Bondage Series

Degrees of Control

James and the Giant Dilemma

Taunt (A Why Choose Romance)

Captivated (with NYT Bestseller Tessa Bailey)

The Bennett Sisters series

Locked Box

Open Hearts

Paying For It

Baby Talk

The She's on Top Series

Something Borrowed

Something Else

Dysfunctional

Sweeter

Printed in Great Britain
by Amazon

45439507R00158